DARK LADY

DARK LADY

Richard North Patterson

ALFRED A. KNOPF   NEW YORK   1999

THIS IS A BORZOI BOOK
PUBLISHED BY ALFRED A. KNOPF, INC.

Copyright © 1999 by Richard North Patterson

All rights reserved under International and Pan-American
Copyright Conventions.
Published in the United States by Alfred A. Knopf, Inc., New
York, and simultaneously in Canada by Random House of
Canada Limited, Toronto. Distributed by Random House, Inc.,
New York.

www.randomhouse.com

Knopf, Borzoi Books, and the colophon are registered trademarks
of Random House, Inc.

Library of Congress Cataloging-in-Publication Data
Patterson, Richard North.
Dark lady : a novel / by Richard North Patterson. — 1st ed.
p.   cm.
ISBN 0-679-45043-2
I. Title.
PS3566.A8242D37   1999
813'.54—dc21   99-23565
CIP

Manufactured in the United States of America
First Trade Edition

A signed first edition of this book has been privately printed by
The Franklin Library.

For George Bush and Ron Kaufman

PART ONE

ARTHUR BRIGHT

ONE

IN THE moments before the brutal murder of Jack Novak ended what she later thought of as her time of innocence, Assistant County Prosecutor Stella Marz gazed down at the waterfront of her native city, Steelton.

At thirty-eight, Stella would not have called herself an innocent. Nor was the view from her corner office one that lightened her heart. The afternoon sky was a close, sunless cobalt, typical of Steelton in winter. The sludge-gray Onondaga River divided the city as it met Lake Erie beneath a steel bridge: the valley carved by the river was a treeless expanse of railroad tracks, boxcars, refineries, cranes, chemical plants, and, looming over all of this, the smokestacks of the steel mills—squat, black, and enormous—on which Steelton's existence had once depended. From early childhood, Stella could remember the stench of mill smoke, the stain left on the white blouse of her school uniform drying on her mother's clothesline; from her time in night law school, she recalled the evening that the river had exploded in a stunning instant of spontaneous combustion caused by chemical waste and petroleum derivatives, the flames which climbed five stories high against the darkness. Between these two moments—the apogee of the mills and the explosion of the river—lay the story of a city and its decline.

By heritage, Stella herself was part of this story. The mills had boomed after the Civil War, manned by the earliest wave of immigrants—Germans and British, Welsh and Irish—who, in the early 1870s, had worked fourteen hours a day, six days a week. Their weekly pay was $11.50; in 1874, years of seething resentment ignited a strike, with angry workers demanding twenty-five cents more a week. The leading owner, Amasa Hall, shut down his mills, informing the strikers that, upon reopening, he would give jobs only to those who agreed to a fifty-cent cut. When the strikers refused, Hall boarded his yacht and embarked on a cruise around the world.

Hall stopped at Danzig, then a Polish seaport on the Baltic. He advertised extensively for young workers, offering the kingly wage of $7.25 a week and free transport to America. The resulting wave of Polish strike-breakers—poor, hardworking, Roman Catholic, and largely illiterate—had included Stella's great-grandfather, Carol Marzewski. It was on their backs that Amasa Hall had, quite systematically, undercut and eventually wiped out the other steel producers in the area, acquiring their mills and near-total sway over the region's steel industry. And it was the slow, inexorable decline of those same mills into sputtering obsolescence which had left Stella's father, Armin Marz, unemployed and bitter.

Recalling the flames which had leaped from the Onondaga, a brilliant orange-blue against the night sky, had reminded Stella of another memory from childhood, the East Side riots. Just as the West Side of Steelton was home to European immigrants—the first wave had been joined by Italians, Russians, Poles, Slovaks, and Austro-Hungarians—so the city's industry had drawn a later influx of migrants from the American South, the descendants of former slaves, to the eastern side of the Onondaga. But these newcomers were less welcomed, by employers or the heretofore all-white labor force. Stella could not remember a time in her old neighborhood, Warszawa, when the black interlopers were not viewed with suspicion and contempt; the fiery explosion of the East Side into riots in the sixties—three days of arson and shootouts with police—had helped convert this into fear and hatred. A last trickle of nonwhites—Puerto Ricans, Cubans, Koreans, Haitians, Chinese, and Vietnamese—felt welcome, if at all, only on the impoverished East Side. And so the split symbolized by the Onondaga hardened, and racial politics became as natural to Steelton as breathing polluted air.

This divide, too, shadowed Stella's thoughts. In the last six years, she had won every case but one—a hung jury following the murder trial of a high school coach who had made one of his students pregnant and who, devastated by Stella's particularly ruthless cross-examination, had thereafter committed suicide. It was this which had led a courtroom deputy to give Stella a nickname which now enjoyed wide currency among the criminal defense bar: the Dark Lady. But only recently had they become aware of her ambition, long nurtured, to become the first woman elected Prosecutor of Erie County.

Though this was a daunting task, it was by no means impossible. Stella was a daughter of the West Side, a young woman her neighborhood was proud of—an honors student who had worked through college and law school; had remained an observant Catholic; had not turned her back on Steelton and its problems, as had so many of her generation;

had already become head of her office's homicide unit. Stella was not a vain woman, and had always seen herself with objectivity: though she lacked the gifts for bonhomie and self-promotion natural to many politicians, she was articulate, truthful, and genuinely concerned with making her office, and her city, better. She was attractive enough without being threatening to other women, with a tangle of thick brown hair; pale skin; a broad face with a cleft chin and somewhat exotic brown eyes, a hint of Eurasia which Stella privately considered her best feature; a sturdy build which she managed to keep trim through relentless exercise and attention to diet, yet another facet of the self-discipline which had been hammered into her at home and school. And if there were no husband or children to soften the image of an all-business prosecutor or, Stella thought ruefully, her deepening sense of solitude, at least there was no one to object or to say, as Armin Marz might, had he not lost the gifts of memory and reason, that she was reaching above herself.

But her biggest problem, Stella knew, was not that she was a woman. It was as clear to her as the river which divided her city: she was a white ethnic with no base on the black East Side. And with that, her thoughts, and her gaze, moved to the most hopeful, most problematic, aspect of the cityscape before her—the steel skeleton of the baseball stadium Mayor Krajek had labeled Steelton 2000.

It was not the first improvement in this vista: the lake and river were cleaner; the air less polluted, if only because the mills had declined; the once seedy downtown area, formerly the preserve of prostitutes and muggers, now featured shops, theaters, and restaurants which were slowly drawing suburbanites and young people; some new glass office towers had kept clean industry from leaving. The public mall along the lake remained intact, the center city's only expanse of green, across which stretched City Hall and the County Courthouse, two beaux arts masterpieces from the turn of the century, the age of monumental architecture and municipal self-confidence. But it was the stadium-to-be which, for Stella and many others, symbolized the battle for the soul of their city.

The Steelton Blues baseball team dated back to 1901. Starting with her great-grandfather, four generations of the Marz family had gone to its games; *five*, Stella corrected herself, if her younger sister, Katie, and her husband had begun to take their kids. The Blues were part of the city's fabric: a voice on the radio; an argument in a bar; a conversation between a father and son who might have little else to talk about; years of statistics documenting a futility so epic—the Blues' last World Series appearance was in the 1930s—it had created a perverse fascination that a baseball team could so perfectly mirror its home.

But now *that* was a problem, too: attendance was off, the franchise was depressed in value, and the spoiled superstars who were baseball's princes could demand far more money to play in better media markets. Peter Hall, the heartless steel baron's great-grandson and current owner of the Blues, had threatened to sell the team to a group from Silicon Valley who would move the team to California. But, just as Hall did not relish being vilified as the callous owner who sold the Blues, Thomas Krajek, the young and ambitious mayor of Steelton who had risen from Stella's own neighborhood, was determined not to be the once-promising politician who had let Steelton's identity be sold to a pack of computer-chip millionaires.

The upshot had appeared, week by week, before Stella's eyes. Once it had been an artist's rendering, used by Krajek and Hall to sell their vision of Steelton 2000 in a hard-fought special election to float $275 million worth of municipal bonds. Now it rose, skeletal against the featureless gray canvas of Lake Erie: the ghost of a ballpark, its steel girders in place; the cement which would encircle it taking shape in stages; its timeless geometry imposed on bare earth. Above it, cranes stood watch like the bones of prehistoric animals; beside it, the trailers of contractors and subcontractors, though they were deserted today, a Sunday, had proliferated as Stella watched. It would be a modern classic, another Camden Yards or Jacobs Field—in 2000, when the Blues took to the field, the spirit of Steelton would be reborn. Or so Mayor Krajek promised, and Stella wished to believe.

And this, Stella knew, was her biggest problem of all.

Krajek was up for reelection this November. But, first, he faced a bitter Democratic primary. That this was inevitable stemmed from the race of Krajek's opponent, Arthur Bright, and one of Bright's principal contentions—that Steelton 2000 was a shameful diversion of public financing from such pressing needs as better schools, better housing, and safer streets. Bright was the first African-American ever elected Prosecutor of Erie County, and it was he who had made Stella his head of homicide. She owed him loyalty; more important, she admired him. And *her* political future depended on his: the prosecutor's office would be vacant only if Bright defeated Krajek; Stella could win election only if Bright supported her among the East Side voters who were his base. In either case, much depended on whether Bright could persuade voters to take a second, harsher, look at Mayor Krajek and his field of dreams.

It was *this* thought which, finally, drove Stella from her brooding inspection of Steelton 2000, and back to her desk.

She saw the usual mess: a coffee cup with cold, half-bitter dregs; her gym bag; status reports on homicide cases; police files. But squarely facing her was the one document so delicate that she had discussed it with Bright himself—the police report on the death, three days earlier, of Tommy Fielding.

She had not known Fielding but, from what little she knew of him, it was not a death she would have predicted. His maid had found his body in the bedroom of his town house, naked, next to a dead black prostitute named Tina Welch. Fielding's kitchen sink contained the primitive chemistry set—lighter, spoon, cotton balls, glassine Baggy with a white residue of powder—used to cook heroin. The police lab could find no fingerprints on these implements, and no prints traceable to Welch anywhere; the initial police canvass of the neighborhood turned up no one who knew Fielding well, but no one who had imagined him using heroin or hookers. His former wife, the mother of his only child, had, according to the police, been too shocked to be coherent. Nor did his status in life square with the meanness of his death: Fielding had been Peter Hall's lieutenant, an officer of Hall Development Company, and the project supervisor for Steelton 2000. Stella had barely read the headline in the *Steelton Press,* "Ballpark Official Found Dead," when Arthur Bright appeared in her office.

Stella, he said, must handle this herself; he had already called Nathaniel Dance, Steelton's Chief of Detectives, to make sure that everything went through her. The inquiry would be straight down the middle: thorough, impartial, professional. Most likely, Tommy Fielding had been the victim of an accidental overdose. But whatever the cause, only a fool could ignore that a man at the center of Steelton 2000 had died a puzzling death. And then, as Stella knew it would, their talk had turned to politics.

"I SUPPOSE," Bright said in a sardonic voice, "it's a welcome example of racial amity. 'Hands Across the Onondaga'—black hooker teaches white executive to shoot up. How will that play in Warszawa, Stella?"

Stella did not have to answer: Bright knew, almost as well as she, that most of her parents' generation, and many in her own, were so mired in bias that Tommy Fielding's death would merely buttress their suspicion of all blacks. Never mind that Arthur Bright had devoted much of his professional life to a relentless fight against drugs—tougher enforcement, stiffer sentences, more education, better treatment facilities. All was lost in the neighborhood's deepest fear: that, should Bright become mayor, "the blacks" would take over Steelton for good. Finally, Stella replied, "You could get some votes there, Arthur. If you can make them see past race."

"What they see," Bright answered wearily, "is just another black man—the predator they cross the street to avoid." He leaned forward in his chair, restless. "I'd run stronger in a dress. White voters can cast black women in a nurturing role, like cook or nanny or housekeeper, at least if they're older and fatter than Tina Welch. Sort of like Mammy in *Gone With the Wind*."

"I can find you the dress," Stella rejoined, "but you'd better start eating." Her tone grew sharper. "You've been fighting this for years now. Why all the self-pity?"

Bright frowned at Stella's tile floor. He was wiry, smooth faced, much younger looking than his fifty years, and wire-rimmed glasses gave him a scholarly appearance. Stella had seen him fire up an auditorium with an impassioned speech, reminiscent of Malcolm X at his incisive best. Yet, for Stella, his hidden core had a certain tenderness—wounds that Stella could sense but not see, and which would never quite heal.

"Polls," Bright said bluntly. "My own. I've got ninety percent support on the East Side, less than sixteen on the West Side. And stuck there." He looked up at Stella. "So how's *your* campaign? You've been very decorous—I'd even say ladylike, if I didn't know you better. But I hear you've been popping up among the ethnics, eating pierogi and giving speeches."

Sensing where Bright was headed, Stella forestalled him with a smile. "I *am* a lady," she responded, "who wants to run for a law-and-order job. So I'm changing my name to Duke."

Despite himself, Bright laughed. "Duke Marz," he mused. "How does old Duke feel about the death penalty?"

"Still against," Stella answered crisply. Her distillation of Catholic teaching had its disadvantages, she knew, among them a stubborn consistency regarding what "life" meant—that it was sacred for a fetus, and even for a murderer. "But it's the law in this state," she continued, "so I'm bound to apply it fairly and judiciously. Which is what I tell people on those grim occasions when they ask."

"If you run," Bright responded, "they'll ask. Charles Sloan will make sure of *that*—it's his ticket to a few votes in your neighborhood."

Bright was playing her, Stella knew, like a fish on the line. And the mention of Charles Sloan was the bait—Sloan was Bright's First Assistant and oldest associate, a veteran black lawyer now positioning himself as Bright's political heir. But it was too early for either Sloan or Stella to push for a commitment and Bright, with an earlier race to run, was using that to keep them off-balance. Knowing this, Stella remained silent.

"So," Bright continued. "How do you make a virtue of being a woman? And who votes for you on the East Side?"

The first question, though the easier, nettled Stella. "Since I joined homicide," she answered, "I've put twenty-four murderers in jail for life, and three more on death row. My religious beliefs didn't stop me, and neither did my sex. Where gender and religion help me is with other causes I believe in—like Catholic Charities or Big Sisters, or taking kids out of abusive or neglectful homes before they're warped or murdered or tossed out on the streets." Her voice slowed. "Women on the East Side know what *that's* about, Arthur. A lot of them are already raising other people's kids, and doing the best they can. By the time I'm through, they'll know that I'll be there for them."

Bright gave her a dubious look. After a time, he asked, "Who's advising you?"

"Dick Feeney," Stella responded, naming a veteran political consultant. "Unofficially—I can't pay him yet. But there are other friends I talk to, people who know other people. I've lived here all my life, remember."

Bright fell silent. The defensiveness of Stella's tone underscored his silent message—Stella was an amateur. "So has Charles Sloan," he observed, "and he's got a good ten years on you. That's about a thousand church socials, United Way banquets, and speeches to cops, just waiting for his time to come." His voice grew soft. "You know the problem. If I'm elected, the end of the rainbow is a special election—two thousand Democratic precinct committeemen jammed in an auditorium, voting for who gets to be interim prosecutor. Charles Sloan knows each and every one of them, from the blacks to the last Lithuanian."

Stella gazed at him equably. "As you say," she answered, "I know the problem."

Bright hesitated, and then smiled a little, acknowledging that, in this verbal game of chess, Stella had forced his hand: his election, after all, *did* come first. "And you know mine," he said at last. "Charles is one of my oldest and most loyal friends in public life. And my core constituents in the black community, as loyal as they are, have taken to the idea of an African-American prosecutor. Support a white candidate over Charles, and some will say that I'm not as black as I used to be."

There it was, Stella thought. "We *all* run those risks," she answered, "when we cross the Onondaga."

Bright studied his cuff links. "Someone has to run them," he murmured, "or this city will stay the way it is. God knows I've been trying."

Despite their fencing, Stella felt an answering wave of sympathy. "I know."

The quiet stretched, and then Bright looked into her eyes. "I need your help, Stella."

"What can I do?"

"Campaign for me against Krajek. In Warszawa, and on the West Side. Talk to those friends of yours." His voice grew soft again, "I need you, and you need me to win."

Suddenly, Stella thought, she was not quite such an amateur. "And if you do?"

"No promises. But I'll have a better idea of how you'd fare in an election. And so will you."

This was the most she could expect, Stella knew—a door left ajar which, if she refused, would be slammed in her face.

"I won't attack the stadium," she told him. "You and I disagree about that."

Bright watched her face. "I don't need you to. What I need is you telling your friends and neighbors you believe in me."

Stella paused for effect, and then gave the answer she had been prepared to give for months. "Of course I will," she said with a smile. "I was just waiting for you to ask."

Bright laughed in recognition of what was, quite plainly, the truth. "I'll talk to my campaign people," he answered easily. "They'll be back to you soon."

Stella nodded. "Good."

Bright stood, then paused, studying the newspaper on Stella's desk. "About the ballpark," he told her, "that's what makes you perfect to monitor this Tommy Fielding thing. People might think I'm trying to sling mud on Steelton 2000. You could soften that a little."

With that, Bright left for an appearance at a day care center, and Stella resumed staring at the headlines.

. . .

N o w , o n Sunday, Stella read the police report again.

There were no signs of robbery or, in the first inspection of the bodies, of violence. It seemed that Fielding had eaten dinner before Welch arrived, leaving remnants of a ham sandwich and a beer. Tina's clothes were carefully folded on a chair, and the bedroom lights were low. In the drawer of Fielding's nightstand was a soft-core porn magazine, *Black Beauties.*

His autopsy had been delayed at the request of his wealthy parents, tracked down while on a luxury cruise of Southeast Asia. A few hours before, Stella had met with them—a courtly, soft-spoken father, a diminutive mother whose patrician facade concealed her intensity, and for whom death had not diminished her fierce sense of maternity. Tommy was the victim of a murder, she insisted: he had been orderly since childhood, a principled boy who had become a principled man with a deep aversion to drugs. Appalled by the prospective wreckage of an autopsy, drawn by Stella's sympathy, they had extracted from her a promise she gave with some reluctance: to attend Fielding's autopsy tomorrow.

Tina Welch, of course, had been autopsied at once. Although Stella did not yet have the report, Coroner Kate Micelli had called Stella with her tentative conclusion—that Welch was an addict, and had died from a massive overdose. Not that this ruled out murder, Stella reflected, but a double homicide by injection would be quite a complex task.

Pensive, she studied the work of the crime scene photographer.

In their nakedness, as pitiful as the camera was pitiless, Fielding and Welch lay on the bed, Fielding with his eyes shut, Welch staring back at the camera. Perhaps it was the apparent incongruity, Stella thought, or her own vestigial prejudice, but even in death they did not look like a couple. Unless it was her parents, she thought with sudden irony, sleeping with their backs turned to each other.

There were other photos, close-ups. Welch appeared much older than her twenty-three years evidenced by her driver's license: there were the bruises of fatigue beneath her eyes, and her body, though slender, lacked muscle tone. Her skin looked ready to collapse upon the bone, the work of drugs and malnutrition.

Twenty-three, Stella thought, and began to examine the close-ups of Fielding. At thirty-four, he looked younger than that, with slicked-back black hair and sculpted features, and his body appeared fit and well muscled. She could imagine him at a picnic with a sporty pair of slacks and the sleeves of a pastel sweater, taken off in the warmth of summer, tied loosely around his neck. Here her admitted prejudice involved class, not race—to Stella, he looked like a friend of Peter Hall's.

Whatever else, she concluded, these two were no one's idea of Romeo and Juliet. But then Juliet was not a hooker, or Romeo enamored of *Black Beauties.* And Stella herself, she felt confident, had seen too much to be surprised by much of anything: she had long since learned how little we know about anyone's life, even those we believe we know well.

Her telephone rang.

The sound, on a Sunday, startled her. It was Nathaniel Dance, the deep-voiced Chief of Detectives. The call was a surprise—it *was* a Sunday, and Dance seldom troubled himself with routine matters.

"I have a homicide," he said. "A big one."

Beneath the calm, something in Dance's tone suggested that he had taken a trip to hell, and was reluctant to describe it. Reflexively, Stella answered, "It never rains but it pours . . . "

"It's Jack Novak."

At first, Stella could not speak. But even in her disbelief, her rebellion against what Dance had said, the professional in Stella understood his call.

"Does Arthur know?" she asked.

"Not yet. They say he's out campaigning, on the way to a debate in your old neighborhood. I've been trying to reach him, but this is a message I can't just leave with anyone." His voice lowered. "I don't want the press to find out before he does, somebody ambushing him. Especially at this debate."

This, too, did not surprise her. In theory, Dance was above politics. In truth, no cop—black or white—would have risen so high without an acute political sense. Dance was buying Arthur time, no doubt because he wanted Bright to become Steelton's first black mayor, perhaps because Dance wanted to be Steelton's first black Chief of Police. Whatever his motives, Dance had seen at once what Stella saw, too—that most homicides matter only to the victim's family but that, every few years, a murder comes along which can ruin the prosecutor who touches it. This could be that case: the killing of Steelton's leading drug lawyer, an old classmate and friend of Arthur Bright's who, despite their roles as legal adversaries, was one of Arthur's strongest white supporters.

"Who killed him?" Stella asked tonelessly.

"We don't know. Homicide got an anonymous call, and went to Novak's apartment. They knew enough to get me out here."

Stella closed her eyes. Finally, she said, "Then I should come out, too."

Dance himself was briefly silent. "The crime scene's pretty rough, Stella."

Did she only imagine, Stella wondered, a trace of compassion? But Nathaniel Dance knew many secrets. Even, perhaps, hers.

"Fifteen minutes," Stella said, and hung up.

She could not permit herself to feel, she told herself. She did not have time, and the tears, when they came, might be difficult to stop.

She put on her coat and left the office. Only then did it occur to her that she had not needed, and Dance had not offered, directions to Jack Novak's home.

TWO

FROM THE time that Stella had first known him, Jack Novak had lived in Lincoln Park.

Like Warszawa, it had begun as a working-class district, and bordered on the western plateau of the Onondaga River valley. Even now, the modest two-story homes seemed overshadowed by the mills, the miles of blast furnaces and smokestacks Stella could see as she approached. The center of the district, the park itself, also was an outgrowth of industry—the first Anglo-Saxon workers had gathered there after church on Sunday afternoons and, in the early 1860s, had drilled on its tree-shaded green, four city blocks long, before going south in the war to free the slaves. The arrival of Eastern Europeans, too, was reflected—in the steepled Polish cathedral, St. John Cantius, and in the beautiful onion domes, painted gold, of the Russian Orthodox church built with money sent by the martyred Czar, Nicolas II. But in contrast to Stella's neighborhood, which clung stubbornly to its working-class character, Lincoln Park had become an uneasy mix of artsy and ethnic, bohemian and trendy, shabby stores and fashionable restaurants. Its character seemed unsettled, without clear definition, just as, for Stella, Jack Novak remained a kaleidoscope of glittering fragments that never quite formed a whole.

Novak lived—Stella could not yet put this in the past tense—in another artifact of the blue-collar past, the Lincoln Park Baths. A tan brick structure with an elegant facade, it had begun in the 1920s as a public bath for weary steelworkers, now converted into a chic redoubt for professionals who had the money to buy one of six large units with high ceilings, open floor plans, and a panoramic view of the park itself. Or so Stella remembered it.

She parked one block away. She would need time to steel herself, breathe some fresh air; she felt disoriented, almost feverish, and not only because of what she would witness here. There was also the memory of another disorientation, long ago: leaving Jack Novak late one Tuesday night and driving, in a mere ten minutes, to what suddenly seemed another world—Warszawa, and her parents' home. Just as Jack had implied in the hours before, the trip had become too far to go.

Stella had been twenty-three years old.

SHE LAY against him lightly, the first man she had ever slept with, her breasts against his chest, the tendrils of her hair damp from their love-making. Then, shyly, she had looked into his face again.

He was older, thirty-eight, and flecks of gray had appeared at his temples. But his eyes were, as always, alert and preternaturally bright, their blue looking into Stella in a way that suggested he could read her thoughts. His nose was slightly bulbous and his face somewhat round, but this softness was offset by a long chin and neat mustache, which, combined with the piercing eyes and his thick shock of brown hair, gave him the rakish look of a Tartar horseman. And though he scorned exercise for its own sake, a heightened metabolism and a restless quest for new experience seemed to keep him thin and youthful. At the corner of his full mouth, Stella saw the hint of a smile.

"Curfew time?" he inquired. "Or has your parole been revoked for good?"

Though his tone was mild, his implication—that their relationship existed at her father's sufferance—stung her. "It's late," she said. "I've got *your* work to do tomorrow, and my first midterm next Monday night."

The smile became a frown. "Then I guess I won't see you for a while."

Was his undertone a threat, Stella wondered—that there were other ways in which Jack Novak could amuse himself? When she searched his face again, he murmured, "Poor Stella."

Stella closed her eyes, listening to Led Zeppelin on Jack's expensive stereo system. "It's not that simple," she said. "Moving out. They barely accept that I'm going to law school."

The strain in her voice was an unspoken plea: Jack, too, had grown up in Warszawa—better than anyone, he understood her life. "Because you should be having babies now," he answered. "Working as a clerk-typist for the parish. Hoping against hope that your husband won't get laid off like your father did, sit muttering into his vodka and cursing the little woman out of the sheer injustice of his life." Pausing, his tone was softer yet. "I've been there, Stella. It's a shame that you still are."

She stared at him. Beneath his words, Stella heard a fathomless anger,

Jack's utter rejection—even fear—of his own past. "That's not *my* life," she said with vehemence. "I'm making my own, like I've always planned I would —"

"*Your life*," he cut in. "I know all about your life, even the parts you haven't told me. The money hidden under the mattress. The admonitions to be good—to go to Mass and get good grades in school. The silent message that went with that: but not *too* good, or you'll go so far beyond us that you'll forget your place." His voice rose in a strange combination of mockery and bitterness. "Oh, and the Sodality of the Blessed Virgin, the endless worship of your own virginity that requires every little Polish girl to keep her knees together until she's married.

"That's the cardinal rule of them all—no sex, and no mention of it. That's what this is about, isn't it?" Pausing, Jack's eyes swept her naked body. "To leave your parents' home is to admit you're sleeping with me. And in the Islamic State of Warszawa, that's never, ever done."

Stella inhaled, sliding back from him so that their bodies no longer touched. Her life felt more complex than that, her childhood and neighborhood far richer, though what he said about her family was painfully close to the truth. "It's changing, Jack. And my life was always more than that. It still is." Her own voice became bitter. "I go to law school at night, and work for you to pay for it. There aren't enough hours to pay rent, too."

"*Or* enough hours for me."

"No." The flat declaration surprised Stella herself. "Not when you're this selfish."

Instantly, Stella regretted this; though determined in pursuit of her goals, she had no gift for conflict, at least with Jack. But his face seemed to soften. "If money's the problem, I'll pay the rent myself."

Flushed with shame, Stella looked away. Suddenly, their surroundings—the stark white walls, the spare modern furnishings, the span of mirrors in which they lay reflected—filled Stella with the sense that she did not belong here. "Isn't it enough," she said in a lower voice, "that I'm your paralegal, and I'm with you? Or that your secretary suspects I'm sleeping my way through law school? Maybe you *are* keeping me, Jack. Maybe I don't want to face that."

Jack gave her a complex, unfathomable look. "When I hired you, Stella, I didn't know you'd sleep with me."

"Didn't you?" *Why*, Stella wondered, *don't you just tell me that my work is good?* "Whatever your reasons," she added more quietly, "there are other people in my life. Not just my parents—Katie."

"Your sister?"

"Yes. Once I leave, Katie deals with them by herself."

"Left to bear the purdah alone, you mean? I suppose I should feel more shame."

Far from shame, Stella sensed the resolve of a Jay Gatsby, an intense desire to erase the ways in which she reminded Jack of his own origins.

"Shame," she finally said, "is too much to expect from you. But I could use some understanding."

For a moment, he watched her, and then gently touched her face. "I'm sorry," he said. "You're twenty-three, and so was I once. I'm fighting my old battles all over again, at your expense. It isn't fair."

Despite her wariness, it was these sudden moments of tenderness which led Stella to hope that Jack's comprehension could become the wellspring of compassion, of closeness instead of conflict. All her life, she had somehow felt alone, apart—even so young, Stella feared that this would always be true, and prayed that it would not. Tears came to her eyes, unwanted.

Jack kissed her forehead. "I'm your friend, Stella. Always."

Confused, she rested her face against his shoulder. He was uncharacteristically still, as if, for once, time were not his enemy. "Stay," he murmured at last. "Just another hour."

Perhaps, for his sake, perhaps because her loneliness and doubt were so painful that she needed to escape them, Stella felt desire stir again. In silent answer, her lips grazed his chest, the light tuft of hair between his nipples. She heard, rather than saw, his hand slide open the drawer of his bedside table.

Once more, Stella closed her eyes.

When she opened them again, she saw the cause of another argument, two weeks before, which had finally left her shaking her head in silence, unable to give words to her embarrassment.

In his hand was a garter belt and black stockings.

Stella's mouth felt dry. Again, despite herself, she wondered whether some other woman had worn this.

"For us," he said. "Please."

Without answering, Stella took them from his hand, and got up.

She stood at the end of the bed. Silent, he watched her put them on. She forced herself to look into his face.

"I *am* your friend," he said softly. "With every night, everything we do that you've never done before, you're that much closer to leaving them. To becoming who you really are."

Stella did not answer. On the stereo, Led Zeppelin was playing "Stairway to Heaven." Desire faded to numbness, the feeling of anesthesia; she saw herself, moving toward him in the mirror, as if she were someone else.

"You're beautiful," Jack Novak said, and then she saw that he, too, was watching their reflection.

NOW THERE were squad cars in front of Jack's building, a uniformed cop guarding his door. Stella handed him her identification card. "I'm Stella Marz," she said. "Head of the prosecutor's homicide unit."

Nodding, he handed back the card. She waited one more instant, then entered.

Whatever had happened to Jack Novak, she saw with transitory relief, had not happened in the living room.

Two men from the crime lab were there, one bent over a half-finished glass of what looked like whiskey, the other peering into a dish bisected by a line of white powder. As she would have expected, the decor had changed, reflecting Jack's restlessness: the upholstered furniture was more colorful, as was the painting which dominated the cavernous room, a splashy oil reminiscent of Jackson Pollock. One of the crime lab team looked up at her. Then other voices broke the silence, and Stella no longer had to wonder where Jack was.

Stomach souring, she walked slowly toward the bedroom.

"Leave him up there," she heard Dance say. "We can't hurt his feelings now." And then she saw Jack Novak, reflected in the mirror.

THREE

STELLA HEARD her own sharp intake of breath, then felt the palpitation of her heart, a sudden damning nausea. The terrible scene became a tableau—Dance and a homicide detective watching her; the crime lab photographer, also still, filming Jack's body; their images reflected in his mirrors. The only sound was the soft whir of the video camera.

Stella steadied herself in the door frame, struggling to bring reason to what she saw.

Jack Novak hung suspended from his closet door, his feet dangling inches above the carpet, kept there, Stella realized, by a leather belt around his neck. Drawn taut over the top of the door and secured by a metal coat hook on the other side, the belt strained with his weight. But its work showed in his face—eyes bulging with shock, filled with the red pinpoints of burst vessels; mouth twisted open, the tip of his tongue protruding. Below his waxen torso, sagging with middle age, he wore a garter belt and stockings. A pair of black high heels had fallen from his feet into a carmine pool.

Stella's eyes shut tight.

Someone had castrated him. On the rug, a kitchen knife was caked in dry blood.

All that Stella could do was stand immobile, hand braced against the door frame. When she opened her eyes again, Nathaniel Dance had stepped between her and Jack's body.

He towered over her. From his granitic face—harsh planes and angles which seemed to have been hewed and shaped—Dance's yellow-brown eyes looked down into hers. His impassivity had always felt faintly ominous to Stella, enhancing her sense of his power, of secret knowledge. Yet it seemed on this occasion an act of grace. "The man never felt that," he told her. "He was already dead."

His deep voice was close to gentle. Dully, Stella asked, "How do you know?"

"The blood." Stella realized that Kate Micelli, the coroner, stood behind her. "Blood droplets obey the laws of physics," Micelli went on. "*If* he'd been alive, you'd have arteries pumping—the blood pattern would be a series of arches, getting closer to his feet as the pumping leveled off. This is drainage, the work of gravity. I'd put my money on strangulation."

Micelli seemed completely in character, one professional briefing another, distanced by experience from the horror of what she saw. It felt otherwise with Dance. Perhaps this was a trick of the mind, a projection of Stella's confusion on the stoicism which, in Dance, was surely meant to suggest omniscience while obscuring the direction of his thoughts. But Stella had the sudden certainty that Dance knew what Jack had been to her.

Black stockings.

Across the years, she saw herself again, reflected in Jack's mirrors. Then she forced herself to look at how the years had ended.

He had lived too well and too carelessly, and now the indulgence which had softened his body was not concealed by hand-tailored Italian suits. He had died, Stella saw now, with his hands tied behind his back. Near his dangling feet, toes pointed Christlike to the floor, a low metal stool lay on its side.

Stella remembered it. Its purpose was to help Jack reach the shelf atop his closet. He kept his luggage there: he had mounted the stool while packing for their final weekend. But he, or someone, had used it to suspend him from the closet door—feet supported by the stool before, in an instant, the stool was gone.

Stella's voice was toneless. "How did it happen?"

"With love." The voice belonged to Detective John Burba. Crossing the room, he stood beside Dance. Though both were big, Burba was redhaired and blocky and proletarian, with a crude perfunctory manner. "This is a full-on, fist-fuckers-of-America, male-on-male scene."

No one answered. Stella looked past Burba into the rictus of Jack Novak's face. An odd detail struck her, which made the rest seem all the more pitiable: that Jack's mustache was dyed black. *Tell me,* she wanted to say. *Tell me how you came to this.*

Gradually, the sounds of others drifting through the apartment seeped into Stella's consciousness. Collectively, the crime lab team would gather evidence—dust; hunt for fibers which did not belong here; search out fingerprints; look for signs of robbery or break-in; remove the traps from the bathroom drains; and slowly, systematically, take the place apart. Dance would ensure that they missed nothing.

Stella faced him. Without speaking, Dance seemed to dismiss Burba's comment, and then turned to Micelli in inquiry.

The coroner was a hawk-nosed woman in her early fifties, with her hair dyed jet black, and the deep-set eyes and sunken cheeks of a Spanish inquisitor. But she was relentlessly competent, and Stella had learned to trust her. "I'm just getting started," Micelli said. "But I'll show you what occurs to me."

Briskly, she took Stella by the elbow and steered her past Dance and Burba until they stood three feet from Novak. For Micelli, the grotesque was a problem to be solved; her tone was flat, that of an anatomy professor dissecting a cat. Focusing on Novak's stockinged legs—anything but his face or her own flashbacks—Stella made herself concentrate on the science to be learned, the facts to be remembered. Her skin felt damp.

"It *looks* like an autoerotic scene," Micelli began. "Self-asphyxiation to stimulate ejaculation. But, like any of us, the autoerotics have their ways.

"Self-asphyxiation tends to be a solitary act, secret even from wives or lovers. And one way to get caught is to hang yourself by accident. So a committed autoerotic tends to be self-sufficient, and quite practiced at surviving.

"They don't do this to die—the point is to produce a heightened orgasm. So you never want to be fully weight suspended. You have to remain conscious, and be able to escape.

"That's where *this* scene begins to deviate, as it were." A surprising shaft of sunlight entered the room; it struck the mirror, bathing Novak's tormented body in gold and causing the coroner to blink. "Usually," she said after a moment, "they don't use a stool. It's too risky if you're by yourself, and one mistake may hang you. Standing on your tiptoes is enough."

Stella looked from Novak's feet to the belt around his neck, the flush which stained his face. Imagining his last moments, she felt a piercing agony.

"Next there's the belt," Micelli said. "The real pros use leather thongs—they buy them in sex shops, or through catalogues, or even on the Internet.

"Then there's the hands." Micelli walked decorously around the pool of blood and placed her palms on Novak's hips, turning him so that Stella could see his hands, lashed together at the cleft of his buttocks. "Only two options here," Micelli went on, "other-tied, or self-tied. The solitaries self-tie, of course, and leave themselves a means of escape.

"Not so here. This rope is so taut his palms are white. The decedent had a friend."

Micelli's didactic tone aroused just enough antipathy to keep Stella from throwing up. She could feel Dance watching her again. In a thin voice, she asked, "What about anal penetration?"

Micelli released the body. It twisted in the light and shadow of the mirrors; Jack's red-speckled eyes appeared to stare in shock at Stella. "No sign of it, externally. And no semen I can see. Nor, based on the spatter pattern, did he castrate himself and climb up here to finish off a suicide."

Stella felt Dance beside them now. "There's no padding around the neck." His tone was measured, calm. "Most of these folks have to show up for work on Monday. No point having rope burns above the collar— people might talk about you."

Laconic as it was, Dance's observation carried something more human, a sense of how these foibles worked in real life. "No wear and tear on the top of the closet," Dance went on. "Or on the belt . . ."

"That's not dispositive," Micelli cut in. "But it brings us to the neck." Reaching up, she placed her thumb and forefinger beneath Jack's chin, raising it to expose the neck. "Autoerotics put the rope beneath the chin, not the neck. In a hanging accident, the rope slips, leaving two marks." The deep-set eyes squinted slightly, making the coroner in profile appear even more aquiline. "The only mark I see here is the one beneath the belt."

A sudden wave of repressed vomiting made Stella shudder and turn away. But the mirrored room became a kaleidoscope in which her ex-lover hung at different angles, again and again. "So," Burba said to Micelli, "you don't think our pal Jack was getting it in the ass."

It was the first clear evidence of what Stella knew instinctively: that the grisly death of a prominent drug lawyer would fill Steelton cops with satisfaction, their contempt for the enemy enhanced by a blue-collar envy of the affluent. "Not that I can see," Micelli answered. "But love is strange, as they say."

Stella stared at the carpet, arms folded, caught between waves of sickness and a grim determination not to flinch. The repeated image of Jack's death—bowels voiding; body writhing and kicking, then twitching; the anguish in his eyes becoming fixed, timeless—made her swallow convulsively.

It was Dance who brought her back. "There's only two choices," he said.

His tone, practical and disinterested, came to Stella as a lifeline. "There's only one choice," she answered. "Someone murdered him."

Dance's yellow-brown stare seemed to underscore her disorientation. In the same phlegmatic voice, he said, "I meant before that."

Stella looked down again, briefly touching her eyes. "Why don't we talk in the living room," Dance suggested.

Stella turned her back to the mirrors, and left.

There was a couch facing the fireplace. Sitting stiffly, Stella studied the glass coffee table: the line of what appeared to be cocaine; two cocktail glasses with a thin film of amber liquid which, if Jack's tastes remained the same, would prove to be a single-malt scotch. With what manner of person, Stella wondered, had he shared his final hour, and what pathology had transmuted drugs and alcohol into the death endlessly reflected in his bedroom.

Dance and the coroner sat in chairs on either side of her; Dance watched as Burba inspected the apartment door. "No signs of a break-in," Burba told him. "Whoever was here, Novak let in. Unless they had a key."

"*So,*" Stella said to Dance, "what are your two possibilities?"

Dance turned to her. "Novak could have had a partner who played these games with him. But this time he—or she—kicked out the stool . . ."

Micelli laughed softly. "Such a dirty trick."

"*Or,*" Dance continued, "someone executed him."

Stella inhaled. "First they had to get him up there." Facing Micelli, she asked, "Any bruises, or signs of a struggle?"

"Not on first inspection. It doesn't look like he was strangled, either." Micelli glanced at Dance. "Think there was more than one of them?"

"Maybe. If this was an execution, someone would have to dress him up, then hang him while he was still alive. Not easy for just one person, even a man." Pausing, he addressed Micelli. "Novak *was* alive, you think."

"At that point, yes."

"But dead before they castrated him."

Micelli gave a thin smile. "So why bother, you're asking? When people castrate themselves, it's out of self-hatred, or sexual confusion. This . . ." She paused a moment, glancing toward the bedroom. "*This* could be sheer rage. Which I'd associate more with a homosexual affair."

Briefly, Dance glanced at Stella. For her, an awkward moment passed before Dance said to Micelli, "Then I'd expect a sloppy crime scene. Maybe some hysterical boyfriend blubbering in the corner after the drugs wore off, wondering how Jack could be so cruel."

Micelli nodded in recognition. "Such a tease. Maybe your boyfriend's our anonymous caller, though I guess whoever called disguised their voice enough that it could have been a man *or* woman." She paused, then added, "Or maybe your killer just wants to send a message."

Stella found her voice again. "If this is an execution, why do all the rest?"

"To make it look like what it isn't?" Pensive, Micelli folded her hands. "I don't know, Stella. As murders go, it's pretty baroque."

Stella forced herself to keep on thinking. "What size are the heels?" she asked.

"Big enough, it looks like. You'll have noticed the stockings fit him, too."

Something in Dance's silence drew Stella. His eyes had narrowed, and he was staring at the white powder on the coffee table. "Some of these guys turn rancid," he said. "The drug lawyers. Their lives get as dirty as their clients."

The remark, Stella sensed, carried an unspoken warning—certainly for Arthur Bright, perhaps for her—about where this murder might take them. "Nat," Burba called out from the bedroom. "I've got something to show you."

The Chief of Detectives stood heavily, directing a brief, inquiring glance at Stella. After a moment, she rose, her movements rote, mechanical; together, they returned to the serial nightmare which had been Jack Novak's bedroom and where Stella, estranged from her family and the life she had known, had finally come to sleep. Once she had imagined it as a refuge.

With mock delicacy, Burba dangled a pair of handcuffs from one finger. "Can't wait to find the climbing gear," he said. "And there's enough amyl nitrite in the bathroom to start a pharmacy for faggots."

Stella stared past him at Jack Novak's chest of drawers. The lower drawers were open wide; the top drawer, she saw, only a crack. "The upper drawer," she said to Burba. "Did you look in that?"

He put down the handcuffs and began sifting through the top drawer. But Stella's question had not been a directive; she had remembered just how tidy Jack had been. "See something?" Dance asked.

Did you *see something?* Stella wanted to ask. "I was wondering if someone had searched the place," she answered. "Before we got here."

Dance remained impassive. "You'd have to be nerveless. What with Novak hanging there."

For a moment, Stella was quiet. "Still," she murmured, "you're guessing this was all planned out, aren't you?"

Dance considered her. "That's all it is. A guess."

Suddenly, the sound of music startled Stella. And then, listening further, she shivered.

It was the first few bars of "Stairway to Heaven."

Burba, she realized, had switched on Jack's stereo. Still watching her, Dance said, "That's what was playing when they found him."

For a moment, the haunting sounds came to her from another time, and she could feel her lover's skin on hers. But when she looked again, Jack Novak was still suspended there, lifeless.

"I'd better go find Arthur," she said.

FOUR

TEN MINUTES later, Stella entered Warszawa, following by instinct the route she had taken that night long ago, when she had traced the Onondaga River valley, in those years still lit by the orange glow of the mills, from Jack Novak's spacious apartment to the only home she had ever known.

This night it was early evening, dusk sifting like mill smoke into Warszawa, and into Stella's soul. But even now, the two-hundred-foot spires of St. Stanislaus, looming above the low-slung houses and cobblestone streets, felt like twin beacons summoning her to prayer; even now, fifteen years after she had left here, Warszawa felt like home to her.

The sensation was both spiritual and sensory, an immersion in the earliest impressions of childhood: the closeness of small houses and of narrow streets; the smell of fried fish, prepared in the bars and restaurants every Friday, long after the Church had lifted its ban on meat; fathers with push mowers, carefully tending the postage-stamp lawns; the popcorn vendor with his orange pushcart; the drift of voices from the small front porches on a sweltering summer night; the noisy wedding parties in the St. Stanislaus Social Hall, with polka bands, beer, stuffed cabbage, and endless platters of food; the church school with Lent, Prayer, Fasting, and Almsgiving lettered in its windows. And, always, the church itself.

Stella could not remember when she had first entered the church. But her most vivid memories were of a child's awe: at the sense of God's design in its massive, neo-Gothic brick; the shadowy vastness of the sanctuary; the damp, sudden coolness on her skin as she stepped inside; the multicolored richness of the stained-glass windows and intricate statuary; the reverence she shared with the children and adults surrounding her, their respect showing in the suits and dresses they wore. But this humility commingled with pride: four generations ago, out of the pennies scraped from the $7.25 a week that Peter Hall's great-grandfather had paid them, the first Polish workers had built St. Stanislaus from the ground. As miserable as their lives had been, the church was their own, as much a monument to their existence as the mills were to Amasa Hall. Even now, Stella Marz felt a solidarity with those who lived here, a oneness with those who had come before.

But, though she now worshipped here again, few others among the two thousand parishioners might be considered professional. They were workers still—older, poorer, or, like Armin Marz, cast off by the mills. A divide had opened between Stella and the others, one she had not wished for. Yet since she was old enough to imagine a future, she had fought fiercely for a future of her own; she would not be pregnant at nineteen, or a chattel under her stolid husband's thumb. She would not become her mother.

It was this, well before Jack Novak, which had made Armin Marz her enemy.

She did not think he had ever known this. Her father was not a reasoning man—things just *were*. Because of that, the depth of his own bitterness had remained concealed from him, and his rage at Stella, in his own mind, was a reaction to her willfulness. But what was, for her, a battle for survival was, to Armin, the last stake to the heart. The only dominion left to him lay within the walls of his home.

It was three blocks from the St. Stanislaus Social Hall, where Arthur Bright was debating Mayor Krajek. But the primary race was heated, both within Warszawa and without; tonight the narrow streets were jammed with cars. And so Stella, already laden with sorrow and remembrance, parked in front of her parents' house.

The modest two-story was no longer theirs, of course. The last time she had set foot inside was when it had been sold, over her sister's bitter objections, to pay for her father's care. He was no longer angry—the house had begun to frighten him, for it was filled with objects he no longer knew.

Now only Stella remembered that last scarifying night, her return from Jack's. Only Stella recalled—as, in spite of everything, she did now—parking the battered Honda she had bought with her own money. Then slowly climbing the few steps to her parents' front porch; hearing the soft creak of the floorboards beneath her feet; feeling the half prayer on her lips as the door clicked open, the hope, as she entered the darkened living room, of a twenty-three-year-old woman, with the moisture of her lover inside her, that her father had fallen asleep. Then he switched on the lamp by his chair.

· · ·

HIS FACE in the half-light was craggy and worn—veined, fleshy nose; deep hollows below his cheekbones, stained with drink; scraggly, graying hair which had retreated from his forehead; his skin so etched with furrows that, to Stella, it had become a relief map of his failures. But his black eyes glowed with anger.

Despite herself, Stella shivered; to fear him was the first instinct she had learned. "Where were you?" he said.

It was a demand, not a question. Though Armin Marz had been born here, to Stella his low voice had the guttural sound of another place and time, a feudal authority which was his by right. To lie would be to defy him and, she now knew, to betray herself. "With Jack," she answered simply.

There was silence. Up the darkened stairway she could sense her mother listening, too cowed to intervene, too much her husband's avatar to fight for Stella, or even to understand her. Katie, three years younger, would listen, too, grateful for her role as good daughter, yet praying, for her own sake, that Stella's willfulness would continue to shield her. Then Armin Marz said softly, "You're a whore."

Stella flushed. Despite herself, a shiver of guilt passed through her. "I'm not."

Armin Marz half rose from his chair, thick torso straining his T-shirt, exposing the sag of his body. "Are you saying, Stella, that you don't spread your legs for him?"

"No," she answered. "I'm saying I do it for free."

Armin Marz's lips trembled. He stood with a surprising grace and quickness, and then walked toward her, eyes filled with a smoldering fury.

Stella made herself stand still. As he raised his hand, she stared into his face, so close to hers that she could hear the raggedness of his breathing.

His palm cracked across her cheekbone. She staggered back, eyes stung with tears, tasting blood on her lip.

Armin Marz stood frozen in front of her. His eyes had a wild, uncomprehending look—that of a horse, caught between anger and fear of the force that might humble him. He was breathing hard.

"You're a whore," he said again, and this time the word held a stubborn self-justification. "You work for him, and he pays for you. You whore to become a lawyer."

Stella's temples throbbed with pain. For an otherworldly moment, trapped like a prisoner in this darkened room, she wondered why a people who had created the magnificence of St. Stanislaus lived in such bleakness. But then that was why she was a whore.

"I work," she said in a trembling voice, "because *you* don't. And I still live here so someday I won't have to live like you."

Years of molten rage suffused her father's face—the silence of his shame broken, his humiliation thrown back at him by his daughter's words of contempt. The terrible hurt in his eyes ravaged Stella more than the force of his blow. She could scarcely comprehend what she had done.

He grasped her wrists in a grip so merciless that she winced. His face was inches from hers, and she caught from his breath the medicinal smell of vodka. "*You* won't finish law school," he said hoarsely. "Whores don't become lawyers. They get pregnant."

Suddenly, there was no turning back; in her resentment of a lifetime spent planning to escape his rule, Stella heard him wish for her failure. "Whores know how to protect themselves," she answered. "I won't disgrace you by having Jack's baby. I'll disgrace you by succeeding."

The room was poisonous now. Her father's hands were like twin vises, and his face contorted with the sense of his own impotence—the gift of words, mysteriously granted his older daughter, had failed him. When he slapped her again, there was a weariness about it, a confession of failure.

Shrinking back, Stella felt her neck snap. She bowed her head, wiping blood from her lip, struggling against faintness. Her voice was hollow. "That's twice," she said. "Twice more than you'll ever hit me again."

She saw him take in her meaning, eyes widening.

"Tonight," she told him, "I'm going back to Jack's. Then I'm getting my own place . . ."

"To whore for him."

"To *whore* for him?" Her voice rose. "Is that any worse than being your daughter?"

He flinched, stepping back. Stella felt sickened. This man had taken her to the zoo, to Blues games, had watched her play basketball with quiet pride. All his life he had wanted a son and instead been given daughters, the older of whom was inexplicable to him. And so she had concealed her desire to escape, out of fear and tradition and even respect: until the mills had closed and his nights of bitterness had begun, somehow they had managed. Until the mills had closed, and until Jack Novak.

"You're *not* my daughter." His own voice shook. "Once you leave this house, Katie is my only daughter."

Even then, Stella knew that she was abandoning her sister to a fate she did not want for her. But her guilt was overtaken by the wrenching certainty that this rupture would never heal—that, when she left, the flawed mosaic of her family would shatter. She imagined her powerless mother crying upstairs, the enormity of what Stella had done filling her sister with fear. Then Stella realized that the fear and grief were hers.

Tears ran down her face. "I never *was* your daughter," she managed to say.

She turned before he could answer, before anything else could happen. For years afterward, she wondered whether the sheen in Armin's eyes were tears of his own.

Yet she was still his daughter, though he could not recall their life together. And the woman she would always be, the child of this neighborhood, wished to enter the vast cathedral to pray for the salvation of Jack Novak's soul, then for the soul which had fled the shell who was now her father. And, were there time, for guidance.

But there was no time. As dusk enveloped her, Stella hurried to the Social Hall, to tell Arthur Bright of Jack Novak's murder.

FIVE

SLIPPING INSIDE the ballroom, Stella wondered how much time Bright had until the press learned of Novak's death.

She stopped, gazing around. The room was the same as it had been in her teens—large, plain, and well lit, with brown-stained wooden floors worn by years of school dances and wedding parties. But today the floor was covered by four hundred metal folding chairs, many occupied by people from the neighborhood. There were television cameras; cables; photographers; the claque of reporters to one side; police to provide security; and, at the front, the candidates and the moderator, a gray-haired veteran from the *Steelton Press*. The atmosphere was hot, close, and tense: while Krajek spoke, addressing a crowd as partial to him as it was hostile to Arthur Bright, Stella saw the sheen of sweat on Bright's forehead.

She felt for him in this place. After the night that Stella left her family's home, never to return while her father lived there, her mother, Helen, would visit her in secret. Though no one spoke of it, her father knew this; he would pass judgments at the dinner table, supposedly for her mother and sister, meant for transmission to Stella. Since she was small, Stella had heard from him that Jews were venal and that blacks were lazy, corrupt, and licentious. So Stella was not surprised when her mother confided that working for Bright was, to her father, the ultimate degradation of his daughter the whore, despoiling whatever else she might accomplish. This was Stella's fault, her mother implied; once more, Stella had erected a barrier which prevented Armin Marz from acknowledging her success. But Stella was quite certain that he had never wished to do so.

Now, leaning against the wall, she scanned the crowd.

Many, she knew, shared her father's attitudes, and their faces were taut, unsmiling. Stella spotted her late mother's closest friend, Wanda Lutoslawski, peering at Bright through her black-rimmed glasses. From girlhood, Wanda's two daughters had been Stella's and Katie's playmates, and Stella remembered her as filled with kindness: along with other women in the neighborhood, Wanda had functioned as a self-appointed surrogate parent, watching out after the Marz sisters once their mother went to work. But now Wanda was older, living on slender means, and the look on her face, as on that of her husband Stanley's, was grim. Next to them were two of the handful of blacks scattered through the crowd; Stanley leaned away from them, toward Wanda. When will it end? Stella wondered, and then focused on Mayor Krajek.

He was no older than Stella, and, though he was the neighborhood's pride and her schoolmate, she had never liked him. Even as a teenager, Tom Krajek's activity of the moment seemed undertaken not for its own sake but because it was the next point on a map of ambition which existed in Tom's head. Where the map ended, only Krajek knew for sure; then, as now, he had an energetic, quick-speaking manner which gave away nothing, and, to Stella, his eyes remained like those of Krajek in his teens—alert, soulless, and opaque.

Perhaps she felt jealous that a man she thought so narrow had come so far so quickly. Perhaps, too, it was because the boyish aura older women cooed over was distinctly unattractive to her: the slight, slender build; the adolescent face, beaky and unlined. His slick new taste in double-breasted suits—which, Stella reflected with renewed sadness, Jack Novak had adopted with success—reminded her on Krajek of a salesman out to upgrade his image. The inner man, Stella still believed, was as mean as a snake. But she would give him this—he was smart, cool, and no one would ever outwork or outplan him.

And there was one other thing: Tom Krajek was lucky.

His luck had begun at twenty-two, when his predecessor on the City Council, a true creature of the neighborhood, had collapsed of a heart attack at the annual Polish Street Festival. Still a student at Steelton State, Krajek had jumped into the race and won, managing to endear himself to Warszawa while persuading the downtown interests that he, unlike his limited predecessor, understood their needs. He and his new friends had waited for twelve years—three terms on the City Council—and then Krajek had run for mayor at the age of thirty-four.

His opponent was George Walker, the longtime black politician who was City Council President. Though sometimes arrogant and cursed with multiple marriages, Walker was masterful—as eloquent as a street preacher, yet a man who understood the city, and its interest groups, in a way that Krajek never would. Had he been white, Stella believed, Walker would have beaten Krajek two to one. As it was, a poll one week before election day showed Walker ahead by 6 percent.

Two days later, Stella picked up her *Steelton Press* and knew that George Walker was finished.

On a tip, two cops from narcotics had raided Walker's upscale apartment and found five kilos of cocaine. Walker declared himself drug free, the victim of a frame. So many rumors attended his personal life that few believed him. On the East Side drugs were a scourge, and enough of Walker's political base stayed home to give Tom Krajek the election. Five months later, the case was thrown out on the basis of a faulty warrant. But that was Walker's only consolation. In Warszawa, his downfall reinforced the folk wisdom about blacks, drugs, and minority politicians, making Arthur Bright's task that much harder.

But not as hard, Stella reflected, as Jack Novak's murder might make it—the association, however unfair, of another black candidate with the bizarre death of a drug lawyer, his friend and supporter, might prove fatal. And not as hard as Krajek had *already* made it, by staking his reelection on Steelton 2000: Tom Krajek—the man who, by uniting with Peter Hall, had launched their tarnished city on a new era of revival. Perhaps its greatest epoch, Stella thought with sudden irony, since Amasa Hall had brought the Poles to Steelton.

Eyeing her watch, she read a little past six, and turned her attention to Krajek.

As was his custom, Krajek stalked the speakers' platform with a hand-held microphone, gaze sweeping the audience as, suddenly, he stopped to make a point.

"Steelton 2000," he said sharply, "is *not* a welfare program. It is a break from the past which pays for itself in new jobs, new revenues, and a new future for our city.

"It is *not* rehab centers in settled neighborhoods, spreading drugs and social pathology where they have never been before."

"It is *not* affirmative action, which further divides us into competing groups . . ."

As though, Stella thought to herself, *we weren't divided long before.* But she noticed many in the audience look up in approval, Stan Lutoslawski nodding, could see the alertness of the press corps to points being scored. Quickly, Stella glanced at Bright. Despite his gift of self-control, he frowned; quite effectively, Krajek was touching on the accumulated fears and resentments, some justified, of many Steelton whites. More insidious, to Stella's mind, was the skill with which, through code words, he appealed to racial bias. As if to drive this home, Krajek spun on Arthur Bright.

"If *this* is what Arthur Bright offers us," he asked, "how can he claim to have the tools to run our city? Why should we promote him when, as prosecutor, he has failed to stem the scourge of drugs? And why should City Hall be a hunting preserve for favored groups, and favorite cronies?"

Stella watched Bright absorb the thinly veiled accusation: that he was unqualified and that, by backing him, blacks were trying through politics to exploit the city for themselves. *This* was why Bright needed Stella, in Warszawa and elsewhere—she could speak out for him in a way that he could not. But suddenly there was so much more to worry about: the Fielding case, and now Novak's murder. Fretful about time, she repressed the desire to pace.

"*Arthur Bright*"—here, Krajek faced the crowd again—"*claims* to be a visionary. But he *sounds* like a bean counter, nitpicking Steelton 2000 because he has no vision of his own. Including the *very people* he claims to represent."

Read "blacks," Stella thought sardonically. But most of those present, she noticed, listened closely.

"The real friend to minorities," he went on, "is *not* Arthur Bright—it's Steelton 2000." He began pacing again, speaking faster.

"This project benefits *all* races, *all* neighborhoods.

"It changes the image of Steelton from a burning river to a city with a glowing future.

"It keeps Steelton's money in the hands of Steelton's workers, through a state-of-the-art ballpark built by local contractors, supplied by local vendors, and played in by a team with local ownership."

Abruptly, Krajek began speaking directly to a TV camera which carried the debate live. "And *here* I want everyone in this city to listen closely: Steelton 2000 helps benefit our citizens of color, both this generation and the next."

As Krajek's voice slowed, Stella could imagine his face on a television screen, could hear the emphatic sincerity of each word.

"The *project manager* is a partnership which includes a minority contractor.

"*Thirty percent* of all contracts on Steelton 2000 will go to minority businesses.

"*Thirty percent* of all those who help build Steelton 2000 will be minority workers.

"We are building our future together, and *no one* can stop us."

It was brilliant, Stella thought. She could imagine black viewers taking note, just as she could feel her white neighbors saying to themselves, *What else could* they *want now? What more could* they *ask for?*

As if to confirm this, more in the audience began to nod. "I'd like to introduce," Krajek told them, "someone whose support I'm very proud to have. Peter Hall, could you stand up?"

As Krajek looked to his left, Stella saw Hall rising from the front row. In Stella's mind, his great-grandfather, Amasa, was a painting in the museum which bore his name—bald and mustached, with a stern Calvinist visage which brooked no doubt that the mills were his by right. But four generations of inherited wealth and elegant wives had bred the imperious mien out of the Halls who followed. Peter Hall was trim and sandy haired, a youthful man in his early forties who looked like what he was: a graduate of prep school and Princeton, with a guaranteed career in business and long weekends spent sailing—a man whose life was as privileged as his face was handsome, with the even features and blue eyes of a gracefully aging film star. Now, unlike Amasa, Peter Hall was popular as well.

"Peter Hall," Krajek said as the applause lowered, "is a guarantee of integrity. Because Hall Development is sharing any savings in construction with the city.

"*Peter Hall* will keep this below cost. And, when the ballpark is done, the city will own it.

"We will keep our old team, in a new home." Krajek paused again, flashing a quick smile. "But something else is new, something which Peter has asked me to share with you . . ."

It was then that Stella noticed a black man next to Hall. His hair was flecked with gray now, his upper body thicker, but he was still recognizable at once—one of three Hall of Famers the Steelton Blues had ever produced. He looked alert, at the ready, as he had been when Stella saw him take off at the crack of a bat, spearing a line drive on the dead run.

"As of next month," Krajek went on, "the ownership of the Blues will include one of Steelton's first citizens, whose pride in our community is second only to our pride in him: Larry Rockwell, the greatest center fielder in the history of the Blues . . ."

Mother of God, Stella thought to herself.

Larry Rockwell stood. Amidst the greatest applause of the evening, so did many in the audience.

It was a coup, Stella saw at once, for both Peter Hall and Krajek.

Blacks saw Larry Rockwell as a homeboy hero from the streets of the East Side; for whites, Rockwell was a precursor to Michael Jordan, a man who had given them a pleasure which transcended race. The former center fielder stood ramrod straight.

In contrast, Arthur Bright looked winded—Bright plainly had not seen this coming. Now, as he watched from a metal folding chair, three strands of Steelton's past had come together—the mill owner's descendant, the Polish mayor, and the son of migrant blacks—to secure its future. Against her will, Stella felt herself respond, old emotions stirring with hope for the city.

"Together," Krajek said when, at last, the applause had died, "we will build this park. And then *all* of us will help Steelton become what Ronald Reagan envisioned for America—'a shining city on a hill . . .'"

As the crowd stood to cheer, Krajek sat down.

Arthur Bright remained still. For all his talents, Stella thought, for all he had given to the city, Bright suddenly looked overmatched. Her heart went out to him—Bright was a good man, she believed, in a way that Krajek never would be. But politics was too seldom about goodness.

"County Prosecutor Bright?" the moderator prompted, and Arthur rose to answer.

SIX

QUICKLY, STELLA checked her watch.

It was six-fifteen. Soon the police would seal off the crime scene and transfer Novak's body to the morgue; soon after—if the press had not already overheard it on police radio scanners, they would release the news of his murder. Stella and Dance had not needed to discuss what that meant. The Chief of Police, Frank Nolan, was beholden to Krajek for the job Dance wanted: in dealing with the media, Nolan would take his cues from the mayor, and Dance could not overtly serve Bright's interests.

Nor could Stella help him now; until the debate was over, Bright was in the open, and all that she could do was watch. Thereafter, her hope was to spirit him away before some reporter asked why his friend and political ally Jack Novak had wound up wearing a garter belt, murdered, with his testicles on the bedroom floor and cocaine on the coffee table.

She closed her eyes again.

She would have given much to be in the cool quiet of St. Stanislaus, prayerful, removed from the crosscurrent of death and politics. Instead the thought made her search out Lizanne Bright.

Lizanne was in the first row, on the opposite side from Peter Hall. But she, like Stella, surely wished to be elsewhere. Lizanne was a slender woman with tightly coiffed hair and a serious manner, an ex-teacher devoted to her children, her husband, and her church. She was much too shy for politics, and seemed to stay within a narrow range of experience, far different from the active, questing life of her very public husband. As Arthur took up the microphone to face a hostile forum, Lizanne had a tight, pained expression.

And then Arthur smiled.

"I'm guilty," he said, raising his hands in mock surrender.

"*Yes*, I'm for affirmative action. Because I know that *all* of our citizens deserve a chance, and that to *live* with each other, we have to *know* each other.

"*Yes*, I'm for more drug-rehab centers. Because we can bust dealers from here to eternity—and I *will*—and still not save our kids from drugs.

"*Yes*, I'm for helping people from welfare to work, and not just folks from the East Side. Because most unemployed are *white*, abandoned by the companies they've worked so hard to build." Bright gave a quick, sharp glance at Krajek. "*Tom* knows it, and *you've* seen it—right here in this community, as the mills have slowly died."

Stella felt, in spite of everything, a slight lifting of her spirits. In this traumatic hour, when her past and present had collided, it was good to remember why she admired Arthur Bright. As she watched the crowd, Bright's unflinching style commanded their attention.

"*So*," he asked them, "what are we talking about here?

"Two hundred seventy-five million dollars of *your* money to build a new ballpark for Mr. Hall.

"Two hundred seventy-five million dollars for a stadium *you* can't afford to take your kids to, crammed with luxury boxes that go for a *hundred thousand dollars a year.*

"Two hundred seventy-five million dollars to keep the wealthy downtown interests—folks who have no interest in *your* neighborhood, or *your* lives, but a very generous interest in *Tom's* campaign—happier with their own lives."

Arthur was using his orator's gifts, Stella saw, to rise above his nervousness. Now he had settled into a rhythm, combining humor with the sharp edge of a social critic.

"What else could we *do*, Tom wonders, with two hundred seventy-five million dollars?

"Tom says he's worried about *crime.*

"With two hundred seventy-five million dollars we could do for Steelton what Mayor Giuliani's done for New York—put cops back on the beat keeping *you* safe, rather than stuck back at the station filling out police reports.

"Tom says he's worried about *schools.*

"For two hundred seventy-five million dollars we could rebuild our public schools, start new charter schools with rules that make sense to *you*, not some overpaid bureaucrat.

"Tom says he's worried about *jobs.*

"With two hundred seventy-five million dollars we could fund job-training programs for displaced workers, to help give back our families the security they deserve."

His voice had a rhythmic cadence now, a seductive touch of the

South—even Wanda Lutoslawski, Stella saw, was listening closely. Then Stella thought of Novak's body, headed for the morgue, and checked the time again.

Six-twenty.

"*You* all," Bright was saying, "*know* all this. So how does Tom Krajek sell you this deal?

"He can't very well put Mr. Hall's face on a billboard and say, 'For two hundred seventy-five million dollars, you can feed this boy.'" There was a ripple of nervous laughter, and Bright, flashing a quick grin, played to it. "I mean, Mr. Hall could write out a check for *that* much, on the spot, and hand it up to Tom right now."

Despite all that weighed on her, Stella almost laughed. Sitting straighter in his chair, Krajek looked genuinely annoyed, though Hall, glancing at the mayor, assumed the bland expression of a man unfazed.

"So," Bright said with irony, "Tom takes some black kid nobody knows, and makes him the poster child for a ballpark neither you *nor* the kid will ever see.

"Now, the mayor tells you that there will be jobs galore for African-Americans." Pausing, Bright flashed a brief, sardonic smile. "Well, Tom was too polite to mention it, of course, but I *am* one."

There was more laughter now; whatever their sentiments, many in the audience looked amused by Bright's witty dissection of Krajek's tactics. And there was something more at work, Stella knew: by reminding Warszawa of the history of the mills, the gulf between their hardship and the public largesse which Krajek had granted Peter Hall, Bright suggested that blacks and white ethnics had more in common than they knew. The clump of reporters had begun watching Bright's performance with open enjoyment.

"And," Bright continued, "I can promise you that when this project has come and gone, things in the black community will be the same as before. Just like in Warszawa.

"So ask yourself—'Will spending two hundred seventy-five million dollars of *my* money to help Mr. Hall help *me*?'" Bright smiled again. "*That's* what you need to answer. Don't be building him a ballpark to save some poor black child."

He paused, letting his irony sink in, and then its underlying seriousness. And now Bright, quite suddenly, was serious, too.

"You deserve better. We *all* do.

"It's not too late. I say renegotiate this deal. Let Mr. Hall pay some of the costs. Then take the money we'll save, and put it where it helps you, and this city, the most." Looking across the audience, he finished softly, "Thank you all for listening to me."

With that, Bright sat down.

The applause was respectable, Stella thought—not as great as the cheers for Krajek, or for Larry Rockwell, but better than she had hoped. Perhaps Bright might yet mine support in Warszawa.

As Krajek stood to answer him, Stella ducked into the hallway and fished the cell phone from her purse.

D A N C E   W A S alone in his squad car, driving to police headquarters.

"Does the media know yet?" she asked.

"No." Dance paused, then he added, "I just told Nolan."

His words conveyed much more: that the Chief of Police had not known before; that Dance had waited as long as he could to tell him; that the time remaining to Bright was however long it would now take Nolan to decide whether to inform Krajek first, or to bring in the media at once.

"It'd be better," Stella said, "if Nolan told the press as little as possible. The more we say about what we know or guess, the more we tell whoever murdered Jack."

"I know. But I don't think that's what's going down. Give yourself an hour, tops."

Stella thanked him, and slipped back into the hall.

"P E T E R   H A L L ," Krajek was saying, "deserves our thanks. But make no mistake—*I* negotiated this deal and *I'll* take the credit, or the blame.

"Blame *me* for the fact that Hall Development will pay for any and all cost overruns.

"Blame *me* for the fact that Hall Development Company makes money if the city *saves* money.

"Blame *me* for the fact that if *Peter Hall* brings the Blues' new home in for less than two hundred seventy-five million dollars, the city gets a rebate."

Krajek's small frame was tense with the look of a man accused; he had always lacked humor, Stella recalled, or any perspective on himself. She thought this a weakness in a politician, which went beyond an absence of charm: it hinted that there might be no limit on his ambitions, no ability to distinguish between his interests and the public's. Nervously, she scanned the press, searching for evidence—reporters fumbling for beepers or cell phones—that the news of Novak's murder was out.

"The two hundred seventy-five million dollars," Krajek said assertively, "is as good as paid for—in new tax revenues from jobs created and more baseball tickets sold, *and* from more new events like rock concerts, All-Star games, and someday, I devoutly hope, even a papal Mass . . ."

Was the Pope signed on to throw out the first ball? Stella wondered. Or was he hidden next to Larry Rockwell? But Krajek was mining a well of sentiment which existed, too, in her: she still remembered the moment, sacred to the seven-year-old Stella, when the future John Paul II, then the Polish Cardinal Karol Wojtyla, had performed Mass at St. Stanislaus and briefly touched her hand. No Pope had been here since.

"We once were great," Krajek finished. "We can be great again . . ."

Stella felt the cell phone buzz in her purse. She took it out again and punched the button, murmuring, "Yes?"

"You've got maybe twenty minutes," Dance said. "Nolan's contacting the press."

"'As GOOD as paid for?'" Bright asked in a tone of incredulity.

"Not from construction jobs—they're temporary.

"Not from money people would have spent on leisure activities somewhere else in Steelton—at movies, restaurants, or department stores—instead of at the ballpark.

"Not from rent—Mr. Hall will pay hardly any.

"Not from luxury boxes, or tickets, or concessions—Mr. Hall controls all that."

Stopping, Bright placed one hand on his hip—the teacher, leading his class to the light. "As you know, the mayor and Mr. Hall dreamed up this deal in private. They're financing it by selling two hundred seventy-five million dollars in bonds that the *city* has to repay. Add interest, and repaying those bonds will cost you almost *four hundred fifty million dollars.*

"*They* will build it, and *you* will pay.

"*That's* why this deal was done in secret.

"*That's* why there was no competitive bidding.

"*That's* why they haven't told you about the millions upon millions *more* you will sink into this ballpark—in new access roads, new sewers, new utilities, new bus routes, more security, and the endless costs of maintenance." Bright smiled again. "Mr. Hall doesn't even have to pay for *lightbulbs.*

"No, *they* will build it, and *you* will pay. And pay and pay and pay and pay, long after the construction jobs have vanished."

Pausing, Bright grew serious again, his voice quiet. "A stadium isn't a steel mill. The mills helped build this city. But it's the *city* who's building this ballpark, *Peter Hall* who will profit from it, and *you* who will pay for it." Bright touched his chest. "*I* will pay. We *all* will pay. And that's the thing about this project which unites us."

Amidst respectful applause, greater than before, Bright sat down.

For the last time, Stella checked her watch.

The debate was over.

QUICKLY, THE candidates shook hands, contriving smiles for the media. And then the press enveloped the two men, their managers and handlers trying to act as intermediaries.

Hurrying through the crush, Stella was struck by how fragile Bright looked, how diminished from the energetic figure who had just faced a hostile crowd. But that was what the process seemed to do, and, reflecting on her mission tonight, Stella experienced a flicker of doubt about the price of her ambitions. A few feet from Arthur, Lizanne Bright, looking as cornered as a deer, mouthed platitudes about her pride in Arthur, how hospitable she found Warszawa.

Finally, Stella reached her boss. "Excuse me," she said to the young woman from Channel 3, interrupting a question.

Sharply, Bright appraised Stella. "Whatever it is . . ."

Plucking his sleeve, she pulled him a few feet away, dismissing his annoyance, saying softly and quickly: "I need to get you out of here. Jack Novak's been murdered."

Reflexively, Bright glanced over his shoulder. A series of emotions seemed to fight for control: fear, surprise, calculation—everything, Stella thought, but grief. Then his body sagged and slowly, almost reverently, he murmured, "*Fuck* . . ."

To Stella, it sounded something like a prayer. "Oh," she told him, "it's much worse than that."

SEVEN

BRIGHT SAID a few words to Lizanne, then he and Stella walked to Stella's car in silence.

Sitting in the semidark, sealed from the audience trickling out of the Social Hall and into the streets of Warszawa, Bright was in shadow. "How did it happen?" he asked.

"Badly." Stella's voice came out flat. "He was hanged from the closet door, with his own belt, wearing stockings and high heels."

Bright stared at Stella. His lips parted, but no sound came out. Then he turned from her, gazing emptily at the darkened windshield. He seemed hardly to breathe.

Softly, Stella told him, "We don't know who. Or why."

For moments, Bright said nothing. "Then how," he asked slowly, "do you know it was murder?"

The question surprised Stella; wherever his thoughts had drifted, Bright seemed to imagine an accidental death, his friend overtaken by hidden desires. With equal quiet, Stella answered, "They'd castrated him, Arthur."

In profile, Bright froze. Then his head bent, hands covering his face.

Stella was faintly aware of footsteps on the sidewalk, the voices of passersby. In her attempt to be practical, she had repressed emotion; now, watching Bright, her own anguish returned. She placed one hand on his shoulder, seeking comfort as much as offering it.

After a time, Bright straightened in his seat. "What else is there?"

"There was an anonymous call, saying Jack was dead—the voice was disguised, and they're not even sure if it was a man or a woman. When they arrived, Jack's door was unlocked, no sign of a break-in. He'd been drinking with someone, it appeared, and there was a line of coke on his coffee table. Jack was in the bedroom. They also found amyl nitrite and a pair of handcuffs." Oddly, Stella realized, the recitation helped her; her voice was clipped, passionless. "It's either a scene turned violent, or a planned execution tricked up in drag."

Bright rubbed his eyes. "Why," he murmured, "would anyone do *that*?"

"I don't know, Arthur. I just stared at him, and wondered, 'How could you die like this?'"

Something in his face changed; for the first time, turning, Bright seemed fully aware of her. "Were you *there*? At Jack's?"

"Yes."

"*Sweet Lord.*" He covered her hand with his own. "You didn't need to do that."

She searched his face for meaning. They had discussed her relationship with Jack only once, and long ago; now she wondered how much he knew. As if sensing this, Bright met her gaze. "You want off this?"

Stella shook her head. "Nothing could be worse," she answered, "than what I saw tonight." She hesitated, and then said with quiet vehemence, "This doesn't feel right to me. Whatever else Jack was . . ."

The words stuck there. Was she, Stella wondered, trying to keep some corner of her memories free from tarnish? Or was she simply trying to tell Bright that *they* weren't like that? And how far Jack might have traveled in fifteen years?

Bright had turned from her again. "What," he asked wearily, "do we really know about anyone?"

Stella did not answer. "Drive me to the office," Bright ordered. "I'll call Sloan."

Stella handed him her cell phone. After he reached the First Assistant, they fell quiet for the rest of the trip, caught in their separate thoughts—trying, Stella sensed, to restore themselves.

FIRST ASSISTANT Charles Sloan was already in Bright's office, talking on the telephone to Bright's campaign manager and media spokesman.

"Say we have 'full confidence in the police,'" he directed. "Which is more than Krajek's dickhead chief deserves, with what he's done. Fax me a draft as soon as you've got one." Brusquely, he put down the phone, and said to Bright, "That asshole Nolan told them everything, right down to the garter belt. When I got here, there was already a voice-mail message from Leary at the *Press,* asking how much money Novak's raised for your campaign." Sloan shook his head, adding with muted disgust, "Black stockings. They'll love *that* with their coffee and cornflakes."

To Stella, this said everything about her rival. Sloan was shrewd, assertive, unsentimental, and distrustful of anyone who—like Novak or Stella herself—might impinge on his relationship to Arthur Bright. Her own antagonism involved more than who succeeded Bright; it was born of a fundamental clash of temperaments between the master office politician and a woman who believed that she still wanted, above anything, to be the best at what she did. To Stella, Sloan's tireless antennae were misused, his desire to control the flow of information to the prosecutor a disservice; for Sloan, her affinity with Arthur was a threat to his own preeminence.

To look at them, the two men were opposites. Sloan was short, round-faced, mustached, and paunchy, with snub features, rumpled suits, and a voracious appetite for fast food and the Pepsi he drank now, one of a dozen or more cans, close observers claimed, that he consumed each day. Compared to Sloan, Bright, sliding into his leather chair, looked like a wraith. But, glancing from one to the other as she sat in front of Bright's desk, Stella had the uncomfortable feeling of being three times an outsider—white, a woman, a stranger to their shared history.

"They're drafting a statement about Novak," Sloan told Bright. "The political people want you to hold a press conference tomorrow—to tell the voters you're on top of this, and that all this office wants is the truth. Just like always."

Bright's expression was curiously distant. The only sign that he had been listening was his quiet, belated question, "Is *that* what we want?"

"Among other things. We also don't want this to get any dirtier than it already is. Or weirder." Abruptly, Sloan turned to Stella. "What are *your* plans?"

Stella marshaled her thoughts. "Keep close to Dance—thank God he's running this himself. I'll be there for key interviews, help with strategy. Not that Nat needs much help." She faced Bright. "How visible do you want *our* office to be?"

Bright frowned, pensive. "That," Sloan interjected, "depends on where Nat's going. And what he's doing."

Stella shrugged. "Everything, he tells me. Investigating neighbors, friends, girlfriends, the paperboy, the mailman, people in his office. With what we've found, you can add sex shops and the S and M scene. And Nat will look at Jack's cases for problems or unhappy clients." She looked at Bright again, speaking more quietly. "The public may not know that his biggest client was Vincent Moro. But Dance knows."

There was a palpable change in the room—Bright staring at the desk, Sloan studying Stella. In their silence, she became more aware of details:

the flickering of a spent bulb in the fluorescent panel above them; the framed picture of Lizanne and the kids on Arthur's desk; papers which seemed to be precinct-by-precinct polling figures from the last mayoral race between Krajek and George Walker; the irregular grid of Steelton's skyline, appearing in the darkness like an electronic game board with some lights punched out. Somberly, Bright said, "No one *knows* that, Stella. Jack never represented Moro in court."

"But Moro controls the drug traffic," she answered, "and Jack represented the biggest dealers whenever they were busted. Do you think *that* could have happened without Moro's blessing?"

"Novak was *good*," Sloan broke in. "Do *you* think these dealers are stupid? They could afford the best."

Sloan looked and sounded angry. Unflinching, Stella answered, "I know what I know. Fourteen years ago, I saw Moro in Jack's office. At night, when no one but Jack was supposed to be there."

Sloan leaned forward. "Vincent Moro," he said, "runs organized crime in Steelton—drugs, gambling, prostitution, everything. He has for twenty years. If Arthur knows Jack is Moro's guy, no way we take his money. Period."

Beneath the words, Stella heard Sloan's second message—*and that's the way it's staying, so stay away from Moro.* "Drugs," Stella retorted, "are a nasty business—way too much money at stake, and the feds pressing dealers to rat each other out. Suppose Jack pissed off a client . . ."

"*Vincent Moro?*" Sloan's eyes widened in a pantomime of annoyance and incredulity. "Moro's a businessman—he doesn't butcher people, he disappears them. If Jack *was* his guy, why kill him? And how do you ever prove it? You don't." His voice turned low and chill. "But once you even ask the question, you start rumors, right in the middle of the mayoral race. Last time around, rumors were the beginning of *George Walker's* end."

Sloan, Stella knew, was playing to an audience of one. Bright's glance at Stella was veiled. "If there were problems with clients," he said, "it won't be Moro who tells you that. And no dealer anywhere is stupid enough to say 'Vincent Moro' aloud. You can ask about Jack's clients without mentioning Moro's name."

Stella nodded. "Before you ask anyone about anything," Sloan told her abruptly, "ask *yourself* whether you should handle this case at all."

Wondering whether Sloan had known of her true relationship to Jack, Stella felt herself flush. "I'm the head of our homicide unit," she answered. "This is a major homicide . . ."

"You worked for Novak," Sloan said in his most unimpressed voice. "He helped you get a job here. And now you're bringing up Vincent Moro, even though it makes no sense. So I have to ask, Stella—are you objective enough to do the job?"

Was he setting a condition for her keeping the case, Stella wondered—drop the subject of Moro? Or was he setting her up, in Bright's presence, in case the inquiry went sour? "Doing the job," she answered coolly, "is all I care about."

Eyebrows raised in a pantomime of skepticism, Sloan turned to Bright. The prosecutor seemed inscrutable; even now he exploited, while refusing to acknowledge, the rivalry between Stella and Sloan. "Just keep Charles informed," he told her. "Everything goes through him."

It was typical of Arthur, Stella thought—her place preserved, Sloan's primacy maintained. "If that's your decision," Sloan said to Bright, "Stella should be with you at the press conference."

Stella was surprised; Sloan was at pains to keep her profile as low as possible, her face off the evening news. In this case, she guessed, Sloan wanted Stella to take some of the heat in case Novak's murder went unsolved. And, she supposed, the presence of a white woman next to Bright might have its political uses.

Weary, the prosecutor unknotted his tie. She half expected a change of mood, perhaps some reflection about Jack's murder. To Stella's surprise, he asked her, "Where are we with Tommy Fielding?"

Though she had last examined the crime scene pictures perhaps six hours ago, it seemed to have taken place in some other, more rational life. But, quite suddenly, Bright was thinking ahead. "The autopsy's tomorrow," she answered. "I'm sitting in. Maybe that'll tell us something—his parents are in the dark. They keep saying he was murdered."

Bright steepled his fingers. "Tread lightly," he told her, "with Peter Hall. After tonight, especially."

At the corner of her eye, she saw Charles Sloan, narrow-eyed, fold his hands across his paunch—pondering, she guessed, what the death of Hall's aide and a drug-addicted black prostitute might mean to Arthur Bright. And, by extension, to him.

"Anything else?" Stella asked.

There was silence. "'Sufficient unto the day,'" Bright finally murmured, "'is the evil thereof.'"

It was a signal, Stella knew, for her to leave. When she did, Bright barely seemed to notice.

EIGHT

IT WAS close to midnight before Stella reached her home.

It was near the western border of Steelton, with a stone porch, brown-stained wood, and a second floor with dormer windows which afforded Stella a distant city view. She had bought the house for its sense of space and light, so different from the dark, cramped home of her childhood. But its solidity, and the bright colors of her furnishings, gave Stella a refuge from the harshness of her job. And the house was *hers*, with all that implied—bought with her own money, a testament to her pride in years of work as well as a concession, squarely faced, that she might always have to do things for herself.

She shared it with a cat. Star was lean and cool and black—to look at her, the epitome of the cat who walked alone. But Stella would be home for only minutes before Star would come to find her, rubbing against her leg. Stella did not know the ways that animals knew things, but Star seemed to know that Stella had saved her life.

The neighbors' ten-year-old had found her in their basement, barely more than a kitten, scrawny and dirty, with a feral look and the smell of skunk spray. The boy's mother had found Star unsettling and faintly diabolical and, as quickly as she could, had shipped her to an animal shelter and a near-certain death. Hearing the story, Stella had asked the boy to go with her to identify the cat; though it was irrational, no other pet would do, for the story of the cat's rejection had touched Stella's heart. So Stella had paid for a battery of shots, and set about the business of giving affection to a cat.

Locking the door behind her, she felt Star's soft forehead nudge her leg. Stella flicked the wall switch; a lamp cast its light from the living room to the black cat at her feet. Stella picked her up.

Tired, she stood there in the alcove, Star cradled beneath her chin.

On a walnut table beside them was a porcelain statuette of the Baby Jesus—wearing an ornate crown and a robe with gold ruffles—known for reasons now lost to Stella as the Infant of Prague. When Stella was young, many homes in Warszawa had an Infant; Stella and Katie had given this one to their mother and, on Christmas and Easter, would please Helen Marz by wheedling money from their father to buy the statuette a new robe. They had bought the gown it wore now when Stella was ten, and it had been her mother's favorite; as she lay dying of cancer, she had given it to Stella.

Though Stella had visited her mother daily, sometimes holding her hand for hours, they found little to say. She sensed that her mother's bestowal of the Infant symbolized for the older woman a time of certainty and order, before so much was lost between them, and the hope now, however different they were, that her older daughter would remember her. To Katie's resentment, Stella had retrieved the statuette when the house was sold, and placed it in her new home with a mixture of nostalgia, respect, some humor, and simple wonderment that she could reflect so little—in looks or in her essence—the woman who had given birth to her.

She had said this to Jack Novak once, in bed, years before her mother had died. With a certain cool edge, he remarked, "You've outgrown her, Stella. You looked at her life, and at all those nuns in school. Then you realized that the *Sisters* never got to be a *Father*." A faint smile touched his mouth. "You don't want to be your mother, or even Mother Teresa. You want to be a Cardinal, or maybe the Pope."

Perhaps as Jack had intended, Stella felt an unwanted fear: that her hesitance in giving herself involved a deeper ambivalence about being a woman. And so on that night, as on other nights, Stella had tried still harder to prove she had become one.

Cradling Star, she climbed the stairs to her bedroom.

THERE WERE framed pictures on her dresser—her parents, her sister. They stared at her from the past, unknowing. Now her mother was dead, her father dead in spirit, Katie estranged since the night Stella had left them for Jack Novak. But the night that Stella had left her parents' home for good, she had not foreseen this.

The evening had begun on the tide of Jack's elation, celebrating a victory over dinner at a flashy downtown nightclub. Jack had ordered a bottle of Roederer Cristal with the same air of sangfroid that he took to the opera and the ballet whenever the New York companies passed through town, or to piloting the trim new sailboat he had acquired on a whim. Life was good for Jack, and seldom better than that night: to

Arthur Bright's quite evident disgust, his case against Jack's client—George Flood, a big-time East Side drug lord charged with distributing five kilos of cocaine—had vanished with the coke itself, destroyed by what the police had called "an administrative error."

With the champagne a silken buzz on her tongue, Stella had said, "I don't understand how you and Bright can be friends. To me, he seems so idealistic."

"And *I* seem so cynical?" Jack answered with a smile. "Arthur and I are friends, and we're also professionals who accept that we're part of each other's ecology. But let me tell you what an idealist I really am. Because if I were God, Stella, I'd legalize the drug trade.

"Think about it. You could have drug treatment instead of drug addicts. Believers like Arthur make the chain of drug distributors possible, and make *me* necessary. Whereas I'd put myself out of business if only Arthur would let me." His smile faded. "But instead, I have to beat him. That's the *only* principle Arthur permits me. That, and to never represent anyone who wants to cut a deal with Arthur by selling out the next guy up the chain."

Stella sipped more champagne. "Why not, if the deal's good enough?"

Jack shrugged. "Because, in the end, it's bad for everyone. Some people start lying. Others just get killed."

Stella had fallen silent. Even then, she saw who stood to gain the most from Jack's policy: the man who supplied the drugs. But Jack's clients were plentiful—blacks, whites, Asians, Haitians, Latinos. They would call from jail; later, a wife or brother would appear at Novak's office with an envelope of cash. Stella collected her paycheck, and went to school at night, and said nothing. Just as Jack's clients said nothing to Arthur Bright.

Where did the money come from? Stella had wondered then. And why cash, when Novak made no effort to hide his affluence or, she was confident, to evade taxes? Jack seemed to be at the heart of an elaborate game to which, of the two of them, only he knew the rules. But the rules Stella had learned in law school—innocent until proven guilty, and that even the worst criminals were entitled to a competent defense—had, for a time, stemmed the qualms of a soul which believed that laws should be obeyed, order maintained, goodness encouraged.

"The cocaine they lost," Stella had asked Jack over dessert. "How could that happen?"

Jack smiled. "Bureaucracy. Thanks to people like Arthur, there are so many drug prosecutions that their storeroom is jammed with evidence.

Once the case is over, they have to destroy it, or they'd be swimming in white powder. So they fill out a form, and the coke goes up in smoke." Softly, he laughed. "Looks like somebody misread the form. But then some of our cops have a literacy problem."

"Lucky for you."

Jack sipped his brandy. "Luck," he said blithely, "is a talent." Putting down his glass, he looked into her face, serious again. "What's truly lucky, Stella, is that I get to share it with you. Knowing I'll be lucky for hours."

He just assumed this. And yet, Stella knew, he was right. That night, walking toward him in the mirror, unaware that within two hours her family would shatter, the unsettling sense came over her that Jack made his *own* luck, in court and with her.

Fifteen years later, she saw herself in that moment, naked before him, naked in her confusion. And then saw Jack as he had been tonight, his luck at an end, hanging in the reflection of those same mirrors.

Undressing, Stella settled Star on the pillow next to her and turned out her light. The cat put her nose in Stella's hair and purred, its body vibrating with satisfaction. Then the purring stopped, and the cat was asleep.

Only then, in the quiet of her room, did Stella cry. She was not sure for whom.

PART TWO

JACK NOVAK

ONE

THE NEXT morning, sleepless and spent, Stella attended Tommy Fielding's autopsy.

She still recalled her first: the man's organs had no sooner been exposed by Micelli's swift scalpel than a lab tech, grinning, had chirped, "Another Kodak moment," and began snapping Polaroids. Since then, her lasting impression of the autopsy room had always been of metal—Micelli's silver instruments; the dull gray sink and cabinets; the hanging scale used to weigh internal organs; the steel tables on which they placed the bodies. Tommy Fielding lay on one; on the other, staring emptily at the ceiling, was Jack Novak.

Leaving Micelli, Stella walked over to him.

At best, for Stella, witnessing an autopsy was something to be endured. But this was too much. Gently, she placed a gloved finger on each eyelid, cool to the touch, and closed them over Jack's red-speckled eyes. This made the final moment, a last look at his face, slightly more bearable. Then she drew a sheet over his naked body, consigning him to memory.

Stella offered no explanation, nor did Kate Micelli ask for one. Micelli and her assistant stood over Fielding's body, exchanging laconic observations; except for their voices, the room was silent, and their movements had the sparing efficiency of surgeons in an operating theater. Stationing herself beside the coroner, Stella steeled herself, and considered Tommy Fielding in the last moments that he would resemble the person he had been.

As she did, Stella felt a vivid empathy for Fielding's parents, and a quiet awe for what the absence of an animating spirit did to mere flesh. The man she saw had already traveled far from the one his parents had known, or thought they knew; he was white and stiff and pallid, and it was not easy to imagine him alive, worrying over the spectral ballpark materializing through Stella's window. But he had been as handsome as the crime scene photos suggested, with large brown eyes and the sculpted features of a Greek statue. His body, too, was a statue's—sinewy and well defined—bespeaking a rigid adherence to exercise and diet. Even now, there was something fastidious about him, an aura of cleanliness; studying him, Stella could appreciate Marsha Fielding's shock and disbelief.

"Consider yourself lucky," Micelli observed. "The one we did last Friday had been dead for three weeks."

Stella still gazed at Fielding. "Tell me about Tina Welch," she said.

"The report's on my desk. But I can give you the essence—she was a junkie, a textbook case. Needle tracks on the arms and beneath the fingernails, subcutaneous hemorrhages caused by numerous injections, dried blood surrounding the last one." Pausing, Micelli inspected Fielding's torso minutely, then his arms, stiff and unyielding. "Here, there's nothing but the one puncture."

She dictated some clinical observations into a tape recorder, then began speaking to Stella again. "Tina Welch," Micelli continued, "showed a thickening and sclerosis of the subcutaneous veins typical of the habitual user. I don't expect we'll see that here." With a gloved finger, Micelli opened Fielding's lips, tilting his head. "What I *do* see, in both of them, is a thin white froth. Consistent with a massive overdose.

"But the differences are obvious. At twenty-three, Tina Welch was worn, unhealthy looking. If the body's the temple of the soul, these two weren't exactly soulmates." Micelli dictated a few terse sentences, then added, "Oh, yes, Tina was HIV positive. And she had the beginnings of focal lesions in the white matter of the brain, indicative of AIDS."

"In short," Stella said, "a walking tragedy."

Micelli nodded. "Who was fated to die a very unpleasant death. By comparison, her actual death was a mercy—an acute respiratory depression, consistent with an overdose of heroin. Which everything about her body would lead you to suspect."

"Then what," Stella wondered aloud, "would Fielding want with her?"

"'The heart is a lonely hunter'? You're thinking, I imagine, about Mom's homicide theory."

"Yes."

Micelli angled her head toward Novak. "In *that* respect, this man's like your friend over there—no bruises, no scratches, no signs of violence on the body itself, or to the skull. Nothing to suggest that Fielding wasn't as cooperative with Tina Welch as, on the surface, Mr. Novak was with *his* unknown friend. Nor did Tina's body suggest rough treatment—other than what she'd been doing to herself for years."

"Did Fielding have sex with her?"

Micelli shook her head. "There appears to be no residue of semen on his penis, and all of Tina's condoms were still in her purse. Perhaps they planned to shoot up first. A fatal dose of coitus interruptus." She spoke to her machine again, then told Stella, "We've sent all the paraphernalia to be tested, of course, and fingerprinted if possible. Maybe that will tell us something more.

"But remember this—killing someone with an overdose of heroin requires unusual sophistication, someone who knows drugs. And anyone who does would also know how unpredictable that is."

"How so?"

"Heroin converts to morphine in the body, acting as a respiratory depressant. But even a massive dose won't necessarily cause death—especially with a Tina Welch, who's habituated to heroin. Your murderer would have to stick around, maybe sit on their chests to make sure they both died." Micelli reached for her scalpel. "That's *two* homicides. How many *murderers* would that take, and what presence of mind?"

Stella followed Micelli's hand. "That's what I've been asking myself."

Narrow-eyed, Micelli made a Y-shaped incision in Fielding's chest and abdomen. "I can only tell you what the medical evidence is, Stella. But we both know that most murder is butchery. Here, even Fielding's bedroom was as neat as a pin. If this is a double homicide, it's really quite elegant. And it would seem to require multiple killers."

The coroner held a hand saw now. Body taut with effort, she used it to open the dead man's ribs, exposing his internal organs.

Stella winced at the sound. "Can you establish time of death?" she asked. "Even in a relative way?"

"Not from their bodies. They were both cold."

Carefully, Micelli removed Tommy Fielding's heart and lungs. Her bespectacled assistant, a young Chinese man, took the severed organs to be weighed. Stella forced herself to concentrate on Fielding's face.

Why? she silently asked him, just as she had with Novak. *How did you end up here?* That was what she found so unsatisfying about an autopsy, Stella realized; Micelli could extract this man's heart, but she could tell her nothing about his soul, or even how his life had intersected with that of Tina Welch. As Micelli sectioned the heart and lungs, Stella thought of Fielding's mother.

"Tommy hated needles," she had said . . .

Carefully, Micelli inserted a pink sliver of lung beneath a microscope. "What are you looking for?" Stella asked.

Micelli squinted into the lens. "With habitual heroin use, the lungs often contain fibers: they're long and slender and, in close-up, they glisten. Tina's were actually quite beautiful. But Tommy's lungs are standard issue."

"And so," Stella prodded, "there's nothing to say that he'd *ever* shot up."

"Not yet." Micelli turned to her assistant. "Cut a sample of his hair," she instructed.

Stella looked into Fielding's eyes, as blank as marble. "I keep wondering why Tina Welch went home with a stranger. Street hookers tend to have a workplace—hotel rooms, cars, even alleys. A place where they have a little control, to minimize the risk that some psychopath will cut them into pieces."

"Yes," Micelli said dryly. "At least *I* wait until they're dead." She shrugged. "Maybe he'd picked her up before. But Nathaniel Dance and the boys and girls from vice will have to survey Tina's colleagues.

"All *I* can tell you is what, as corpses, she and Tommy have in common—cause of death." Solemn, the coroner surveyed the bloody wreckage of Fielding's internal organs. "What we see here is consistent with a classic drug overdose. The lungs are filled with blood; the heart has failed as a pump; and the man's respiratory system simply crashed. Tommy literally drowned in his own blood."

The odors rising from his body had begun to bother Stella. She backed away a step; seeming not to notice, Micelli concluded, "We'll check the *content* of his blood for heroin, of course. And we'll find the residue of a serious dose, maybe a bad batch."

Stella considered this. "Tina had to shoot *him* up first, right? That's how she ended up with the needle in her arm."

"One would think."

"And he wasn't an experienced user, you believe. So wouldn't it hit him right away? It killed *her*, and she *was* experienced."

Micelli fixed Stella with a speculative look. "In other words, wouldn't watching Tommy die discourage even the most ardent smackhead? I suppose it would. Only there's no way for me to tell you how quickly he reacted, or how quickly she shot up."

"But *she* died," Stella retorted, "so quickly she barely got the needle out of her arm."

Micelli frowned. "So who held them down?" she asked. "How many were there? Why aren't there any signs of a struggle in his bedroom, or on his body? This man was an athlete, after all."

"Exactly."

Micelli gave her a thin smile. "And here you are, thinking that *my* job's hard."

"It is to me."

The coroner's smile faded; she glanced at Novak, and then turned her attention back to Stella. "You've got a lot to do," she said quietly. "You've kept your word now, Stella. If there's anything more of interest here, I'll call."

Grateful, Stella left—she had no need to impress Kate Micelli. The metal doors closed behind her, cutting off the harsh scraping sound of Micelli's saw on Tommy Fielding's skull.

TWO

THE PRESS room at the County Prosecutor's office—tile floors, bare walls, metal chairs—was crowded and hot. Arthur Bright and Stella sat at a folding table facing minicams, photographers, sound technicians, crime reporters, and players that Stella was less accustomed to, the political media. Jack Novak's financial support for Bright had combined with his murder to create a room tense with incipient scandal: as soon as Bright finished his statement, Dan Leary of the *Press* was on his feet.

"How much money," Leary called out, "did Jack Novak raise for your mayoral campaign?"

Wiry and aggressive, Leary leaned into the question. Bright's own demeanor was quiet, composed. "Mr. Novak gave a thousand dollars, Dan, the limit on individual donations. He also helped sponsor a dinner which raised $47,000 more, and included some of his friends. They were also *my* friends—as you know, I have broad support in the legal community . . ."

"But wasn't it a mistake to accept money from a lawyer whose *own* money came from defending drug dealers?"

Edgy, Stella thought again of George Walker's downfall, and of its unsettling parallel to Bright's dilemma now. She saw First Assistant Charles Sloan, arms folded, following each exchange from a corner of the room. "It was not," Bright answered promptly. "Lawyers believe in the right to a fair trial. Because of this shared belief, some of us prosecute cases, and others defend them. That's the way our system works." His tone became, to Stella, a shade defensive. "For over twenty years, I've prosecuted drug cases to the limit. *No one* has ever questioned that— *especially* Mr. Novak."

"*Arthur?*" Turning, Stella saw a tall blond reporter—Jan Saunders of Channel 6. "Novak's murder seems to involve drugs, sexual perversion, and extreme brutality. Doesn't it disturb you that a friend and supporter would die in those circumstances?"

"It more than *disturbs* me." Bright looked from face to face. "Noth-

ing I knew about Jack Novak suggested that his life would end this way.
More than anyone here, I want to know why it did."

"But won't a murder this bizarre," Jan Saunders persisted, "hurt your
chances of becoming mayor?"

Bright stared at her. "Absolutely not," he said. "Why should it?"

The room was momentarily quiet. "Do you have any information,"
Chet Winfield of Channel 2 asked, "about *who* it was that reported
Novak's murder?"

Stella reached for the microphone. "Not yet," she told Winfield. "But
the police investigation is barely eighteen hours old . . ."

"What responsibility is *your* office taking for the investigation?"

Involuntarily, Stella glanced at Charles Sloan; it was the question he
had wanted to finesse, and she was certain he would criticize any answer
she gave. "I'm the head of the homicide unit," she said. "That makes me
responsible, along with the police, for what we do or don't do—"

"Do you feel added pressure," Jan Saunders interjected, "because Mr.
Bright is running for mayor?"

Stella shook her head. "Any pressure I feel," she answered, "is
because *Mr. Novak* is dead."

"But aren't you *also* concerned," Leary cut in, "that a failure to
resolve this case could hurt *your* political aspirations, which seem to
depend on Mr. Bright's?"

Dan Leary, Stella suddenly recognized, had surfaced the new com-
plexities of her own position, the nascent contest between Sloan and
Stella which would erupt should Bright succeed. "A man has been murdered," Stella responded evenly. "I'm concerned with why." Resigned to
a long siege, Stella settled in, knowing that Charles Sloan would get his
wish now—her face on television, for better or for worse.

Two hours later, Stella and Sloan sat with Bright in his office.

Sloan slumped in his chair, his posture suggesting a weary tolerance
of error. "Why not tell them," he asked Stella, "that this is a police matter, and that our role is to give them input when they ask for it."

"In *this* case?" Stella demanded. "*You* saw those people, Charles. I
couldn't have gotten by with that answer if I believed in it." She turned
to Bright. "And *we* can't get by now without checking into Jack's clients.
How will it look if we don't?"

"How will it look," Sloan retorted, "if Novak was offed by some
drug dealer?"

"As opposed to a fellow transvestite?" Stella asked coolly. "With choices this lousy, I'll go with whatever the truth is."

Sloan frowned. "You've given them their press conference," he said to Bright. "Now go after Krajek on *your* issues, and let Nathaniel Dance worry about Jack Novak. At least until we see how the facts play out."

There was a knock on the door. Stella's secretary, middle-aged and efficient, peered with hesitance into Bright's office. "You've got two messages," she told Stella. "From Captain Dance and Coroner Micelli. I knew you'd want them right away."

STELLA HAD just finished with Micelli and had hardly begun sorting out her emotions when Arthur Bright entered her office.

"Jack died," she told Bright, "with cocaine up his nose. As for the kinks, his fingerprints were on the handcuffs we found in his drawer, and his maid remembered seeing a black garter belt and stockings in his nightstand. But not the heels. Which is strange, I think."

Bright sat across from her, chin resting on folded hands. "Why is that?"

"Wouldn't he have the whole outfit? Also, Micelli says there's no medical evidence that Jack was ever sodomized."

Bright lowered his eyelids, reflective. "There are two sides to that, Stella. Giving, and receiving. What was the amyl nitrite for?"

"We know all about J. Edgar Hoover." Her voice hardened. "If Jack was into gay bondage, someone else will know. Besides whoever killed him."

Bright crossed his legs, carefully rearranging his suit coat. "You're asking me," he said at last, "whether you can go wherever Jack's life takes you."

Stella stared at him fixedly. "*I* can live with it, if you can. Charles is so busy mapping out the angles, he's forgotten what he's here for. Or maybe," she added with quiet contempt, "he hasn't."

Bright looked up, permitting a faint irritation to show through his impassivity. "I have my reasons for keeping Charles in his job. And you in yours." His tone grew crisp. "Tell me about Fielding."

"He ODed, period. Maybe that's all there is. But we can't just accept that." Idly, she began scribbling on a legal pad. "The immediate questions are under what circumstances; how did he know Tina Welch; and whether there's any prior indications he'd used heroin. Dance is talking to his ex-wife, to hookers who knew Tina, to narcotics cops, and to the people at Steelton 2000. Including Peter Hall."

"What if he finds nothing?"

"Then it's like Jack's secret life: if Fielding's life is a secret from *everyone*, something's wrong. In the meanwhile, at least we'll have done our job."

Bright's lips formed a perfunctory smile. "Sometimes, Stella, your world is a very simple place."

Stella shrugged. "That way I can concentrate. And so should you, Arthur—on running for mayor. Sloan's right about that much. After all, we both want you to win."

The sardonic reference to everyone's ambitions produced, in Bright, a probing look. "And *your* way is to be aggressive. Including—maybe especially—digging into Jack Novak's drug practice."

"That's right. I think it's better for you to solve this case than hide from it. Go with what got you here, Arthur."

The veiled look returned along with Stella's sense, fleeting but quite strong, that Arthur's thoughts had slipped away. Finally, Bright said, "You should talk to Johnny Curran."

"The narcotics cop?"

Briefly, Bright looked impatient. "Is there *another* Johnny Curran?"

Surprised, Stella sifted her memory. She had only seen Curran once— when she had still worked for Novak, and Curran had testified for Bright against one of Jack's clients. Yet she remembered him vividly: a broad, powerful frame; ice-blue eyes; thick hair and mustache already gray in his early forties; the self-assured, slightly contemptuous air of someone reflecting on a cynical private joke. But then Curran had survived for years in the paranoid world of the undercover cop, where the rules were unwritten and error could be fatal. Among his peers, he was somewhat of a legend—the white cop who worked the black East Side.

"Remind me about Harlell Prince," Stella said.

Bright wiped his glasses and then, replacing them, considered her squarely. "Curran killed him."

"Killed, or murdered?"

Standing, Bright walked to the window, seeming to study the skeleton of the baseball stadium, swarming, on a Monday, with workers in hard hats. "The only murderer we know about for sure," Bright said at last, "is Harlell Prince. He was from Detroit, a contract killer—so vicious and psychotic that he'd murdered a couple of Vincent Moro's people and set up his own drug network on the East Side. Smart, too: not even Moro could get to him."

He faced her again. "But Curran did. He'd flipped Prince's chief lieutenant, had him ready to turn Prince in. Then one night Curran found the snitch on his doorstep: murdered, with his tongue cut out.

"Curran worked alone then. He went looking for Prince. Prince's bodyguard wound up dead. So did Prince: they found him with a gun in his hand, shot through the eye from about two inches away. It was self-defense, Curran said."

Stella studied him. "And the only 'witness' was the bodyguard Curran had killed already."

Bright nodded. "What cop was going to lean on Johnny Curran? Harlell Prince was what the police call a public-service killing—no one missed him." Pausing, Bright rested his hands on the back of the chair. "Curran scares the hell out of me. But he doesn't trust *anyone*, and he knows *everything* there is to know about drugs in Steelton, even more than Dance. If you want to ask around about Jack Novak, start with Johnny."

THREE

AT SIX o'clock, Stella sat waiting for Saul Ravin in the bar of the Steelton Club.

She was not a member—it was barely a decade since the club had been opened to women—and the atmosphere was distinctly male and middle-aged. The ornate bar had been hand carved from oak; the walls were made of thick oak panels, stained dark, decorated only with discreetly spaced black-and-white photographs of eminent members—judges, business leaders, and mayors—who, besides being male, were dead; the chairs were upholstered in soft green leather; and there was a faint, persistent odor of tobacco. But, to Stella, the view was the most telling detail of all.

The club sat on top of the Steelton Trust Bank, twenty stories high, and the perspective was both proprietary and detached: from this height, the urban grit was less apparent, and the glow from the few mills still operating, red-orange in twilight, created an illusion of vitality. The membership, too, seemed caught in a time warp: the fractious ethnicity of the city had been strained out—Stella saw no blacks, no faces she would associate with Eastern Europe—and the members, clustered tightly around small tables, were either graying and WASPish in aspect or the younger, vainly aspiring male mediocrities, largely Protestant as well, with which the club had lately filled its ranks. Here, Stella supposed, it was still possible to believe in the cosseted privilege of Anglo-Saxon males, passed from generation to generation. But blacks and ethnics ran the city government now, and the calculus of power was changing. A Peter Hall, clever enough to find new outlets for old money, was rare; the forerunners of change, the large law firms, were peppered below their most senior ranks with women, blacks, Italians, Eastern Europeans, and Jews. As if on cue, Saul Ravin appeared.

He was past seventy now, with an angelic nimbus of yellow-white hair, a sloping stomach, and the ponderous gait of a man who had never exercised much and now was feeling the effect. But his blue eyes were clear and lit with a certain ironic humor: three years ago he had stopped drinking, halting a discernible downhill slide, and preserved the respect he was due as the dean of the city's defense lawyers. Then, reinvigorated, he had married the bright and charming widow of a wealthy stockbroker.

Stella, who believed in redemption and respected Saul's strengths, had been glad. At Saul's instance, they began to see each other for lunch now and then; Stella sensed from Saul the answering respect of a fellow professional mingled with an attraction which was harmless and even flattering.

Sitting, Saul smiled at her across the table. "It's good to see you, Stella. You remind me of what's missing from the place—aside from Jews."

"What's that?"

"Youth, and beauty. I can make myself comfortable, knowing that you won't die before I finish my club soda."

For the first time since Jack Novak's murder, Stella managed a sardonic grin. "Then I'll try not to go into cardiac arrest. Or menopause."

A spectral black man appeared, their waiter, as old as most of the members. Saul ordered his club soda, and Stella a glass of red wine.

"So," he said. "Jack Novak. A bad death."

Stella picked up her wineglass. "*Too* bad, I keep thinking."

Saul's face was serious now. "You're wondering, I gather, whether Jack got crosswise with a client. As opposed to a member, shall we say, of the 'leather community.'"

"I'm wondering about a lot of things." Pausing, Stella sipped her wine. "I used to work for Jack, you know."

Saul's answering gaze held no surprise. "I remember. Around that time, Jack and I tried some drug cases together."

What, Stella wondered, might Jack have said about her: Saul's absence of expression was that of a lawyer who wished to show nothing. "I was thinking," she explained, "about one of them in particular. You represented the dealer. Jack had the supplier, George Flood."

Above a faint smile, Saul's expression was speculative. "Flood was charged with distributing five keys of cocaine to my client. The evidence disappeared."

Stella nodded. "Arthur was the prosecutor, and the arresting cop was Johnny Curran, right?"

"That's right."

"So who was George Flood?"

Though Saul's expression did not change, his eyes were bright with interest. "Vincent Moro's guy."

"You knew that."

"No one *told* me. But no one had to. Moro needed a black man to run the East Side for him. If Flood wasn't *his*, Moro would have killed him—Flood was too big, and he'd lasted too long."

"If you're right, then Moro needed Flood cut loose."

All humor had vanished from Ravin's eyes. "Yes. Setting up a distribution network like Flood's is a lot of trouble and, if you're Moro, there's damned few people you trust." Slowly, he put down his drink. "Even more important, Flood was up high enough he might actually *know* something about Moro. Moro couldn't risk Flood cutting a deal with Arthur."

Stella let a moment pass in silence. "So," she quietly asked, "how did the evidence get destroyed?"

Saul's smile returned. But it was mirthless, and his gaze was cool now. "Do you expect me to know that?"

Stella's own gaze was unflinching. "What *do* you know?"

Saul turned to the window—a scattering of lights in the darkness, and beyond, the inky blackness of Lake Erie. Silent, Stella watched him weigh the benefits of helping her against the code of the defense lawyer, his own habit of silence. Finally, he said, "My client's dead, and I never worked for Vincent Moro."

"But Jack did."

"Of course. Moro's people weren't coming to Novak on their own. Moro tells them who their lawyer is and who he'll pay for."

Even now, hearing this made Stella's skin feel cold. "So what happened in the Flood case?"

Saul still looked past her. "Off the record?" he said at last.

"Yes."

Briefly, Ravin glanced around them. The others seemed absorbed in their own conversations; Stella felt confident that they could not imagine *this* one. "What I can tell you," Saul began, "is that my guy was willing to make a deal with Bright.

"*We* had the toughest defense *and* the biggest opportunity. My client was the one Curran had caught with the drugs: Flood had some bullshit story about just being in the neighborhood. So Arthur needed us. And because Flood was much bigger than my guy, I had some real leverage.

"My client was willing to make a deal—*if* Arthur gives him a lighter sentence, he'll roll over on Flood. So Arthur and I begin talking. It was looking pretty good when my client pulls the plug."

"Why?"

Saul sipped the club soda, licking his lips. "I was never sure. I could guarantee him a short sentence, but I couldn't guarantee he'd live when he got out." He shrugged. "What he *said* was that he'd gotten the word— the case was going away. He wouldn't tell me why."

"But you think Jack *knew* why."

Saul sat back, drink cradled in both hands. "A man like Vincent Moro has a thousand ways of doing things—crooked cops, crooked judges, bribing evidence clerks, paying a court clerk to rig assignments to get a judge that's better for him, even a prosecutor paid to go in the tank. Or, maybe, evidence gets destroyed by 'accident.'" He looked directly at Stella now. "It could have been that Jack was just the incidental beneficiary. But he never ran away from the word out on the street—that he was the lawyer who could make things happen. A reputation like that is good for business."

Stella placed a fingertip on the rim of her glass. "Until you disappoint someone," she said at last.

Saul smiled. "Maybe if Jack made a promise and couldn't deliver?" He rested his face on one liver-spotted hand. "You're right about one thing, Stella—since the early nineties, it's a different world.

"Jack was Vincent Moro's lawyer in big drug cases. That means at least two things. First, Jack has to keep all of his clients from snitching— his loyalty is not to them but to Moro. Second, Jack takes his fees in cash, because Moro can't be writing checks which can be traced back to him or one of his 'legitimate enterprises.'

"After 1990 or so, the pressure was on. Not only do the feds have electronic surveillance down to an art form, but now there's mandatory life sentences for serious drug offenses. It's not so easy to tell your guy not to flip, that he ought to risk going to trial. *If* Jack promised somebody the case would get taken care of, and then the guy gets life—yeah, one of those mean sons of bitches might want to take him out.

"And now the briefcases of cash are a problem, too. These days, if you take over ten thousand in cash, the IRS requires you to say who gave it to you. Someone like Novak may have to lie, and if a client *knows* he's lying, then the guy can deal *Jack*. Or maybe Moro has the guy killed before *Jack* is under pressure to deal *Moro*.

"It's like a hall of mirrors—everyone's watching everyone else, and everyone's paranoid. Something goes wrong and . . ." Saul gave Stella a long, considering look. "Yeah, that's one thing that could happen to a drug lawyer. But another is that they get to like the life too much—the drugs and easy money and any kind of sex you can invent. Then they start to fall apart. Maybe *that* was what happened to him."

"Do you think it was?"

Saul shrugged. "I hadn't seen Jack much lately. But he always struck me as capable of flying a little too close to the sun—that he was a guy who lacked a regulator." He picked up his drink. "What I *never* heard was that he'd started blowing off his cases. When the wheels come off a drug lawyer, that's what follows."

Stella finished her wine; its aftertaste was tart, tinny. "And if it did?"

"Maybe he dies like Jack appeared to—a victim of his own bent tastes. Maybe a client kills him. But not Moro, I think. Firing would be enough." With a ruminative air, Saul settled back in his chair. "What I never figured out was why Moro canned his old *paisan* drug lawyer, Jerry Florio, and started passing the word to big guys like Flood that Jack was the one to call. Florio was in his prime, and Jack was just a punk. What was his magic? some of us wondered.

"Suddenly all the dealers Moro protected had Jack's card in their wallets and were calling him from jail as soon as they were busted. Though I have to admit Jack took the proverbial ball and ran with it."

For a time, Stella was silent, staring at her empty wineglass. "Do you have time for a second drink?" she asked.

Something in her tone made Ravin cock his head. "Why?"

"I have a story to tell you."

FOUR

STELLA HAD met the Haitian dealer only once, but she always remembered him—a smooth face, a two-day growth of beard, liquid pleading eyes. Only his hair, sharply receding above the temples, suggested that he was past thirty.

His name was Jean-Claude Desnoyers, and his high-pitched, faintly musical accent contributed to his youthful air. He showed Stella school pictures from his wallet—two bright-eyed twin girls in an East Side kindergarten—and told her he could not stand to be deported.

"There is nothing for me in Haiti," he said. "Only poverty, and death."

They sat together in Novak's minimal library. Jack had posted bail the day before; as sometimes happened in recent months, he was held up in court, and had called to ask Stella to interview his new client, charged with possession of five kilos of heroin after being busted in a motel parking lot at midnight. Listening to the Haitian, Stella wondered at the moral deadness, only dimly imaginable to her, which would lead a father of two to see America as a precious opportunity to sell lethal drugs to others. And, inexperienced as she was, Stella had no doubt that Desnoyers was an important East Side dealer—the street value of five kilos was considerable.

"How did they catch you?" she asked.

The Haitian looked around him, as though the library were a prison. The small shrug he gave resembled a nervous twitch. "I did buys there. Maybe they watched, before."

Stella put down her pen; watching her take notes seemed to make the Haitian nervous, and his high forehead showed a thin sheen of perspiration. "Tell me how the buys worked," she asked.

He looked down. "I would park there," he said at last, "and go into the bar. My supplier has a trunk key. I have a drink, he puts the smack inside my trunk. Ten minutes, then I leave the motel and he passes me in the parking lot. I slip him the envelope—two seconds, tops."

"This time he's not there." The Haitian hesitated, body taut with remembered fear. "Right away, I know there's something wrong.

"The only thing is to leave.

"I go to my car, and get inside." The Haitian's eyes shut. "There's a guy hunched down on the passenger seat. Before I know what's happening, he puts a gun to my head.

"The first thing I think is it's Harlell Prince, poaching on our territory. But this is a big white man with a gray mustache.

"'Open the trunk,' he tells me, and then sticks a rolled-up piece of paper under my chin."

"A warrant," Stella said.

The Haitian's chest, scrawny beneath a thin cotton shirt, vibrated with a quick, swallowed breath. "I'm not a fool. My supplier is not a fool. I figure he's seen what's going down and the drugs aren't there. So I open up the trunk . . ."

The sentence died there. Sorrowing, the Haitian shook his head.

Stella knew the rest. Jack had only two choices she could think of: hope the warrant was legally defective, or try to cut a deal with Arthur Bright.

Hesitant, she asked, "Who's your supplier?"

The Haitian became still. "If I rat him out . . ."

He had already considered it, Stella knew at once. She could feel him weighing the risks; though this conversation was privileged, perhaps she should reserve anything else for Jack. Then, staring at the conference table, Desnoyers murmured, "George Flood."

George Flood, Stella repeated to herself: the black man, Jack's client, who had gone free after the police "lost" five keys of coke. The thought of this left Stella quiet.

The telephone rang.

Jack had returned, the receptionist explained—he wanted to see her in his office. With a few words of reassurance to Desnoyers, Stella left.

Unlike the library, the decor in Jack's office was carefully composed—Japanese vases, delicate Japanese watercolors by an expatriate Frenchman named Jacoulet—and its studied foreignness to Steelton was intended, Stella suspected, to set Jack apart. She sat in a spare black chair and explained what she had learned; only at the name George Flood did Jack's air of amused alertness, an appreciation of the human comedy, vanish.

"That's a problem," he said.

"Why?"

"George Flood was a client, and may be again. There could be a conflict." Novak sat back in his chair, reflective, and said to Stella, "Bring him in."

Stella did that. Half expecting Jack to ask her to stay, preserving the tentative rapport between her and Desnoyers, she lingered in the doorway.

"Come back in a while," Novak told her. As she left, the Haitian glanced up nervously, and then Jack shut the door.

A half hour later, watching from the library, she saw Desnoyers walk quickly through the reception area, head down. He did not seem to see her.

She returned to Novak's office. "What happened?" she asked.

Jack frowned. "He's too afraid of deportation."

"Wouldn't you be?"

Novak cradled his chin in his hands, gazing up at her. "He asked about going to Arthur, Stella. What did you say to him?"

Stella felt herself flush. "Nothing." Her defensiveness became a more undefined emotion, somewhere between curious and accusatory. "What did *you* say to him?"

"That if he wants to rat out Flood," he answered, "he'll have to find someone else." He seemed to study her expression, and then his tone softened. "It's a clear conflict of interest and, yes, it's also against my *own* code of ethics.

"The man has a family. And no jury will believe a word he says without more proof. So what's Arthur going to do—put a body wire on him to entrap George Flood? How many seconds would Desnoyers last then?"

In spite of her own aversion, Stella felt a nascent sympathy for the Haitian and his family, trapped between competing forces. "There must be a way," she said.

"Not *that* way." Jack's voice grew softer yet. "He'll get himself killed, Stella. But not on my watch."

Stella said nothing more. That night, she did not sleep at Jack's.

PART OF the reason had been second-year finals.

Two nights later, Stella found herself staring numbly at the notes from her taxation course, deeply discouraged. Then the law librarian flickered the lights in warning, and she realized that it was closing time.

She rubbed her eyes. If she returned to her tiny apartment, she would lie down on her bed and fall asleep. The best option seemed one that she had never used—to drive to Jack's office, make a fresh pot of coffee, and hope that the wooden chair and table in the library would serve to keep her upright.

Entering Jack's reception room, she froze.

There were soft voices, too hushed to overhear. A shaft of light came from Novak's office.

Stella stood there, indecisive. Then, nerve ends tingling, she walked softly across the carpet toward the light.

Jack's door was merely ajar; Stella could not see inside. "Have you done all you can?" she heard someone ask.

It was a man's voice—businesslike, dispassionate, and somewhat cold. "I left nothing to the imagination," Jack answered. "But he's out of my control."

Jack's tone was new to her—far different from the clipped, cocky manner he adopted with most clients. "And?" the calm voice asked.

Jack's voice was muted. "There *is* no 'and.'"

Stella took two more steps, and peered through the door.

Only Jack's desk lamp was on. The other man sat with his back to her. He was not big, she saw, and even at this hour, past midnight, he wore a charcoal gray suit and crisp white collar, and his graying hair was carefully and, she thought, expensively, trimmed. Still facing Novak, his head raised slightly.

The visitor had noticed Jack's eyes, she realized. They were fixed on Stella with a look of alarm.

Awkwardly, she stepped inside. "I saw your light on," she told Jack. "I thought someone had broken in."

The man turned to face her. In the half-light, his black eyes were penetrating, and the skin around them, though the man appeared in his early forties, was seamed with concentration. "This is my paralegal," Jack managed to say, "Stella Marz."

The man stood. While slight, his body was well proportioned, and each movement seemed sparing, yet silken. And so, she realized, was the new softness of his voice. "You're a very pretty lady, Stella Marz."

Before Stella could react to the antiquated, somewhat patronizing compliment, the visitor stepped more fully into the light.

His looks were unusual, she thought: the skin of his face, as sparing as his movements, was stretched across taut cheekbones, thin lips, a slightly pointed chin, forming a geometry of planes and angles, light and shadow. As he held out his hand, staring intently into her eyes, Stella kept herself from flinching.

Though she had never met him, she knew this face.

The man took Stella's hand, cradling it in both of his, dry and cool on her skin. "Very pretty," he repeated softly. "Now, if you'll excuse us . . ."

Silent, Stella backed from the office.

MINUTES LATER, Jack Novak entered the library.

Stella looked up from the notes she had tried, without success, to study. Under his breath, Jack asked, "What were you doing here?"

Stella's mouth was dry. "That was Vincent Moro, wasn't it."

It was not a question, and Novak did not answer. He leaned in the doorway, arms folded. "It was business." His voice lowered. "I don't want you worrying about him, or talking about him. As far as you're concerned, he was never here. Do you understand?"

No, Stella thought. It was too much to understand tonight—sleep deprived, without family to confide in, needing the money Jack paid her. But, even now, she knew that Jack, and his practice, would never be the same to her. What she needed was time alone.

Mute, she nodded.

Circling the table, Jack kissed the nape of her neck. "Go home," he told her. "It's too late to do yourself any good."

THE MORNING after her tax exam, tired and depressed, Stella unfolded the morning paper. She read in a desultory way, sipping coffee at her breakfast table. Then she noticed the short article on the last page of the Metro section.

"Suspected Drug Dealer Murdered," the story began.

Stella put down her coffee.

Jean-Claude Desnoyers had been found floating beneath a steel pier in the Onondaga River. There was a bullet in his head.

For whatever time it took her to accept this, Stella sat there. Then she folded the paper and drove to Novak's office.

Jack was at his desk. Closing the door, Stella flung the paper in front of him. "You sold him out," she said, "and Vincent Moro had him killed."

Jack bolted from his chair, then looked past her at the door. This fleeting hesitance, an admission of his own fears, deprived his anger of its force. "How can you say that?" he asked. "Don't you know me at all?"

Stella stood in front of him. "No," she said with quiet fury. "I don't think I do . . ."

Jack flushed. "Why do you think I tell them never to go down that road? Because it ends at the bottom of a pier.

"Vincent Moro doesn't need *me* to tell him when some dealer's about to flip. Steelton's a sieve—other dealers, the cops, maybe even the prosecutor's office. Desnoyers wouldn't listen."

"But Moro did," Stella answered stubbornly. "He owns you, doesn't he?"

"*No one* owns me." Clasping her shoulders, Jack slowly shook his head, as if to calm them both. "It was a one-shot deal," he said more softly. "Moro wanting me to talk to Arthur, tell him his antidrug crusade is a hopeless waste of time and money—not to mention his political future. You overheard me explaining there was nothing I could do."

Stella gazed at him, thoughts muddled. "That wasn't what I heard."

For the first time since she had known him, tears formed in Jack Novak's eyes. In her confusion, Stella hesitated.

"Please," Jack murmured. "I've never said how much you mean to me. Please, Stella, believe me . . ."

Stella closed her eyes.

FINISHING HER wine, Stella looked across the table at Saul Ravin. The bar around them had begun to empty, members drifting toward the dining room.

"I always wondered," she said quietly, "whether Jack turned Desnoyers in."

Saul's expression held the bleakness of a recording angel's. "Never wonder, Stella. That was part of Novak's job."

Silent, Stella turned to the window.

"And," Saul continued, "since yesterday you've wondered who else besides Desnoyers's family might have reason to hate Jack Novak enough to hang him, then cut his balls off."

Stella faced him again. "Yes."

"Then let me give you some advice." Saul leaned forward, his face displaying a deep seriousness, a solicitude Stella had never seen. "This job is your life, and your ability to do it depends on your idea of yourself—that you're honest and play by the rules.

"I don't laugh at that, Stella. Sometimes I even wish I could remember ever having it. If I were you, I wouldn't fuck with it, either. It's hard enough to stay clean once you've decided you want Arthur's job. This case is too much about you. Even a saint could lose her bearings."

Stella smiled, though her spirit felt leaden. "I'm no saint, Saul. I lost my chance at canonization when I went to work for Jack." Her smile vanished. "Maybe this *is* about me. But I have to see it through."

Saul's expression did not change. But he shook his head slightly, as if in warning. "Before you do," he answered, "ask yourself why."

FIVE

AT TEN the next morning, Stella stood with Nathaniel Dance, waiting at a shabby preschool for Tommy Fielding's ex-wife.

Stella had driven there through the ravaged streets of the black East Side, thinking as she did about Arthur Bright—the way in which these streets must have shaped him, the qualities it had taken to become who he was and then to face what Stella saw all around her. Since the riots of thirty years ago, much of the area seemed stunted. Spacious homes had become boardinghouses occupied by the threatened, the impoverished, the unemployed, the transient; others were boarded up, turned to crack houses or magnets for delinquency. A once-respectable shopping area, started in the twenties, was now a garbage-strewn street of laundries, liquor stores, corner groceries which welcomed food stamps, repositories for secondhand clothes, and check-cashing businesses, their signs lettered in fading paint or outdated cursive script. Within two blocks, Stella had seen a cluster of teenage boys who belonged in school, their breaths misting in the chill winter air as they passed a joint; a homeless man, his face cadaverous, pushing a battered shopping cart with a sleeping bag stuffed inside; a bus stop where three black women in heavy coats waited with weary patience for a bus which, from its direction, would take them to clean houses in the white eastern suburbs; another woman passed out in the caged doorway of a liquor store.

After that there was public housing, a Stalinist cinder-block monolith covered with indecipherable graffiti, where hopelessness festered and intact families were rare; then a tan brick school with broken windows and a playground with two basketball hoops without nets and Bloods Rule splashed in red paint on the bare cement. For the last six years the Steelton schools had been in receivership or administered by the state under "emergency" laws which had no deadline, and basic literacy was as random as the safety of those who entered them; several recent cases handled by Stella's unit had involved gang shootings outside schools, and one in which a drug-dealing student killed a female teacher for refusing to grant a bathroom break.

Here and there Stella noted signs of hope: rehabbed houses, or spacious new homes built on once-vacant lots, sold by the city for one dollar to policemen or firemen or civil servants and their families, willing to take chances in the hope of saving an embattled neighborhood. The still-vigorous black churches offered day care, after-school recreation, tutoring, training in basic job skills, the presence of strong role models, male and female, and the balm of faith and community on Sunday morning. A growing middle and professional class existed at the edge of this depressing vista, but—regrettably, in Stella's mind—many more had fled to the safer streets and schools of suburbia.

Of course, she could not blame them. It was hard to find clear answers to so much poverty, dependency, discrimination, substance abuse, familial breakdown, and, by now, at least three generations of social pathology. This reinforced for Stella how much she admired those who, like Arthur, had risen from these conditions, and how clear her own path now seemed to her by comparison. The thought made her glad that Bright had stayed to dedicate himself, within the complex calculus that politics allowed, to the salvation of this area and the revival of his city. And it also made her curious as to why the former wife of the smooth-faced Ivy League executive she had first seen in the morgue had come to teach at a preschool in a district so dangerous that drug dealers like George Flood held more sway than the police.

The center, when she arrived, held no surprise. Standing with Dance in a hall outside the playroom, Stella felt—as she sensed Dance did—the contrast between the spirited colors of the paintings and posters on the walls and the flickering fluorescent lights above worn linoleum, gray with scuffed-on dirt, or the hand-me-down clothes, pale with repeated washing, worn by the children themselves. They were mainly African-American kids under six, with a handful of Asians and Latinos, and a bright-eyed Haitian girl in pigtails who made Stella wonder, briefly, about the fate of the girls in Jean-Claude Desnoyers's school photographs. Many were still curious and eager: Stella followed for several minutes the progress of the Haitian girl in building a precarious tower of blocks. Despite her foreknowledge of their probable fates, Stella deeply enjoyed watching them in the remaining moments of their childhood. But Amanda Fielding, emerging from the classroom, was a shock.

·   ·   ·

AMANDA APPEARED much older than her ex-husband had been, and she was tall and rawboned, with an awkward gait and a figure in which each proportion seemed a little off—chest too flat, hips too broad, ankles too thick. She wore a shapeless print dress and no makeup; her hair was a nondescript brown cut in careful bangs; her skin was pale; her face was gaunt; the loose skin beneath her eyes added a touch of weariness. Amanda's contrast with the young Adonis awaiting Micelli's scalpel held, for Stella, some of the same dissonance as the pictures of Fielding dead with Tina Welch. Only Amanda's unsmiling gray eyes—level and probing, suggestive of quiet intelligence—hinted at what the attraction might have been.

Amanda held out her hand to Stella, then Dance. "I have an office down the hall," she said without preface. "We can talk there."

Her refined voice had the accents of the East Coast: this was a well-educated woman, Stella surmised, perhaps upper class and intellectual, who scorned marginal adornments. Dance and Stella followed her to an office, barely more than a closet, and sat in two plastic chairs. Watching Dance settle into a seat far too small for him, wincing as one of his knees creaked, afforded Stella a moment's amusement, as, she sensed, it did Amanda Fielding.

"Perhaps I can find you a larger chair," Amanda said dryly.

"Thank you," he answered. "I think it's better if I don't try to get up."

The deadpan remark, taking the edge off Dance's intimidating presence, reflected for Stella what a subtle man he was. When he switched on his handheld tape recorder and placed it on Fielding's desk, Amanda did not object.

Dance began with routine questions: When had Amanda last seen her ex-husband? What had their recent relationship been like? Polite but not intimate, Amanda responded. When he asked whether she had ever known Fielding to use drugs, the firm answer was no. Amanda volunteered nothing: Stella found her apparent absence of emotion unsettling, and wondered how she had processed the sordid death of the father of her seven-year-old daughter. Instinctively, Stella inquired, "How is Julia taking this?"

The subject seemed to distress Amanda Fielding. "This is her first day back at school," she answered quietly. "Peter Hall has been very kind, coming to see her, taking her out to his place to ride horses. He knew how much Tommy adored her, and she adored him. She would wait for her father at the door, all dressed up. Then Tommy would drive up and

Julia would run to him . . ." With a short shake of the head, Amanda cut herself off. "She just can't comprehend it."

Stella had a swift series of mental images: the beloved father who has become a guest star in his daughter's life; the mother, responsible day to day, who watches a seven-year-old become her surrogate in the affections of an ex-husband. "Can *you*?" Stella asked.

"No."

"Because of the heroin?"

Amanda lowered her eyelids and then, angling her head away from Dance, fixed Stella with a look of painful candor. "Because they were naked."

Dance was still now. The atmosphere in the room had changed: Stella placed a pensive finger to her lips, still gazing at Amanda, head tilted in inquiry.

Silent, Amanda crossed her arms; to Stella, it seemed as if she were hugging herself, creating a sudden, sad image of widowed sexuality. "Tommy didn't like sex," she said at last.

Stella lowered her own eyes, signaling respect for so personal a subject. "With anyone?"

Amanda breathed in; her gaze slid to Dance, then away, and Stella saw her renewed awareness of the circumstances—the unblinking black detective, the spinning tape, a woman she did not know asking questions about her life. Then her wounded gray eyes filled with resignation.

"I don't know why Tommy died like that," she said at last. "But I can help you understand him. And that starts with why he married me."

Stella nodded. "Anything you can tell us . . ."

Glancing at Dance, Amanda faced her again. "I was thirty-three, Ms. Marz. Seven years older than Tommy.

"I'd come here from college—Smith, actually—with a degree in social work. Even then, I knew I couldn't save the world. But I thought I could help someone, perhaps salvage some small piece of the next generation."

Stella heard a trace of nostalgia for the young woman Amanda had been, and remembered feeling similar emotions on the day she had joined the prosecutor's office, grasping for what was most fundamental to her nature. "I understand."

"I thought *I* did," Amanda said flatly. "But *this* had no end—the child abuse, the crack cocaine, the unwanted pregnancies—and I had no resources for it." She bit her lip. "And I was lonely, and could hardly give myself away.

"So I drank." Arms still folded, Amanda stared at the ceiling. "I drank at night, alone, and when I couldn't face work anymore I called in sick and drank in the morning. Because *then* I felt better. Finally they gave me a choice: either I went to an in-patient clinic for substance abuse, or they'd let me resign.

"I knew what I had to do. I quit my job, and found another one." She summoned a quick, bitter smile. "Working as a travel agent in the suburbs, so I could keep on drinking. I'd arrived at the truth: vodka wasn't about my job—it was about loneliness, and isolation. The things I took with me wherever I went."

The candid eyes lit on Stella again, and Amanda seemed to reenter the present. "You're wondering," she said with surprising evenness, "what the fruits of six years of psychotherapy have to do with Tommy. Everything."

Amanda folded her hands in front of her and began to study them, as if this distraction calmed her. "I volunteered to help run a travel club the agency had, for singles. I was going to meet someone—I didn't care how old anymore—get married, and have the child that I wanted. Then I wouldn't need to drink.

"But I've never attracted anyone—young or old—and there were ten sad, long years where I tried to be so efficient at work that they'd overlook my bouts with the flu. And then there was Tommy.

"The first time he came into the agency he took my breath away." Amanda exhaled, and her voice freshened with the remembered moment. "He was clean and gorgeous, and he dressed like someone in a magazine. He seemed so cheerful—relentlessly so—that I almost heard the first false note, and wondered why a man like this wanted or needed a travel club which was a magnet, frankly, for people who were older and *far* less attractive. We'd go over travel brochures and what trips the club offered and I'd think 'Why not go find some beautiful investment banker with a figure like a swimsuit model and take your own damned trip? Rather than sit here and torture me.'

"Tommy had clearly thrived in what I thought of as the real world—Princeton, an MBA from Michigan, a good new job at Hall Development. The first time he asked me to dinner, I was shocked and scared and excited.

"Maybe, I told myself, he just wanted the company of someone more mature. We were both Easterners, from good schools, and seemed to read so many of the same books. We'd had such good talks by then."

Amanda's voice filled with weary self-contempt. "Waiting for him to pick me up, I even tried imagining we were soulmates. But I couldn't make it last."

Suddenly the seesaw of recollection seemed to exhaust Amanda, to draw her back toward despondency. Quietly, Stella asked, "What happened?"

Amanda still studied her hands. "I began to drink at dinner, and became talkative, then vivacious. Then I just got drunk."

Dance listened, Stella noticed, with his customary opaqueness: Stella could not help but wonder whether he considered this the maundering of a privileged white woman with too few problems of her own. But the detective in him seemed alert, as Stella was, to where this story was headed.

"And so," Stella said, "he asked you out again."

Amanda gave her a brief look of surprise, then nodded. "And again, and again, and again.

"He didn't *mind* when I drank, I thought. The first time he kissed me, I hoped he would make love to me." Stella could hear Amanda's remembered wonderment, filtered through the disillusion which followed. "Instead he asked me to marry him.

"Finally I had what I wanted—an engagement—and more. Except that he barely touched me. He was always at work or out training for a marathon, or just too tired. When I tried to talk to him about it, he wouldn't.

"Tommy could tell me about books and movies, work, and all the places he had been. But he had no talent for intimacy. " Her tone became thin and bitter. "When I met his mother, I finally realized why. Tommy lived his life under military occupation."

Recalling her impression of Fielding's mother, Stella felt a piece fall into place. "She smothered him?"

"Smothered?" Amanda gave a short derisive laugh. "It was more like a laser. She would ask *him* anything, ask *me* anything, make slighting comments about me even when I was there, although not *so* slighting that Tommy felt he could confront her. The thought she couldn't stand was that *any* aspect of his life might be closed to her.

"From childhood, Tommy had perfected the only defense he had—to go into hiding, from Marsha and every woman he knew. The charm, the perfect dress, the fanatic devotion to work and fitness, were all an expression of fear. He not only didn't want sex, he was *afraid* of it. What Tommy wanted was for some part of him to be left alone."

Stella glanced at Dance. The detective watched Amanda with deep concentration, and Stella wondered whether he had the thought that she did—that shooting heroin with a woman was, in a peculiar way, as intimate as having sex. "Still," Stella interjected, "you and he got married, and had a child."

Amanda leaned back. "One night, when I'd consumed enough vodka to be brave, I confronted him—all the loneliness and rejection spewing out. I couldn't marry a man who wouldn't touch me, I told him, who wouldn't give me love or give me children.

"He turned pale. Without saying anything, he kissed me. I helped him . . ." Amanda's face became pinched. "And then Tommy fell asleep, and I lay there. Drunk as I was, I finally understood.

"We had reached an arrangement, without anyone saying a word. Tommy had tolerated my weaknesses because he sensed that I would tolerate *his*, that I was in no position to drive a harder bargain. He was that rare man for whom my alcoholism served a purpose: coming home late at night to a wife who had passed out from drink and loneliness made things *easier* for him.

"We would marry, and I would go with him to social functions. It wouldn't matter how incongruous I was—as long as I was articulate and sober, Tommy didn't have to date, or have some younger, prettier woman badger him about their relationship.

"He had a wife for dear old mom—although she was visibly appalled when she met me—and for Peter Hall, and I could drink myself to oblivion in the privacy of our home. Just so I didn't answer the telephone until I'd sobered up." Amanda hunched her shoulders. "And *I* could ask for sex when I was fertile. After all, a child would give Tommy the cover he so desperately needed, and Marsha the grandchild *she* so insistently wanted."

Abruptly, Amanda Fielding stared at Dance's tape recorder, as though awakening from her self-lacerating reverie. She looked from Dance to Stella. "*Pay* some woman to have sex with him? Tommy would have paid her *not* to."

"Then what ended your marriage?" Stella asked.

"Julia." For the first time, Amanda's tone of irony commingled with pride. "The day I learned I was pregnant, I stopped drinking. I didn't want my child to have a drunk for a mother, nor did Tommy. The only problem was that now I saw my situation with merciless clarity.

"I stood it for three years after Julia was born—for her sake, I told myself. Three years of Tommy's indifference, of Marsha Fielding trying to seduce our daughter away from me, to make Julia see *her* as the most important person in her life. And I came to understand *that*, too. The senior Fieldings had a marriage as loveless as ours: if Marsha left us alone, then she would have nothing.

"Well, *I* planned to raise an adult, not an adult child. And I refused to make my daughter a pawn in this Freudian nightmare. So I left, and tried to be someone Julia could respect, rather than forcing her to worry about filling her *own* mother's void." Pausing, Amanda smiled without humor. "Deep down, I think Tommy understood that, too. Because what scared him most of all was to face how much he reviled *his* own mother."

The harshness in Amanda's voice made Stella's skin go cold. The only antidote, she knew, to the disease of a family which has metastasized is to escape, and then to pray that it is not too late, that somehow you have not become a carrier. "What kind of parent did *Tommy* turn out to be?"

Amanda's expression became softer. "Devoted. And he was *grateful* for her: she proved that he was heterosexual, which made it more respectable to become a workaholic with no social life. She was the safest relationship he'd ever had, and she could hardly have reminded him of *me*." Now Amanda's smile was merely sad. "She's beautiful, like Tommy. He never missed his Sunday."

Dance leaned forward. "Was he the kind of man, Mrs. Fielding, to put his life at risk? Maybe he was unhappy."

Vigorously, Amanda shook her head. "Things had worked out for Tommy, at least as well as they could. But even if he *were* unhappy, Tommy was too self-protective to use drugs—he did *not* like being in an altered state. He only drank for appearances, perhaps a glass of wine. And fitness—diet and aerobic exercise—was second only to work."

Stella recalled the autopsy, the sculpted body on Micelli's table. "His mother said that Tommy had always been afraid of needles."

"Did she now? I don't think Tommy much liked shots. Of course, it *is* the kind of story Marsha loved to tell—her son as a child, needing her to cope. And never more than to other people when Tommy was in the room, forced to listen." She seemed to catch herself. "The *real* impossibility is that Tommy would share a needle with some prostitute he didn't know. Tommy was the ultimate clean freak, and *that* scenario is unthinkable.

"And then there's the idea of Tommy drooling over a magazine filled with naked black women—absolutely incongruous."

Dance appraised her. "Maybe," he said in his flattest voice, "your ex-husband got off on naked black women, and just forgot to tell you."

Watching Amanda Fielding flush, Stella suppressed a smile, and then

Amanda shook her head. "It's not the 'black,' Captain Dance. It's the 'women.'"

Dance's expression did not change. Even to Stella, the unblinking blackness of his eyes felt daunting. "Did he ever talk about work?"

"Yes. That was a safe subject for us, and Tommy seemed genuinely excited about the ballpark. It was the infectious part of him that still seemed charming—he brought Julia a scale model and set it up in her bedroom." Amanda's voice, for the first time, held nothing but sorrow. "He made me promise Julia could skip school on Opening Day, to see the Blues' first game there. He even traded in his license plate for one that spelled PLAY BALL."

"Was there *anything* in his life," Stella asked, "any problem that could have changed his behavior?"

Fielding stared at her desk. "I'd *like* to understand this. I want Julia to understand, someday, and to think as well of Tommy as possible.

"He *did* seem depressed, the last couple of weeks. He said *something* about problems with the stadium; he was responsible for bringing it in under budget, you know, to make it appear a better deal for Mayor Krajek and the city, and to protect Peter Hall from overruns." She glanced up at Stella. "With Mr. Bright challenging the whole concept, I'm sure he felt political pressure as well. But I'm guessing—I have no idea *what* Tommy's problems were, if any."

Curious, Stella leaned forward. "If the pressure got bad enough, how might Tommy react?"

"By throwing himself into his work even more, not by running from it. And certainly not by taking a walk on the wild side, as it were. That's wholly out of character." Amanda looked up at Stella again. "So," she finished, "how Tommy died is inexplicable, at least to me. Unless . . ."

"Unless what?" Stella asked.

Amanda gave her a last bitter smile. "If he was with this black woman, it wasn't for the drugs, or for sex. It was so Tommy could imagine making his mother watch."

STELLA AND Dance stood in front of the school. An arctic wind scoured the street, biting into their skin. "Those kids in there," Dance said. "By the time they're old enough to vote, a lot will be pregnant. Or dead." He turned to Stella. "About Fielding, did you believe her?"

"Yes. Did you?"

Dance looked into her face. "I don't believe anyone," he answered.

SIX

"So," Johnny Curran said in his lyrical voice, "Bright sent you over."

Stella sat down. "I need a short course—drugs in Steelton."

Curran stroked his mustache, appraising Stella. He made no effort to be polite about it—his cool, slightly clinical assessment seemed intended to remind her that she was a woman, and a supplicant. Curran was a big man, bulky in his blue jeans and crewneck Irish sweater, and his belly protruded like a small, hard cannonball. He must be well into his fifties, Stella thought; his thick longish hair had turned white, and a red tinge in his face, combined with a blue-veined nose, suggesting that whiskey helped relieve the tensions of his job, briefly reminded Stella of the tormented man her father once had been. But his pale blue eyes were clear and cold, peering from the incipient wreckage with a heartless lucidity. Stella had no trouble imagining him firing a bullet from two inches away into Harlell Prince's eye: even the faintly accented voice—soft and light, with the musical undertone of an Irish tenor—had a lethal quality.

"Because of Novak?" he asked. "Why bother?"

Stella had known this man for less than two minutes; already she knew better than to waste her time on moral argument. "Because it's my job."

Curran sat back. *And why bother with you?* his expression said. Bluntly, Stella asked, "How did Novak wire cases?"

The only change in Curran's face was a cool stare, then a glint in his eyes. "Now, that's a deep subject."

"How so?"

Curran inspected his brown leather boots; part of his persona, Stella realized, was indifference to any imperative but his own. "Twenty-three years spent doing this," he said, "ten years in vice before that, and I don't know the answer. *You* don't even know the question."

Many cops were storytellers, Stella knew, and some developed a vivid, profane gift for narrative. But Curran had spent years undercover;

he treated words as if they were traitors, and even his bare office revealed nothing of his life. "Then what *is* the question?" Stella asked.

Slowly, Curran looked up from his boots. Amidst the blood red of his face, the white surrounding the chill blue eyes was startling. "How *Vincent Moro* fixes cases."

Stella cocked her head. "And that's how he's survived."

Curran settled in, half shutting his eyes with palpable weariness and boredom, as if someone had forced him to watch the same movie for the rest of his life. "Back in the old days," he finally said, "some guys from Chicago tried to move in on the Steelton mob. The locals met them at the train station, took them for a ride, blew their heads off with a shotgun, and shipped what was left back to Chicago in a freezer car. The cops didn't mind—what did they want with more hoods from Chicago, when the ones they already knew paid them well enough. Life was simple."

Despite its familiarity, the story suddenly seemed to amuse Curran in the telling—a thumbnail sketch of how things had worked in a more primitive time. Stella watched him. "Drugs changed all that," he continued. "There's too much money. More people want in on the business, and they'll kill for a piece of it. And *we're* supposed to do something about that. So now Vince Moro has to deal with the competition *and* us.

"The mob still whacks competitors, same as before. Only now they're smarter. When I took out Harlell Prince, I could hear Vince laughing. A Christmas present, from me to him—George Flood gets his territory back." Curran put his boots up on the desk. "Of course, when I got my snitch's tongue in the mail, I was laughing, too. Because Prince was already dead."

Curran, Stella sensed, was not talking figuratively; she could see him smiling at the severed tongue. She sorted out the sour joke beneath the joke, the chain of death and its consequence, Curran solving Moro's problems for him. "You *know* Vincent Moro?"

Her surprise seemed to amuse him. "From the old neighborhood. We used to steal cars together, before I turned cop and Vince went professional."

The first part did not seem unusual—the line between cop and criminal was sometimes a fine one, walked by wild, barely formed kids who, whatever course they chose, wished to make their own law. But the link between Curran and Moro intrigued her: two tough and shrewd survivors who had known each other well, when few people could claim to know either man at all. "What was Moro like?" she asked.

The mordant humor vanished from Curran's face. "Nothing scared him," he said at last. "He never talked much, but what he said he'd do, he did. Most of all, he's smart. No one ever caught him stealing cars. Just like no one's caught him fixing cases."

His voice held an unwonted respect—perhaps, Stella thought, because he could have been describing himself. "Why does he never get caught?" she probed.

Curran appraised her again. Softly, he answered, "Because he's got too many people."

She thought of Saul Ravin's belief that Moro had a network—Novak, judges, clerks, cops, maybe prosecutors. With equal quiet, she asked, "How would a *cop* protect Moro?"

His eyes were chill now. "Other than destroying dope by 'accident'?"

Once more, Stella felt off-balance. "Other than that."

Curran's eyes became slits again. Feeling him slip away, Stella imagined him reviewing thirty years of history, deciding how much, if anything, to say. When he spoke, his voice was a monotone. "You can tip off a dealer. You can sell out someone else's snitch, so Vince can have him killed. You can tell the prosecutor to go light on a defendant, because he's really *your* snitch. You can use some other cop's password and get into our computer, find out what your pals are working on. You can do a bad search, get the warrant thrown out. You listen. You never leave a trace."

This was not academic, Stella thought: the accretion of betrayal on betrayal had a poisonous quality. "And you think all those things happened," Stella said.

There was silence. When Curran's eyes opened more fully, they had a deep alienation, the look of someone whose life had set him apart. "Working undercover," he said, "you lie to people. You sell them out. You learn to imitate junkies. You learn to read faces. You learn never to say you were in the joint somewhere, because the dealer you're trying to burn may kill you if you don't know every inch of the place. You don't trust anyone." The tone of buried anger returned. "You get smarter than Jack Novak ever dreamed of being. And you don't want the attention."

"But you think this guy exists. A crooked cop."

Curran stirred in his chair, giving the lazy shrug of a cat. "Did I say one guy? Maybe two, maybe three. Over twenty years, maybe different guys." He paused again. "We don't talk about it. I don't want *you* to talk about it. Maybe it's stopped now—last couple of years, Vince doesn't seem so lucky anymore. The only reason I'm talking to *you* is that you're so far over your head that you don't even know it. Or you wouldn't come here asking about Jack Novak."

Stella stifled her resentment. "Or about a Haitian dealer named Jean-Claude Desnoyers? You busted him in a motel parking lot, remember. After George Flood didn't show."

Curran stared at her. "Novak was a whore," he finally said. "I was going to flip Desnoyers."

Stella's tone grew cold. "We've been talking for twenty minutes, and already Flood's been lucky twice. How many more times *were* there?"

Straightening, Curran looked past her at the wall. "One more," he said tersely, "that I know of."

"What was that?"

"A raid. We got the drugs, and the headlines. But Flood was gone."

"And you've never talked about any of this," Stella said with asperity, "with any of your colleagues. You're just not curious."

"*Curious?*" Curran crossed his arms and he seemed to bite each word. "I'm at least 'curious.' We've got fifteen undercover cops in narcotics, and nine with twenty years in. Five other cops who're still on the job spent time here, including the Chief of Detectives. There's a good chance at least one of them belonged to Vince." His voice moved between sarcasm and disgust. "Which one should I ask to confess? Because none of them is so stupid that they're living large like Novak, spending Vincent's money. They're waiting for retirement and then they'll just disappear." He paused, adding softly, "Unless I catch them first."

Stella felt the force of Curran's reality—a paranoid and violent world, devoid of trust. "Like Harlell Prince," she said.

Curran gave her an enigmatic look. "Prince," he answered, "died fast. So you might say he was lucky. Just not as lucky as Vincent."

The musical lilt of Curran's voice, renewed again, was more frightening than his anger. Another dimension of Curran's world was becoming clearer, its organizing principle—a twilight struggle between boyhood friends through which, after forty years, Curran and Moro remained bound to each other. Harlell Prince seemed to have died too fast for Curran's liking, and whoever crossed Curran next might pay the price.

"So who killed Novak?" she asked.

Curran shrugged again. "His dressmaker, maybe. If you're looking for pissed-off clients, or even one who's going down, I can't think of any."

"You used to be in vice. Ever hear anything kinky about him?"

"Kinky? No. Only that Novak liked hookers. Not street whores—Moro's girls, from the escort services." Curran sounded so bored by the range of human desire that nothing impressed him. "Novak was into scenes, the word was, and sometimes you have to pay for what you want."

"'Scenes,'" Stella repeated.

Curran spread his fingers in front of him, wincing in pain. They were gnarled, arthritic looking, and the joints were red and thick; to Stella's surprise, his fingernails were immaculate. He began twisting a heavy metal ring with a large red stone which seemed to grow from the flesh of his left hand. "Threesomes," he answered. "I heard Novak liked to give direction. Like an auteur."

Stella's skin felt warm. "He liked to watch?"

"So I hear."

"Did that include guys? Or bondage scenes, someone helping to hang him up?"

Looking up from his hands, Curran fixed her with a penetrant gaze. "You tell me," he said. "We weren't that close."

The ambiguous comment left Stella momentarily off-balance. Watching her, he smiled, a quick show of teeth. "Some things," he added lazily, "are a man's job."

This insult, clearly, was intentional: Curran was leaving her to guess whether the "man's job" was hanging another man in a garter belt, or prosecuting the murder which resulted. Coldly, Stella answered, "Like rape, you mean."

Curran gave a short laugh. "Like a lot of things."

Folding her hands, Stella stared at him. "Ever hear anything about Tommy Fielding?"

Curran's bushy eyebrows twitched upward. "The stadium guy who ODed with the hooker? Nothing."

"What about *her*—Tina Welch? Dance tells me she was busted a few times near the theater district. On Scarberry Street."

Curran looked into the chipped coffee mug on his desk, as if to reaffirm that it was empty. "Don't know the names anymore," he said. "Too long since I worked vice—the whores I knew are probably toothless, or dead. But Scarberry's still the same—hooker alley. They'll fuck you behind a garbage can."

His contempt for women, Stella was certain, did not end with prostitutes. Calmly, she said, "Narcotics works Scarberry, too."

Curran put down the mug. "I don't do undercover now—too old, too many people know me. But sometimes I'll cruise the place, maybe send my people there."

"Looking for what?"

"Smack. A lot of the hookers are addicts, and they're easier to turn than dealers." Curran's tone was contemptuous. "They're more afraid of jail—why lose business *and* go through withdrawal? Problem is that they usually buy from low-level dipshits not even Jack Novak would touch, or sometimes just make trades." The smile flashed again. "Promise most of these girls smack, and they'd suck Rock Hudson's dick. Maybe help dig him up."

"But would they just drive off with him?" Stella responded coolly.

With a weary sigh, Curran settled back in his chair. "So you want to know about hookers."

"I know about hookers. I want to know about the Scarberry District."

Curran paused, as if forcing himself to continue. "Dance can tell you—him, and the people from vice. But Scarberry's basically a sewer—you can buy drugs and whores, the low end of both markets. Some of the whores will rob you, a few are run by pimps, most of them are outlaws, fending for themselves." He twisted his ring again. "It's dangerous down there. Some of the whores look out for each other, make sure a psycho doesn't rip one of them apart with a steak knife. Dance knows to ask—if Fielding picked her up there, chances are someone saw his car."

"Where do they turn tricks?"

"Cars. Alleys, like I said. Cheap hotels, but they've got to pay the guy at the desk. Why split five bucks for a five-minute blow job, which is all you'd pay for it if you've got any brains at all. And a *hooker* with any brains won't drive off with a stranger." He looked up again, his eyes speculative. "So does she go home with him? Not unless he offers drugs. Maybe not even then, unless the guy pays extra, and she knows him from before."

Stella opened her briefcase. "When were you last down there? Thursday, by any chance?"

"The night he died, you mean?" Curran asked. "No. Maybe a couple of days before. Last Tuesday, I think."

Stella took out the crime scene photographs and handed them across Curran's desk. "Recognize either of them?"

Curran spread the pictures in front of him. Reaching into his desk, he put on half glasses, squinting at the two naked corpses. "Him, no," he answered. "Not in the Scarberry. Her, I couldn't say—maybe in the dark, when I'm driving through. Vice will know her."

Curran handed back the photographs. "Last Tuesday," Stella asked, "What time was this?"

"Not late. Nine, nine-thirty. I don't remember."

Stella tossed the pictures in her briefcase. "How are you at remembering cars?" she asked.

"*Cars?*" The impatient tone returned. "That's how you recognize dealers."

"Do you recall seeing a white Lexus? A 1999 model."

Curran was quiet. "A suburban housewife's car," he said softly. "The kind you see parked at the country club. It cruised the block a couple of times, like the driver was looking for something, and drove away. Maybe his curfew was up." His eyes grew keen. "This one have a personalized license plate?"

Stella felt anticipation creep through her, a tension in the nerves and muscles. "'PLAY BALL,'" she answered.

Curran sat back and began to laugh, as if at the relentlessness of human folly, mirth rippling the small mound of his stomach. The blue eyes seemed to dance now. "No extra innings for that boy," he said.

"WE'VE ALREADY been through the Scarberry," Dance said over the telephone. "No one remembers Fielding at all. Or seeing his Lexus, either."

From her desk, Stella watched the stadium, the workers creeping through its iron frame like soldier ants. "If Curran's right, maybe Tina knew him from before."

"Curran." Dance's laconic voice carried an indefinable note. "Did you two bond?"

"Not particularly." Stella hesitated, weighing how much she wanted to reveal about Curran's suspicions. "But he thinks Jack Novak was into hookers. And scenes."

Dance was silent. "Maybe you should come over," he said at last. "I'm about to go see Novak's girlfriend. She claims to be the last one to see him alive. Except, if you believe her, whoever killed him."

SEVEN

I T W A S three o'clock when Dance and Stella reached Missy Allen's penthouse, and her panoramic view framed pale winter sunlight, barely lightening the dull gray of the lake.

Dance and Stella sat on the couch. Allen remained standing; she had quick darting movements—snatching an empty glass from the coffee table, straightening a pile of fashion magazines—and her speech was disjointed, sentences tripping over each other, reflecting her awareness that she was a potential suspect. She was a model, she explained, but work was hit and miss, and there were younger girls—Missy had too much time to herself, to think about Jack and that phone call. "I'm so glad you're here," she blurted. "Ever since Jack—I feel like such a mess. I mean, the phone rings, and I think it's whoever killed him—"

Abruptly, she stopped, extending her arms in a stagy gesture of helplessness and distress. She had long streaked-blond hair, a face too smooth and lineless for a woman in her late thirties, and dramatic red nails which accented the fan of her outspread fingers, reminding Stella of a mannequin. What traits, she found herself wondering, could she and Melissa Allen possibly have shared which had drawn Jack Novak to them both?

"Tell us about that night," Dance said in his phlegmatic way. "Everything you remember."

Allen became still, as if she had not heard, and then nodded belatedly. "Everything," she repeated and, stalking the living room as she spoke, began a nervous torrent of admissions.

She was going to stay over with him that night. Yes, she used cocaine—a lot of girls in her business still did, it got them through the endless shoots and call-outs, the curt rejections for not having the right look. But cocaine wasn't a problem for her or Jack. Mentally, Stella dismissed this; when Missy began crying, Stella wondered if she were coked right now. Then Missy sat abruptly, as if she had crashed.

Dance and Stella simply watched her. As though abashed by their silence, Missy started talking again, harassed now, her words shadowed by fear as she described the night Jack Novak died.

JACK WAS a little high. They had stayed until the restaurant closed, Jack demanding samples of single-malt scotch and complaining about the service, and Missy knew that he'd coked up in the men's room. He was becoming more unpredictable, and he scared her. So when he shut the apartment door behind him and demanded that she strip, Missy did not argue—his eyes were too bright. All she asked for was cocaine.

With exaggerated patience, he used a razor to sculpt a thin white line on the coffee table. No sooner did the cool powder hit her nasal passages than Missy felt better; the cocaine surge cut through all the white burgundy she had drunk, and the room took on a chill clarity, Missy still in it, but not of it.

The lights were too bright. When she reached for the lamp at the end of the couch, Jack said softly, "Leave it on."

She turned to him. The harshness of the light exposed the ravages of middle age—Jack's face had become more fleshy now, separating into segments, and the darkening bags beneath his eyes made him look like an evil badger.

Leave him, Missy's brain told her, but her body would not obey. The modeling jobs were fewer now and, as long as she did as he wanted, Jack kept her in an apartment the other girls coveted. When he was tender, rubbing her back or reading her sinuous lines of poetry by Verlaine, Missy thought maybe she loved him . . .

Jack vanished into the bedroom. When he returned, the handcuffs dangled loosely from his fingers.

Silent, she undressed, her movements so automatic that her mind drifted away. She had eaten too much chocolate—tomorrow, she would do an hour on the exercise bike. As he slipped behind her, Missy gazed down at the flat plane of her belly, and wondered how much longer this would last.

Gently, Jack kissed the nape of her neck. Missy recognized the signal; docile, she slid her wrists behind her back. As the handcuffs clicked, she froze, staring at the carpet.

The sound of Jack unzipping his pants made her sad, and the light across her body yielded a moment of bleak honesty. She had traveled too far with him, and this was never what she'd imagined. What she had always wanted was to be beautiful, and desired, and then, after the excitement faded, to be cherished by a man who would take care of her. When she had first met Jack, time was running out, and she had hoped he was that man . . .

Awkwardly, she fell to her knees. The carpet abraded her skin—strange what the handcuffs did to balance. She righted herself, skittering toward him on her knees.

Jack sat on the couch, pants around his ankles. He was not hard yet—he was having more trouble with this, though sometimes the amyl nitrite seemed to help, or watching her with someone else. Depending on what Jack wanted, it helped *her* . . .

Bending forward, she took him in her mouth. Slowly, she closed her eyes, drifting.

The telephone rang.

She felt Jack flinch. In the hush of the apartment, the ringing sound was harsh, intrusive.

To her surprise, he rose to answer. Missy rested her face against the couch, grateful for the respite.

Tomorrow, after working out, she would call her mother. Maggie Allen had always told her she was beautiful—like Maggie herself had been before the babies. Long before Missy developed breasts, her mother taught her how to use makeup, how to dress, how to model clothes. Maggie would smile at Missy in the mirror: it was like seeing herself again, Maggie said, and soon Missy began gazing at her reflection, alone, searching for the quality of beauty her mother so clearly saw . . .

"*Now?*" she heard Jack ask.

What time *was it?* Missy wondered, and became anxious, fearful that he would invite someone she did not know to join them. Jack's voice sounded tense, newly alert. "Give me ten minutes," he said. When she heard his footsteps on the carpet, Missy shut her eyes again.

She felt a light tug as Jack grasped the handcuffs, then heard a click as the manacles slid from her wrists.

"You have to go," Jack said.

His tone had a rough urgency. But Jack would not explain, she knew—he never did.

As Missy dressed, Jack began pacing as if she were already gone. Silent, she unlatched the door to leave.

Once more, she felt Jack's lips on the nape of her neck. Softly, he asked, "Are you all right to drive?"

She turned to him. In her surprise, tears came to her eyes. Mute, she nodded.

Jack seemed to search her face, to really see her. "Call me," he said gently. "Tomorrow, whenever you get up."

Quickly, Missy kissed him, and slipped into the cool night.

THERE WAS a knot in Stella's stomach—not simply at the stirring of shameful memory, but of doubt. She could too easily imagine the repressed hatred of an abused girlfriend, fueled by alcohol and cocaine, igniting an unreasoning rage. It did not take a man to kick out a stool, or castrate a corpse. "When you left," Stella asked, "did you see anyone?"

"No." Missy looked exhausted. "I remember there were cars outside. But there always were."

Stella drew a breath. "You *know* how Jack died."

Nodding, Missy looked away. She really *was* quite beautiful, Stella realized: high cheekbones, luminous brown eyes, a fleeting ethereal look which lent vulnerability to the model's sheen. But plastic surgery would steal this in time; already her skin was too tight, and eventually her face would have the porcelain, affectless quality of a doll's. Part of Stella felt deeply sorry for this woman. But for all she knew Missy Allen had wiped her own fingerprints off the knife. In the silence, Dance appraised this woman, his presence massive on the small couch. Quietly, he asked, "Novak ever ask you to tie him up?"

Allen's eyes flew open. "No."

"Or maybe hang him?"

"*No*." Allen's voice became brittle. "I don't know anything about that."

There was a practiced indignation in her words which gave Stella pause. Missy Allen was insecure, neurotic, without a core; in Stella's experience, such women lied habitually, believing that lies were a tool of survival, and, when confronted, often told further lies with the dramatic, wounded air that Allen used now.

"You mentioned people watching you," she said in a neutral voice. "Did you mean men?"

Allen shook her head back, the wave of hair flowing down her neck. To Stella, the gesture had a dissociated quality, a model collecting herself to walk down a runway. "And women," Missy answered.

Stella hesitated. Softly, she asked, "Did Jack have sex with them?"

"The women." Allen bit her lip. "Mostly Jack liked to watch me. He'd ask me to do things for him, with people I didn't know. Sometimes it was with women Jack would pay for." Her voice became a constricted whisper. "At least they never hurt me. Not like the first time, with his client . . ."

This time it was Stella who closed her eyes.

I T W A S summer, and the narrow strip of sand fronting Jack's lake house was damp, glistening.

Stella sat with her feet in the water, tossing pebbles into the gentle waves. Though this was early afternoon, she had already drunk too much wine, and her thoughts were scattered, her movements sun stunned. The string bikini Jack had given her felt less skimpy now— perhaps she simply felt less. She was not that used to wine.

She had always liked coming here; it seemed their refuge from the treadmill of work and law school, the jittery rhythms of Jack's life. But now she was drinking to numb her unease—with Jack's practice; with who she felt herself becoming; with the sense that Jack himself was becoming restless, needful of fresh excitement. With last night.

Stella drew the chilled bottle from the cooler and refilled her plastic cup. She watched the waves which swirled at her feet, the afternoon sunlight coloring the water's deep blue . . .

In the darkness of his bedroom, his question had carried an undertone of pleading, of desperation. "What kind of fantasies?" she murmured.

"Different ones." Once more, Jack kissed her neck, his voice low, quiet. "Let me tell you."

Stella's head began to spin; she had drunk too much wine, she realized. She lay back on the bed, confused, and then she felt Jack's lips on her stomach. Perhaps, tonight, she would learn what was in his heart.

After a time, he entered her. She moved with him, only half listening to Jack's whispered tale of the stranger, watching them from the darkness. Only when Jack climaxed with the climax of his story did she realize that, in his fantasy, the stranger was inside her . . .

On the beach, Stella drank more wine, remembering. "That was beautiful," Jack had told her. "Watching you."

He was waiting inside the house. Over lunch, she had asked for time to be alone. To her relief, Jack did not argue; he had sent her off with a second bottle of white wine.

Fantasies. What was there about Jack Novak that made Stella's seem so mundane?—a law degree, a home, a partner who understood her as well as Jack could at his best. Perhaps, someday, a husband, a daughter of her own, a bright-eyed girl who would feel the love from Stella, a sense of her own value, that Stella herself had craved. Why did she lack the courage to say these things to Jack?

For moments—Stella did not know how long—her thoughts seemed to merge with the sunlight in the water. When she picked up the bottle of wine, it was empty.

She rose, slowly heading for the house.

She was drunk, Stella discovered. Each step felt halting, desultory; the sunlight was too bright, and the world—the rose garden, the shade trees above the cedar house—seemed to narrow to the next few feet in front of her.

Reaching the rear porch, she placed a hand on the railing, steadying herself. Then she opened the screen door and stepped inside.

The living room was dark and cool. The faint whir of an overhead fan entered Stella's consciousness, then the dirge of the Verdi Requiem from Jack's stereo. The house was not what Stella imagined as a vacation home: it was carefully decorated, and the floor-to-ceiling shelves were filled with art books, recent hardcovers, leather-bound collections of the classics. The sight made Stella feel momentarily peaceful, secure.

Looking around for Jack, Stella started.

A tall, handsome black man with startling green eyes had risen from Jack's sofa. His body in the tight jeans and T-shirt was sinewy, and his sensual mouth had a smile at the corners.

"Where's Jack?" she asked him.

She was frightened, Stella realized, her voice tight. Then she saw Jack watching from a corner with a smile of his own, and wondered if this was as he wanted it.

"Meet Diego Carter," Jack said easily. "He's a client. And a friend."

Stella could not move. She fixed Jack with an imploring look, seeking some explanation. Then she realized that there would be no explanation, and that she did not need one.

Softly, she said, "Can I talk to you?"

"Of course." Jack took her hand as though she were a child, leading her to the bedroom.

She stood there, arms at her sides.

Gently, Jack kissed her forehead, then looked into her eyes. "Is it that he's a black man?"

Stella shook her head, unable to express herself. Slowly, with the reverent touch of a lover, Jack unhooked the top of her bikini.

It fell to the floor. Stunned, she stared at it, head down. The sense of their downward flight stole over her.

"It's all right, Stella." Jack's voice was soothing, yet suffused with his own urgency. "I'll never let anyone hurt you."

Stella felt a wrenching nausea. She took one stumbling step backward.

Jack reached out for her. With all the shock and anguish of her apartness—from her family, and now from Jack—Stella raised her arm and slapped him across the face.

He reeled sideways. In a trembling voice, she said, "Give me your car keys, *now.*"

Jack touched his lip. Tightly, he said, "You're not fit to drive. I can't let you."

She was finished with him, Stella was certain. But the fear that Jack was not done with *her* filled her with fresh panic. She saw herself as a plaything caught between two men—nothing to her lover, desperate to be something to herself—and knew that her sense of who she was, and could be, was as much at risk as her body. As calmly as she could, Stella answered, "Then get rid of him."

Jack said nothing. In the shadows of the room, they watched each other.

"*Do it,*" Stella said between her teeth.

For another moment—endless agony to Stella—Jack was still. Then he left the room, closing the door behind him.

Still half-naked, Stella began to cry.

THIRTEEN YEARS later, she gazed at Melissa Allen.

"These men," she inquired at last, "the ones Jack shared you with, did any of them become angry with you—*or him?*"

"I don't know." Reflexively, Missy seemed to curl in on herself, knees close together. "Not while I was with them—I mean, I can't *remember...*"

"Do you remember names?"

"He never told me names." Allen looked away. "Sometimes they wore a mask."

Quiet, Stella glanced at Dance. As usual, he looked impenetrable—Allen could have been describing the art on Novak's walls. But Stella's palms felt damp.

"Did Novak ever wear stockings?" Dance asked. "Or heels?"

"Jack?" Missy's voice became lower, throaty. "No. *I* did."

Stella inhaled. "What about that night?" Dance continued. "At the apartment, did you drink more scotch?"

There was a pause, and then Allen's face screwed tighter in seeming concentration. "I didn't. I don't think Jack did, either."

They would have to fingerprint her, Stella knew. Dance folded his hands in front of him. "On the telephone, did Novak sound scared? Or worried?"

Missy looked pensive. The contrast between her frenetic behavior earlier, and her lassitude now, deepened Stella's unease. "Not exactly," Missy answered. "More like cautious, or respectful. I couldn't see why Jack would answer the phone at all . . ."

Nor could Stella, were Missy telling the truth. "Do you know if he had problems at work?" Stella asked.

Nervously, Allen flicked back her hair. "He never talked about work. I don't think he liked me to know too much." Her voice softened. "I just wanted to be there for him, to give him what he needed to be happy."

Stella paused, feeling her doubt at Allen's story collide with the memory of her own delusion, the hope that she, somehow, would be enough to bring Jack Novak peace. And then she recalled that final weekend, her last words as she opened the car door, looking back at Novak in the darkness. "There's a hole in your heart, Jack. I can hear the wind whistling through it." She had not known, then, how much he had damaged hers.

EIGHT

"I f i t's a relationship you want," Martin Breyer said half an hour later, "the man you're describing is not a very good risk. Unless your notion of 'relationship' is fairly elastic."

"It would have to be," Stella answered. "This particular man is dead."

Breyer considered her through horn-rimmed glasses. To Stella, the glasses, like Breyer's office—monastic, impersonal, painted a pale blue— were standard issue for a psychiatrist, a breed which, in her personal life, inspired in Stella an unease akin to fear. But, as a lawyer, Stella sometimes was confronted with the insanity defense, and in Breyer she had found an expert witness whose beliefs in personal responsibility and moral choice were consistent with her own. Raising his eyebrows, a habit which accentuated his long, thin face and white-fringed pate, Breyer inquired, "Would we be discussing the unfortunate Mr. Novak?"

"We would. Between us."

Breyer placed a thin silver pen to his lips. "You've mentioned an interesting variety of personal characteristics—charm, grandiosity, a disdain for social norms, a first-rate ability to manipulate, deep fear of the ordinary, a desperate need to fill the void inside. At bottom, there's something rather sad about him." His eyes narrowed. "Am I correct in assuming that you knew him quite well?"

Stella hesitated. "Yes. For a time."

The eyebrows raised again. "Enough to have experienced some of this at first hand."

It was not a question. Stella met his gaze directly. "Enough," she answered brusquely, "to find out what my limits were."

The psychiatrist's gray eyes were keen. "And *not* enough," he said at last, "to know what *Mr. Novak's* were."

Stella paused, and then nodded. "If any. The experience of more recent friends suggests there weren't many left. And then there's the way he died."

Breyer crossed his legs, still idly twisting the pen he held. The gesture called attention to his long fingers, which added to the ascetic, scholarly impression of an aging professor. "You've mentioned voyeurism, and a taste for group sex. So we'll start there.

"To me, that bespeaks not only a craving for excitement—that's obvious enough—but for control." He compressed his lips; Stella sensed a new delicacy, an appreciation of her embarrassment, and of her resolve to conceal it. "To force a 'lover,' if that's the right word, to give herself to other men is the opposite of love, or intimacy. It suggests that part of *his* pleasure involves erasing her boundaries to conform to his *absence* of boundaries. Anything to enhance *his* own need to be different, special— potent." Breyer's voice softened. "That was a need, I expect, which transcended sex. And to fulfill it, the man you describe would be very, very seductive, with an uncanny instinct for the weaknesses of the woman he chose."

After a time, Stella became aware of her own silence. "I came to realize," she said at last, "that nothing was beyond him. Even tears."

Breyer gave her a look of veiled inquiry. "How old were you when you knew him?"

Beneath his detachment, Stella heard an unaccustomed compassion. "Early twenties."

Breyer looked up from his pen. "Anyone who escaped this man," he said, "at any age, did well."

Was her self-questioning that obvious? Stella wondered. But the note of understanding was balm to her soul. Perhaps, she admitted to herself, that was part of why she had come, though she did not think she could ever return on her own. "Jack showed me who I was," she said. "At least in one way."

Breyer nodded. "We live by rules. We need them." He frowned, thoughtful. "But even deviance has rules, of a kind. And that's where your description puzzles me."

"How so?"

"The bondage fantasies are consistent enough. But I have some trouble with the garter belt and heels—on *him*, that is. As well as the auto-erotic gamesmanship."

Stella shifted in her chair. "I'm a little at sea," she said. "The only evidence of that, so far, is how we found him."

Breyer twirled his pen. "Well, here's my problem, and see if this makes sense to you.

"As your Dr. Micelli seems to have intimated, autoerotics tend to be somewhat pathetic loners, even more so if they like to dress in women's lingerie. They're solitary and ashamed—in many ways, it's a metaphor for the ultimate loneliness. Which the flirtation with death, whatever the stimulus involved, suggests.

"I don't mean they *never* find partners—some do. Perhaps there's a certain solace in having another person feel their pain. But by the time they do that, they should have developed a high degree of sophistication. They'll have S and M manuals, their own leather straps, scarves to prevent bruising, and they'll know just how far to go. Which means they usually don't risk using stools—tiptoes will do nicely."

Involuntarily, Stella relived the moment Micelli had turned Jack Novak's naked body to show how tightly bound his hands were. "So what you don't accept," she said at last, "is that Jack had a partner."

"I accept that whoever killed him was quite possibly a sadist. I have a harder time with Novak as a masochist. The idea of him cooperating, and the somewhat primitive tools at hand, don't feel quite right to me. Also, the man you describe strikes me as someone with a very keen survival instinct, someone who had a good sense of whom to exploit, whom to avoid, how far to go at any given moment. *Not* someone likely to misread a partner with a burning desire to murder him." His tone grew contemplative. "Your dilemma puzzles me. I wish I could tell you exactly how this happened."

"That's what's bothering me. I can't see it."

For an instant, Breyer seemed to hesitate. "And, perhaps, don't want to. So I should inject a note of caution.

"Novak was a thrill seeker. And his sense of imperviousness would only be heightened by cocaine. So it's not impossible that his death occurred exactly as it appears to have, and that he simply misjudged his partner." He paused again, as though considering whether to say more, and then his voice became almost paternal. "This is not a case I'd have wished on you, Stella. Whatever the truth is, I hope it's no more painful than what you've learned already."

Recalling Saul Ravin's admonition, Stella, too, was briefly quiet. "How can it be?" she answered.

THE OFFICE, Stella thought when she returned, seemed unusually busy—two uniformed police officers rushed past her down the narrow hallway, and the secretarial pool outside Charles Sloan's office, a polyglot mix of every ethnic group in Steelton, looked overburdened and resentful. The acrid smell of burnt coffee hung in the air.

Stepping into Sloan's office, she closed the door behind her—the rivalry between them was already rumored, as was the prospect that they would run against each other to succeed Bright. She had no desire to make things worse.

Sloan regarded her. In his most neutral tone, he asked, "What can I do for you, Stella?"

Though uninvited, Stella sat. "I need help in the Novak case."

His eyes narrowed. "What kind of help?"

"The crime scene still seems contrived to me. Dance thinks so, too. Suppose, for the sake of argument, Jack didn't have a playmate. That would make it a straight-out murder."

"*That,*" Sloan answered curtly, "is why Nathaniel Dance exists."

"It's more than that. Someone was helping Jack to wire cases, I think. So do Saul Ravin and Johnny Curran. Not many cases—a few big ones."

"*Someone?*" Sloan repeated coldly.

"Maybe the cops. Remember the George Flood case?" Her gaze met his. "It's not every day that five keys of coke just disappear."

Sloan said nothing. But Stella saw the memory register in Sloan's eyes. "George Flood was a killer," Stella continued. "So are others of Jack's clients. Suppose Jack promised another miracle, but this time couldn't deliver."

Sloan leaned forward. "The night after the murder, Stella, you suggested that Jack Novak—a man who gave Arthur campaign money—was Vincent Moro's lawyer. Now you're implying that he fixed drug cases. Why don't you just walk down the hall and blow Arthur's brains out. Or just as good, endorse Tom Krajek."

Stella stifled her own anger. "Curran, Ravin, and me. I doubt that we're the only three people in Steelton who wonder about Jack Novak. Are we better off if someone *else* figures this out? The *Steelton Press,* for example?" A note of sarcasm crept into her voice. "I know I lack your sophistication, Charles, but I've always thought that integrity sells. At least consider it as an option."

Sloan stared at her. "My only interest is in electing Arthur mayor, so that *his* integrity gets put to better use than making *you* feel good. That's more important to me than one dead lawyer who *I* had no relationship with." Pausing, Sloan bit off his next words. "If *you* have a fucking problem with that, go look in the mirror."

Stella flushed. At considerable cost, she answered calmly, "How about us going to Arthur instead."

Sloan's usually restless body was still. Her response, she sensed, hit

Sloan where he was most vulnerable—his concern with the uniqueness of his relationship with Arthur Bright. "Arthur," he said disgustedly, "is not a playground monitor. As I mentioned, he's running for mayor."

"Which is why we can't decide this for him."

Sloan crumpled the fast-food wrapper into a tiny ball and then slowly released it from his hand, studying the remains. At length, he asked, "What do you want?"

"Someone who absorbs paper well enough to help me sift through Jack's records." Stella hesitated. "It would also help if he understood organized crime. That's not Nat Dance's usual beat."

"'Help.'" Sloan's tone, though quiet, was acidic. "Why do I keep forgetting that we're 'helping' Arthur Bright."

Stella did not answer. Sloan turned away, as though, when backing off, he could not stand to look at her. "The 'help' I'll give you," he said grudgingly, "is a few hours of Michael Del Corso's time. Very few." He clutched the telephone, and then his hand paused in midair, and he stared at her again. "I want to know everything you do on this, Stella. Every goddamned thing."

Leaving, Stella returned to her office. She had another difficulty to face, one she relished least of all. But Sloan had reminded her of its necessity.

BY THE time Stella reached her sister's house, it was nearly eight at night.

Katie Derwinsky answered the door. "Come on in," she said to Stella.

With her reddish hair and snub features, Katie was a plumper replica of their mother. But her tone, neither welcoming nor hostile, was all her own. Stella was certain that Katie had worked on it, and had decided that indifference pleased her most.

This fit the attitude of withdrawal Katie had adopted since their mother's death, their father's decline. Even her move from Warszawa to a suburban tract of fifties ranch houses and postage-stamp lawns, Stella had always believed, was in part a protest against her older sister's cruelty in selling off their parents' home. Stella had left the family, Katie had made quite clear, returning only to destroy its roots. Stella still found it astonishing that sisters, raised by the same parents and only three years apart, could hold two versions of all they had in common—their parents, their family life, even the simplest of memories—so at odds as to be inimical.

She followed Katie into the kitchen, hearing whoops issue from the family room. "He's a choke artist," she heard her brother-in-law pronounce. "A gold-plated, million-dollar candyass."

Stella paused in the entryway to the family room. Since Steelton had lost its basketball team, her indifference to the sport was such that she had forgotten that Bobby was a fanatic. He sat with two other men—from the Ford plant, Stella guessed—while the object of his opprobrium turned out, to Stella's utter unsurprise, to be a well-paid black point guard noted for his clunky jewelry and constant braggadocio.

Bobby himself could hardly be called flashy. With his sagging belly, Fu Manchu beard, and the Steelton Blues baseball cap he wore indoors and out, he looked like a refugee from an ad for Miller High Life. Though, from the evidence of their two children, Katie let Bobby have sex with her, Stella had always found the image appalling; she could only hope, for her sister's sake, that it did not involve the missionary position.

Glancing up, Bobby noticed her. His familiar, chip-on-the-shoulder grin appeared. "Lady Stella," he announced—his pointed reference to the upscale life of an Assistant County Prosecutor and also, Stella knew, his first line of defense against what he guessed must be her mission here. She felt embarrassed, edgy.

"Princess Stella to you," she answered, and then added more amiably, "Hello, Bobby."

Remembering his manners, Bobby introduced her to the others as "my sister-in-law, the next County Prosecutor." After brief pleasantries, the men refocused on the game, and Stella followed Katie to the kitchen.

"Coffee?" Katie asked.

She filled two cups and they sat together at the kitchen table. Once more, it struck Stella that the decor—a ceramic eagle, benign peasant figurines—derived from a Poland with which Katie helped embroider their family's mythic past. Far more accurate, Stella thought, to have a still life of a vodka bottle next to a defunct ceramic steel mill.

She let the awkward silence stretch until Katie asked in a reluctant tone, "How is he?"

"Oh, fine," Stella said. "Two Sundays ago he recited the entire Gettysburg Address. I'd forgotten that he knew it."

When Katie frowned, Stella chastised herself for the irony she brought into this house. More evenly, she said, "He's the same, Kate. He hasn't spoken in months. I doubt we'll hear his voice again."

"But he's healthy?"

"Very. Or so they tell me. "

Katie took a long sip of coffee, carefully setting it back in its saucer. "You *sold* the house, Stella. And fired the nurse."

Stella willed herself to be patient. "That's part of how we've kept him going. You know that."

"I don't know that. *You've* made all the decisions."

Stella had the familiar sense that conversation with her sister was not communication but a series of thrusts and parries. "Someone had to," she answered. "It's like a problem in eighth-grade math—how long will he live, and what will it cost. Except that no one knows the answer."

With elaborate delicacy, Katie poured more cream into her coffee, stirring it until satisfied. "You must know *something*. Or else you wouldn't have called."

No, Stella thought with sudden anger. *I'd have stayed as invisible as he is.* Quietly, she said, "I'm sorry for the intrusion. But Dad keeps breathing, and they keep billing. Funny how that works."

Katie gave her a pinched look. "We all keep breathing, Stella. We were breathing all the years you didn't talk to us. While you were making headlines, Bobby and I got married and had kids. We don't send you the bills, do we?"

The unfairness of it cut through Stella's unease. "You could have given them a choice, Katie. Something like, 'Stella comes to the christening or no one does.' I didn't stay away because I wanted to, but because you needed me to. So you could stay part of 'the family,' as you used to call it." Pausing, Stella lowered her voice. "We're still a family. But Dad's not awarding points anymore. He can't remember you, and he needs his diapers changed. Neither of us can do that for him."

Katie crossed her arms. "It's not just about Dad. It's about Deb and Jimmy." Her voice took on a weary patience. "Bobby won't see ninety thou a year, ever. You've never had to deal with this, Stella, but the public schools are shit. We're paying for Holy Name because we want better for the kids."

Stella put down her coffee, still battling her own reluctance. "I don't want to consign my niece and nephew to the Dark Ages, Katie. You must know how I hate asking. I just need a little help. This won't be forever."

"Maybe not. But you've talked to the doctors, haven't you, and you figure it *will* last to 2001. And you need money to run for County Prosecutor."

Whatever else, Stella thought, Katie was not a fool. "The world's such a simple place, isn't it. This isn't about our father. It's motherhood versus ambition, with me cast in the role of selfish bitch. Katie Marz's personal home movie."

Katie stood abruptly. "You *left* them, Stella. You left *all* of us." She stopped herself, as if to fight the tremor in her voice. "You went to law school, and you live alone. So now you can afford to take care of him. As far as I'm concerned, it's the least you can do." Her tone became soft, venomous. "Or does it take too much time to write a check."

Stella felt the dam break inside her, the last restraints of self-interest and civility. Only the sense of her own superiority, she realized, made her choose contempt over shouting. "I've thought about our childhood a lot," she said. "How unfair it was that I got typecast as the smart sister, and you as the nice sister. I used to think, no matter how hard it was, that I got all the breaks. Because the smart one got to leave, and the nice one had to stay.

"I had it wrong. You're too smart to care when no one notices. And not nice enough to feel ashamed." Stella stood, facing her sister. "Who you are isn't my fault, Katie. It's not even *their* fault anymore. You're a self-made woman. You've chosen who you are."

Katie stiffened with anger. "Get out," she growled.

Stella had a sudden memory from their childhood—Katie crawling into bed with her because she was frightened by a nightmare. Even then, Katie had known that Stella was safe. But there was no going back.

"I'm sorry," Stella said. "I'm sorry for us both."

She turned and left. Katie and she would not speak again, she felt sure, until their father died.

NINE

STELLA AND Michael Del Corso ate lunch on a bench in Steelton Square beside the statue of Marshal Pilsudski, its cast iron befouled by pigeons. The day was unseasonably warm, and street vendors had appeared to sell hot dogs and warm pretzels. Briefly relieved of winter's bone-deep bitterness, office workers drifted from the ill-matched glass towers and weather-worn buildings from the thirties, squinting with mixed suspicion and pleasure at the thin noonday sun. Stella nibbled a pretzel.

After his first bite of Polish dog, Michael observed, "This is how we'd meet if you were Vincent Moro—outside, where you couldn't be wire-tapped, and eavesdropping's harder. Except it'd be dark, somewhere the cops hadn't thought of." He peeled off a piece of bun, tossing it to a pigeon. "Unless I was naked, you'd *still* worry I was wearing a gun or a wire."

Stella sipped her apple juice. "Paranoid."

"Disciplined," Michael corrected her. "You never relax, never drink too much, never let anyone get close to you. Your first rule is 'No new people'; you don't even trust the ones you've known for years; you kill whoever might sell you out before they've had the chance. You last because no one else has been that vigilant, for that long."

Stella considered Michael more closely. He was perhaps six feet two, with a large frame and broken nose which hinted that some football coach had seen a big, willing kid and stuck him on the line. But his curly jet black hair was flecked with an early gray, and the stillness of his body, thickening with the first fleshiness of a man entering his mid-thirties, bespoke a disinclination to react too quickly. Dark liquid eyes, hooded and contemplative, added to the air of someone who had faced hard truths. Suddenly he laughed at himself, which made him look almost boyish, and Stella's impression of sadness—sentimental and wholly uninformed, she decided—vanished.

"If I make Moro sound like the last gunfighter," he said, "it's to pump up my role as the Don Quixote of bureaucrats."

The self-deprecation took Stella by surprise. "But I'll never nail him," she said flatly.

Michael appraised her. "Maybe the feds," he answered. "Not you. Especially for a murder he had nothing to do with."

"Why *not* me? Or—it sounds like—*you*?"

The response was more abrupt than she had intended; there was amusement in his eyes, as though perceiving an unspoken clash of egos. "Okay," he said. "We'll leave Novak hanging there for a while, and focus on Vincent Moro."

That the remark was delivered with a low, street-accented flatness—derived, Stella guessed, from immigrant parents who spoke only functional English—underscored its mordant reference to the manner of Novak's death. "Moro's virtually untouchable," Michael went on blandly. "At most there's maybe three or four people who can get him. *Them* he protects like his own life depends on it, at least until he has to kill one. 'Cause he's Mafia through and through."

Michael's Polish dog, Stella observed, remained uneaten. "Forty-odd years ago," he continued, "Moro drops out of high school and starts working for the mob. A few years later they take him to a secret room lit by candles. The when or where doesn't matter; for centuries the ritual hasn't changed.

"They put a saint's card in his right hand. Then they light it. Moro lets it burn until the flame goes out." Michael gave her a first, fleeting smile. "If that sounds like the Godfather, shake Moro's hand sometime. His fingers are puckered with scar tissue."

Stella took another bite of her pretzel. The near intimacy with which Michael spoke of Vincent Moro reminded her of Johnny Curran; it was as if Michael, too, had grown up with Moro. She did not mention meeting Moro in Novak's office; it had been dark, and she had noticed Moro's eyes, not his hands.

"Next they prick his finger," Michael told her matter-of-factly. "While his flesh is still burning, to remind him that betrayal means death. Of course, he already knows that. The only way into the Scalisi Family was to kill whoever they told you to. For Moro, his own cousin.

"He learned the rules, and he lives by them still. If his people betray him, they know they'll die, unless they kill him first. Like Moro killed Tino Scalisi." Pausing, Michael seemed to rediscover his hot dog. "They say the lesson Moro never forgets is the one he taught Scalisi."

"You sound as if you know him," Stella countered.

Surveying the pigeons, Michael took another bite, chewing with deliberation. Stella knew nothing about him except his credentials—degrees in law and accounting, six solid years as a soldier in the uphill fight against white-collar and organized crime. But he struck her as a mix of the proletarian and the refined, the prideful and the sensitive, with humor tinged with darkness. Even his attitude toward Moro seemed ambiguous, his professional enmity at war with a deeper familiarity, close to respect and perhaps more.

Michael turned to her. "I grew up in Little Italy. People *deferred* to Vincent Moro—not just because they feared him, or even because he lent them money, or found them jobs. They *knew* him, and he knew them." His voice became soft. "His father came from Sicily, like mine. The first time I met Moro, I was on a Little League team he sponsored, and won the championship game with the longest homer I'd ever hit. Afterward, he gave me an old baseball, signed by Yogi Berra, and said that he respected what I'd done. He didn't need to say who he was, or why I should care."

"And he knew you'd always remember."

Michael nodded. "He knows people's weaknesses, how to seduce them. But it's more than that. What he thinks of you matters."

Once more, Stella found herself curious. "Then how did you go bad?"

Michael gave her a fleeting smile. "Law school. My parents had a strong sense of right and wrong, so it wasn't a stretch for their good Catholic son to believe that the laws are for everyone—or *should* be, anyhow." He gazed out at the square again. "There must be things *you* feel that you don't like yourself for feeling. Admiring a man who sells drugs and women, then murders to protect his profits, is worse than ignorance. It's evil."

This abrupt severity of tone struck, in Stella, a disconcerting chord. Perhaps she, too, clung tightly to the rules as an expression of self-contempt, a protection against the moral erosion she had seen in the mirror Jack Novak had held up to her. Perhaps Michael Del Corso, knowing himself, was as afraid as Stella.

"Moro," Michael went on, "preys on the worst in us. Take his escort business—high-priced prostitution. Moro's limo service drives the girls where they need to go, helps them sell drugs to clients who also pay them for sex. If the client's important enough—a rich businessman, or maybe a politician—the girl takes him to an apartment where Moro's got a

Handycam hidden in the bedroom wall. After the guy's finished feeling frisky, then maybe talkative, Moro gets the tape." Michael's voice held more weariness than anger. "It's stuff he can use for blackmail: kinky sex, cocaine use, or something the poor fool shouldn't have said. But *Moro's* totally insulated: he collects his take through intermediaries.

"We're left trying to prove he's laundering the cash through his limo service. But there's no paper trail, the books are cooked, and the company's nominal owner knows if he's caught ratting out Moro's go-between, he maybe dies." Michael turned to her again. "It's like a flow chart of human weakness. Except it never ends."

Listening, Stella could feel his disillusion. Though she had prosecuted the occasional Mafia hit, where the defendant never talked except to give an alibi, homicides were generally far simpler—rooted in the lust or greed or anger of a single murderer—and ended in a lengthy sentence or, for a few, death. Compared to that, Michael labored in the Augean stables, and had earned his skepticism about convicting Vincent Moro.

"So why do it?" she asked bluntly.

He shrugged. "It's existential. Which guy said you have to live like it matters—Sartre or Camus?"

Stella sensed the semifacetious remark might conceal something more fundamental than despair: the dogged determination of an immigrant's son to do the best that was in him. Combine that with a fear of the worst in you, Stella knew, and the fear can enter your soul.

"Tell me about Moro's drug network," she said.

Michael took the last of his hot dog bun and tossed it to a strutting pigeon. "You already understand that pretty well.

"The structure's simple, designed for Moro's protection. He's at the top: the only person he talks to is his capo, Frank Falco. Falco deals with the distributors, and Moro never sees them.

"Take your East Side drug lord, George Flood, and this Haitian dealer you met, Desnoyers, the one that got whacked.

"To Moro, Flood's absolutely key—a black guy who distributes drugs for an Italian to Latins, Asians, and other blacks. But Flood's only contact's with Falco, and your Haitian's only contact is with Flood.

"Every street dealer below the Haitian is level five—the highest Moro wants our busts to go. It's Novak's job to help by keeping his clients quiet. But Johnny Curran's a very smart guy; somehow he flips one of the Haitian's street dealers, who rats out the Haitian, who Curran rolls in a parking lot to try and get George Flood.

"Moro can't have that. He especially can't have your Haitian dealing

Flood, because the next step is Frank Falco. Sure, Flood and Falco know better than to drop the dime—but it's still too close. So when the Haitian says to Novak *he* wants to deal Flood, it's all over for him.

"All Novak has to do is tell Moro." Michael snapped his finger. "Just like that, your Haitian's dead. Fourteen years later, he's *still* the closest we've gotten to tying Moro to drugs. A memorial to Novak's loyalty."

The last was said with such contempt that, for an instant, Stella sensed it spilling over onto her, could feel his unspoken questions about a woman who once had worked for Novak. Dismissing this, she asked, "Then how do you know *anything* about Moro?"

"The feds, mostly. They've got manpower and resources we've never dreamed of: agents to spare, surveillance, wiretaps, video cameras, a network of informants who hear things, records of who people like Falco call, what businesses he has contact with. They've even got a hierarchy of the Moro Family which seems pretty accurate. But there's a difference between *knowing* and *proving*. I mean, the feds can film Moro and Falco getting into a private plane. But they can't hear what Moro says to him once the plane takes off, which is why Moro uses it." As though impelled by his frustration, Michael's speech came quicker, his street accent falling into a sardonic rhythm. "And *us*: Arthur and the cops—even Johnny Curran? At worst we're a nuisance to Moro, and sometimes we even help him."

"How so?"

"Drugs are Darwinian—only the toughest and smartest survive. But there's so much money in it every psychopath with an attitude wants his share.

"Take the East Side again, George Flood's territory. Years ago, Flood's only worry was Harlell Prince, the black guy Curran took out. Now it's the gangs—the Bloods, the Crips, Hell's Angels—plus skinheads, blacks, and a boatload of Jamaicans with no respect for tradition. Sometimes Moro has to eliminate a few. Sometimes we do it for him. Because they're still amateurs who don't have Moro's sophisticated distribution system—parking lots, limos, warehouses, whorehouses, the people to run all that—along with whatever network of crooked cops or judges or court clerks Moro uses to make sure Arthur Bright doesn't roll *his* system up. The wannabes, Arthur can get. But the feds don't trust us, or even respect us."

Michael stopped abruptly, as though hearing his own bitterness. He hunched on the bench: now Stella thought not of a young football player but of a boxer who had learned that he would never rise in his division, perhaps was afraid of knowing that he despised the sport that had defined him. Then Michael shrugged, and Stella wondered if she saw more than there was.

"So when they say the Mafia's dying . . ."

For a moment Michael was silent. When he spoke again, his voice was quieter. "It's a very slow death. But what Ravin told you is right: all the pressure on lawyers and street dealers has made the feds tougher for the mob to deal with. That, plus wiretaps and the witness protection program, where someone like Sammy 'the Bull' Gravano can allegedly kill twenty people and still get a new face and a new life for selling out *his* Vincent Moro. The feds' whole idea is to make Moro a walking get-out-of-jail-free card." Michael laughed again. "Maybe that's why Moro's son, Nick, wound up sitting next to me in torts class. But it's also why Moro didn't string up Novak. Someone that amoral is too valuable to lose."

Stella pondered this. "Suppose he saw Novak as a threat somehow?"

"You mean as in he might try to deal Moro? *Novak?*" Perhaps Stella only imagined that, words etched with disdain, Michael looked at her more closely. "An hour ago, I called a guy I know at the DEA. If he's telling the truth, the feds had nothing on Novak. Besides, taking Moro's money requires a whole lot less guts than selling him out."

Briefly, Stella thought of Jack's elation on the night of George Flood's acquittal, following the "miracle" of the vanishing cocaine. Jack had been many things she had understood but dimly: lonely, mercurial, perhaps tormented by his own emptiness. But in the end, too late to avoid her own scars, Stella had been right about what was most important. Character counts, and Jack Novak had none.

Michael was glancing at his watch. "I've got to get back," he said, and stood abruptly.

Inwardly, Stella bridled at this; his manner lacked the deference owed one of Bright's lieutenants, and as a young female lawyer she had long ago experienced enough condescension for a lifetime. But she had also learned to take her time, to find the right moment to assert herself so that the assertion was irrefutable, the condescension never repeated.

Silent, they walked beneath a graying sky into the building, took an elevator, and went to Michael's office.

Stella paused at the doorway, looking inside. She had never stopped here before; with its metal desk and bare walls, its tile floor, Michael Del Corso's work space was as monastic and impersonal as Stella's own. Except, she noticed, for a small, framed photograph on the credenza behind him: a dark-eyed, dark-haired girl, perhaps seven, of striking delicacy and beauty. What unknown woman did she resemble? Stella wondered, and then realized that Michael wore no ring.

"Still," she told him, "I need your help with Novak's records. I'd like to be sure he wasn't killed for business reasons. So humor me."

The last phrase, delivered with dry understatement, was meant to remind him that humoring Stella was compulsory. A change in his eyes, a slight narrowing, signaled that he understood this and perhaps more—that she and Charles Sloan were rivals and that, if Michael wanted out, he had a place to go.

"Sure," he answered.

TEN

THIRTEEN YEARS after leaving him, Stella sat in Jack Novak's office.

It was a little past seven at night. The room had no windows; Stella felt estranged from the outside world, hermetically sealed in her own past. It was as if the years between had vanished.

In front of her lay a stack of five files culled from the past, the work of several hours.

They were under subpoena, obtained by Stella. From the first, a thin file labeled "Jean-Claude Desnoyers," Stella had extracted her interview notes, written in a tight coiled script which had not changed over time. "Deal?" she had scrawled, and then had underlined the word.

Two days later, the Haitian was dead.

The office door opened, and Nathaniel Dance entered.

He sat in the visitor's chair, his large frame dwarfing it. Hands folded, Dance viewed her with his accustomed impassivity.

"What did you find?" he asked.

"These files. They're all from when you were in narcotics, I think." She placed one aside. "This was for Jean-Claude Desnoyers, a dealer who wanted to flip on George Flood. It's Curran's case—I already know what happened. The rest I need some help with."

Dance said nothing. His silence, Stella thought, was both weapon and defense, a habit cemented by the twilit world of the Steelton police, where trust was carefully rationed.

"All five involve Flood's network," Stella told him. "In the oldest one, Saul Ravin represented Flood's dealer, and Jack Novak had Flood."

Dance's smile was faint, unamused. "I busted the dealer, Louis Jackson. The evidence was five keys of coke."

Stella flipped open the file. "There was an 'administrative error'— someone in the evidence room destroyed the coke, and everyone walked. Saul tells me that Jackson was ready to deal Flood."

Slowly, Dance nodded as he considered Stella.

"Who," Stella asked, "authorized the destruction of the coke?"

Dance folded his arms. "The log in the evidence room showed them receiving a routine authorization, saying that the case had been pled out. But we never found the authorization form. So we never found out whose mistake it was."

"Was it a mistake?"

Dance watched her. Stella felt quite confident that he would not ask why she wanted to know; Dance would follow her questions until he reached his own conclusion. "Mistakes happen," he said. "Maybe this was one."

Stella did not push this. "The next case," she went on, "was also Johnny Curran's. He got a warrant to search the apartment of another of Flood's dealers. According to the warrant application, an unnamed informant told him the coke was stuffed inside his couch." Stella's brief smile was pointed. "When the couch turned up empty, Curran took the guy's keys, went to the garage, and found the coke in the trunk of his car, ready for transport. The case got assigned to Judge Freeman, the East Side's champion of civil liberties. You know what happened *then*, of course."

Dance nodded again. "Freeman tosses the case for a bad search. Curran exceeding the scope of his warrant."

Stella placed the file on top of the first two. "Tidy, isn't it."

Dance settled back in the chair. "You're thinking Moro rigged the assignment to Freeman."

"Or someone tipped the dealer, told him to move the coke somewhere the warrant didn't cover. Curran wouldn't have much of a choice—if he goes back to the judge to expand the warrant, maybe the coke's gone. At least this way it's off the street."

Dance leaned his arm against the arm of Novak's chair, propping his chin in the palm of his hand. "Who was the prosecutor?" he asked.

The question reminded Stella, though she did not need it, of how perceptive Dance was. "Charles Sloan," she answered.

Dance laughed softly, and said nothing.

"The fourth case," she went on, "was Curran's again—and Sloan's. Once more, it's Louis Jackson, for possession of cocaine. But this time Sloan lets Jack plead him out." Casually, Stella tossed the file atop the others. "He got off with a year, and out. Not much tougher than a trip to Disney World."

"What was Novak's defense?"

"Illegal search, like the last time. But this time his motion papers look lame, and it's not before Judge Freeman." Stella picked up the remaining file. "This last one's yours, too."

Dance had summoned an equanimity which was close to benign. "Let me guess which one," he said. "It happened when Jackson was in jail. I busted the guy Flood put in his place, Morgan Beach, for distributing heroin. Beach was willing to give us Flood. Novak got the bail set low—something like fifty thousand. We never saw Beach again."

It was interesting, Stella thought, how much he recalled. She set the file atop the others. "Remember the prosecutor?"

Dance nodded. "Sloan."

His face was expectant, as though waiting for Stella to pursue this. Instead, she asked, "So what have you found out? Was Jack really *that* kinky?"

Dance folded his hands. "He didn't keep a P.O. box for gay porn, or bondage magazines. No one remembers seeing Novak at leather shops. Nobody—his secretary, his associates, his neighbors—admits to believing he was into scenes like the one with whoever killed him." He gave a lazy shrug. "What he *was* into was coke and videos. His apartment and weekend house were full of them—every kind of man doing it in groups with every kind of woman. But no gays or kids or animals."

Involuntarily, Stella remembered her last weekend at Jack's lake house. "What about Jack's cases?" she asked.

"His *recent* cases? Nothing new. No big ones, no real problems, still no word from our snitches about anything unusual. Nothing that would trouble Vincent Moro. Nothing that says his murder *wasn't* personal, whatever the motive."

"Then who had a 'personal' reason to kill him?"

Dance gave her a shrewd glance. "Except for someone like Missy Allen? I just talked to Kate Micelli. The only prints the crime lab got from Novak's apartment were Novak's, Missy's, and the maid's—an old Czech woman. Kate thinks one glass was wiped clean, along with the handle of the knife that cut his balls off. Maybe it's Missy Allen, but only if he cooperated and then she kicked the chair out from under him." He paused, then asked slowly, "Think she hated him that much?"

When Stella did not respond, his stare moved to the files in front of her. "Those cases are *old*, Stella."

"Those cases were *fixed*," Stella retorted. "One of them got someone killed."

Dance's gaze met hers again. "Jean-Claude Desnoyers," he said. "May he rest in peace. His family left town right after they found him in the Onondaga. There's no one left in Steelton who cares, or even remembers. Except for you."

And *you*, Stella thought. "I guess you checked."

Dance nodded. "Yesterday. I remembered Desnoyers, too."

By now, Stella was not surprised. She rested her hand on the files. "So," she said, "who wired these, Nat? Besides Jack."

Dance leaned forward now. "It was a conspiracy," he said. "Between Novak, Curran, Sloan, Judge Freeman, a guy in the police evidence room, and me. Once a month, we'd have meetings. Oh, and Arthur took attendance."

Stella emitted a harsh laugh.

"I don't believe in conspiracies," Dance said flatly. "They're too complicated. You've got five old files, three with Charles Sloan's name on them. So what?"

"Because *I* don't believe in coincidences, at least not five in a row. Someone's rotten here. That's why Flood's still in business, making money for Vincent Moro."

Dance's stare turned pointed. "I thought you were head of homicide, and we were investigating a murder. This feels more personal—or political."

Stella shrugged, meeting his eyes, waiting him out. *He* was Chief of Detectives, and her unimpressed silence was sufficient reminder. "What does Curran say?" Dance asked at length.

"That maybe it's a cop. But he doesn't know."

Dance looked past her, silent, as though his mind were somewhere else. "There was only one I know about for sure," he said finally, "and he's dead."

"Who was it?"

Dance seemed to consider whether to answer; it was long moments before he spoke. "An old bull named Steckler. Buffalohead, they called him."

"How did you catch him?"

"We'd heard stories from snitches that Buffalohead would bust dealers and sell the drugs himself." Dance turned to her again. "Then a couple of dealers turned up dead, their apartments ransacked before we could raid them. Not Moro's dealers, freelancers, where the risk was less. And it smelled like a cop; someone who had access to records, wiretaps, snitches, who maybe heard things from other cops. But Buffalohead was smart—all the captain could do was pair him up with someone."

Stella watched him. Dance's eyes narrowed slightly; she had the sense of his remembered tension, his recall of danger.

"You," she said.

Dance tightened the knot of his tie, a gesture which, in him, seemed unusual for its absentmindedness. "Buffalohead," he said, "gets a tip that a dealer named DeJesus was selling a lot of heroin. So one night the two of us go to his place to bust him.

"The only thing on DeJesus is a Saturday night special and a key to a storage locker at a bus station downtown. Buffalohead puts a gun to DeJesus's head and asks if he'd 'mind' showing us what's in the locker.

"We've got no warrant for this. But once we cuff DeJesus and put him in the backseat, Buffalohead mutters, 'He gave his consent, Nat—I mean, who'll the judge believe, us or this asshole?'

"I don't say anything, because I already know what's going down.

"It's past midnight, and there's almost no one at the station. Buffalo-head tells me to stay with DeJesus. I sit with him in the car: he's skinny, and sweat runs down his face, even though it's cold. And I know if there's anything in the locker, he's a dead man."

Dance was *there*, Stella knew, not here. "When Buffalohead comes out," he continued, "all he says to me is 'Nothing,' like he's disgusted. Then he turns to DeJesus in the backseat and tells him, 'Lucky for you, punk. Guess we'll have to take you home.'

"DeJesus just gapes at him.

"There's no one on the street: Buffalohead checks, just to make sure. Just as he pulls DeJesus's gun on me, I shoot him in the face.

"The locker key's still in his overcoat pocket. I leave him there, brains all over the windshield, DeJesus crying and jabbering, and go back inside the terminal.

"Inside the locker is a duffel bag with over a million in cash.

"I know it's the cash that'll save me. I go back out, shove Buffalohead into the passenger seat, drive him and DeJesus to the station, dump the bag on the captain's desk, and say Buffalohead's outside with his face missing."

The pit of Stella's stomach felt tight. "Buffalohead planned to murder you *and* DeJesus," she said. "There was going to be a 'shootout,' maybe back at his apartment, where you two killed each other. Then Buffalo-head keeps the money."

Dance stared at her now. "A million dollars," he said softly. "I thought about that all the way to Central Station."

The point of his story, Stella understood at once, was different than she had expected: *Don't ever accuse me.* But the way he had made it was more searing than anger.

"If there's Buffalohead," she responded blandly, "maybe there's somebody else. Or was."

Dance's eyes remained fixed on her. "After him," he answered, "things changed. We partnered up more, used polygraphs, even psychology tests. We rotate people in and out, check their bank accounts, monitor who gets seen at places owned by Moro and his people. And the feds have so many wiretaps now that a crooked cop is likely to pop up on one. Besides," he finished flatly, "the last case in your pile is over ten years old. Now narcotics reports to *me.*"

"So if someone besides Buffalohead was crooked, he's gone?"

Dance jabbed a thick index finger at the files. "There are maybe nine guys in narcotics who were there when these cases went down. If one of them belongs to Moro, and he's survived, he's someone very special.

"He hides his money, never talks on the phone, confides in nobody. He lives in compartments—there's only one contact between him and the Moro Family. He can pass a lie detector test without sweating. And he's a stone cold killer." Dance's voice softened. "Maybe that's what's pissing Curran off. Wondering if there's somebody out there as tough as him. Or Vincent Moro."

"But ten years ago," Stella persisted, "there was. These files say so."

Dance frowned. "It doesn't have to be a narc. Take a look at your list of players. Even with the evidence room, people have access who aren't cops at all."

"Like Sloan."

Dance shrugged, still watching her. "Like any DA, and that's just for openers. Unless Sloan killed Novak himself. *That's* why you're here, after all."

Eyes hooded, Stella gazed at the files. Once more, she sensed that Dance wished to head her off.

"Why don't we talk about baseball," he said. "And Tommy Fielding. You were wanting to go with me to Peter Hall's, remember?"

ELEVEN

PETER HALL, whose great-grandfather had brought Stella's to live in Warszawa and work in the mills for seven dollars a day, himself lived where it was possible to forget the smokestacks, rusted and obsolete, which could no longer support men like Stella's father.

Peter Hall was a developer; his income, like his father's, came from the suburban malls and office complexes which had helped suck the life out of Steelton. Leaving the guardhouse at the head of Hall's driveway, the black Chief of Detectives at her side, Stella thought it ironic that Hall had reinvented himself as the savior of Steelton's baseball team, and its inner city.

The village of Stonebrook, where Hall chose to live, was a New England theme park: its parcels were zoned to a five-acre minimum, the rolling hills dusted with morning frost or covered with swatches of dense woodland—oaks and birches became silver shards, leafless in winter—and homes of a colonial style meant to suggest New England, but swollen in scale by money and ostentation. Crossing a wooden bridge above the swift stream which bisected Hall's estate—perhaps a hundred or more acres of land, Stella guessed—she and Dance drove another quarter mile through an undulating landscape which offered distant glimpses of a white horse barn; white-fenced fields; low, decorative walls of heavy stone; a tennis court; more woods. Only the house itself departed from this pastoral theme: it was hewed from stone and wood and glass in a style reminiscent of Frank Lloyd Wright, suggesting that Peter Hall, the modernizer, here had prevailed. Approaching, Dance and Stella took this in. They parked in a circular stone driveway and were met by a neat young man in a blue blazer and turtleneck, a twenty-first-century butler.

With an air of brisk deference, he led Dance and Stella through a massive living room with skylights, stone floors, bright abstract paintings; Stella, who had an amateur's interest in art, thought she recognized a Diebenkorn and a Kandinsky. Tall glass windows revealed, behind the house, a carefully maintained Italianate garden surrounding a covered swimming pool. Traversing a long hallway, they passed hundred-year-old black-and-white photographs of the mills; Polish workers; Amasa Hall, in a starched collar, or at table with his family. The journey ended at a roomy but sparely appointed office where, in a leather chair oriented toward a field in which three horses grazed, Peter Hall sat reading business papers. He rose from the chair, his gaze suggesting a solemn curiosity, thanked his young aide, and shook hands with both Stella and Dance.

They sat on a couch, angled to the side of his chair. Hall turned to them, legs crossed, fingers steepled. His black leather shoes were brightly shined and his khaki slacks neatly pressed; his black sweater was cashmere. The same polish seemed inherent in the man himself: his teeth were white and even; his handsome face, tan from vacation, had just enough lines and angles to suggest character; his thick brown-blond hair had no touch of gray; and his eyes, a clear blue, regarded Stella and Dance with complete attention. Stella found him attractive; few women, she supposed, could be oblivious to a beautiful man—the word was appropriate—who looked at them so directly.

"I admire your record," he told her. "How many years without a loss now—six?"

There was nothing obsequious in his manner, Stella thought, no taint of artifice; it was as though, because the compliment was earned, he did not mind extending it in front of Nathaniel Dance. Hall was involved in the affairs of Steelton, the remark suggested, and advisers—political and otherwise—kept him abreast of who was who: given his interests, Stella had become a person of note, a County Prosecutor in waiting.

Smiling, she answered, "Six and three-quarters."

Hall returned her smile. At the corner of her eye, Stella felt Dance watching them both. As if noting this, Hall sat back, more serious now, looking from one to the other.

"Tommy Fielding," he said. "His death's hard for me to accept."

Dance remained silent. "What can you tell us about him?" Stella asked.

Hall considered her for a moment. "Do you remember the poem 'Richard Cory'?" he asked. "By Edwin Arlington Robinson?"

This, though subtle, Stella recognized as flattery, an assumption of shared culture across the social divide. "The perfect man," she answered, "admired by everyone in town. Then he goes home and puts a bullet through his head, and no one knows why."

Hall nodded. "That's how I felt about Tommy overdosing on heroin with a prostitute. That he'd no more do that than *I* would."

Dance, Stella sensed, had determined to observe them. "All the tests aren't back," she told Hall. "But it seems pretty clear that heroin killed them both."

Hall stared at the rug, pensive. "I thought, or flattered myself, that I knew him. We went to the same college, belonged to the same clubs, were racquetball partners. More than that, we were friends. To me, he was a completely reliable personality—punctilious, orderly, compulsively fit, extremely organized, and utterly competent. Once Tommy took charge of something, I quit worrying. I knew if I needed to worry, he'd be the first to tell me."

"*Was* he worried about anything?" Stella rejoined. "Or under some particular stress?"

Looking up, Hall smiled faintly. "Tommy was always under stress," he responded. "The one thing that worried *me* was that he seemed to have no regulator—he worked like if he ever stopped, he'd crack. I'd make him take a vacation, and he'd have a cell phone on the beach." This was not Hall's way, his tone suggested; there was a balance in life that had to be observed. "The ballpark," he continued, "was our biggest project, something wholly new to our company, and which our *city* depends on us to do right. For Tommy that was all-consuming; he couldn't help himself."

"*Amanda* Fielding," Stella said flatly, "thinks there were problems."

Hall tilted his head. "Did she say *what* problems?"

"No. Just that he'd seemed very troubled."

Hall raised his eyebrows. "For how long?"

"The last few weeks."

Hall turned from her, contemplating the framed photograph of a lovely ash-blond woman who appeared, to Stella, to be in her late thirties. Stella recalled that his wife had died in an accident; seemingly aware that Stella was watching him, he turned to her again.

"Maybe," she suggested, "you could explain Tommy's job to us."

He rested his elbows on the arms of his chair, careful to look at both Stella and Dance. "Tommy was our project manager. Which means that he was the one who supervised the partnership between our white- and minority-owned general contractors." Glancing at Stella, he said, "You were at the debate, I remember, when Mayor Krajek explained the deal. Hall Development guarantees to deliver Steelton 2000 for two hundred seventy-five million dollars. We bear any expenses over that; bring it in *under*, and we share any savings with the city.

"That motivates *us* to keep the contractors' costs down. Whereas their motive, naturally, is to make all the money they can. Part of Tommy's job was to make sure there *was* a savings—for which, if he succeeded, he would personally receive ten percent of our share. So there was an inherent—healthy, I would say—tension between him and our contractors, and perhaps within himself. Because he also had to make sure that quality wasn't sacrificed to savings."

Out the window, Stella saw, a doe and fawn skittered toward the denuded woods. Facing Hall again, she asked, "As a practical matter, what did Fielding do each day?"

Promptly, Hall began ticking off his points on the fingers of one hand. "First, approve bills from the general contractors, or question them—which was also true for the architects and all the subcontractors. Approve any change orders—increased costs for changes that needed to be made, but weren't provided for on the architect's detailed plans. And, of course, make sure the minority contractor and subcontractor get the percentage of work Tom Krajek promised they would." Hall smiled again. "All while ensuring there'd be money left at the end."

For the first time, Nathaniel Dance spoke. "But there weren't any problems," he said in a voice so uninflected that it bespoke a profound, if habitual, skepticism.

"Have you ever paid for a kitchen remodel?" Hall inquired pleasantly. "There are *always* problems, and you *always* get overcharged."

The faint amusement with which Dance regarded Hall seemed far less friendly. "I wouldn't know," he answered. "I remodeled the kitchen myself."

The humor in Hall's eyes did not fade, Stella saw; it merely changed, to acknowledge the differences between Dance and himself. "Tommy complained about change orders all the time. And well he might have—they ate into his share of the savings clause. But that wasn't a problem. It was the way I wanted it to work—"

"What about women?" Dance cut in.

"Women?" Hall's face became serious. "I knew his ex-wife, that's all."

"Did his marriage surprise you?" Stella asked. "Or his divorce?"

"Neither." Turning, Hall fixed Stella with his candid blue gaze. "We're talking about one of life's great mysteries—nothing men and women do surprises me anymore. Perhaps *dismays* me, but . . ." In reflection, the corners of his mouth turned down. "Amanda wasn't whom I expected, it's true. Not because of her age or appearance, or her intelligence; she was clearly bright and cultivated—enough to interest Tommy. But the divorce wasn't startling: there was a neurasthentic quality about Amanda, a bitterness, and she was married to a workaholic . . ."

"Was she married to a homosexual?" Dance asked.

Turned toward Dance, Hall's expression was unsurprised, unchanged. "Not that I know about. And Tommy wasn't the kind of man who'd tell me about other men. Or other women."

Hall was unerringly graceful, Stella reflected—unruffled, philosophical, responsive. "Or prostitutes?" she inquired.

Hall shook his head. "No. But if you asked me to imagine Tommy paying for sex, it would be with a two-thousand-dollar-a-night call girl with a degree from Wellesley who practiced safe sex." Smiling a little, Hall added, "And spoke French like a Parisian."

Hall's small irony bespoke fondness, bewilderment. Then the smile vanished altogether. "You've seen the ballpark," he told Stella with a new intensity. "It's rising before our eyes, and we've seen nothing like it anywhere in the country. By April of 2001, the Blues will be playing there, and we'll have started to remake the face of Steelton.

"As much as anyone's, that achievement would have been Tommy's. He'd have been there in my skybox, with the beautiful daughter he very much loved, watching Larry Rockwell throw out the first pitch. Instead, we have this tragic waste." His voice became softer. "Don't ask me to explain it to you."

"But if you had to," Stella persisted.

Hall emitted an audible sigh. "Maybe," he said at length, "it's that Tommy spent his life trying to be more perfect than God grants us the right to be. And that, in the end, it killed him."

The room was quiet for a moment, and then Hall smiled again, faintly and without humor. "I hope you'll excuse me," he told them. "Whatever his reasons, Tommy left me his job to do."

LEAVING, DANCE remained quiet, watching the landscape of Peter Hall's world, so different from his own.

"You know what's bothering me," she said at last.

Dance gave a mirthless smile. "That Curran's got Fielding cruising the Scarberry? Or that he *in-dub-it-ably* died of a drug overdose, with an

AIDS-infected hooker, and not one person who knows him admits to believing it?"

"That his life was the stadium," Stella answered. "But we don't understand Steelton 2000 at all."

Dance continued to stare out the window. "Assuming it has anything to do with anything," he said finally, "for that you'll need an accountant."

I'll need Michael Del Corso, Stella thought, and then imagined, without pleasure, appealing to Charles Sloan.

ENTERING HER office, Stella gazed out at the stadium. The steel skeleton was more complex now: its black girders had begun to resemble the bowl which would surround the green diamond envisioned by Peter Hall. Stella imagined herself working late at night, watching the white-yellow glow which signaled a game still in progress and, she hoped, the revival of Steelton. Then it struck her that, though she had watched the stadium take form at a distance, she had never been to the site.

She picked up the telephone and called Kate Micelli.

"About Fielding and Tina Welch," she asked, "are the lab tests back?"

As always, the coroner answered crisply. "Point eight zero micrograms of heroin per milliliter. A typical overdose—one that *can* kill you, but with no guarantee that it will."

"But this one did," Stella rejoined. "Both of them. Are there prints on the syringe?"

"No. But that's not surprising—a plastic surface that small doesn't lend itself to prints. It wasn't wiped clean, though." A short pause. "Why are you asking?"

"I'm not sure. On one side there's no medical evidence to say that this wasn't an accidental overdose. Plus Johnny Curran thinks he'd seen Fielding's car in the Scarberry before, which suggests that cruising for hookers wasn't new for Tommy. But there's no indication that he'd ever used heroin before, or ever would."

"Lots of people have secret lives, Stella. In some sense, *all* of us do."

Who else had said that to her, Stella wondered, and then remembered Arthur Bright, pondering Jack Novak's death. *What,* he had asked, *do we really know about anyone?* There was much, surely, that Stella never wanted anyone to know about her.

"Stella?"

Micelli's note of impatience jerked Stella back to the present. "But you've still got nothing," Stella prodded, "that suggests that Fielding had shot up before this. And neither do we."

There was a short pause, Micelli reflecting. "I took that hair sample from Fielding. There's a test I can run on it—that'll tell us whether Fielding had used heroin in the last month or so. Other than on the night he died, of course."

Stella considered this. Even if negative, the result would not change the direct cause of Fielding's death. But a positive test would ease her mind; whatever the mysteries of Fielding's inner life, she would know that before his death he was not a stranger to heroin.

"Run the test," she said.

TWELVE

WHEN STELLA hung up, her thoughts returned to Arthur Bright.

She called his secretary, Brenda Waters, and learned that Bright was out campaigning. He would be back for an hour, at around four o'clock—perhaps Stella could steal a few minutes then.

Stella put down the phone. But Brenda's voice, the comfortable tone of an amiable woman—black, round, and sixty—still echoed in her mind.

They had met when Stella was still in law school. Then, as now, only a lucky few department heads had reception areas, relieving their secretaries of the need to work in a noisy, crowded room. As head of the narcotics unit, Bright had been lucky. So Stella, twenty-five and apprehensive, had waited for Bright in Brenda's cubicle, sent there by Jack Novak.

"I can't work for you," she had told Jack.

It was two days after their last weekend together. "*Why?*" he asked.

"*Why?*" she repeated with quiet anger. She should have quit long ago, on principle, after she had seen Vincent Moro and then the Haitian had been murdered. Her hope of dignity, she decided, rested on silence, on staring at Jack as steadily as she could.

His hands fell to his sides. "All right," he said with weary resignation, "so last weekend wasn't *you*, you think, or want to think. So now you're afraid. But that has nothing to do with work. Let's try to be adult about this, okay?"

He had become her enemy, Stella thought, like her father. "I never want to be that 'adult,'" she answered stiffly. "Not in my work, and not in my life."

Her voice, though it quavered at times, sounded sturdy enough. Resplendent in his Armani suit and blue pocket square, Jack studied her. "What do *you* want?" he asked.

After two sleepless nights of pitiless self-scrutiny, her need to break with him felt desperate. "To work for the County Prosecutor," she answered. "Vincent Moro belongs in jail. Not somewhere he can murder your 'clients,' or pay for your suits."

Jack laughed softly. "So *that's* it. 'Will these hands of mine ne'er be clean?' Poor, dear Lady Macbeth. You never have believed me, have you?"

Stella flushed. "It's more than that. I need a *job* I can believe in."

The retort seemed to sober him. "Maybe so, Stella. But how in the world do you get one?"

She did not know. "I'll find a way," she insisted. "I'm third in my class and on moot court."

After a moment, Jack smiled a little. "I can always call Arthur Bright, if that's what you want. You can start in on Moro right away."

Why should she believe, Stella wondered, that Arthur Bright would hire her on Jack's word? A call from Jack might hurt, not help, and, if not, would tie her to him still further. "I'll do it on my own," she answered stubbornly.

Jack shook his head. "No offense, Stella. But there's a line of bright young ethnics from here to Lake Erie who want in at the County Prosecutor's office. The ones who get there have a letter from the Democratic County Chairman, or whatever city councilman helped deliver his ward for Arthur's boss, the esteemed Francis X. Connolly. When it comes to hiring, not even Arthur has a free hand. What you need is a patron." His voice became soothing. "I helped raise money for old Francis, even though he's running on fumes. Equally important, I've been Arthur's friend since law school, and I understand his ambitions. He knows I'll be there for him when Connolly goes to a better place."

Even as she tried to leave him, Stella realized, Jack was confronting her with fresh temptation; his mordant summary of hiring practices in Francis Connolly's office had the sound of truth. As if reading her thoughts, Jack added, "Just one more bite of the apple, Stella, and you're free. What hold will I have on you when we're not lovers anymore, and I'm not signing your paycheck?"

Stella sat straighter. "I'd always know how I got there."

"Because you're good. All I'd have done was to make sure Arthur takes the time to see that." His voice became warm, almost intimate, and his eyes locked Stella's. "It hurts me to lose you, Stella, no matter how poorly you think of me now. If you let me do this, maybe I can tell myself we ended well. And if you do as well as you deserve to . . ."

His voice trailed off, leaving the rest unspoken. To her surprise, Stella felt her eyes mist. Seeing this, Jack smiled: all at once, Stella feared that, if she took his help, her life thereafter would bear his stamp. And that this knowledge, ever with her, was what Jack Novak wanted.

Staring at the floor, she slowly shook her head.

She heard, rather than saw, Jack stand and circle his desk. Gently, he rested his hands on her shoulders, and kissed her on the forehead. "Please," he said. "Let me be selfish, one last time."

A WEEK later, Jack called her to his office. "I talked to Bright," he said. "He likes your résumé, and he'll see you."

Stella did not tell him of the nights she had spent debating with herself, the uneasy compromise she had reached before accepting his help. "But will they hire me?" she wondered aloud.

Jack smiled a little. "Of course," he answered. "I've told Arthur just how motivated you are."

His tone was rueful. He leaned on his elbow, gazing at her with a look of regret. "I've been missing you, Stella."

Stella looked away. "It's over," she said quietly. "For good."

He made no argument. Nor did he then, or at any time thereafter, try to touch her in any way that was not respectful, the greeting of one lawyer toward another to whom he was well disposed. But his expression in that quiet moment was softer than she had seen from him, before or after.

At last, he murmured, "I'll always remember you."

And I'll always remember you, she silently answered, and knew that it was true.

THIRTEEN

AT FOUR-FORTY, Brenda called. Bright had five free minutes, she told Stella—hurry on down.

There was much on Stella's mind as she rushed down the tile corridors. But what struck her was the difference between her mission now, as Bright's chief of homicide, and thirteen years earlier when, tentative and edgy, she had come to him as a supplicant, uncertain of her future or what Arthur Bright might think of her . . .

Brenda had closed the door behind them. Feeling stiff in her navy suit, the only one she had, Stella sat in front of Bright's desk, trying to appear smart and energetic as Bright, unwelcoming, marched her by rote through her résumé.

She had seen him in court, and knew that he could be eloquent and persuasive, with a nascent gift for showmanship. But in this context he seemed preoccupied, as though compelled to spend time with someone he did not wish to see. Was Bright even hiring? she wondered. Or had Jack told him they were lovers and, man to man, Bright had agreed to give her an elegant brush-off, a place in bureaucratic limbo, waiting for a job that would never open?

Bright looked up from her résumé. He had a scholar's delicacy, she thought, and something else—a sense of deep caution which suggested not just prudence, but distrust. "Why," he asked finally, "do you want to leave Jack Novak to join the good guys? For experience?"

Stella shook her head. "I worked with Jack for almost two years. It was interesting, and I learned a lot that I can use here. But I'm not a defense lawyer."

"You're not."

Stella hesitated. Though Bright had acknowledged Jack's role in getting her here, he had spoken of him with no more warmth than he extended to Stella. But the safe course, for now, was to tell the truth at its simplest. "Most of Jack's clients are guilty," she answered. "He knows it, and you know it—the system entitles them to a defense, and that's what their lawyer provides them. I believe in that, too. But it's too abstract for me to live with, when the harm drugs do is so real."

Bright frowned, seemingly unimpressed, though he studied her closely. His voice held a trace of skepticism. "So you're especially interested in narcotics."

Stella inhaled. "No," she answered. "I'm hoping you can help me find a job in another department."

Bright stared at her with a small, humorless smile. "You don't want to work with me?"

Though it was a moment Stella had to face, she also dreaded it. "I'd like to," she said at last. "But I don't think I should." She looked at him directly. "Jack and I were *involved*, Mr. Bright, for most of the time I worked there. And without his help, I wouldn't be here at all, would I?"

Bright raised his eyebrows. "That doesn't sit well with you."

"Now that I'm here, it's fine with me. I think I'm as good at my work as Jack's letter told you I was, and that my record in school qualifies me for a job here." She was speaking too quickly, she realized, and forced herself to slow down. "But I may always have feelings for Jack, complicated ones. And, if I take a job with you, I'll not only feel indebted to Jack, I'll have cases against him. Maybe that's not an ethical problem, but it seems like a bad place for a prosecutor.

"That's all I really want to be—a prosecutor. I don't care where I start."

Bright folded his hands, his expression of surprise arranging itself into something more pleasant. "Well," he said at length, "you're admirably candid."

If she was telling the truth, Stella decided, she might as well tell all of it. "I thought you might already know."

"Jack never mentioned it." Bright paused, and then added, "A true gentleman, Jack Novak."

The last comment, marked in its irony, was surprising in a man who seemed so guarded, all the more because he didn't know her. "Jack wanted me to stay," she said simply. "But I couldn't do that, either."

Bright seemed to appraise her further; whoever worked with him, Stella thought, must learn to withstand silence. "I think you were right," he said in a softer tone. "I think you're right all around. Which is too bad, because there's an opening in my unit."

Despite her resolve, Stella felt a crushing disappointment; her tenuous self-respect, so hard won, had exacted its price. She folded her hands. "I'm sorry, too. But I don't think it can be helped."

Bright's eyes narrowed. This time his quiet had the feel of weighing, judging her, reaching a decision. "Maybe it can be," he said. "I heard there's something in misdemeanors. Think you can mount a crusade against jaywalking?"

His smile seemed genuine now. It was the expression of someone who, perhaps to his surprise, had decided he liked her, and would do her a favor to which Jack Novak was irrelevant.

"Jaywalking?" Stella answered in a resolute tone. "Let them do that, and the next day they'll be littering."

To *her* utter surprise, Arthur Bright began laughing.

THIRTEEN YEARS later, she opened Bright's door.

He was near the window, gazing toward the stadium in the encroaching winter twilight. Perhaps, despite his opposition, Bright shared Stella's fascination as Hall and Krajek's monument rose before their eyes. Turning, he said, "You've found Novak's killer, right? If I can announce it before Krajek does, it's worth three percent in the polls."

Stella sat down. "We've got nothing," she answered. "But I've been over some of Jack's old files. He was wiring cases, it looks like."

Bright stared at her. "How?"

"I don't know. But they all involve Moro's guy on the East Side, George Flood. Or at least Flood's people."

Briskly, she described the cases. Bright watched her intently, unblinking. When she was through, he asked simply, "What does this have to do with Jack's murder?"

"Zero, probably. But we've also got nothing to say that Jack was into bondage, asphyxiation, or any S and M scene heavy enough to kill him . . ."

"But he was into groups, wasn't he?" Though Bright's voice was soft, his question was pointed, and Stella surmised he had been talking to Dance. "And strangers. And ever new thrills. There's always a first time, when things get that much weirder. And there's also Missy Allen." His voice grew softer yet. "You were well out of that, Stella. However Jack was then."

Though it was true, Stella felt manipulated, her past unfairly used against her. She did not need to answer.

Bright walked to his desk, sitting wearily into his chair, as though feeling he had gone too far with her. "Just tell me, if you can, that Jack couldn't have ended that way. Tell me he was impossible to hate."

"I can't. What I've told you is that Jack was fixing cases. Did that make any kind of impression, Arthur?"

He looked up at her. "They were my cases, Stella. They made an 'impression' at the time."

"But?"

"The reasons were all over the map. A bad judge, a witness who jumped bail—"

"What about *low* bail," Stella interjected, "and a dead witness?"

Bright folded his arms. "Missing witnesses—and dead ones—are what happen in drug cases. I didn't see a clear pattern then, and I don't now." His voice grew quiet again. "Dance is right, you know. Too many people would have to be involved."

So they *had* been talking. "Including, maybe, someone in your narcotics unit?"

Bright was very still now. "If someone in my unit threw a case, I'd know it." He snapped his fingers. "*That* fast, and they'd be out of here, looking at a stretch in jail. I knew *everything* about these cases—any call that was tough, I made myself." He paused, then said emphatically, "Including setting bail so low that the defendant was certain to skip town."

Startled, Stella stared at him. "He was a *snitch*," she said.

"*My* snitch. He was scared, and begged me for a way out." Bright's smile was sardonic. "In the moral code of the drug wars, I owed him a debt of honor. So I told Charles Sloan not to oppose Jack's bail motion. But I couldn't tell anyone why, not even Dance. My guy was too afraid that Moro had a pipeline to the cops, though I never found any proof of that."

Stella felt deflated, foolish. "That's one case," she answered. "There's at least four others. Are you telling me that *only* you could screw up a prosecution?"

"In the narcotics unit, yes." He gave her a keen look. "Except maybe for Charles Sloan. But you've assumed that all along."

Bright's veiled accusation—that Stella might be after Sloan—silenced her. Dusk had fallen quickly; the fluorescent lights above Arthur's desk gave the room a yellow cast, accenting the dark circles beneath his eyes. "You know what bothers me the most?" he finally said. "These cases have hair on them, they're so old—too old to relate to Jack's murder. But they *do* relate to the time you spent with him.

"I don't mind your rummaging your own conscience, Stella, on your own time. But this act of necrophilia you're committing has potential implications in the here and now. For *me*." He leaned forward. "Do you think Krajek—or the press—will show a fine sense of discrimination if they learn that *you* think one of my leading supporters was fixing narcotics cases?

"Never mind that, as an officeholder, my personal finances have been turned inside out and upside down, or that Charles Sloan has even less money than I do. Krajek and the media won't need bribery; Jack's fundraising will be enough to damn me." Bright's monologue ended abruptly, with a clear reproof. "Charles is dead right about that. As he usually is."

Stella stiffened. It was a reminder, if she needed one, that her own political hopes depended on whether Bright would favor her over Sloan—and that Stella was doing herself no favors here. Quietly, she said, "Whoever helped Jack may still be out there. We can't ignore that."

"I'm not asking you to. It's a question of priorities, and unintended consequences. For every minute you spend wondering what Novak did when you were with him, you're no closer to who killed him." He smiled more easily now. "Worrying about *that* is not just your actual job, Stella. It's the only thing that can do us *both* some good."

His smile faded. She had clearly taxed his patience and, despite his oft-demonstrated pride in her achievements, disappointed him. This discouraged her in her other resolve: to ask Bright, rather than Sloan, if Michael Del Corso could examine Hall's stadium deal. It was hard to play office politics when you questioned your own motives.

Stella thanked Bright for his time, and left.

IT WAS close to six when Stella went to Sloan's office, and the floor was quiet, the secretarial pool empty, and the lawyers' offices mostly dark. But Sloan might be there for hours yet; in this, if little else, Stella knew they were alike.

"I have a favor to ask," she told him.

Her tone, precatory and modest, seemed to surprise Sloan, particularly given their last, acidic discussion. He took a sip from the ever-present cola can and said, politely enough, "Another piece of Michael Del Corso, to look at the ballpark deal."

Were there any secrets in this office? Stella wondered—she had not mentioned her idea to anyone. But to Sloan, information was power, especially where it concerned Stella; he must have debriefed Dance on their interview with Hall, and, divining her thoughts from there, had chosen to remind Stella of his obsessive vigilance. As if this were unremarkable, Stella said, "Fielding's wife thinks there was trouble at Steelton 2000. Maybe it's nothing—that's what Hall says, and Fielding comes off as a compulsive worrier. But we don't know enough about how the deal worked to know what 'trouble' might be."

Sloan took another swig of soda. "Or why Steelton 2000 made him overdose on heroin, or troll for hookers. If Johnny Curran remembers seeing his license plate, you can take it to the bank."

Unlike his reaction to her suspicions of Novak, this seemed more probe than put-down. "Fielding's a blank," she said. "We know he died of an overdose, but can't be sure of how, or why."

Sloan frowned at this. "What about the medical evidence?"

Stella shook her head. "All Kate can say is that there's nothing *inconsistent* with accident—no sign of force, for example. But that doesn't rule it out. And even if Curran saw him in the Scarberry, that doesn't tell us how these two people wound up dead, two nights later." Pausing, she stared through Sloan's window at the stadium, a shadowy vault among the scattered lights of Steelton. "The one thing we do know, as a practical matter, is that Tommy Fielding was building our ballpark."

Sloan gave her a searching smile. "I thought you liked this deal."

"I do. But what does that have to do with Fielding?"

His expression openly dubious, Sloan seemed to weigh Stella's motives. That was his weakness, she thought; Sloan understood himself too well, and so measured everyone else in the same terms. Here she partly agreed with Bright—money might not corrupt Charles Sloan, but ambition and self-interest could have done that long ago. At length, he asked, "What do you want from Del Corso?"

Sloan was tempted, Stella saw; as with Stella, his ambitions rested on Bright's becoming mayor, and any problems at Steelton 2000, as long as they did not seem politically inspired, might tarnish Mayor Krajek. "An economic analysis," she answered. "Who, besides Peter Hall, stands to gain or lose from building and operating the ballpark. Then maybe a look at Fielding's files, the paper crossing his desk."

Sloan pursed his lips, expelling a silent breath. "This could back up on us," he said.

"Not if we're careful. And neutral."

Sloan's eyes narrowed in thought. "Well," he finally answered, "I like this idea better than your last one."

Stella smiled. "Thank you."

Her muted sarcasm induced, in Sloan, a short bark of a laugh. "I'll let Del Corso know. I'm sure he'll be happy to help."

His tone suggested that, in the secret code of males, Sloan had reason to know better. Stella hoped this was projection; after all, she was having dinner with Michael Del Corso.

FOURTEEN

LITTLE ITALY was a white enclave on the near East Side, a neighborhood of narrow brick streets, lined with dogwood, and brick double-decker houses surrounded by carefully trimmed hedges. Its pulse seemed much stronger than Warszawa's. The principal shopping street, Naples Boulevard, reflected the main tributary of its immigrants, and the influence of southern Italy in the flavorful mix of shops, restaurants, trattorias, dolcerias, delicatessens. The neighborhood was largely free of conventional crime: though Vincent Moro, like Peter Hall, lived in a suburban compound, his sway in Little Italy continued and, while Moro exacted his own tribute, no one else dared disrupt it. The streets seemed little changed from the twenties or thirties—it was where Michael Del Corso's immigrant parents had settled and where Michael still lived, Stella had learned, with his daughter, Sofia.

Sofia was the reason for this dinner. Michael had called from Novak's office in midafternoon; following Stella's instructions, he had gone over Novak's books and records—scrupulously maintained, lest the IRS come calling—and found something odd. There was no time to explain, he continued without apology; his seven-year-old had a dance recital. But tonight was Sofia's weekly supper with her grandparents, leaving Michael free for dinner in Little Italy. If Stella didn't mind, that was fine with him.

It was also fine with her. Given her designs on his time, they would need a working rapport, better than the one she sensed they had. In and out of trial, she had eaten with any number of male colleagues, protected by the iron rule she had adopted ever since Jack Novak—no romances with office mates, not even a hint of flirtation.

Michael had suggested Guardino's, the Neapolitan mainstay whose current proprietor, a gnarled ex-boxer named Frankie Scavullo, greeted customers at the door in a black tuxedo. To Stella, the outfit made Scavullo look like an aging, uncomfortable father at the wedding of his fifth and final daughter, grinning maniacally at the celebrants while worrying about the bill. He gave her a bright smile—a perfect mouthful of white, capped teeth—and, though she had never been there before, told her it was a pleasure to see her pretty face again.

"I'm so flattered you remember me," Stella assured him. Upon learning that she was Michael's guest, Scavullo shepherded her to his corner with compliments and ceremony, a chivalrous hand on Stella's arm. As if to complete this burlesque of gallantry, Michael Del Corso stood and, Stella could have sworn, bowed slightly at the waist.

"Such a beautiful woman," Scavullo told Michael and scurried off, leaving Stella, amidst Michael's plain amusement, to wonder what chord this last remark had touched.

Sitting across from her, Michael said, "Frankie's a trip, isn't he? And so's this place."

It was surely that. The waiters were tuxedoed, and the wallpaper a flocked deep red which was suitable to a steakhouse or a bordello. Beneath an elaborate chandelier, a baroque fountain featuring a naked child from the age of the Caesars trickled water into an enormous bowl. "I may not be beautiful," she said, "but I *am* curious."

Michael seemed, just for an instant, put off. Then he shrugged; this was Stella's reputation, the gesture said, impersonal and businesslike. "I took your five cases," he said evenly, "and looked for whether Novak received and/or disbursed unusual amounts of cash at around the same time. Which you might expect if he was paying somebody off."

"And?"

Interrupted by their waiter, a florid man with his hair dyed auburn, Michael looked up. "Cocktails?" the waiter asked her.

"Perrier. Lime, no ice."

Michael seemed to note this, as though her avoidance of alcohol must be part of her ethic. Which it was.

"Chianti," Michael told the waiter. "Thank you."

He watched the man leave, then began speaking in an undertone. "Let's take this one case at a time. Starting with your murdered Haitian, Desnoyers.

"They found his body on a Tuesday. On Thursday, Novak received fifty thousand dollars—in cash."

Though not truly surprised, Stella felt a jolt. "From whom?"

"Crown Limousine." Michael paused. "It's a Moro front. According to Novak's books, the money was a fee for 'business advice.'"

Stella shook her head emphatically. "There's no way. Jack was a drug lawyer—all he knew about limousines is that they took him to the airport."

Michael nodded. "It *looks* bogus—from what I saw, only Crown was in need of Novak's business acumen."

Their drinks arrived. Stella glanced around them, then asked, "This 'fee'—did Jack pass any of it on?"

"There weren't any large withdrawals." Michael leaned forward, expression curious. "And in the context of this murder, a pass-through makes no sense. I mean, who would Novak be siphoning money to? Moro wouldn't need him to hire a hit man. And Novak sure didn't whack Desnoyers himself."

Stella stared at the table. "Maybe it was a tip," she said at last.

"For what?"

"For selling out his client."

Michael studied his wineglass, a thoughtful half smile touching his eyes. The smile was not amusement, Stella thought, but a knowledge of betrayal so deep, born of fruitless years of pursuing men like Moro, that he could not reject her theory out of hand.

"In the next case," Michael finally said, "Novak makes a motion for low bail, which we don't oppose, and Flood's dealer skips town. A guy named Morgan Beach"

Stella nodded. "Since we talked, I asked Arthur about that one. Beach was a snitch—we protected him by rolling over."

Michael was quiet for a moment, and then looked at Stella directly. "A few days later, Novak gets twenty grand. Again from Crown Limousine; again, there wasn't any disbursal. Novak just banked the money, like an honest citizen who was reporting every dime."

This time, Stella was genuinely startled. "Why?" she asked. "Jack didn't do anything—it was *us*."

"That assumes your theory's right—that the cash was Novak's payoff for something." Michael sipped his wine. "One thing's certain: these payments weren't for bribing people. If they were, we'd see cash going out—or, more likely, the payments wouldn't hit the books at all."

Stella ignored her drink. "Two good results," she said. "One dead man, one missing witness. Two inexplicable consulting fees—"

"But no payoffs. Maybe in the second case, Novak just got lucky—he may have wanted his client to skip town, but I'll bet he didn't know that Beach was Arthur's snitch. Or Moro would have had him whacked, too."

"Of course Moro didn't know," Stella rejoined. "He thought Novak had performed another miracle. I'm sure that's what *Jack* believed."

Pensive, Michael touched the broken bridge of his nose. "So Moro's a grateful client, paying extra for extraordinary services."

"Was he 'grateful,'" Stella inquired, "in any other cases?"

"Two more." Casually, Michael opened his menu, continuing in a voice audible only to Stella. "The first was where Johnny Curran exceeded his warrant, and the case was reassigned to Judge Freeman—*after* Novak challenged the original judge for bias. Freeman boots the case, and Novak gets another thirty grand from Crown Limousine."

"Which also stays in his bank account?"

"Yes." Michael perused the menu. "The last payment involved Flood's boy Louis Jackson—the *second* Jackson case."

Charles Sloan's case, Stella thought. "Where Jackson plea-bargains, and gets off with a year."

"Uh-huh. If you're right about the fees, that was worth forty thousand more to Novak."

Stella pondered this. "What about the last case," she asked, "where the police evidence room 'inadvertently' destroys five keys of coke, and the charges against Flood and Jackson get dismissed?"

Michael shook his head. "For that, Novak gets nothing. Just his usual fee—in cash, of course, from Jackson."

Stella picked up her glass, tasting the sparkling water. "And other cases Jack may have won? Any bonuses there?"

For the first time, Michael seemed unsure of himself. "*That* was what seemed funny to me. In the two or so years I looked at it, Novak won several jury trials. No bonus."

Stella put down the glass. "But he did get a 'bonus' for unusual results—dead witnesses, bail set too low, a lenient plea bargain, a reassignment to our most criminal-coddling judge."

"Exactly."

Stella looked around the room. The other diners—old couples, families, a large table filled with what appeared to be three generations of Italian-Americans—seemed happily occupied. "What these records may not show," she said, "is that Jack was Moro's bagman. But they don't prove that he couldn't have been passing bribes."

Michael nodded. "Probably Novak wouldn't have entered bribe money on the books—if he gets audited, it not only looks weird but he's got a tax liability unless he says where the money went. Or maybe someone besides Novak could have passed it out. Or no one." Frowning, he closed his menu. "Ask yourself this, though. If Moro was bribing some-one else, why use Novak as bagman? Or pay Novak extra for other people's work? And this: Why would Vincent Moro risk letting any one person—especially a chickenshit like Novak—know that much?"

Stella remained quiet. Analysis done, Michael had let discouragement enter his voice. This exercise might be interesting, his manner said; in the abstract, it might even mean something. But the hand of Vincent Moro would stay hidden.

It all came back to Jean-Claude Desnoyers, Stella decided. Novak had betrayed him to Moro, she was certain, and been rewarded after some-one else had dumped the Haitian's body in the river. What remained obscure in the last three cases was the nature of the connection between Jack and the result and, perhaps, the identity of the "someone else" who had helped Moro protect George Flood. And, as Bright, Sloan, and Dance would all be quick to say, why should they believe that the answer was related to Novak's death?

"I don't know," Stella said at last.

FIFTEEN

THE WAITER took their orders: carpaccio and saltimbocca for Michael, a garden salad and vegetable pasta for Stella. "Wine?" Michael asked her.

Stella hesitated. "Maybe a glass."

Michael smiled. "You can drive me home," he told her, and ordered a bottle of Chianti.

While the waiter filled their glasses, Michael surveyed the restaurant with satisfaction; it was festive now, its tables full, decibels of talk and laughter rising. When the waiter vanished, Michael asked, "While we're talking about Crown Limousine, what do you know about money laundering?"

Stella took a perfunctory sip of wine, harsh but, as it lingered on her tongue, pleasing. "That it's how Moro makes his profits look legitimate. But I've never followed the ins and outs."

"Okay." Beneath the rising din, Michael's tone was normal, relaxed. "The 'fees' Novak got may have come through Crown, but you can bet the money was from organized crime.

"Drugs, prostitution, and gambling generate huge amounts of cash—you can't put these on your Mastercard, and you can be sure that Moro's people won't take personal checks from drug dealers . . ."

"So little trust."

"Sure. And why leave a paper trail? But cash leaves a trail, too: Moro can't stuff it under the mattress, and his lifestyle makes him a prime target for the IRS." Michael smiled. "That's what they finally got Al Capone for—not all those bodies in the Chicago River, but tax evasion.

"Moro has the same problem. Like anyone else, he has to bank his cash, and make investments. And financial institutions have to report it when he does. Maybe he can smuggle cash offshore, but for sure not all of it—after all, his reported income has to square with his standard of living."

Pausing, Michael took a deep swallow of wine. "So," he continued, "he buys into lawful enterprises, including whatever cash businesses he can get his hands on—caterers, limo services, vending machine operations, parking lots, bars, and restaurants. The illegal money gets siphoned into all these different fronts, which scrupulously report every dime, then fiddle the books to make the proceeds of heroin look like they came from, say, a zillion plates of saltimbocca."

His eyes, Stella realized, sparkled with quiet laughter. Stiffly, she put down her wine. "*This* place."

Michael nodded. "Moro's. The food's good, by the way."

His sangfroid angered her. "What are we *doing* here?"

Michael looked at her, unruffled, his amusement still in place. "Because it's the perfect illustration. Guardino's and Frankie Scavullo arc neighborhood institutions—no one wants to see them closed. And they generate enough real profit to make laundering drug money easier to conceal.

"Frankie's the leading restaurateur in Little Italy—his restaurant gives to Catholic Charities, sponsors CYO teams, and donates meals to shut-ins. No one tries to shake Frankie down or give him any trouble. And Frankie never, ever wants to piss off Vincent Moro.

"That's another part of what we're up against. For too many people, it's too easy just to go along. The only safe thing, actually."

Stella put down her glass. "*What,*" she repeated, "are we doing here?"

Michael stopped smiling. "I've *always* come here, ever since I was a kid. I know what Frankie's up to, and he knows I know. We've established the rules long ago—I don't take free meals, and he gives me useful tips as long as they don't shaft Moro.

"You may not like that. But it's practical, and it's the best I can do. Because Frankie and I also know that I'll never have the resources to spend the months and months it would take to try and figure out his books. If someone gets Frankie—and that probably will never happen—it's the feds, not us. But for every waiter here, there's probably a ghost employee, someone Frankie pays who never shows up for work. 'Cause the guy really works for Vincent Moro."

"As in soldiers, like Moro was?"

Michael shrugged. "Soldiers, leg breakers—for all I know, the guy who whacked your Haitian was on Frankie's payroll. But Frankie wouldn't know a thing about that, either. Which is another part of Moro's genius."

Staring at him, Stella tried to sort out the anger she felt. He had compromised her—smugly, without asking, because he was used to small corruptions like eating at Guardino's. And, however realistic, his attitude toward Moro was defeatist.

In her silence, Michael's face turned serious. "You look pissed."

"I *am* pissed. Being here makes me feel like a professional opponent, like the team of chumps the Globetrotters used to tour with." Her voice lowered. "How do you even know that this booth isn't bugged?"

Michael's fixed stare signaled his own anger. He seemed to be fighting back a retort when their first course arrived.

Carefully, deliberately, Michael spread the mustard across his carpaccio and then, looking up, said, "I'm not a fool, Stella. The feds tell me this restaurant isn't wired, and that's not a chance Vincent Moro would take. After all, electronic eavesdropping's against the law." Though quiet, his words were biting. "You've just discovered how organized crime works, even though you worked for Novak. So you're filled with outrage. I say fine—show me how we put Moro away, and I'll give you all the time I've got. But until you do, at least try to appreciate what you don't understand. And don't ever call me a 'professional opponent.'"

Stella bit her lip, staring back at him. There were reserves of pride in him—or at least male ego—that she ignored at her peril. And, as chief of homicide, it was not as if she'd never cut deals with one murderer to get another, or courted potential witnesses who, in any other context, she would have scorned as mendacious scum. The bottom line was that she needed Michael Del Corso.

"I'm sorry," she said evenly. "I appreciate the work you did today. I just didn't like discovering in midmeal that I was eating at a Mafia front."

Michael folded his hands. "Understood," he answered finally. "I'll never bring you here again."

In its ironic reversal of their real relationship, the sour joke made Stella smile. She began picking at her salad, feeling his silence across the table. "Actually," she ventured, "I'm not doing this very well. Because I may need your help with something else."

Finishing his carpaccio, Michael gave her a look which was neither hostile nor enthusiastic. "What is it?"

"Steelton 2000. I've got a project manager, Tommy Fielding, who died of a heroin overdose no one can believe, and an ex-wife who claims that he was bothered by problems with the stadium. But I don't understand how the deal works, who's making money, or what Fielding's job really was."

Michael's expression changed to one of mild interest. "There's a whole class of people," he said, "who make their living packaging ballparks—accountants, investment bankers, construction companies.

That's where you need to start. Then, maybe, someone like me could look at the nuts and bolts."

It was best not to push him, Stella told herself. "Can you at least find out where I should go?"

Michael hesitated. "I guess you've talked to Sloan."

"I have."

His look of amusement briefly returned—the strains between Sloan and Stella were, by now, as well known within the office as the political complications involving Bright, Mayor Krajek, and Steelton 2000. Bluntly, Michael asked, "Are you running for prosecutor?"

His directness startled her. "Why do you ask?"

Michael watched her face. "Because Sloan is. And there are a lot of nervous employees—people who the next County Prosecutor could fire at will—wondering which one of you to support, which one to risk offending, or hoping the winner won't mind if they just stick to their jobs. Steelton's not the best place to be pounding the pavements."

Especially, Stella thought, *the single father of a seven-year-old daughter—if that's what you are.* "First Arthur has to win," she answered. "A lot depends on how voters wind up viewing Steelton 2000. You can bet Charles Sloan hasn't missed *that*."

Michael laughed at this. "So I'm safe."

He did not sound terribly worried: beneath his apparent discouragement about his work, Stella had begun to detect a certain self-confidence. "Very safe," she answered, "though Sloan's interest is political and mine's professional. *He* wants the ballpark discredited and Arthur elected, and *I* want Arthur elected and the Blues to be playing in Steelton when I'm eighty. Just as long as I know for sure why Fielding died."

Their waiter returned. Smiling, he asked them if all was well, then spread their entrées on the table. The smell of cheese and veal from the saltimbocca made Stella wish she were less conscious of gaining weight.

"So you're a baseball fan," Michael said after the first bite.

It was small talk. They needed some, Stella thought, and it could not hurt to offer a small piece of herself. "More than a fan," she answered. "I played softball all through high school—pitcher and center field. Until I turned fourteen, my fantasy was to replace Larry Rockwell. It was hard to accept that the Blues wouldn't take me." Briefly, she smiled. "I'm still not sure I accept it."

Michael gave her a speculative look. "County Prosecutor," he said, "is not a bad substitute."

Stella's smile faded. "Maybe," she said simply. "But first Arthur has to win."

Michael regarded her further, then glanced at his watch. "Nine o'clock," he said. "I should call my folks." Plucking a cell phone from his pocket, he murmured to Stella, "Before Sofia, I used to hate these things," then hit the memory button and the number 1.

Stella focused on her pasta. "Mom?" she heard Michael say. "I'll be there pretty soon. How is she?" There was silence, Michael listening, and then he answered, "Good. You gave her a bath, right? Her hair needed washing."

The answer, Stella guessed, was affirmative, followed by a monologue from Mrs. Del Corso; throughout, Michael nodded to himself, as though to rush her to conclusion. "Thanks, Mom," he said. "Love you," and got off.

Stella put down her fork. "Everything all right?"

"Fine." Flipping the phone shut, Michael added, "Sometimes she can't believe that a man's raising her granddaughter. Like I'm genetically incapable of taking her to the dentist."

So he *was* a single father. "How was the recital?" Stella asked.

Michael smiled again. "Ever seen a bunch of second-graders in tights, trying to dance in unison? But I only had eyes for the Sugar Plum Fairy. Who was dazzling." His expression grew more serious. "For Sofia, the basic thing is she felt proud of herself. That's all I really care about."

To Stella, this last remark suggested that there were difficulties, or at least had been in the past. But she did not feel free to ask.

They finished quickly. "*Do* you need a ride?" she asked.

"If you don't mind. I left the car at my parents'—it's just a few blocks from here."

At Stella's insistence, they split the bill before hurrying out. After the warmth and noise of the restaurant, the night felt chill, the drive to Michael's parents' quiet.

They lived in a modest two-decker which, though different in structure, put Stella sadly in mind of the home where she had spent her first twenty-three years. Through the first-floor living-room window, Stella saw a dark-haired girl in dim light, arms draped over the back of a couch as she watched for her father. Her mother, Stella thought again, must have been quite beautiful.

In the car, Michael turned to her. "Thanks for the lift," he said, and went to collect Sofia.

SIXTEEN

STELLA WAS busy Friday morning: a preliminary hearing; a meeting with the homicide unit to review pending cases; job interviews with third-year law students; two calls from potential supporters inviting her to speak. It was past eleven before she could phone Dance about Tina Welch, the prostitute who had died with Tommy Fielding.

They had finally found Welch's mother, Dance told her, a domestic on the East Side who helped care for Welch's five-year-old son. The woman was shamed by Tina's life and mystified by her death. Yes, she knew about Tina's heroin problem, and what she did for a living. But she had no more information about Tommy Fielding than about whoever her grandson's father was—Tina hadn't come home one night, and the next day she was dead. Dance's account was weary; he had seen this all before, his tone suggested, but it had never quite ceased to depress him.

"What about the Scarberry?" Stella asked. "Any luck there?"

"Nobody remembers Fielding or his car. All we've got on that is Curran."

"There's also Tina. Hookers tend to be territorial, work the same block. Someone saw her that night."

"Not that they're saying. The vice cops knew her, and we've been all over her usual turf. But most hookers hate cops—vice especially. None of them recall anything; one night's pretty much like the next, you know, a dozen ten-buck blow jobs."

His deep voice had carried, for a moment, the ghetto-inflected imitation of a jaded prostitute. "I guess you've passed out flyers," Stella said.

"Fielding and Tina both. Nothing."

Stella riffled through her unanswered messages: one from Jan Saunders at Channel 6 and two from Dan Leary of the *Press.* "But you've found Jack Novak's killer, right?"

Dance emitted a sound, part grunt, part laugh. "Any day now." His voice had an undertone of frustration. "We've questioned Missy Allen again, turned her life upside down. No bloody clothes, nothing at the dry cleaner or in her garbage, no one who says she's capable of murder. All she keeps saying is that the phantom caller must have killed him, and that she misses him like crazy."

"What do you think?"

Through the telephone, Stella heard the same harsh sound. "That there's no accounting for tastes." Dance fell silent, then said, "An impulse killer would have left something at the scene, like prints, maybe been seen or heard leaving in a panic. For a messy killing, this was real clean: show up, hang Novak from the closet, cut off his nuts, and disappear without a trace."

Once more, Stella glanced at the copy of the *Press* sticking from her wastebasket. "Few Leads in Novak Murder," the headline had read; as she expected from a paper which supported Krajek and the stadium, the article called Novak a "close confidant of Arthur Bright."

"If it wasn't about sex and rage," Stella answered, "how did whoever it was get Jack to go along?"

"Stuck a gun to his head, maybe?"

He sounded dubious, and so was Stella. "I'll run it past Kate," she said.

KATE MICELLI was performing an autopsy—a six-year-old girl who had been raped and murdered while her mother was at a bar—and it was lunchtime when she returned Stella's call.

"At gunpoint?" Kate asked, and pondered the question. "It doesn't sound right," she said at length. "No one's *that* docile. Once the killer kicks the stool out from under him, Novak starts to fight—it's a reflex, no matter how scared you are of getting shot. There'd be marks on his wrists where he struggled with the bonds, maybe more abrasions on the neck . . ."

A question occurred to Stella, and from the coroner's abrupt silence, it had struck Micelli, too. "That would also be true," Stella said, "if a sex partner did it."

Michelli paused. "True enough."

"What was Jack's blood-alcohol level? And how coked was he? Allen says they'd had a skinful of wine and then did some coke at his place. And we know, from the cocktail glasses, that he also wound up drinking scotch with someone. Though Allen swears it wasn't her."

"So do you pour your killer a drink?" Micelli asked skeptically.

Stella leaned back in her chair. "Maybe if you know him. Allen says he took a call and suddenly sent her packing."

"About the alcohol, Novak was well past the legal limit—point one six. But I'd guess from his history and body mass he wasn't falling-down drunk. Allen says he wasn't, right?"

"If you believe her."

"I don't need to. The coke would act to keep him up."

Stella thought of Jack as he hung from the closet, face hideously distorted. "If you're out of questions," Micelli said, "I've got something for you."

"What?"

"The test on Fielding's hair. He's the polar opposite of Novak: I figure we're looking at a month's worth of growth, and no drug use at all. For that matter, according to his blood test, no alcohol worth worrying about. Maybe that half glass of beer we found in his sink."

Stella stood and began pacing. "If you had a heroin problem, even a new one, do you go a month?"

"Probably not. Then there's always the first time. No way to be sure, but I'd guess this was his debut."

Novak, Fielding, Tina Welch—all questions, no answers. Hanging up, Stella stared out, as was her habit now, at the stadium in progress.

"Damn," she said aloud.

BEFORE SHE noticed, she had spent a half hour at her window, minutely examining the steel girders; the enveloping bowl partly filled with concrete; the men in hard hats, dull metal beneath the sunless sky—30 percent minorities, Thomas Krajek had assured the voters, a veritable rainbow coalition. And for that half hour, Stella had procrastinated.

It was a fault she recognized: to feel beset by so many frustrations, a plethora of loose ends and unsolved problems, that it stymied her. She also knew the antidote—to pick any one thing, no matter how trivial, and do it. Momentum recovered, the next thing would follow.

To her surprise, she chose to take the elevator to the basement, to the dead-records room.

It was in the bowels of the building, airless, sunless, dusty and dank, with a light switch on the cinder-block wall beside the door. Using her office key, Stella opened the door, then flipped the switch.

Overhead, the shuttered fluorescent lights flickered, then came on.

The room was filled with ten-feet-high metal shelves, row upon row across the dirty linoleum floors. There was utter quiet. This was the mausoleum of expired prosecutions—cases dismissed or pled out; trials won or lost, the last appeals exhausted—and no one came here unless some scrap of history might illuminate the present.

The room reminded Stella of a graveyard without a caretaker: though a file clerk maintained an index, entering new arrivals in thick binders which dated to the seventies, neither the trickle of visitors nor Arthur's overtaxed budget suggested the assignment of anyone to work here. Prosecutors removed files on the honor system, writing their names in a log, then the file by name and number. According to the log, no one had been here since Jack Novak was murdered.

It was Novak's files—the five George Flood cases—which had brought Stella to this cavernous room. There was much those records had told her, but much they could not. Perhaps here were notes regarding the vanished snitch, Morgan Beach, and his relationship to Arthur, or to Charles Sloan. Or an entry showing why Sloan, or Bright, had accepted a plea bargain sentencing Flood's lieutenant, Louis Jackson, to only a year for possession of cocaine. Or a paper trail disclosing how the *Green* case—where Johnny Curran's seizure of cocaine was found to exceed the scope of his warrant—had been transferred from the original judge to the hostile courtroom of Judge Freeman. Or, if Stella was lucky, a memo tracing how five keys of coke had vanished from the police evidence room. Or something to show whether the prosecutor—Sloan again—had known that Jean-Claude Desnoyers wanted to rat out Flood; rereading her own notes, with the scribbled word "deal," had made the dead Haitian's desperate hope as vivid to Stella as yesterday.

She scanned the index. Each case was listed: *State v. Flood; State v. Desnoyers; State v. Green; State v. Jackson;* a second *State v. Flood.* A litany of failed efforts to roll up Moro's network.

Stella was not sure, precisely, why she had come. Perhaps the instinct—and it was only that—that someone was lying to her about one or more of Jack's cases, or at least concealing the truth. Perhaps simply the desire to be certain that this room held nothing she should know.

With the file numbers scribbled on a scrap of paper, Stella began searching the metal shelves.

They were arranged like a primitive library—a strip of tape was stuck to each shelf with the span of dates and file numbers written in magic marker. Carrying a stepladder, she stopped at the shelf which should contain the file for *State v. Desnoyers*.

It was the highest row. Climbing the ladder, Stella peered at it: though the shelves were otherwise jammed, there was a small crack of light, a file leaning sideways. She checked its number, then that of the file it leaned against.

State v. Desnoyers was missing.

Stella paused, taking in the musty smell of dust and aging paper. Systematically, she removed each file to assure herself that nothing was out of order. Nothing was.

Climbing down, she moved through the shelves until she found the one for *State v. Flood*—the first case, where the evidence had vanished. This was easier; the shelf was eye-level.

Stella found another leaning file, another crack of light. It took perhaps a minute to confirm that *State v. Flood* was gone.

Motionless, Stella gazed down at the paper in her hand.

On the next shelf, the index had told her, was *State v. Jackson.* Except that it was not.

The room was stifling, the forced air from the ancient heating system far too hot and close. With a discomfort which bordered on apprehension, Stella searched for the last two files, certain now—as proved to be true—that these were also missing.

Stella returned to the log. Flipping its pages, she determined that the entries went back to 1996. On the list of her colleagues, Michael Del Corso's name appeared, next to the file of a convicted embezzler. But there were no entries for Arthur Bright or Charles Sloan. No one, according to the log, had removed the files Stella wanted.

She stood there, hands on hips, surveying the shadowy room. Its quiet felt oppressive.

Opening the door, Stella left.

MICHAEL WAS in his office.

Stella stopped in his doorway. He looked up from a stack of papers.

"How was Sofia?" Stella asked.

"Fine, thanks." Michael smiled wryly. "Except she kept me up last night trying to crawl into bed with me. Sometimes she does that when I've been out."

Where was the mother, Stella wondered—dead, or just gone? Michael's comment carried intimations of insecurity in the girl, perhaps a sudden loss. Maybe that was why she had watched for him in the window.

"I've been searching," Stella said, "for our office files on those drug cases. You don't have them, do you?"

Michael's expression was, at most, mildly curious. "They're missing?"

"And not logged out. Though it's possible someone did that years ago and never put them back."

"All five?" Michael's eyes became more sober, and then he shrugged. "Anyhow, don't look at me. I've never even had a library fine."

Stella smiled faintly. "Were you ever tardy?"

"Never."

"Neither was I."

Stella turned to leave. "Have you heard of Megaplex?" Michael asked. "They're America's leading builder of sports facilities. I just talked to one of their vice presidents, Paul Harshman."

He was certainly efficient, Stella thought. Or perhaps he simply felt it prudent to impress a woman who might someday be County Prosecutor. "Is Harshman willing to help us?" she asked.

"As long as it's off the record—he doesn't want to get caught up in Steelton politics. But he seems to know all about Steelton 2000. It might be good if you went to New York, sat down with him."

Stella considered this. "Maybe you can go."

Michael looked doubtful. "I can translate," he answered, "but *you're* the one who's got to understand this."

Stella hesitated. "Maybe we both go," she finally said. "We're only talking a day, right?"

Michael eyed the desk. "There's Sofia. I'd have to see."

Stella felt awkward: she had cornered a man who neither wanted to go with her nor wanted to refuse her. A man who was responsible for raising a seven-year-old girl.

"I forgot about Sofia," she said.

"And Sloan," Michael answered dryly. "He may not want the staggering expense of two airplane tickets in coach."

"To check out Steelton 2000? Didn't you tell me Sloan wants to be County Prosecutor?"

The comment made him smile. "I'll talk to my parents. *You* ask Sloan."

"Thanks," Stella said.

She went to find Sloan. But her thoughts refocused on the void of evidence surrounding Novak's death, and what she feared was the hidden skein of his corruption. Before reaching Sloan's office she decided not to mention the missing files.

Sloan heard out her request, a suggestive light stealing into his eyes. "You and Del Corso," he said.

"It's only a day, Charles."

He folded his hands across his stomach. "Think that's long enough to find out why this ballpark sucks?"

SEVENTEEN

FROM A corner table, Stella watched the busy SoHo street scene. The trip to Manhattan had come the same day Sloan approved it; Paul Harshman of Megaplex was available the next morning, or not for weeks. And so Stella found herself eating dinner at Raoul's—a pleasant bistro with good food and an eclectic crowd—while Michael paced the sidewalk, talking to Sofia on his cell phone.

At length, Michael returned. He twirled his wineglass absently. "I'm feeling guilty," Stella told him, "about taking you away."

He looked up at her, an ironic self-awareness stealing across his face. "Sometimes I'm not very good at this. I worry that if I don't make her feel important enough . . ."

He did not finish the sentence. Stella was torn between respect for his privacy, and fear that disinterest would confirm for him how cold she was. "I'm sorry," she said at last, "but I can't help wondering what happened to Sofia's mom."

She's dead, Stella half expected him to say. Instead he answered, "She's living in Australia."

Unexplained, his response imposed on Stella an awkward silence. Michael looked narrowly at the table; Stella wished that she had never asked. "Do you believe in precognition?" he finally said. "That you can see a person for the first time and know, without knowing why, that she's going to change your life?"

His tone commingled remembered awe with the sad knowledge of how his marriage had ended. "That's never happened to me," Stella said honestly. "I'm just as glad. For someone to have that kind of power, it would have scared me."

Michael nodded. "I think of that," he finally answered, "when I watch Sofia sleep at night, and she looks so much like Maria. And I imagine saying to her, 'It's okay, you're why it all happened.'"

What a burden, Stella thought, for father and daughter to carry. "What *did* happen?" she asked.

He smiled at one side of his mouth. "Do you really want to hear this?"

"I asked, didn't I?" Reading the doubt in his eyes, she added quietly, "Yes. I really do."

Michael gazed out the window. "That first day," he finally said, "we were in sixth grade. Twenty-two years later I couldn't remember a time I didn't love her. It sounds retrograde, but there was never anyone else for me. I'd look at Maria, and just feel lucky.

"Our parents came from the same region, we had the same friends, and we went to the same church. We knew everything about each other. I remember Maria getting her first period, for God's sake, and how embarrassed she was." Pausing, he shook his head in bemusement. "Most people can't imagine growing up with the person they're going to marry. We couldn't imagine anything else."

Once, Stella supposed, there would have been pride in his voice, not this sense of two unwitting people marching toward a fall. "But then you started to," she said.

"Maria started to." Protected by their location in the corner—a cocoon of privacy in the noisy closeness of the restaurant, its crowd of yuppies and young couples from the neighborhood—Michael seemed absorbed in memory. "We had a plan. Maria got her business degree and went to work for British Petroleum, to put me through grad school. Then we'd have a family, and live in the 'burbs, with a nice house and good schools. But we'd still take the kids to Mass in Little Italy, at St. Peter and Paul's, and to Sunday dinner with their grandparents. Just like our folks had done with us."

Stella smiled. "Was it John Lennon who said, 'Life is what happens while you're making other plans'? I've never wanted to believe that."

Michael studied her, curious. "Have you always had a plan?"

"I'm still living it."

Michael began playing with his silverware, absently aligning and realigning. "So were we. I got out of school, and took a job with Arthur— for experience, I thought—and Maria had Sofia. And then she said she wanted to go back to work.

"That was okay—we could deal with it, our folks would help, and I didn't want her to feel stifled. But it worried me a little. I adored Sofia. Maria didn't seem to take the same joy in her, or in our life. Like this person I knew so well—funny and affectionate—had gone somewhere else.

"Maybe I'd begun to bore her. Maybe she'd had a baby and didn't love it like she'd planned, and suddenly realized that she was thirty, living a life she'd chosen when she was twelve. Still telling me things were fine because she didn't know how not to.

"All *I* knew was she was different. Then one night she came home and told me she was in love with a guy she worked with, from Australia, and that's where she was going.

"I just sat there, wanting to throw up. All those business dinners, all those trips out of town, and I'd been too stupid to see it. 'Cause the girl I'd known since sixth grade would never, ever lie to me." His voice was soft. "I told myself she was still a good person, that she couldn't just change like that. But it was like looking at a stranger. The Maria I loved was dead."

Though quiet, the words had an immediacy Stella could feel in her soul. Michael was in mourning, and it had caused him to question the worth of everything in his life, except for the daughter he loved.

"Do you ever see her?" Stella asked.

"No." He sipped more wine. "I think, for Maria, moving was the only thing she could do. She had a whole lifetime of people she couldn't face, not just a husband and kid but our families, everyone who'd known us. If anything, Sydney wasn't far enough away."

This formulation had the sound of something Michael had spent months to understand. "What about Sofia?" Stella asked.

For a moment, Michael closed his eyes. "Eleven months," he said, "and still she asks when Mommy's coming home. How can I tell her Maria's never coming back, that she's in love with someone else?"

"What *do* you tell her?"

Michael put his elbows on the table, and his body seemed to sag. Despite the gray at his temples, he still looked young to Stella, but at times he had the burdened quality of a man who believed the best was behind him. "That Maria took a job, to help us. So we don't know when she gets to come back." There was suppressed anger in his voice now. "Because I prod her to, every month or so Maria sends Sofia a postcard. They're chatty, filled with information, like an aunt would write to a niece she doesn't know all that well. Except that they're signed, 'Love, Mom.'"

What to say? Stella wondered. Dinner arrived amidst her silence; two glasses of wine down, Stella looked at her steak au poivre gratefully. When the waitress filled her glass again, she realized that she felt more of a glow, a greater freedom than she tended to have with someone she did not know. "I don't have kids," she ventured, "only a niece and nephew.

I'm the aunt who doesn't know them all that well. So anything I say has zero basis in experience."

Michael looked up. "Go ahead."

"I just wonder if it's right for Sofia to believe that vanishing is how mothers treat daughters. Or, later on, to learn that you've been covering for Maria."

Michael finished his first bite of lamb. "What would you suggest?"

Stella remembered her family's silences, the solitude which had deepened in herself. "Maybe the truth," she answered. "As gently told as possible."

Michael stared at her. "That her mother left us for someone else?"

For an instant, Stella felt his anger at Maria had merged with resentment of Stella's advice. "Maybe there's no good choice," she conceded. "But, for Sofia, Maria's become a fantasy person who may come walking through the door. And you know that's not true.

"Maybe it's best if Sofia sees things as they are. Maybe, when she gets older, she'll understand her mom's behavior is not her fault, and she can start detaching. Sometimes detachment's all you can hope for."

The words were out before Stella knew how much they said about herself. For the first time that evening, Michael studied her keenly. "It sounds like you've had experience."

Stella hesitated, silenced by her instinct for privacy. But tonight, at least, her past might have value for someone else. "My family left all the important things unspoken," she finally told him. "My father drank, because he was frustrated and angry. My mother was so frightened she pretended not to notice. Katie and I were supposed to pretend along with her.

"From the time I was young I remember watching the three of them like I was an anthropologist. But Katie developed the Stockholm Syndrome." Stella cocked her head. "You know what that is, right?"

"Uh-huh. Where a kidnap victim starts to identify with her captors. Because she's frightened to see them as they are."

Stella nodded. "Katie invented a home that never existed, filled with warmth and sentiment, expressed in the Marz family's own unique way. And I walked out.

"Katie's still angry at me for not living her lie, and at my father for not being himself anymore. While my mother, by dying, became the saint of Katie's invention." Stella took a sip of wine. "Hard as it was, I'd rather be me than Katie. And maybe Sofia's better off if she understands

it's down to you and her. Facing reality screws you up less than deny-
ing it."

This seemed to make him pensive. Finally, he asked, "When you say
your father's not himself? . . . "

"He has Alzheimer's."

Her tone was not inviting. "That's hard," Michael said simply.

"Not for him. At least not anymore."

Michael considered her. "Hard for you, I meant."

Stella felt the familiar pressure on her chest. "It was a shock," she said
at last. "One day he just called me at the office, out of the blue, to com-
plain about how I'd shamed him. But the woman who answered the
phone was thirty-four, and the daughter he was complaining about was
twenty-three. And he didn't know the difference."

Michael's mouth framed a low, silent whistle. The memory, Stella
found, was as vivid as yesterday. Driving to Warszawa. Entering the
darkened house, heart pounding, as she had on the night she left. Imagining what she and Armin Marz might say to each other eleven years after
she last had heard his voice. But the man she found was bent, his hair a
thinning yellow-gray, his body a husk which seemed to hang from his
bones. Cackling, he watched *Family Court*. The blankness in his eyes
was terrifying.

For eleven years, she had wanted to scream, *you refused to speak to
me. Until you just forgot about that.*

"Once I saw him," Stella told Michael, "I didn't need a diagnosis.

"He just went downhill from there. Even though she was dying, my
mother had been caring for him, covering up as always. It was almost a
relief to see my father at the funeral Mass, honestly grieving. Then we
went home with a few friends from the neighborhood."

His eyes, Stella remembered, had gone as dead as burnt-out bulbs.
"He waited until they left," she told Michael. "Then he grasped my wrist
and said, 'Your mother's changed on me.'"

Michael rested his elbow on the table, his brown eyes, deep set in his
rugged face, more sympathetic for the contrast with his features. But she
could not tell him that when she explained again that her mother had
died of cancer, Armin Marz had snapped, "She left because you whore
for Novak."

"So you put him in a nursing home?" Michael asked.

"Katie still wanted to keep him in the house; it was the source of
Dad's memories, she said. But I'd see him look around and not recognize
someone in a photograph, or recall where something was, and get fright-

ened and angry. Forgetting his own house was torture." Pausing, Stella stared out the window. "Katie couldn't accept it. Finally, I told her I wasn't paying for a nurse anymore . . ."

"*You cold-blooded bitch,*" Katie had answered.

"Who pops for the nursing home?" Michael asked.

"I do."

"Your sister doesn't help?"

Turning, Stella surveyed the restaurant. Two new couples at nearby tables reminded her, uncomfortably, of how much time had passed. "She says they can't afford it," Stella answered. "But I think Katie sees this as my just reward for moving out, maybe for leaving her stranded. I'm doing penance for my sins against her imaginary family."

Michael tilted his head. "And your father?"

"Remembers nothing, and no one. The last time I saw him he was sitting in a circle with the other patients, holding hands with a black man." The memory made Stella laugh. "It shocked me. Then I realized he'd forgotten he was a racist."

Michael smiled at this. She could never tell him that on Sundays, she sat with the shell that her father had become and imagined, in his artificial serenity, that they could reconcile. That, even now, the hardest part was to accept that, as important as he still was to her, she was nothing to him at all.

At length, she said, "We've talked about everything, it seems. Except tomorrow's meeting."

Michael fiddled with his coffee cup. "True."

"To start, my agenda isn't Sloan's. I'm not here to prove that Steelton 2000 'sucks.'"

Sitting back, Michael looked curious. "Even if it helps Arthur?"

"Doing our job helps Arthur. What I want is to identify the pressure points in Fielding's work life, and who he might be crosswise with."

Michael glanced around them. In a dubious tone, he asked, "You're not thinking someone killed him, are you? For sure they wouldn't hire a hooker with a heroin habit to do the job. Besides, she wound up dead."

"All good points," Stella responded evenly. "So tell me how she wound up with Tommy Fielding."

"Not a clue."

"*That's* our problem. And as long as Arthur understands it's why we came here, we don't need to worry about anyone else."

His head cocked, and there was a slight narrowing of the eyes. "Not Sloan?"

Stella reminded herself that Michael had a daughter and a mortgage; and that, in the crosscurrents of office politics, both might be at risk. "Sloan's not a fool," she answered dryly. "He knows that good people make him look good, even when he's not trying. And to my knowledge, you've never questioned whether Charles Sloan ought to be in charge of dispensing justice in Steelton."

The look Michael gave her was long and serious—the expression of someone, Stella thought briefly, who wished to be a friend. "But you do," he said at last. "So what's to stop you from running?"

My father. For every month he lives, my savings—the nest egg I need to borrow against to help start my campaign—shrinks a little more. And, with it, my hopes. Because the usual donors belong to Sloan.

"Humility," Stella answered.

AFTER COFFEE, they took a cab to their modest hotel in the East Fifties. The driver, a transplanted Russian in a New York Yankees baseball cap, shifted lanes maniacally, observing yellow lights by running them, red lights by braking with a sickening lurch. To distract herself, Stella focused on the velvet canyons of Manhattan at night, the street life, pulsing at all hours.

The cab braked to its final stop.

Entering the hotel, they took an elevator to the sixth floor. Their rooms, Stella had discovered, were across the hall from each other.

They stopped in front of Stella's door. Hands jammed into his pockets, Michael looked suddenly awkward. Their conversation had veered from business to the deeply personal; Stella sensed that he wanted to acknowledge this but was not sure how.

Finally, he told her, "What you said at dinner really helped me. I didn't expect that."

Nor had she. The trip out of town, the wine, seemed to have unsettled her. Stella managed to smile. "I don't usually treat people to my family history," she said. "I'm not sure it's any favor."

At once, Stella regretted saying this. The man worked for her, and yet she liked him enough, or had said enough, to want reassurance. Gently, Michael said, "It was, though."

He was standing closer to her, Stella realized. She looked into his face.

Briefly, tentatively, he rested one hand on her shoulder. "Thanks," he said. "For all of it."

"Sure." She turned from him, opening the door, and stepped into the darkness of her room. She could still feel his touch on her shoulder.

THAT NIGHT, Stella dreamed of the dead-records room.

The cavernous space was dark, and she was frightened. But she could not leave. Jack Novak had promised to meet her there, to tell her the truth, at last. Until he did, she would never be free.

Blindly, Stella felt her way from shelf to shelf.

Jack had been murdered. She knew that. But he had promised to meet her this last time.

Touching a shelf, she felt a gap left by the file closed after the murder of Jean-Claude Desnoyers. Dead records, dead Haitian, dead end.

Dead Jack.

The only sound Stella heard was her own breathing, ragged now. Her skin felt clammy.

There was someone behind her.

Fearful, she closed her eyes. He was a man, someone she knew; why else this sudden feeling of intimacy. But not safety.

Why, if it was Jack, did he not speak? She could feel his breath on the nape of her neck.

"*You're a very pretty lady, Stella Marz.*"

Cool fingers touched her arm . . .

Stella started awake, caught in a tangle of damp sheets.

The room was dark. But she knew where she was—not in dead records but New York, caught in the aftershock of a nightmare. Tendrils of hair stuck to her forehead.

Stella looked around her, reorienting.

She placed little stock in dreams, seldom remembered more than fragments, scraps of nonsense which told her nothing. But it was easy enough to decipher the strands which connected this dream with waking—solitude and paranoia. Why, when the whispered words were Moro's, did she believe that the fingers which had touched her belonged to someone else? . . .

She drifted to the window, in search of light. But beneath her was a narrow concrete pit, East Fifty-third Street, gray with first light. The only sounds were metal clanging, the hydraulic wheeze of a garbage truck.

Turning, Stella sat on the edge of the bed.

There was a pattern, she was sure—the pattern of the missing files followed the pattern of fixed cases. Anyone in the chain of law enforcement could have helped Moro and Novak and, she supposed, somehow have gained access to the dead-records room. But only prosecutors had the key.

Who had been there before her? Stella wondered. And who had been with her tonight? She did not know whether she felt lonely or unbalanced—a woman who trusted no one, and so had begun to parse her dreams.

Just before the meeting, she called Nathaniel Dance. He had nothing new in Novak's murder. She said nothing of the missing records.

EIGHTEEN

"IT'S LIKE I said," Paul Harshman told them, "I'm happy to put on this little tutorial, but I don't want our name in the paper."

"Understood," Stella answered, and sat down beside Michael.

Though it featured a view of the Hudson, Harshman's corner office had a spareness which suggested that, unlike lawyers and investment bankers, he did not consider sophisticated decor necessary to his business. Perhaps, Stella reflected, this came from having a tangible product—the corridors had a geometric severity, sheets of glass joined to bare white walls, their sole adornment color pictures of what Megaplex had wrought: Camden Yards in Baltimore; Jacobs Field in Cleveland; Turner Field in Atlanta; and, most recently, San Francisco's Pac Bell Stadium. In each city, the structures had become the modern pyramids, symbolizing not only a new pride of place and the hundreds of millions of dollars spent to acquire it but all the civic sweat and blood which became as much a part of these complexes as steel and concrete—the angry ballot battles, the accusations of greed, the clearing of land, the displacement of people, the claims of jobs created or schools deprived, the class warfare, the winners and losers, the beginning or end of public careers. This was big business, as profitable as it was volatile, and Harshman was doing them a favor to meet at all.

He filled two Megaplex coffee mugs for Stella and Michael and pushed them across his conference table. He was a big man, middle-aged, gray haired and heavy lidded, with a midwestern accent and the hearty flush of someone who liked the outdoors and didn't mind a drink. His manner matched the look—smart, straightforward, and tough—of a man who minced few words and believed things when he saw them. "Whining," he added laconically, "is bad for business."

Michael sipped his coffee. "Did Steelton give you something to whine about?" he asked.

Harshman laughed. "Turned us down flat—didn't even let us bid. First time *that's* happened in seventeen years."

"Do you know why?"

"Politics. Your mayor wanted to say he had an all-local deal, and we don't live in Steelton." A smile flickered around his mouth and eyes. "Float two hundred seventy-five million dollars in municipal bonds, like Krajek did, and it takes about *four* hundred million to pay it off. For that amount of money, you need all the selling points you can get, and jobs for local citizens trumps expertise."

"But," Stella said, "you do know how Steelton 2000 works?"

"Yup. Politically, all of these deals are minefields. Before you bid on the next one, you have to know what happened to the *last* one: where there were overruns, what pissed people off, why it succeeded or failed. And Steelton 2000 is unique in the past five years—the trend's for private financing, not public."

Stella gazed out at the Hudson, a chill-looking purple in the sunlight of a January morning. Dryly, she observed, "We were desperate."

Harshman did not smile now. "You should have been. Bad image, small media market, and a ballpark where the descendants of the original rats outnumber the paying customers. If Peter Hall moves the team, he gets a new ballpark and a big tip—a cool fifty million or so, and he's the happy owner of the Silicon Valley Blues, or Laptops, or whatever."

"So by staying," Michael inquired, "he's losing money?"

"Maybe not, in the long run. That's the genius part." He looked from Michael to Stella. "Probably that's where we should start—how the world looks to Peter Hall. In the end, that'll get us to your dead guy, Fielding.

"The first thing you need to know is that Peter Hall was hemorrhaging money.

"When you hear owners wail about losses, it's real. Only four major league teams made money last year—the players cost too much, and they suck up all the money baseball gets from TV." Hunching back in his leather chair, Harshman took a swig of coffee. "That's why you get the Murdochs and the Turners and the Disneys buying up franchises. Who else can afford them?

"For Hall, that's the key. Baseball makes no sense as a business. But a sports team's the ultimate toy for a rich guy with a raging ego. In baseball the teams are in short supply—there's only thirty, and these billionaires keep driving up the price.

"Compared to those guys, Hall's a pauper; he made his money in steel and shopping malls, not from TV and movies and multimedia empires.

The only way for Hall to cash in is to move his team, or to peddle it to the next conglomerate that wants one."

Michael put down his cup. "Either way," he interjected, "the Blues leave Steelton."

"Unless Steelton builds him a stadium." Harshman flashed a grin, revealing a row of surprisingly white, even teeth. "In the nineties, like in the time before TV, baseball revenues are attendance driven. So stadiums aren't *ball*parks anymore. They're theme parks, designed to promote nostalgia but filled with luxury boxes, video games, virtual-reality centers, special effects, convenient parking, and high-end foods—everything that appeals to the corporate crowd and the affluent consumers who've replaced Joe Sixpack. Everything that your old Erie County Stadium isn't."

Abruptly, Harshman stood, stretching with his hands behind his neck. "Build Peter Hall a stadium," he continued, "and he *and* his new African-American minority owner, Mr. Rockwell, will do just fine—at least once they sell to the next Rupert Murdoch. Which I'm sure Hall pointed out to Rockwell when he went looking for a front man to help with black voters.

"Window-dressing like Rockwell is the key. Spending two hundred seventy-five million plus interest to help someone as rich as Hall is bound to raise the furies in a city as bad off as yours." Harshman grinned again. "No offense intended. On the other hand, your Mayor Krajek doesn't want to be the guy who lost the Blues—hell, he might want to be a senator someday. What he needs is to persuade enough voters that all their public money he spends is not only going to stay in Steelton but will help to grow *more* money."

Stella found that the bald summary scalded her pride. She had wanted to see the revival of her city and, with that, the revival of its self-image: she did not like to think of it as low-end property—a Baltic Avenue—in a game of Monopoly played exclusively by billionaires. "The usual arguments," Harshman went on, "are enhancing the downtown and maintaining a 'big-league' profile. But Hall and Krajek took that one step further.

"First, they looked at everyone who stands to make money: the landowners; the folks who clear the site; the architect; the developer—I thought it being Hall was a nice touch; the construction manager; the general contractor; the subcontractors; the accountants; the lawyers; the folks who sell the municipal bonds; the concessionaires who provide all the parking, food, novelties, and video games. Then they decided *every one* of them would have to be from Steelton. And just to make it sing, and cut the legs out from under folks like your Mr. Bright, they made sure there was a minority owner, a minority partner for Hall Development, spots for a minority contractor and subcontractors, and assurances about minority hiring."

"They seem to have found them," Michael said.

"Uh-huh." Harshman sipped his coffee. "Only problem is I've hardly heard of any of those outfits, from the architect to the contractor to the company that's gonna sell the hot dogs. This isn't just a ballpark, it's a Christmas tree for amateurs. Which is probably why there was never any competitive bidding, and why it's costing the taxpayers so damn much money."

"With a cap," Stella pointed out. "If the cost goes over two hundred seventy-five million, Hall's liable for the overruns."

Facing her, Harshman's expression assumed an amiable patience. "I should have mentioned that," he rejoined. "It's the second reason Steelton 2000 costs so much—to make sure Peter Hall never has to pay a nickel.

"Forget 'guaranteed maximum price,' Ms. Marz, and think 'guaranteed minimum profit.' Then you'll begin to see how ingenious this arrangement really is. Everybody in Steelton who touches this deal is guaranteed to profit—except the city itself."

"Peter Hall," Stella interjected, "points out that there's a 'savings clause.' If Hall keeps the construction costs under the two hundred seventy-five million dollars generated by this bond issue, Steelton gets back half the savings, and Hall Development gets the other half. What he says is that, by motivating Hall Development to sit on the contractor, it also saves money for Steelton."

Still standing, Harshman folded his arms. "And that's another selling point for Hall and Krajek. But what you have to understand is that—done right—this is a two-hundred-million-dollar project.

"That's seventy-five million dollars' worth of padding. Some of that defrays the cost of hiring people with no real experience, and all the waste, cost overruns, and just plain screw-ups that result. For the sake of argument, let's set *that* figure at twenty-five million. So half of what's left over—the last fifty million—goes to Peter Hall and Steelton.

"The typical profit for a construction manager is four percent. On two hundred million, that's an eight-million-dollar fee—not bad. But not as good as a twenty-five-million-dollar bonus generated by the savings clause." Harshman grinned again. "What a deal for Steelton. It gets back twenty-five million dollars it never needed to raise, but on which it's paying interest, at the price of a twenty-five-million-dollar bonus to Hall Development. I'm just glad that your Mayor Krajek doesn't manage *my* finances."

Michael glanced at Stella. She might not have come to prove that Hall had screwed the city, his expression said, but the upshot was a gift to Bright and Sloan. Then it struck her that this might not be so.

"Let's assume you're right," she said to Harshman. "That this is a two-hundred-million-dollar project, and that Hall splits fifty million of the overage with the city. Who benefits most from the other twenty-five million?"

Leaning back, Harshman gazed down at her, no longer smiling. Then he went to the window, as though distracted by a tour boat steaming toward Ellis Island and the Statue of Liberty. But his eyes were slits, his mouth pursed, and Stella felt him weighing his answer. When he turned, his face and voice reflected a new seriousness.

"I'm not a racist," he said. "I believe in keeping the construction trades open to minority business enterprises—MBEs. Hiring them is the only way, over time, to make sure they develop expertise and get a piece of the pie. I've worked with too many topflight MBEs to believe any different.

"But there's a dirty secret in my business, one everybody knows and is too politically correct to say aloud: that quotas for MBEs can mean payoffs to incompetents who are hired because of politics. Once Krajek said that a certain percentage of the deal would go to a minority-owned contractor and minority subs, he was stuck—thirty percent had to be local, and they had to be black, Hispanic, or Asian. What they *didn't* have to be is any good."

Pausing, Harshman walked back to the table and sat across from Stella, looking directly into her eyes. "I wager Steelton has realized the American dream—equal opportunity for fuckups of every race, color, or creed taking turns gouging the city for an overpriced ballpark. But you can bet *one* reason this project costs more is because Krajek used MBE requirements to keep Arthur Bright off-balance." His smile was brief and unamused. "You're having an election, I hear."

Seemingly a throwaway, the remark implied that Harshman had seen the underside of Stella's question: that, by interposing minority businesses between Steelton 2000 and its critics, Hall and Krajek had made an attack on its construction costs a serious risk for Bright. "Politics," she observed, "is a contact sport. So where does Tommy Fielding fit?"

"In the crosshairs. As project manager, he approves all the bills from the general contractor and the subcontractors, and all the change orders. Plus making sure the work he's billed for is done right, or done at all.

"His goal is to get Hall Development as big a chunk of the savings clause as he can. But every day he's up against contractors and subs who are after that same money—including minority businesses. And every few weeks Fielding has to certify to the city that the MBEs are getting thirty percent of the project, whether or not they're doing any work. And if he doesn't . . ." Pausing, Harshman gave an elaborate shrug. "All political hell breaks loose, and who knows who gets hurt. Including Hall and Krajek."

"So Fielding's sitting on a pipeline," Michael said, "with everyone else waiting for water. And only Fielding gets to turn it on and off."

"More like a powder keg. Hard not to light it."

Listening, Stella tried to gauge the pressure on the Tommy Fielding she imagined: a perfectionist whose job had become his life, charged with a project which affected not only millions of dollars but the future of a city and the men who wished to run it. Perhaps he had cracked, tried to escape through whatever means, no matter how alien. But he could not have escaped making enemies. "Are you thinking," Harshman asked her, "that someone wanted to kill this guy?"

It was her turn to shrug. "Wanting's one thing. Doing's another. This looks like an accident." She hesitated, reflecting on what she had heard. "You say Fielding reviewed the bills. Give me some examples of when that could lead to problems."

"Lots of ways. Say the change order's inflated, or unnecessary. Or there's phony workmen's comp claims, or overcharges for materials." Tasting his coffee, Harshman seemed to find it cool, and put it down with a somewhat grumpy air. "With the MBEs," he continued, "the prospects increase exponentially, because they've got Fielding—Hall and Krajek, too—by the short hairs. They can threaten not to work, screwing up the reports to the city on MBE compliance. Or they can submit a bill for work they didn't do—rather than fight with them, Fielding pays them off to meet the guidelines, and then pays another contractor to do what they didn't. Maybe they *can't* do the work, because they're billing for minority employees who don't exist except on paper. There's a thousand ways. But you can't know unless you get your fingers dirty."

Michael nodded. "Plow through Fielding's records, find out who the contractors are. Go to the site and see who's there."

Harshman smiled again. "Make yourself conspicuous, in other words."

There was doubt in his voice, and Stella knew why. Bright's critique of Steelton 2000 had been philosophical; to *investigate*, he would have to stick his neck out. Across from her, Harshman glanced at his watch. "Another half hour," he said, "and I'm headed out of town."

Stella turned to Michael for help. "You say everyone makes out except the city," he said to Harshman. "But the city owns the stadium, free and clear, and gets money from operations, including events like rock concerts and maybe the Pope's next visit to Steelton. Break that down for us—*who* else makes money besides Hall and the construction folks, and why operations don't help Steelton pay off the bonds."

Harshman gave Michael a look of new respect. "Let's take the first part—who makes money.

"On the front side, like I said, whoever owns the land for Steelton 2000 does well: you can bet the price went up on *that*, and on whatever land is adjacent to the stadium. Because if downtown *does* come back, land values are gonna skyrocket.

"Next is the construction phase. We've already covered that—the contractors, the MBEs, and especially Hall Development all make out like bandits. What we overlooked is how having a new ballpark makes *more* money for Peter Hall as owner of the Blues.

"First, there's naming rights—the reason why San Francisco's park is named after a goddamned phone company, and Denver's after a beer." Sitting back, Harshman seemed to savor the elegance of Hall's deal. "The Blues retained naming rights, then sold them to MCI. For the next twenty years, for a price of forty million dollars paid to the Steelton Blues, the real name of Steelton 2000 will be MCI Stadium. Almost as heartwarming as Ma Bell Field."

At this, Michael laughed aloud. "Then there's luxury boxes," Harshman continued blandly, "one hundred of them, sold up front for a hundred thousand bucks a pop. That's another ten million.

"*Then* there's income from concessions." Pausing, Harshman faced Stella. "This one's a bit unusual—the Blues are accepting a flat annual fee in exchange for the rights to provide parking, food, and novelties. That's pretty good for the concessionaires, particularly for companies I've never heard of: these are low-cost businesses, where the revenues are in cash, and usually the concessionaires split their profits with the ball club. But the annual fees the Blues will get aren't bad—two and a half million for parking, two million for food, and one million for novelties. That's another four and a half million dollars for the team, from which the city doesn't get a nickel. And that's before the Blues have sold a single ticket." Harshman's voice slowed for emphasis. "Sell out your season tickets, and the Blues are close to actually making money. Which greatly enhances Hall's asking price when it's time to auction off the team."

"And the city?" Michael asked.

"Receives nominal rent—a million bucks a year. Krajek argues that the ballpark also generates tax revenue—ticket taxes and the like—which will help pay off the interest on the bonds. But the city also had to pay for the land, not to mention extra money for new access roads, bus service, security, and all the costs of maintaining a ballpark, right down to the lightbulbs. No way Krajek's numbers add up."

Stella considered him. "If this deal's so easy to take apart," she asked, "why hasn't someone done it?"

"Like Bright, you mean? Who's going to do it for him?" Harshman jabbed the table with his forefinger. "Almost everyone who really understands these deals—us, the folks who secure financing, the consultants who provide Hall and Krajek with all those fancy graphs and cash-flow projections—profits from them. Not one of us has a death wish."

Abruptly, Harshman stood again, hands jammed in his pockets. "If I sound cynical, I'm not. These ballparks become political, and it's only the political arguments I question—whether the benefits to minorities are real, whether the revenues to a city equal the cash it spends, whether more people will spend their money in Steelton. Those are the selling points politicians make to voters and, in any given case, maybe they're ephemeral or even bogus. But, to me, they don't address the real question."

Harshman gazed down at Stella. "This isn't just about money, Ms. Marz. It's about how you feel, how a city feels. What is it worth to Cleveland that its national image—its *self*-image—isn't of an urban dump anymore but of a beautiful ballpark with a backdrop of new buildings? What is it worth that young people go downtown now? What would it be worth to *you* to see that happen in Steelton? And what will it be worth to your kids?

"Life isn't perfect. Probably the Taj Mahal was built on waste and corruption and money which could genuinely have helped the poor. But great cities subsidize art museums, and symphony halls, and all sorts of public monuments. And those don't accomplish a fraction of the psychic good, or touch a fraction of the people, that the revival of the Steelton Blues will."

For the first time, Stella realized, Harshman was revealing the passion which made him care about his work. Suddenly, she thought of her father, of one clear good memory amidst the wreckage—of sitting on his lap at night, past her normal bedtime, listening to the radio as Larry Rockwell homered to beat the Yankees. "Your boss was right about the money," Harshman told her. "Maybe righter than he knew, or wants to know. And God knows why this Fielding died. But whether or not he understands it, Krajek's right about how a city dies, or how it dreams. That's why he deserves to win."

THEY HAD reached La Guardia before either said much. Finally, Michael asked, "So what do you think?"

Stella glanced at the departure board. "That I still can't explain how and why Tommy Fielding overdosed on heroin. I have to stick to that, and let the rest go."

"What about the mayoral race?"

Stella turned to him. It was not a usual question from a subordinate, although, perhaps, she had allowed Michael to be somewhat more. And all that she saw in his eyes, or heard in his voice, was concern. "Sloan and Arthur," she replied, "will take care of the politics. I'd just like us to go where Paul Harshman pointed us. Unless something or someone says we shouldn't."

"Like Arthur?"

"Or Sloan." Excusing herself, Stella went to a pay phone.

It was not yet one in the afternoon: since eight-thirty that morning, although it was Saturday, Stella had received seven messages—one already obsolete, one from Dance, two from the media about Novak and/or Fielding, one from a law student regarding a calendar conflict, one from her putative campaign consultant. It was the last message, delivered in a slurred monotone Stella guessed belonged to a young black woman, which made her press the phone to her ear.

"I saw you on TV," Stella thought she heard. "It's about Tina . . ." There was silence, and then the woman said, "Maybe I'll call back."

The line went dead.

NINETEEN

It was past four o'clock when Stella reached the office; barely fifteen minutes later Charles Sloan, already aware of her return, called to ask that she meet with him and Bright. For the next ten minutes, sitting at Bright's desk, she summarized her meeting with Megaplex. Curtly, Sloan peppered her with questions. Bright merely listened; his air of scholarly reserve—a form of protective coloration, Stella often thought—was more impenetrable than normal.

At last Bright spoke. "Those MBEs," he said succinctly, "will turn out to be Krajek's people. Some of them are getting money for nothing, you can count on it. Without competitive bidding, Krajek could hand Peter Hall a list of pet minorities and Hall would have to go along. The only question is how much public money they're kicking back to Krajek's campaign."

The bald summary caught Stella by surprise. "You *know* that?"

"It just makes sense." Bright folded his hands. "I hear things, Stella. There are qualified minority contractors who tried to get work on Steelton 2000. None of them did. The multimillion-dollar tip keeps Hall from complaining."

"What about Fielding?"

Bright gave a small smile. "His job was to accept reality. And get the stadium built."

Stella glanced at Sloan. "Like Chicago," she said.

"Chicago," Bright answered sardonically, "is not just a place. It's a state of mind."

Sloan had begun fidgeting. He turned to Bright, voice lowered as if wishing Stella away. "What about your base? Start beating on Krajek for using 'unqualified' black folks, and you sound like these crackers always bleating about affirmative action. White folks won't suddenly start voting for you—Krajek's still their man, and most of them want this stadium. And some black voters may decide to stay at home." His tone softened further. "You're better off attacking Peter Hall, like you've

been doing. Hall's the problem here, not a few crumbs for token minorities. The rich always find a way to get richer, so now Hall and Krajek are
playing footsie at the cost of millions of dollars of public money. That's
where the votes are."

"*That*," Bright rejoined, "is why Hall and Krajek gave a piece to
Larry Rockwell, the first great black player the Blues ever had. It's like
recruiting Joe Louis as a greeter at Caesars Palace."

Bright's undertone of bitterness did not obscure his professional
appreciation of Krajek's craft. Stella could appreciate it, too: Krajek was
playing the racial angles with consummate skill, siphoning black voters
while making Bright's best lines of attack as dangerous to him as to Krajek. But the conversation was too rarefied for her liking.

"I've got a couple of dead people here," she said. "What am I supposed to do with them?"

Face cupped in one hand, Sloan gazed at her with mild annoyance.
"They both ODed. Tina had a habit, and Fielding cruised the Scarberry.
One night they met *and . . .*"

His voice trailed off, a testament to human frailty too tiresome to
mention. "*And?*" Stella answered. "What happened next? And why? In
the narrow world of homicide, some of us are curious."

Bright, Stella thought, appeared somewhat shamed. He seemed to
reflect, then turned to Sloan. "Get Nat Dance over here," he said.

AT 6:45, the city had been dark for an hour, and the stadium, through
Bright's window, was a shadow among the lights. The three men and
Stella sat at Bright's conference table, picking at Chinese food in white
cartons. To Stella's surprise, Dance did so with chopsticks.

"Tommy Fielding," Dance summarized, "lived in a town house in
Steelton Heights. Plenty of people up and down the street. But nobody
really knew him, they tell us—he was up early, home late. All they
remember was Fielding's kid." His voice combined frustration with
laconic humor. "He used to give her piggyback rides, a couple of ladies
told me. So I think we can pretty much take *that* fact to the bank."

To Stella, Dance sounded as bemused as she: there was nothing in this
skimpy profile which bespoke a man on the edge. "What about work?"
Stella asked.

The detective turned to her. Instead of answering, he surprised her by
saying, "You don't believe Johnny Curran, do you."

Dance, Stella thought again, was very shrewd. "I believe Curran saw

Fielding's car in the Scarberry," she answered. "Or thought he did, a couple of days before Fielding died. But suppose Fielding was just driving through—"

"You don't get to Steelton Heights," Dance interjected in a mordant tone, "through the Scarberry."

Stella shrugged. "What I'm saying is this: We've got no prior drug use, no change of habits, no woman anyone knows about. Then one night Fielding up and dies with Welch and a syringe. And all that's getting him from *a* to *z* is Johnny Curran."

Dance seemed intrigued by Stella's tenacity. She felt Bright and Sloan watching them, weighing what they heard. "By now," Dance told her, "we've questioned everyone at Hall Development, right down to the night janitor. No erratic behavior, nothing out of the ordinary, except that Fielding seemed tense. His secretary says he'd started getting migraines."

"Was he taking anything?"

"Tylenol. No prescription drugs." Dance sat back, taking in the others. "He'd been working late—according to his parking receipts, he'd been punching out of the garage past eleven almost every night . . ."

"What about the night Curran said he saw him in the Scarberry? Curran put that between nine and nine-thirty."

Dance's expression became unfathomable. "Eight-thirty-six," he answered. "Earlier he'd said he felt sick."

So Dance, too, had wondered. "And the night Fielding died?" Stella asked.

"He left at seven-ten. His secretary says he'd been tired all day, complaining about headaches and not sleeping. The next morning, there was an empty bottle of Tylenol on his desk."

Sloan stuck his plastic fork in a pile of fried rice. "So Fielding was cracking up. One night he goes looking for Tina and some pain relief you don't get from a first-aid kit. The second night, he gets what he wants."

Watching Stella, Dance said nothing. "Maybe," Stella said to Sloan. "Or maybe a demented MBE, embittered because Fielding wouldn't pay him for not working, shot Fielding full of heroin and used Welch to cover it up. A token, you might say." She paused, then added softly, "The truth is, Charles, that you don't know shit. None of us does."

The profanity, unusual for Stella, caused Dance to laugh aloud. The sound seemed to startle Bright from thought. "Where are we with Novak?" he asked.

"No suspects," Dance responded. "No motive. People just keep dying on us, and no one's saying why."

Beyond irony, his tone reflected a knowledge, shared by Stella but not, perhaps, by the others: that homicide, the bluntest of crimes, was seldom this obscure, and when it was, the causes were often deep and complex. Unspoken were Stella's questions about case fixing and Vincent Moro: with renewed unease, she wondered which of these three men, if any, had preceded her to the dead-records room. "What I'm beginning to hope," Sloan said at last, "is that we never know. Let Jack Novak rest in peace."

Politically, Stella knew, it was hard to gauge what hurt Arthur more—that his friend had died in a maze of corruption, or from sadomasochism transmuting into rage. But finding the answer was Stella's job and, in this case, her need. "Tell that to the media," she answered.

Sloan puffed his cheeks. Quiet, Bright seemed to stare into an abyss—whatever pity he might feel for Novak, Stella guessed, his deepest wish was that he had never met him. "What about Fielding?" she asked him.

Once more, Stella had the sense of a reverie interrupted. "Take it slow," Bright told her. "I don't like the idea of Krajek using phony MBEs. But this is about two deaths, not a fishing expedition.

"You and Del Corso can take a look at Hall Development. But unless you can tie Fielding's death to his work, it can't be a long look." Glancing at Sloan, he concluded softly, "People might think you were playing politics."

FOR ANOTHER hour, Stella distractedly shuffled the papers on her desk—arrest reports, a computer run of current cases, a volume of grand jury testimony she could not seem to read. One envelope, the crime scene photos from Novak's apartment, went untouched—they told her too much, and nothing at all. She was about to leave when the telephone rang.

"Stella Marz," she answered.

There was a near silence, a whisper of soft breathing. "Don't want no cops," the woman said.

It was the same voice. The sound made Stella's nerve ends vibrate. "You know about Tina."

Another silence. "I'll talk to you," the woman said. "Not them."

The brittle resolve in her voice gave Stella pause. "All right," she answered. "Where do I find you?"

There was more hesitance now, the sound of her caller weighing her choices, the consequences of each. "Al's Corner," she said. "On Flower Street."

The Scarberry. For Stella, the last doubt resolved itself—the voice belonged to a hooker, someone who knew Tina Welch but had avoided the police. "How will I know you?"

A last brief silence. "You won't," the woman answered. "I'll know you. From television."

TWENTY

THE SCARBERRY District was stark, chill, barren. As Stella parked her car, a biting wind from Canada whistled off the lake through the dirty corridor along the Onondaga River called Flower Street. The name derived from the Scarberry's past, more than a century old, as a place where mill workers like Stella's great-grandfather, Carol Marzewski, might purchase vegetables, or even roses, from carts along the sidewalk.

This usage had passed quickly. The incongruous street name had survived further incarnations—a flickering, somewhat gaudy life in the twenties, with bars and nightclubs serving as an adjunct to the more upscale theater district; then as a darkened neighborhood of speakeasies, fed by bootleg liquor from warehouses nearby; then, in the forties, a last, sputtering saloon life. After that, the suburban postwar exodus had inexorably gutted Steelton's core and, especially, its centers of entertainment; the vast, baroque theaters went dark and fun seekers shunned the Scarberry altogether. Drugs replaced liquor; the district's few hotels, never proud, devolved into flophouses. The Scarberry became a dead end, grimy, graffiti scarred, and thinly peopled by urban ghosts—hookers, street dealers, the chattering half-mad homeless—who awaited the trickle of outsiders whose reasons for coming were, to Stella, as depressing as the district itself.

Looking up and down Flower Street, Stella tried to imagine Tommy Fielding gliding past her in a clean white Lexus.

It was not easy. There were three people on the block: a homeless man with a shopping cart, and two hookers in bright dresses and cheap vinyl boots—one blowing smoky wisps from a cigarette in the darkness, the other with her hands cupped close to her mouth, warming her fingers against the cold. The few commercial signs were dim or flickering neon, and the hotels and bars and Laundromats did not trouble to maintain them. Passing an alley as she walked toward Al's Corner, Stella saw another man sitting against a Dumpster. Like heroin, Stella thought, the Scarberry had been boiled down to its essence.

Al's Corner was part of the residue, a grungy hybrid of bar and restaurant and corner store which offered cigarettes; snack food; a breakfast, lunch, and dinner whose common denominators were cholesterol and grease; and a bar which served up primitive drinks and standard-brand domestic beers. There were few people inside: one, a gaunt young black woman with wary eyes, looked up from a corner table and met Stella's gaze.

Pausing, Stella wished that she could have brought Dance with her. Then she walked across the room. "You drive here?" the woman asked.

Stella nodded.

"Turn around and leave. I'll follow you to the car."

This procedure, Stella realized, mirrored the woman's nightly routine—a man found her, a deal was struck, and she followed him to his car. Most likely she had started her shift at a little before five that evening; her clients would get off work, perhaps drink a little for courage, then stop in the Scarberry for a hand job or blow job on the way home to their families. But prudence made Stella hesitate: she could not know what life had done to this woman, and some prostitutes carried knives. As if reading Stella's doubts, the hooker murmured, "Vice eats here for free."

Hands stuffed in the pockets of her raincoat, Stella looked down at her. The woman's hair was processed straight and, tinted auburn, seemed as unnatural as a wig; her face was a light brown, curiously immobile, and her eyes an almond shape, a hint, like Stella's own, of Eurasia. But the eyes themselves smoldered like burn holes.

Stella had to decide. Without a word, she turned and walked out the door.

She did not look back, heard no one behind her. The only change in the street was that one prostitute had vanished.

Just over a week ago, Stella reflected, Tina Welch had disappeared from these same streets, at the dead end of a life that had gone from abuse, perhaps, to teen pregnancy, prostitution, heroin addiction, and AIDS. A lot to show for a life that short.

Briskly, Stella walked to her car and, getting in, left the passenger door unlocked.

Like a shadow, the woman appeared through Stella's windshield. She glanced to either side, then slipped into the car, softly closing the door. Suddenly she froze, as if some preternatural instinct had warned her of danger; in the rearview mirror, Stella saw two large glowing circles, the headlights of a paddy wagon on patrol. The street was suddenly empty.

Her companion hunched forward. The van slowed, and then moved on, block by block, searching for human detritus.

The woman raised her head. "It's cold in here."

The simple statement, more observation than complaint, put Stella more at ease. She turned on the motor, then the heat.

"Tell me about Tina."

The woman looked around then, her thin face in shadows. "We worked this block," she answered. "Most nights, we tried to be here at the same time."

Homicide had taught Stella lessons most people did not know: one of Stella's early cases had involved a carpenter who had become a serial killer of low-end whores. It turned out that his mother had been one. "For protection," Stella said.

"We keep an eye out." The woman emitted a soft, surprising laugh. "They say there's more murders in marriage than prostitution, and maybe that's so. But you can't prove it by Steelton."

"Are you afraid of anyone in particular?"

The woman lit a menthol cigarette, lighter spitting in the darkness. She did not ask permission—it was a small act of entitlement, like a homeless man jaywalking. Emitting a slow trail of smoke, she answered, "Johns, muggers, murderers. Cops."

The last word was delivered with a harsh emphasis. "Vice?" Stella asked.

The woman stared out the windshield. "What you know about them?"

Cracking open the window, Stella considered the spirit in which she should answer. "That vice is where they send cops too crazy for narcotics. But the ones who hate women volunteer."

Though unfair, the answer had an element of truth. The woman turned to Stella for the first time.

"The ones that don't arrest you," she said flatly. "The guy that rapes you in the backseat of a squad car, then steals your money. The one that cuts off your drugs unless you snitch. The one who takes your driver's license unless you suck him off." Her voice became brittle. "The special one that takes you for a ride, beats and rapes you at night in Steelton Park, and dumps you by the side of the road. Because he can."

"That happened to you?"

The woman's smile was now a feral show of teeth, a stretching of lips which signaled that the question was foolish. "They got rules. What's the word—arr-o-gance?"

"Yes."

"Arrogance is picking up a whore, cutting her into pieces, stuffing her into an oil drum, and dumping it in the river. That was another friend of mine. Never found the one that killed her, did you."

Stella stared at her. The case, though fifteen years old now, was legendary; this woman must have been selling herself as an adolescent. "No," Stella answered. "We didn't."

"That's 'cause it was a cop."

"You *know* that?"

"The girl just disappeared." The woman's voice turned somber. "Someone that crazy, we can tell. No whore's gonna drive off with him. Unless the man's a cop."

"Give me names."

Even through the half-light obscuring the woman's features, Stella felt her black eyes smolder. "No way, Ms. Prosecutor. That trip to Steelton Park was my lucky day. The man told me what would happen if I wasn't *grateful* for his attentions. So I am."

Stella felt an anger of her own, and reminded herself why she had come. "What about Tina?" she asked. "Would *she* go for a ride with a man she didn't know? Someone who wasn't a cop?"

The woman drew deeply on her cigarette, its tip glowing orange in the darkness. "Maybe for drugs," she said finally. "Tina had a habit, a bad one. But she would have tried . . ." Her voice grew quiet, close to valedictory. "Tina knew the rules, and she loved her kid, a whole lot more than she loved herself."

"'The rules,'" Stella repeated. "What are they?"

"Use the hotels," the woman answered. "Five bucks for twenty minutes. Or do it in the alley. Some johns feel safer in the backseat of a car with the doors locked, so the druggies won't roll you. But you don't never drive off with someone you don't know."

For Stella, this matter-of-fact summary underscored the harshness surrounding them: the silence, the dark, the surreptitious, unpeopled aura of a place on the edge of law. As she watched, the remaining prostitute drifted into the alley with a slight, limping man—whether for drugs or sex, Stella could not guess. She wondered why there were no streetlights. "Did Tina have a pimp?" she asked.

"For protection?" The words held contempt. "Most whores in the Scarberry take their chances. Some try to look out for each other—like me and Tina."

But not well enough, the woman seemed to say. "How did you do that?" Stella asked.

The woman took a last drag. "We'd talk about the cops," she said. "What their games are, who had which undercover car. Or how to dope out a trick you've never seen before—the danger signs." Hastily, the woman opened the passenger door, flicked out the butt, and just as quickly closed it. But the surge of cold air, the sense of the world outside the car, seemed to sober her. "Only problem," she said, "drugged out like Tina was, you lose judgment. You OD, you get sick, you get killed. She was dead before she died."

Stella watched her. "Do you know a cop named Johnny Curran?"

The woman was still. Stella could see her thinking.

"He works narcotics," she prodded. "Years ago, he used to work vice."

Silent, the woman surveyed the street. "What's he look like?"

Stella marshaled her impressions. "Mid-fifties. Heavyset, thick white hair, white mustache, red-faced. Cold blue eyes. You'd remember the eyes."

The woman lit another cigarette. "Might have," she said with deliberateness, "if I'd seen him. Sounds like the man's before my time."

What was her time, Stella wondered, and how had she survived? Though the woman seemed older than Tina, she could not be much past thirty, and the immobile face had a seen-it-all look. "We always remember faces," the woman added softly, "and cars. Tina and I memorized plates. That's what I was wanting to tell you."

For the next few minutes, Stella listened, until her vision of the night Tina Welch died became at once hallucinatory and starkly clear.

THE WOMAN had already turned five tricks, the last one in a room at the Royale with a broken lamp and peeling wallpaper. When she returned to the lobby, slipping the desk clerk her money, the clock behind him read ten-thirty.

It was bitter out. Tina was there, slipping from the shadows into the pale light of the Royale's neon sign. Her pupils were pinpoints, her skin had a damp sheen, and her arms were crossed—the look of an addict, holding on tight. She barely spoke.

A dead woman, her friend thought, and wondered about Tina's five-year-old kid. Dead, too, she supposed, in ten, fifteen years; sometimes the woman swore she could feel people's lives closing in. It was the way this block of Flower Street felt, like it was closing in around her.

"You all right?" she asked Tina.

Staring at the sidewalk, Tina shook her head. There were tears in her eyes. But Tina said nothing; by unspoken consent, she drifted away, working her piece of the street. She looked like a wraith, a stick figure in red vinyl boots.

Minutes passed. From the next block, white-yellow headlights came toward them. The woman felt a familiar rhythm: the lights slowed as they drew closer, like eyes in the dark—purposeful, searching. They angled toward Tina, and stopped. No sound of brakes, no motor sound.

Squinting, the woman studied the car. Even in the darkened nether-world of Flower Street, she could see that it was white, unmarked, expensive looking. A car which suggested a safe, regular life.

Arms clasped against her chest, Tina was still.

A moment passed. Tina leaned forward, peering at the car as though its window had opened. She hesitated, then took two steps.

Each movement was tentative, wary; Tina cocked her head, perhaps listening, still keeping her distance. Then she looked down.

From the inside, the car's passenger door opened.

At first, Tina did not move. Then, as if drawn by something she saw or heard, she shuffled toward the car. Watching, the woman felt her face tense, a brief clench in her stomach. Then the shadowy form which was Tina vanished inside.

Noiseless, the car began moving. Weird they could make a motor so quiet.

The headlights grew larger. The woman peered at the license plate, registering the words. As the car passed, she saw Tina's face, the briefest of flickers, staring out at her. Then it turned a corner and was gone.

The woman exhaled. At least the plate would be easy to remember.

STELLA, TOO, felt a tightness in the pit of her stomach. She knew how the ride had ended—she had the pictures to prove it.

"You'd never seen the car before."

The woman shook her head. "Or Tina neither," she said. "Watching her, I could tell."

"Did he offer her smack, do you think?"

The woman began to puff on her cigarette, then paused, tip touching her lips. "Must have. Or money to buy some. Tina didn't have nothing all night."

"Who was Tina's connection?"

Turning, the woman gave her a weary look. "Anyone. There was a guy in the Scarberry sold to her when she had money. But I didn't see him all night."

"And you didn't see the driver."

"Too dark." The woman took a deep drag on the cigarette and her next words emerged in a sinuous curl of smoke and menthol. "That license plate. It belonged to the fool she died with?"

"Yes."

The woman nodded slowly. The soft noise she made was the sound of doubt resolved, of an end confirmed, in all of its sad inevitability. Just as, Stella supposed, it should be for her.

The woman threw out her cigarette.

Stella was silent, reflective. The woman's hand slid into her coat pocket. When she removed it, Stella saw a pair of manicuring scissors, lightly resting in her open palm.

Stella flinched. With a jerky reflex, she clasped the woman's wrist in a grip so strong that the woman let out a brief cry. But the scissors remained steady, balanced in her palm, and she looked at Stella with a bitter smile, smoldering eyes.

"Protection," she said harshly. "You stick it in their eyes." Pausing, she added with renewed quiet, "You still don't know much, do you?"

Slowly, Stella released her arm. "What's your name?"

The woman shook her head. "Back to work, Ms. Prosecutor," she said, and opened the car door.

She was out before Stella could speak. Seconds later, the street was empty; the only trace of her was the swift bite of air as she left, the smell of smoke.

PART THREE

TOMMY FIELDING

ONE

ON SUNDAY, one week after Novak's death, Stella found herself where she had been when Dance first called—at her desk, faced with a stack of papers.

The sameness made her dislocation all the more disturbing. For thirteen years she had found refuge in the certainties of a prosecutor—the boundaries; the rules; the duty to pursue, with the necessary balance of zeal and compassion, the cases which came before her. This routine had cauterized the rupture with her family, helped redeem the moral foundering marked by her affair with Jack Novak. But Novak's murder had made her past painfully central to a present in which she suddenly trusted no one, including herself.

Whatever the reason for Jack's death, he had been part of a corruption which surely involved others. However Tommy Fielding had overdosed, she could not yet explain his apparent mutation from a sexually passive workaholic to a purveyor of heroin to a Scarberry hooker. All Stella knew was that these two puzzles implicated a tangle of ambitions—Moro's, Bright's, Sloan's, Dance's, Krajek's, Hall's—which were years deep. And that those ambitions, in turn, might threaten her own.

Stella often shrank from self-reflection: it seemed at once too wounding and indulgent. But she feared self-delusion more. And she knew that a belief in the rightness of her own motives was a need so deep that, in the wrong circumstances, it could become a form of blindness.

She had begun withholding information from those she worked with, a first in her career. On the surface, her reasons were sound: the missing files, a prostitute's fear of the police. But there might be other reasons. Her need for answers about Jack Novak's past and present and, perhaps, for expiation. Her need to prove herself, again and again. The need which had become the central fact of a solitary life—to succeed Arthur Bright.

Suddenly, she could not stand this office. She could not stand herself. She could not stand that she had nowhere to go, and no one to go to.

Of course, there was always the cat. Or her father.

Despite the darkness of her mood, Stella laughed. Of these two alternatives, the only one who would recognize her had four legs. But she had not seen her father on the Sunday before; for the last time, she thought with mordant humor, Jack Novak had come between them. So she would sit for a time with the shell of Armin Marz. It was less a visit than a ritual—like going to Mass, she supposed, if one no longer believed in God. But sometimes she found a curious comfort in his silence: just as was their hope of love, their war was long behind them. Except, as Jack's death had reminded her, for the damage done to Stella's heart.

Enough. She would see her father, and then she would go home.

Walking through the unlit corridors, Stella thought of what "home" once had meant: a dark house in Warszawa. Then a child's voice startled her. It took a moment for her to realize that the child was not a figment of memory.

THE CHILD began laughing, joined by a man. It was a sound at once foreign and familiar—a father laughing with his daughter—and it came from Michael Del Corso's office.

Curious, Stella went there.

Michael was at his desk. Interrupted from work, he smiled at a picture drawn by the beautiful girl from the window. Her eyes, so serious then, now crinkled with sly triumph. Standing in the doorway, Stella felt out of place, a stranger eavesdropping on an intimate moment.

"If only," Michael said to Sofia, "I could make time work like that."

She should make her presence known, Stella supposed. "Like what?" she asked.

Surprised, Michael and Sofia looked up, and then Michael turned to his daughter. "Show Ms. Marz what you drew."

The girl hesitated, caught between pride and shyness, and then her father's pleasure won out. "Daddy was working," she said, "and I was bored. So I drew the day shorter."

Stella examined the picture. For a seven-year-old, it was a credible rendering of the view through Michael's window—some buildings, a cloud, the lake, a feeble sun. Except that the sun, in reality well above them, was, in Sofia's picture, setting into the lake. "It's time for us to leave," the girl said. "I drew it."

Stella smiled in surprise—as a child, she herself had been prosaic, if not downright literal. "This," she informed Michael, "must be what having an imagination is like. I think I'll try it, and leave, myself."

Sofia turned to him, hands on hips, a pantomime of command. "See?"

This, too, was a surprise. Stella had imagined Sofia as withdrawn and somewhat clingy; on what basis, she asked herself, had she ventured such a guess? Reasonably, Michael told his daughter, "It may be nighttime in your picture, but it's daytime in my office, and I still have work to do."

Sofia's face changed instantly. Her eyes became as grave as Stella remembered; at once she put down her crayon and wriggled into Michael's lap, face pressed against his neck. "Please," she pleaded with him, "I was feeling lonely."

He closed his eyes, and for an instant—it was only that—Stella sensed Michael thinking, too, of loneliness. Then the look turned to empathy for his child, and he kissed Sofia on the forehead.

Interpreting this as a consolation prize, the girl seemed close to tears. "You *promised* we'd go bowling."

Take her, Stella found herself thinking: the word "promised" carried a special weight, a plea for Michael's word to be good. Still, Michael's burden could not be easy—a child, abandoned, as he was, by a woman he still loved. "Sofia," Stella asked, "can you draw another picture?"

Sofia gave Stella a sideways, untrusting look—*you're trying to distract me*, her eyes said, *when all I want is my dad*. "Of you and your dad," Stella explained, "bowling. By the time you're finished, maybe he'll be finished, too."

The girl looked as forlorn as Stella felt clumsy. Quickly, Michael said, "That's a good idea, Sofia. I promise I won't take long."

He's rescuing me, Stella thought, *from my own awkwardness*. Turning, Sofia studied her father's face; at once Stella had a fresh, unsettling impression of a child become preternaturally old, watching out for her father as she wished him to watch out for her. Then Sofia turned to Stella and held out the crayon. "You do it," she said with resignation.

Stella accepted the crayon. For the next few minutes she would take care of this woman-child, whether Sofia wished it or not, by helping her take care of her father.

"Thanks," Michael said to them both.

THEY SAT on the floor, both cross-legged in blue jeans, Sofia a wraith compared to the solid little girl Stella knew herself to have been. After her first few strokes, Stella remembered something else: that even at Sofia's age, she had an intense dislike of passivity, of having anything done for her which she believed she could do for herself.

Completing the bowling alley, Stella said, "I'm not so good at pins," and returned the crayon to Sofia.

Sofia stared at the paper. Then, with surprising care, the girl drew a series of lines that looked more like birthday candles. As she did, Stella became uncomfortably aware of Michael's glance; perhaps he was thinking of when this girl had a mother, not a stranger helping him kill time, a woman who knew little about children beyond what childhood had taught her.

How might her own life have been changed, Stella wondered, had her father been less damaged? Perhaps she could watch the child next to her, and know what to do and say.

Sofia first had drawn the figure of a man, Stella realized. Then, judging by its smaller dimensions and dark curly hair, herself. The Sofia surrogate held a bowling ball in one hand, her father's hand in the other.

At the edge, some distance from the father and child, Sofia began drawing a third figure.

Stella watched, curious. As if sensing this, Sofia hesitated. Then she added more lines—a dress, the flowing curls of a woman's hair.

Quietly, Stella asked, "Who's that?"

"Mommy." Another pause. "She's in Australia, watching us bowl."

At seven, Sofia would know that this could not literally be true, any more than she believed that she could rearrange time by drawing a sunset. But unlike her delight at that touch of fantasy, her voice was toneless. Michael had become quite still.

Stella could think of nothing to say. All that she could do was to watch Sofia complete her mother with the attention this deserved.

Abruptly, Michael turned to them. "I'm through now," he told Sofia. "We can go."

Lost in her picture, the girl did not answer. With a show of busyness, Michael began tossing papers in a briefcase, vying for his daughter's attention. At last, Sofia raised her head and asked, "Can *she* come?"

It took a moment for Stella to realize that "she" was not the imaginary mother of the drawing but Stella herself. The child did not look at her.

But Michael did, eyes somber in his rough-hewn face. "Why don't you?" he asked.

These waters, Stella thought, were impassibly deep, and she had no gift for swimming. Tentative, Sofia turned to her.

Stella thought of Armin Marz, his mind gone dark, unaware that he was waiting for her. "Are you sure?" she said to Sofia. "I'm pretty good at bowling."

THE FIORE Lanes in Little Italy was packed with families, seniors, teens in packs or on dates. As the afternoon wore on, the crescendo rose—shouts, laughter, balls skidding, the thud of tumbling pins. Stella won three games in a row.

"You *are* good," Sofia informed Stella.

Stella smiled. Playing with Michael and Sofia, she found it easy to excel. The child was no athlete: she launched the heavy ball with skittering steps which ended in a ladylike hop as the ball, with agonizing slowness, commenced its unpredictable course. Whereas Michael believed in brute force; if extra points were awarded for the ability to scatter pins like kindling, Michael would be headed for the bowlers' hall of fame. But accuracy was a problem—those pins which remained standing after his initial assault were, too often, quite safe.

"I'm Polish," Stella informed the child. "In my neighborhood, we took bowling *very* seriously. I couldn't help being good."

The truth was somewhat different: in high school, Stella had been an athlete with a relentless determination that came from her fear of losing. The other girls deferred to her. Because Stella was also possessed of a calm self-control and was generous with advice, she became the captain of every team. She excelled at bowling, a marginal interest, only because she could not accept any less. But Michael, picking up on her comment, gave her a teasing smile.

"Tell Sofia," he suggested, "about Mayor Burek's bowling night."

The old story, while true, had never amused Stella that much: it came from the age of Polish jokes, and underscored how provincial—in the ethnic myths of Steelton—were the citizens of Warszawa. But the child seemed content now, happy to be part of the banter between two adults. Stella sat beside her on a bench.

"The mayor used to be from my neighborhood," she told Sofia. "One day the President of the United States asked Mayor and Mrs. Burek to dinner at the White House. Do you know what *that* is?"

Sofia folded her arms, miming impatience. "Sure. That's where the president lives. With all those lawyers."

Though she did not quite know why, Sofia knew she had made a joke;

at the corner of her eye, she glanced at her father, seeking affirmation. He sat down behind her. "Funny girl, Sofia. I may have to lock you up."

Sofia wriggled against him until he put his arm around her. Secure in his approval, she turned to Stella again. "What happened to the mayor?"

With a dry smile, Stella glanced at Michael. "He wouldn't go to the White House. Because it was Mrs. Burek's bowling night."

Sofia looked bemused. "That's all?"

"Not *all*. Just the part your father likes the best."

"What's the rest?"

"The president was Richard Nixon, the embodiment of evil." Catching Michael's eye again, Stella asked with mock solemnity, "Do you know what they used to call him?"

"What?"

"The Godfather."

Michael made a face. Sofia looked from Stella to her father, stimulated by the undercurrent of teasing. "Come on," Stella told the girl. "I'll teach you how to bowl."

Sofia hesitated, giving Stella a look of deep gravity, then burrowed deeper in Michael's lap. "I want Daddy to do it."

Against her will, Stella felt a small stab of rejection. Then she mustered a mild incredulity. "*Him?*"

The girl did not tease back. Silent, she seemed to struggle with emotions she did not understand. In a muted voice, she said, "Then I want you to come to our house. For dinner."

At this, Stella felt uneasy. Neither Sofia nor Michael met her gaze— the child looked confused; Michael's features were still, his eyes hooded. Stella guessed that part of Sofia's confusion was at her own role; she was both Michael's dependent, fearful of sharing him, and her vanished mother's surrogate, the child-wife. Whatever its roots, this was a dynamic Stella wanted no part of. Then, to her surprise, Sofia said softly, "Please."

Without thinking, Stella rested her fingers against the child's face. Michael glanced down at Sofia, the crown of her head resting against his chin, then back at Stella. The plea in his eyes, this gesture told her, was for his daughter.

"It's spaghetti," he said casually. "There's always extra. Sofia eats like her mom."

THE FLAT, though orderly, was small—a front room, a modest dining room, a cramped kitchen with a gas stove and an old refrigerator which wheezed with the strain of cooling. It felt like a memorial to his life with Maria: bought with the residue from paying off student loans; its furnishings less decorative than functional. Stella could imagine many evenings of dinners in, pasta and a bottle of Chianti; of luxuries deferred; of paychecks banked for the dream Maria had run from, a house in the suburbs, brothers or sisters for Sofia. One thing was certain—Stella did not belong here.

While Michael cooked, the aromas of wine-soaked spaghetti sauce drifting from the kitchen, Sofia showed Stella her room.

Its look, Stella realized, was warmer than the rest. Though the room was small, with little natural light, the pillows, bedspread, and curtains lent bright bursts of color; the shelves overflowed with books; the bed was covered with dolls. On the nightstand by Sofia's bed was a picture of Maria.

Stella could not help staring. The woman in the photograph was beautiful, almost ethereal, with flowing hair which offset delicate features, a mouth less sensual than perfectly formed. It was taken in a photographer's studio: in the soft, sentimental lighting typical of family photos, Maria could have passed for a beatified martyr, a sacrificial virgin from medieval lore. Except for the eyes: black and direct, they cut through the gauzy lighting with startling intensity. Was there such a thing, Stella wondered, as the look of an angry saint?

Sofia was watching her, Stella realized. Turning, Stella said, "You look like your mom."

Sofia's head cocked, eyes searching Stella's. She gave Stella a disturbing sense of a child waiting for information, afraid that even a stranger knew things about the real Maria Del Corso, the one who lived outside the picture, that Sofia did not.

For a time, they simply regarded each other. "Let's help your dad," Stella said.

DINNER WAS less easy than bowling.

They ate in the dining room, by candlelight at a wooden table, its leaves removed to make it small enough for a father and daughter. Stella tried to imagine their routine, what they talked about at night; when Stella asked about friends, or school, Sofia gave the perfunctory answers of a child whose thoughts were elsewhere. As soon as she could, albeit politely, Sofia excused herself and went to her room. As though embarrassed, Michael seemed to take a deep interest in the pattern of his china.

What to say, Stella wondered in the uncomfortable silence. But any comment seemed inappropriate. She was simply a woman this man worked for, and she was sorry to have come.

"I think she remembers Maria," Michael said abruptly. "At the end."

If he was trying to lessen Stella's discomfort, this was not the way. "Why do you say that?"

"We always ate together. After dinner, Sofia would bring out a book, and one of us would read it." Pausing, Michael took a sip of wine, watched the candle flickering between them. "A few months before she left, Maria stopped reading stories. For a while, Sofia would put the book in her mother's hands. Then, one night, she just stopped."

Stella was quiet. The flat was haunted by Maria, she thought, more surely than if she had been a ghost. Forgetting her own awkwardness, she wondered whom she felt worse for—Michael or Sofia. Sofia, she concluded: the wounds of childhood, because they were harder to comprehend, lingered. They could not be healed by reason.

It was a moment before Michael, with a father's prescience, glanced toward the hallway.

Standing just outside the light, Sofia watched them.

Once again, Stella sensed she had upset the balance in the house, the pull, invisible but strong, exercised by Maria Del Corso. Then Sofia came forward, stepping into the light, looking from Stella to her father. When she placed the book in Stella's hand, Stella felt her stomach knot.

"Can you read this to me?" Sofia asked.

WHEN AT last she was done, and Sofia was asleep, Stella found Michael in the living room. He was sipping a glass of red wine; another waited for Stella on the coffee table. Handing it to her, he said, "Sorry you got drafted. That's usually my job."

"I didn't mind." Stella sat at the other end of the couch. "Is it always that same story?"

"Not always. But often. It was one Maria used to read."

His words held an undertone, the recognition of, for Sofia, how emotionally loaded her request to Stella might be. But he said nothing more.

"Before you came in," he told her, "I was thinking about Fielding."

The change of subject surprised her, but perhaps Michael had begun to feel, as she did, that she had ventured too far into his life. "What about him?" Stella asked.

"How squeaky clean he was. The only problem anyone thinks he had was running Steelton 2000." Crossing his legs on the sofa, Michael cradled his wineglass. "I'm like you—it just seems weird that he'd up and die like that."

Stella took a small sip of wine. Concealing her trip to Scarberry from him had begun to feel dishonest. "If I tell you something," she said at last, "can you sit on it? At least until I think things through."

Michael considered her. "All right."

Briefly, she told him about the nameless hooker—her fear of police, her account of Tina Welch getting into Fielding's car. As she spoke, Michael listened attentively, asking no questions.

"I guess that clinches it," he finally said. "First, Johnny Curran spots Fielding cruising the Scarberry. Two nights later, a hooker sees Tina Welch drive off with him. For whatever reason, Fielding's life had jumped the tracks."

"But why did she decide to go? Tina's friend says she looked pretty reluctant."

"Probably sizing him up. What Tina sees is a clean guy, in a clean car, flashing money on a night when she needs heroin. She *had* to go." Sinking farther into the coach, Michael contemplated the ceiling, as though picturing what followed. "She's already got the needle in her purse, and she knows where to convert Fielding's cash to drugs. So they go there, and then go to Fielding's town house."

"Where he overdoses on heroin?" Stella asked. "Why? Because Tommy Fielding—who's probably never shot up before—decides he needs a little spontaneity? After all, Tina Welch is a hooker and smackhead, and he's known her for at least an hour. So naturally he trusts her with his life."

Michael laughed aloud. Stella did not. "He goes home at seven-ten," she persisted, "with a migraine headache. He has a bachelor's dinner, a beer and a sandwich. You'd expect him to switch on a basketball game, not drive a half hour to the Scarberry." She put down her glass. "Someone dies like this, and usually you can find half a dozen people to say they've seen it coming. We don't have one."

Listening, Michael's amusement had vanished. "It doesn't have to make sense, Stella. I've read Kate Micelli's autopsy report, and now you've got a witness."

"Who may not have told me all she knows."

Michael shrugged. "Maybe about the vice squad, although she sounds a little paranoid—I don't think too many of those guys go around butchering whores for sport. But it doesn't sound like she held back about Tina."

This was true. Silent, Stella contemplated her wine. "So," Michael said in a cautious tone, "you still want to look at Steelton 2000."

Stella hesitated, then nodded. She did not explain herself.

Michael, too, became quiet. Stella sensed him trying to follow her thoughts. "Those five drug files," he finally said. "Did you ever find them?"

This question surprised her. Though his inquiry could have been routine, she doubted that it was. *Where are you going with all this,* he seemed to be asking, *and who is it you distrust?* But Stella could not have told him had she wanted to. "No," she answered. "I've given up looking."

Still Michael seemed to study her. She felt guarded again, as she had with Sofia. "It's late," she said. "I'd better get going."

Her abruptness appeared to unsettle him. A new expression crossed his face—tentative, and, Stella thought, almost sheepish. Then it seemed to resolve itself in a decision to speak.

"I really appreciated today—how you were with Sofia." He sat straighter, looking into Stella's face. "I know you had other things to do. But I watched her—it's good for her to spend time with a woman who isn't her grandmother. Just a friend, who likes her."

Stella smiled. "I *do* like her. I'm no expert, but it seems as if you're doing all right."

Michael considered this, eyes veiled now. Stella could not help but feel him remembering Maria, still in this house, slipping away from them both.

"Thank Sofia for me," she said. "Tell her I had a nice day."

Quickly, she left.

TWO

Early the next morning, Stella drove to Steelton Heights.

The road curled upward. Behind Stella was the city—the river valley of steel mills the corroded color of rust; concrete highways; low-slung warehouses; the mix of old sandstone office buildings and sinewy glass-and-steel towers; the stadium, rising beside the lake; and, closer, the bleak streets of the East Side. Then she reached a barrier of wooded hills and the city seemed suddenly distant, a specter glimpsed through leafless trees.

Here, the homes were square, massive, three storied, in the style of the early twentieth century. They sat with the sense of weight that time brings: they had been built with the first generation of wealth from the mills, and, though removed, still overlooked the city which brought them into being. It had taken another two generations, Stella reflected, before this proprietary vista had yielded to genteel estates such as Peter Hall's, owned by families which had spurned the city altogether. It was easier to feel no responsibility, she supposed, for what one chooses not to see.

Tommy Fielding's street, Knightsbridge Court, was from the same period, but of a different design—a row of three-story town houses, Bostonian in appearance, which lined both sides of a narrow brick lane. Given their vintage, they lacked garages—a disadvantage in Steelton's harsh winters—but offered a smartness which appealed to young professionals and, on Fielding's side, panoramic views of the city and the lake beyond.

His town house was on the right, second to last in a row of six. Stella parked there and got out.

The door was padlocked, with crime-scene tape across it and, poignantly, a wreath which reflected that, less than four weeks ago, it had been Christmas. Stella wondered if he had kept it there for his daughter; she recalled that the girl was seven, like Sofia, an age when Christmas was still mystical and toys arrived by magic. It had been so in her own childhood, when the mills glowed and Armin Marz, still master of his fate, had hidden presents for his daughters in the home he no longer recalled.

This home, Fielding's, was as well maintained as she had imagined. The shrubs were trimmed, the shutters painted. In the backyard was a brick patio, with a wrought-iron table and chairs, from which, next spring, Fielding could have watched the glow of the stadium at night.

Now the fact of death pervaded his house. It was dark, silent, its curtains drawn. Eleven days before, Fielding had brought Tina Welch here from the Scarberry. No one had seen them; they had slipped like ghosts into this pristine setting and, in the morning, had been found dead. Now that Stella was here, the image unsettled her all the more.

The maid had found their bodies; an anonymous caller had spared Jack Novak's maid the same fate. In either case, Stella supposed, there was no one else with a key. Yet, if Missy Allen was to be believed, Jack Novak's final visitor had also come and gone without a trace. Except for Novak's body.

Stella returned to her car and drove to the Scarberry District.

IT WAS a ghost town. The whores were gone; wire security mesh was drawn across the darkened windows of bleak storefronts. The only constants were the bitter wind, the homeless man Stella had seen, now huddled in the alley beside a Dumpster. She tried to summon an image of Fielding's white Lexus, come for Tina Welch, a whisper in the stillness.

Stella checked her watch. The trip from Steelton Heights, slightly complicated by early morning traffic, had taken thirty-four minutes.

Heading for the office, Stella used her car phone to reach Nat Dance at home.

ANSWERING, HIS voice was neither welcoming nor annoyed.

"Do you remember," she asked, "the porn magazine you found in Fielding's drawer?"

"Uh-huh. Pages and pages of naked black women."

Stella stopped at a red light. "Did the maid ever see that one before? Or anything like it?"

"No."

"Okay. When you were checking out whether Novak was into S and M—sex shops, the mail he got—did you also ask about Fielding?"

She could imagine Dance's stillness, a sign of reflection, as he pondered this. He did not ask Stella's reasons. "It'll take a few days," he answered. "I'll let you know."

THE FIRST thing Stella did at the office was make coffee. The second was to call Kate Micelli.

Waiting for Kate to wind up another conversation, she gazed out at the stadium. It was before eight-thirty, and the bowl was empty, the cranes and earthmovers still. By nine it would come to life.

A Christmas tree for amateurs, Paul Harshman had called it. Everyone who touched it was guaranteed to profit.

Kate Micelli came on.

"I've got a trivia question for you," Stella said. "How long did it take Tommy Fielding to digest his ham sandwich?"

"The Last Supper? I don't think he had, quite. But I'd have to look at my autopsy notes. Why do you care?"

"Digestion stops with death, obviously. If you can tell me, I'd like to know how much time had passed after he ate the sandwich." Stella began pacing. "It would have taken him at least an hour to drive to the Scarberry, pick up Tina, and drive back to Steelton Heights. More if they shopped for heroin."

"Maybe he didn't go home first."

"No? So first he picks up a hooker, goes home, makes a ham sandwich, pours himself a beer, and *then* shoots up with heroin?"

Micelli laughed. "Maybe he was hungry. Maybe Tina wasn't. Maybe he was a lousy host." She stopped for a moment. "No, I guess I see your point. You'd like the sequence to make sense. Assuming you can expect that here."

Tina's hooker friend, Stella did not mention, believed that she had seen Fielding's Lexus at around ten-thirty. "He left work after seven," Stella said, "claiming he had a migraine headache. We don't know what happened after that."

"I don't think the sandwich will tell you much," Micelli answered. "But I'll check and call you back. Give me a couple of hours, though."

IT WAS one of those mornings when Stella felt energized, her nerves pulsing with caffeine, her mind popping with questions. She went by Michael's office three times before she found him.

He was hanging his overcoat on a metal coatrack. Seeing her, he smiled. "That was nice last night," he told her. "Thanks again for coming."

Interrupted in her mission, Stella mustered a distracted smile of her own. "How's Sofia?"

"Very cheerful this morning. But she's a woman of many moods." Detecting Stella's, he asked, "So what's up?"

Stella sat. "I've been thinking about Jack Novak—the unexplained payments, the anomalous case results. We got into all that because I remembered some of the cases from when I worked there. That's why they're so old."

"True. But Dance can't find any recent problems, right?"

Stella nodded. "*Current* problems," she amended. "Still, you tell me—and Saul Ravin tells me—that in the last ten years the drug trade's gotten nastier, that now there's far more pressure on Vincent Moro from both law enforcement and competitors. That had to mean more pressure on Jack to get results, and to keep Moro insulated."

Michael considered this. "Ten years," he said, "is a long time. That's a lot of paper to plow through without knowing what you're looking for."

"Why don't you start with his financial records? If you find a big payment for 'business advice,' like the ones from Crown Limousine, then you can go through his case files from around the same time."

Michael looked dubious. "It's still pretty time-consuming. Some of these cases go on for a while."

Stella reflected. "Stick to the last four years," she told him. What she did not add was that this was the period during which Arthur Bright had been the County Prosecutor, and Charles Sloan, now First Assistant, had stopped prosecuting drug cases. But whether Michael made the connection, she could not tell.

"What you're thinking," he said at last, "is that Novak screwed something up, and it got him killed."

"Or *knew* something that got him killed. What else do we have here?"

"I don't know." He paused, looking at her with open curiosity. "What does Dance have?"

"Nothing."

He was not satisfied, Stella sensed. But he did not challenge her further. "I was going to City Hall this morning," he told her. "Look up the MBE compliance reports on Steelton 2000. Which do I do first?"

It was always like this, Stella thought. The office never had enough resources; even with cases as incendiary as these, she was always choosing one over the other, always preparing to justify herself to Charles Sloan. "Steelton 2000," she finally answered. "When you get through with that, Moro will still be with us, and Jack will still be dead."

THREE

IT WAS past four o'clock when Michael appeared in Stella's office, and spread a sheaf of papers on her desk. "If you believe these," he said, "Steelton 2000 is the epitome of social justice."

"What are they, exactly?"

"The paper trail." Neatly, Michael separated the papers into four stacks, and pointed to the first one. "*Those*," he continued, "are the agreements between Hall Development and the city, committing Steelton 2000 to having thirty percent of the work performed by MBEs, and thirty percent of the workers be minorities.

"The next is Hall's agreement with a minority general contractor, a company called the Alliance Company." His finger stabbed the third pile. "These are Hall Development's monthly compliance reports, certifying that the compliance goals are being met."

Turning the documents so that Stella could read them, Michael pointed out the signature under "Hall Development Corporation"; in neat cursive, as precise as letters on a blueprint, Stella read, "Thomas R. Fielding."

"The last group," Michael concluded, "are certificates signed by the city's MBE compliance inspector, certifying that Fielding's reports are accurate. There's a certificate for every report."

Sitting, Michael waited for Stella to peruse the paperwork. Fielding's reports were precise, she saw, several pages of detailed figures for each month. From what she had heard of him, Stella would have expected no less. But she felt Michael watching her, expectant.

"So what's the catch?" she asked.

"The dates of Fielding's reports, for one thing."

Stella examined them again, one by one. There were reports for the first eleven months of the project, through October, submitted within two weeks of the month's end. But she found no reports for November and December, though it was now the middle of January.

She glanced up at Michael. "He fell one month behind," she said. "But he was dead by the middle of January."

"Take a look at the agreement between Hall and the city. Page two—the date the compliance reports were due."

Stella did that. "'The reports of compliance,'" she read, "'shall be filed within ten business days after the end of each month.'

"What does that tell you?" she asked Michael.

"Only the obvious—that Fielding was late, or had stopped filing reports altogether."

Pausing, Stella thought of her interview with Peter Hall, the stack of papers at his side. "*Whatever his reasons,*" Hall had said, "*Tommy left me his job to do.*"

"The other thing," Michael went on, "is the agreement between Hall and this minority general contractor, Alliance Company."

"I don't know whether or not this is usual. But in return for assuring sufficient minority participation, as certified by Hall and the city, Alliance gets ten percent of Hall Development's share of the savings clause. That could be worth an extra couple of million."

Stella reflected. "What do we know about Alliance—anything?"

"Only the name of their president. The guy who signed the agreement."

Quickly, Stella turned to the last page of the agreement. The president of Alliance, it turned out, was Lawrence J. Rockwell. She found herself smiling.

"Larry Rockwell," she said. "So that's what old center fielders do, besides becoming minority owners of baseball teams. They build things."

Michael hunched forward, hands resting on his knees, watching her. "And rake in bonuses. As long as Tommy Fielding keeps turning in reports."

"Are you saying there's something wrong?"

Michael shook his head. "As far as it goes, Fielding's paperwork's pretty impressive. But like Harshman said, Fielding was in the crosshairs."

Silent, Stella looked again at the date of Fielding's last report. It was November 9—two months before his death. "I'm wondering why he fell behind. Too many headaches? No one calls him a procrastinator."

Michael said nothing. The manner of Fielding's death kept nagging her. The cause was clear: yet it seemed so incongruous, and the one man who could explain it was dead.

Frustrated, she went to the window, staring at the construction site.

"*Everyone who touches this deal,*" Harshman had told her, "*was guaranteed to profit. Except for the city.*"

"You remember what was there before?" she finally said.

"Nothing much. An old warehouse or two, some abandoned railroad yards, a private airport nobody used. The land wouldn't have cost much to buy or clear out—building there must have saved the city money, and it's probably as good a site as any."

"Except that it's windy, and cold in the spring—the weather comes straight from Canada." Turning to Michael, she asked, "Do we know how much the city paid for it?"

"No. But I can find out."

"I'd be curious," Stella answered. "And let's go visit the site. I'd like to see firsthand what Tommy Fielding saw."

WHEN STELLA checked her messages, there was one from Kate Micelli. Quickly, Stella returned the call.

Micelli sounded harried. "I looked over my autopsy notes," she said without preface. "Fielding had hardly digested the sandwich at all. Meaning that he died soon after eating it."

"How soon?"

"Less than an hour, I'd say."

"So," Stella pursued, "he'd have to have eaten the sandwich after picking up Tina. And shortly before they shot up."

"Seems like it. I'm sorry, Stella, but I've got to run out to the Scarberry."

"For what?"

"A whore in a Dumpster. Nat says her throat's cut."

Suddenly Stella felt cold. "I'll meet you there," she said.

DUSK WAS falling, chill and grainy, when Stella arrived.

Squad cars were clustered by the alley off Flower Street, red lights flashing in the dimness. As Stella passed, the chatter of a police radio issued from a car with its door left ajar. The lights of another car, aimed into the alley, turned it shadowy yellow, fading into the darkness of encroaching night.

Dance and Micelli stood together in the half-light, next to a Dumpster into which a crime-lab technician peered. Across the alley two plain-clothes detectives spoke to the same homeless man Stella had seen that morning. In the quiet—muted voices, the drone of the police radio—Stella's heels clicked on the dirty asphalt.

Dance looked up at her. His eyes widened slightly, signaling surprise. *What are you doing here?* his expression said. Stella had the same question for him; this death seemed too low a priority to attract the Chief of Detectives.

"What happened here?" she demanded.

Dance angled his head toward the homeless man. "He found her here, he says, when he was scrounging for food. Says he's got no idea what happened. Except for what's obvious."

Stella took a flashlight from the crime-lab technician and, walking to the Dumpster, aimed it down into the refuse.

The woman lay in a pile of cartons, paper cups, and fast-food wrappers. Stella found the legs first, and then slowly brought the light to her face.

She stared at Stella fixedly. But her eyes were no longer burn holes; the life was gone from them and, with it, the anger.

Stella froze, gazing back at her.

The woman's throat was deeply slashed. Her head twisted away from her neck at an angle impossible in life.

Turning, Stella asked Dance, "Do we know her name?"

"Natasha Tillman, her driver's license says."

"What else?"

Micelli stepped forward in the harsh light. Her hawklike face seemed more severe, a Goya portrait. "She's been here for a while—since sometime last night, I'd say. The body's cold, and rigor's set in."

Stella glanced at the homeless man. "How long has *he* been here?"

"Early morning. He's not exactly sure. Left his watch at home, I guess."

Stella crossed her arms, shivering in the cold. This morning, when she had passed here, Tillman's body had been in the Dumpster for several hours. She must have died the night before, sometime after Stella had left Michael Del Corso's.

The night before that, Tillman had sat in Stella's car. Less to help Stella, she thought now, than to satisfy herself as to how Tina Welch had died.

Had someone seen them? Stella wondered. Silent, she watched the lab technician reach inside the pocket of Tillman's raincoat. A pair of manicure scissors glinted in his hand.

However Tillman had died, Stella guessed, she had made no move to defend herself. A sense of complicity entered Stella's mind, undefined yet haunting.

Dance moved closer. In the chill, his breath was a soft mist. "What is this to you?" he asked.

Stella met his eyes. "Welch worked this block," she answered. She did not explain the rest.

FOUR

EARLY THE next morning, Stella and Michael walked from the office to Steelton 2000.

It was cold; a stiff wind from Lake Erie made their overcoats slap like laundry on a clothesline. Stella's face felt numb. Like Michael, she held a styrofoam cup of coffee in her hand, a centrifuge of warmth as she tasted the thin, bitter liquid.

"It's a bitch out," Michael said. "You wonder if spring will ever come."

The half-built stadium rose before them like ruins, and the barren block in front of it resembled a landscape after a war. The difference was in the hovering cranes, the rumble of cement mixers, the trucks laden with steel and lumber, the distant call of a man's voice issuing commands. To Stella, this was the pulse of revival where, months before, there had been silence and decay.

They stopped in the shadow of the stadium, looking up at the steel frame rising skyward. From her window, the project looked like a scale model, a child's building kit. But at the foot of the project she had a sense of mass and majesty.

"Impressive," Michael murmured.

She nodded. Between them and the stadium was a makeshift chain-link fence, perhaps ten feet high, with a swinging gate large enough to admit trucks, earthmovers, heavy equipment. Stella and Michael went to the gate and showed their identification to the security guard, a uniformed black man.

He looked from one to the other with resentful wariness, the white of his eyes made pink by wind and cold. Then he told them to wait. They did, shivering, until the guard returned accompanied by a white man with a shock of black hair beneath his metal helmet and the lean, weathered look of a strip of beef jerky.

The man was Chuck Panos, he said—a construction supervisor for the general contractor, Farrelli Brothers. His words were sparing, as though the wind made him bite them off.

"We wanted to talk to the Alliance Company," Stella explained. "You can help us find their supervisor."

Panos folded his arms, weight shifting slightly. "Don't know that he's here right now."

Michael stepped forward, bulkier than Panos, half a head taller; with no humor in his face, he gave off a faint, but noticeable, air of menace. "They've got a trailer, don't they."

It was not a question, or a request. Panos looked up at Michael, shrugged, and led them wordlessly inside.

They stood at the foot of an enormous steel pylon. Above was a network of steel and wire from which the voices of workers came; inside the bowl of the stadium cranes and backhoes and cement mixers moved across the scarred, frozen earth. To the left of Stella, Michael, and Panos, a semicircle of trailers bore the names of contractors and subs. Panos led them past several beat-up trailers until they reached one labeled Alliance. Instead of leaving, he opened the door of the trailer and preceded them inside.

The interior was neat and bare—a few laminated-wood desks with little paper on them—reminding Stella of an abandoned schoolroom. The sole person inside was a young black woman, sitting at the only desk with a telephone. Panos jerked his thumb at Stella and Michael, and said, "They're looking for the boss."

The woman peered at him through wire-rimmed glasses. "Mr. Spain?" she asked. "He's not in."

Michael stepped between Panos and the woman. "When *will* he be in?" he asked.

The woman moved her shoulders fractionally. After a moment, Stella put her card on the desk, and said, quietly but firmly, "Have Mr. Spain call me."

Panos opened the door, standing to the side. He waited for Stella and Michael to exit, then closed the door behind them.

"Is Mr. Spain here usually?" Stella asked matter-of-factly. "Or anyone?"

At the corner of her eye, she saw Michael smile to himself, gazing at the workmen on the metal scaffolding above. "Depends on the work," Panos answered curtly, walking toward the gate. Following, Stella discovered that Michael had fallen behind them.

He remained near the Alliance trailer, hands shoved in his pockets, looking about him with an air of leisurely interest. He appeared to be whistling, too softly to hear.

Hands on hips, Panos watched him, a study in impatience.

Michael took no notice. It was a moment before he rejoined Panos and Stella.

Panos opened the gate. When they passed through, Stella heard it clank behind them.

Silent, they walked toward the beaux arts ornament which was their office, a facade which hid the shabbiness inside.

"So what did you notice?" Stella asked.

"That the phone never rang." Michael turned to her. "See any black folks?"

"The guard. The receptionist. One guy up above."

Michael nodded. "Maybe they'll come back tomorrow," he said after a time. "My dad always said that they don't like the cold."

ONCE IN her office, Stella called Dance on his beeper. It took less than five minutes for her telephone to ring.

"Nat Dance," the familiar voice said. Though seemingly neutral, his tone carried, to Stella, a distinct note of coolness.

"Tillman," she said. "Have anything?"

"Not much. Seems like maybe she worked the block alone last night." He paused, then added, "A desk clerk on a smoke break remembers seeing her get in a car last night—an old one, brown, beat-up. He didn't know the make."

"Did he see her get out again?"

Another pause. "It drove away," Dance said finally, "with Tillman inside."

"That's it?"

"Last time anyone saw her. As of now."

Stella pondered this. "Tillman must have come back," she told Dance. "It makes no sense for the killer to cut her throat somewhere else, drive back to the Scarberry, and throw her inside the Dumpster."

"You wouldn't think."

Was there a new note in his voice, Stella thought—a muted reproof? She decided to change the subject. "When you were checking out Fielding," she said, "did you visit the construction site?"

"Sure."

"Did you talk to anyone at the Alliance Company?"

"Uh-huh. Guy named Spain."

"Who else was in the trailer?"

Dance was quiet. "Him. A receptionist. A bookkeeper, I think."

"What about the workforce? Did it look like there were enough minorities?"

"I wasn't counting. But yeah, there were some. About what you'd expect." Dance's voice grew pointed. "I guess you must have dropped in."

Stella hesitated. "I did," she said crisply. "Things were whiter than white. Alliance was a ghost town."

Dance gave a noncommittal grunt. "When you were there," Stella asked, "did they expect you?"

Dance seemed to consider this. "Yeah," he answered. "I'd called ahead. I wanted to see the top people."

"Who'd you arrange it with?"

"Hall."

Stella thanked him, and hung up.

MICHAEL, SHE realized, was standing in her office door.

His look was quite different than it had been moments before—tentative, apologetic. "I hate to ask," he said. "But can I borrow your car? Sofia's school called—she's feeling sick to her stomach, it's my folks' shopping day, and *I* took the bus."

The narrative bespoke cumulative frustration: Michael had been focused on his job and then was interrupted by the reminder, as arbitrary and unpredictable as a child's needs, that what Stella took for granted was a luxury for him. He did not talk much about Sofia to people, Stella surmised, and he seemed embarrassed now. But at least she knew Sofia.

"Sure," Stella answered, and fished her keys from her purse. "I hope she's all right."

"She will be. Kids just get sick." Taking the keys, he said, "I was going to look at the land sales this afternoon. For the stadium."

"It'll keep." Stella smiled. "Just get back before seven. That's got my car key and my house key. I don't want to sleep here."

THE THREE hours until he returned passed quickly—fencing with Leary of the *Press* about the "progress" in Jack Novak's murder. Then a string of phone calls punctuated by fragments of thought: about the connections, if any, between Fielding's death, Tillman's murder, and Steelton 2000; about who in the office might have taken the missing files; about her formless suspicions of Dance. And then, at more leisure, asking herself why she had trusted no one but Michael about her meeting with Tillman.

With the air of a man harassed, Michael came through the doorway, tossing Stella's keys on her desk.

"How was Sofia?" Stella asked.

"Fine." He paused, then sat abruptly, furrows deepening in his fore-head. "You know what I think? It wasn't her stomach. She just wanted to see if I'd come."

Stella studied him. It was remarkable how a man who, hours before, had seemed so confident could become so vulnerable. Quietly, Stella asked, "Or if you'd left?"

Michael's mouth turned down, making the rugged face seem weary. "Maybe that, too. Yeah, maybe so." He seemed to slump in his chair. "All I really want to do, Stella, is buy you a drink. And myself one."

Stella regarded him, feeling caution and friendship at war. "That'll keep, too," she answered.

FIVE

IT WAS two more days—for Stella, frustrating and uneventful—before Michael completed his search of land records; not until five in the afternoon that they gained an audience with Bright and Sloan.

"Explain Lakefront Corporation," Stella asked Michael.

She looked around Bright's conference table. The County Prosecutor sat at the end, a little distant from the others, still sleek and cool after a day of campaigning, his double-breasted suit still crisp looking. Whereas Sloan resembled an unmade bed—rumpled, his tie askew, the soft pillow of his belly straining his shirtfront. The one trait shared between them was intensity.

"Lakefront," Michael began, "owned the land they're building on. And still owns the parcels around it."

Sloan glanced at Bright. "Every one?"

"That's right."

Facing Michael again, Sloan's voice was thick with suspicion. "When did *that* happen?"

"Just in time," Michael answered calmly. "Right before Krajek announced his deal with Hall, and put it to the voters."

Stella leaned forward. "Somebody *knew*," she said to Bright. "They knew Krajek's plan, and where the stadium was going. They bought low, and sold high."

Bright took off his glasses, rubbing them absently, his eyes, though focused on the table, intent with thought. "*How* high?" Sloan asked.

Stella glanced at Michael. "About five million dollars in profit," he answered.

Bright replaced his glasses. Softly, he asked Michael, "Who's Lakefront?"

"The land documents are signed by a Conrad Breem, whoever *he* is." Michael's tone became ironic. "Obviously, a shrewd businessman. You might even say clairvoyant."

"Or a front." Sloan turned to the prosecutor. "Krajek had to know about this, Arthur. I'll bet you a four-year lease on City Hall that Lake-front's a synonym for 'Tom Krajek's pals.'"

"Maybe," Bright answered slowly. "But sometimes people just hear things, especially land sharks. Where *else* would they put a stadium downtown?" He turned to Stella. "Why haven't our friends in the media cottoned on to Lakefront?"

"The paper trail," Michael interjected. "In most cases, Lakefront bought the business which owned the land, and sold it in their name. It took me two days to figure all this out, and I know how to look."

"Does that sound innocent to *you*?" Sloan asked Arthur. "It's a fuck-ing real estate play, and someone's gotten rich off it."

"Who?" Bright asked rhetorically.

"That," Stella answered, "depends on who Lakefront is. Michael says finding out could take a while."

"I'd have to go to the State Bureau of Corporations," Michael explained. "Even that might not help much. You could hit a string of dummy subsidiaries, each owned by the next, going back to some outfit in Bimini owned by God knows who."

"Oh, it would *help*," Sloan said emphatically. "Show me someone who's not a crook who goes to all that trouble."

Bright faced him. "Who?" he repeated softly.

This, Stella knew, was a clash of ambitions, more transparent than the two men usually permitted her to see. The Democratic primary, though clearly dispositive of the mayoral race, was still three months away. Bright feared looking desperate; Sloan feared Bright would lose, killing Sloan's hopes of succeeding him. For once, Stella thought sar-donically, she and Sloan were allies. But she felt sympathy for Arthur; he was still the County Prosecutor, and his prudence did the office credit.

"Ask Krajek," Sloan said stubbornly. "Ask him at the next debate."

"And then what, Charles, after Tom asks *me* to tell him who Lake-front is. Do I turn on him, like Charles Laughton in *Witness for the Prosecution*, and whisper, 'Does the name Conrad Breem mean anything to you?'"

Sloan did not rise to the bait. "You impanel a grand jury," he said, "and put Mr. Breem's ass in the witness chair."

"For what?" Bright's sarcasm became open. "Before you call a wit-ness, you're supposed to know the questions . . ."

"You know the questions," Sloan snapped. "Who owns Lakefront? Why did you start buying land? Who *told* you to buy it?"

"It also would be nice," Stella interjected, "to know the answers. Finding out who Breem *is* seems like the minimum requirement."

"Why don't you do that," Bright said to Michael. "Then check with the Department of Corporations." He turned to Sloan, his tone conciliatory. "I can't use the grand jury for a fishing expedition, Charles. You know that."

Usually fidgety, the First Assistant was still. Slowly, but emphatically, he answered, "That's what they're for."

"Not just before an election. Not without more than we have."

There was silence. "Maybe there is more," Stella finally said. "Something at least arguably connected to Tommy Fielding."

Bright seemed startled, then even more alert. "What is it?"

"The minority general contractor, Alliance. Turns out that Larry Rockwell's its president." She paused, glancing at Sloan. "Two days ago, we went to the stadium. Alliance has a trailer, but almost no one from the company was around. And there were about as many African-Americans on the site as there are in this room."

Bright gave her a wintry smile. "Krajek's saving the black community, Stella. What a friend we have in Steelton 2000."

"That's what Fielding's compliance reports showed, certified by the city. Except that he died owing two months' worth of back paperwork." Her tone became pointed. "You said you'd heard qualified black contractors couldn't get jobs."

Turning, Bright stared pensively out the window. "What you're implying," Sloan said to Stella, "is that Larry Rockwell's an all-purpose front?"

"I don't know that. We *do* know that Alliance gets a big chunk of the savings clause for helping Steelton 2000 meet their MBE requirements. But only if Fielding files the reports and the city inspector certifies them."

Bright, Stella noticed, was listening closely again. "Who stands to make money," Sloan asked, "besides Alliance? If MBEs are getting paid for not working, and Alliance is getting paid for supplying them, Hall Development is getting screwed two ways."

Michael smiled. "Exactly."

"But," Bright interjected, "Fielding *was* submitting the reports, as Hall's representative, and the city *was* certifying them. Unless he and the inspectors were conspiring to screw his boss."

Sloan nodded. "What bothers me is saying, in front of God and everyone, that Larry Rockwell is nothing but a goddamn token."

Stella turned to Bright. "Maybe," she said blandly, "we can put Rockwell's ass in front of the grand jury. That's what they're for."

Bright laughed aloud, a barking, mirthless sound. Sloan stared at Stella with open hostility. "You're the one who brought this up. Where the hell do we go with it?"

Bright raised a hand. In a plaintive, pitch-perfect imitation of Rodney King, he asked, "'Can't we all just get along?'"

The muted sarcasm was more effective than anger. In Sloan's and Stella's silence, Michael said to Bright, "We'd start by going over Fielding's files. Like the backup on his compliance reports—bills from Alliance and minority subs."

Turning from Michael, Bright gazed at Stella. "If Fielding's death looked more like a murder," he said, "we'd be a lot less open to question."

Though Stella looked back at him steadily, she blanched inside. Deceiving Bright was foreign to her nature—it was possible, at times, to forget that she had concealed her meeting with Natasha Tillman from everyone but Michael. Or that, whether from shame or some other motive, she had not told Michael of Tillman's death. In this room, Natasha Tillman seemed never to have existed: whether Bright or Sloan knew of her, perhaps from Dance, she could not tell.

Frowning, Bright let the silence stretch. "Anything new about Jack?" he inquired softly.

"Nothing," Stella answered. "No killer, no motive. No reason."

Bright's look grew distant again. "Find out about Breem," he told her at last. "Then look at Fielding's records. Hall will know what you're doing, but try to be vague about your reasons. And discreet."

That was that, his manner said. Across from Stella, Sloan ran his fingers over his hair, fixated on the table. The angles, she thought without sympathy, must be getting hard for him to figure out. They surely were for her.

MICHAEL FOLLOWED Stella to her office. Looking back into the hallway, he shut the door behind them.

"Well?" she asked.

He leaned against the door. "You tell me."

She shook her head. "I've worked with Arthur for thirteen years now, and I still wonder if I know him. But he's right to be cautious. We don't have very much, and a grand jury on Steelton 2000 could blow up in his face. When it came down to Larry Rockwell, Sloan saw that, too."

Michael smiled at this. "You play pretty rough."

But within the rules, Stella thought. *Until I stopped knowing what the rules are.* Shrugging, she said, "We got what we wanted. At least for now."

For a moment, his look seemed questioning. "Anyhow," she told him, "I've got some calls to make."

He seemed hesitant to leave. "There was something I was going to ask you."

Stella steeled herself for some inquiry about Tillman. "Okay."

"Sofia was wondering . . ." He caught himself, briefly smiling. "We *both* were wondering if you had some time this Saturday. Maybe in the afternoon."

The last phrase was apologetic, a throwaway. *I know you're busy,* he seemed to be saying—*I don't want to interfere.* Stella paused, caught by her own surprise. "I don't know."

She did not claim the press of work; that, and her tone of voice, signaled other doubts. He seemed to consider this, and then decided to speak.

"There'll be new friends in my life," he told her. "And in Sofia's. They don't have to be substitutes for Maria."

His directness, Stella found, was reassuring. But there was still much to ponder. "Let me think about it," she answered.

ALONE, STELLA struggled to sort out her reaction. It would be easier if she did not feel for Sofia or, she admitted, for Michael. But it could go no further: she was not sure what "friend" meant to him, and a friendship, tempered with caution, was all that she could offer a man who worked for her.

She *did* have calls, she reminded herself. The first was to Dance.

"We were talking about Fielding," she said. "Charles, Arthur, and me. Is there anything we should know?"

It was an open-ended question. But Dance chose to interpret it narrowly. "You asked about pornography. Nothing there—no subscriptions, no hanging around porno shops. Maybe *Black Beauties* was a gift."

"Don't you think that's funny?" Stella prodded.

A long silence followed. "Do you?" Dance asked softly. "Like Tillman, you mean?"

Stella sat back. The detective's voice became flat. "You can talk to me, Stella. Anytime you want."

Before she could answer, Dance hung up.

THE DRIVE home seemed long.

Preoccupied, Stella climbed her front steps slowly. Opening the door was a reflex, as was closing it behind her. Then she felt, and heard, the crunch of something broken beneath her feet.

Flinching, she reached for the wall switch. She missed it; then, fumbling, flicked the switch. As it should have, it turned on not only the lamp in the alcove but one in the living room.

The Infant of Prague lay at her feet, his body shattered in sharp pieces, his head decapitated. Only his robe was intact.

Tears came to her eyes. It was the surprise, Stella told herself. That, and the memory of her mother at Christmas, when the wreckage of her family still lay hidden in the ambush of time.

Something else was wrong, Stella realized. Badly wrong. The wall switch.

Stella's skin tingled with shock.

Every night, upon entering, she flipped it up and, with it, turned on both lamps. It was habit of a woman who lived alone; one flick of a finger and the dark house felt brighter, safer. Except for tonight.

The house had been dark, and the switch already up. Whoever entered before her had shattered the statue, turned on each lamp by hand, leaving the wall switch as evidence. By accident, or by design.

The house was still.

Star was not here, Stella realized. By now, the cat should be rubbing her leg, asking for food or comfort. It was only this which kept her from leaving.

Pausing, Stella listened for intruders.

There was nothing.

Taut, Stella began searching the first floor—the living room, the dining room, the kitchen—checking the doors and windows. There was no sign of a break-in, or of her cat.

Slowly, Stella climbed the stairs. At their top, she hesitated, frightened, then turned on the hallway light.

The bedroom was empty. Then Stella saw the disturbance on the dust ruffle of her bed, a slight indentation.

Glancing behind her, she knelt. From the dark beneath her bed, the cat's green eyes stared back at her.

Whoever had come here had driven Star into hiding.

Stella reached out for her. Star licked her forefinger, and then Stella swept the cat into her arms. "It's all right, baby," Stella murmured. "I'm here now."

She stood, still cradling Star, and searched the rest of her house.

No one.

Hesitant, Stella went downstairs, and fed the cat. Alone in the alcove, she stared at the broken figurine.

At last she cleaned up the pieces. She did not sleep until dawn.

SIX

ON SATURDAY morning, Stella sat in her office.

Outside it was as gray as dusk. A chill windblown sleet swirled like fog, obscuring the city, and the steel pylons of the stadium protruded from the mist like some druidical remnant. Strewn across Stella's desk were the crime-scene photos of Tommy Fielding and Tina Welch.

They told her nothing new. Fielding still resembled an Adonis overtaken by sleep; Welch still looked desiccated, weary of life; the hypodermic needle still protruded from her arm. But much had changed; Stella had met two witnesses who connected Fielding to the Scarberry—Curran and a prostitute—and the one who had seen Welch slide into his car was dead. Now someone had entered Stella's house.

Star was a leaper; it was possible that the cat had toppled the statue, frightening herself. But Stella was quite sure about the lamps and, as she reflected, about the intruder's motives. Nothing had been taken, nothing else disturbed. The intrusion was a warning: Stella was meant to feel endangered and, if she went to Bright or the police, to appear paranoid. Not that this was difficult to do, Stella reflected bleakly, to a woman who no longer trusted anyone.

She gazed down at Tommy Fielding. His face was calm; she could imagine him making the ham sandwich and drinking half a beer, but not the drive to the Scarberry which had preceded this, or the moment shortly afterward when Welch had pushed the needle into his arm. No more than she could envision Jack Novak putting on black stockings and letting a venomous sex partner hang him from the closet.

Who had called him that night? Who could have frightened him sufficiently to interrupt his pleasures with Missy Allen, yet been familiar enough for Jack to pour them two glasses of scotch? Or was Allen lying? Stella felt another thought overtake her: that Jack's killer had left no more trace than whoever had entered her home. Only that which the intruder had meant to be found—a shattered statue, a mutilated body.

Stella opened the Yellow Pages and called two home-alarm companies. Then she put away the crime-scene photos and drove to Warszawa.

ONCE INSIDE St. Stanislaus, Stella felt the church enfold her.

Beside her, Michael and Sofia were still, silent. Watching the little girl gaze up at the shadowy vastness of the ceilings, hundreds of feet overhead, Stella remembered herself as a child of Sofia's age, overtaken by the sense of awe she felt only in this place. And then, to her surprise, the child took her hand.

Its smallness startled her, carrying the sense of Sofia's fragility. But then Stella had so little experience of children that now, in the shadows of her own childhood, the moment seemed dreamlike.

Of course, Stella had surprised herself by being here at all. That morning Michael had called her to ask if Stella could meet them for lunch. Standing in the kitchen of her too-quiet house, Stella thought of the empty space which had held her mother's statue, and asked if Sofia had ever visited Warszawa.

Now Stella knelt beside her. "What is it?" she asked.

"It's too big," Sofia answered. "I'm scared."

So am I, Stella thought, *of more than I can tell you, or even know myself.* "I used to be," she answered. "Then I'd think of how beautiful this was, and it made me feel peaceful. Can I show it to you?"

Sofia considered her gravely. Then she held her arms out; inexperienced as she was, Stella remembered this as a gesture of trust, and knew what the child wanted. Easily, Stella picked her up, so feather light in her arms that she could feel Sofia breathing.

Michael forgotten, they stood in the nave of the church.

Soft-voiced, Stella told Sofia the story of how the steelworkers had come here. Of the frescoes and how families like Stella's great-grandfather's had paid for them with years of scrimping and self-sacrifice. Of how the next three generations, including Stella's sister, Katie, had been married in this church. It was a gentle narrative: Stella omitted the harshness of myth, the stained glass portraying the murder of St. Stanislaus; or of reality, that Stella herself had been barred from Katie's wedding. In between she described the childhood she herself had wished for.

It was drawn from life: the weddings, the dances, the school next door, the smells of cabbage or her mother making pierogi—half-moons of soft dough filled with a mixture of potatoes and cheese, the taste such a source of pride that her mother hid the recipe. Left out were her father's bitterness; her mother's fear; their inability to see their daughter as she was; the resolve this bred in Stella. The omissions did not matter, Stella knew; all that Sofia wanted was the softness of her voice.

After a time, they sat in a pew made of hand-rubbed red oak.

Sofia was quiet now, lulled by Stella's story of her own past. However painful the whole truth might be, Stella reflected, this place was still a part of her: the leather-bound books which recorded thousands of Polish births and deaths, christenings and weddings; the memorial at the side of the church inscribed KU WICZNIEJ PAMIECI and bearing the names of seventy-two men, including that of her great-uncle, who had died in World War II; the Poles' ongoing commitment to a city—the by-product of Amasa Hall's avarice—which Hall descendants did not share themselves. A peace crept over her, a feeling of refuge from murder, betrayal, her own fear. And so she sat there, another woman's child nuzzling close to her, the child's father settling beside them. Except for the three of them, St. Stanislaus was empty.

Finally, Michael murmured, "Do you make pierogi like your mother? Or did she hide the recipe from everyone?"

He had heard her, Stella thought, and smiled to herself. "I'm much better at indicting people," she answered. "But if Sofia can help me, maybe I can manage."

STELLA AND Sofia's version of pierogi turned out to be a mutation of Helen Marz's neatly turned crescents. But the smell from Stella's kitchen was credibly like her mother's.

"If you don't tell him how weird they are," Stella said, "I won't."

Sofia didn't know how weird they were. But her eyes lit with the fun of their conspiracy. What children most wanted from adults, Stella remembered, was to matter, to be liked for themselves. With a wooden spoon, Sofia began randomly pushing the misshapen pierogi about a pan. "Is this okay?" she asked.

The principle was much the same as in medicine, Stella thought dryly—first do no harm. By that standard, there was little Sofia could do to ruin their putative dinner. Suddenly Stella wondered if the same could be said of a stranger who, in a moment of loneliness and vulnerability, had looked at Sofia and, perhaps too easily, recalled herself.

"It's fine," Stella assured her.

. . .

AFTER THE meal Michael washed the dishes. Stella and Sofia sat on the couch, with Star stretched out between them. Sofia patted Star as the cat eyed Stella dubiously.

"Where did you get Star?" Sofia asked Stella.

So Stella told the story—how the cat was found starving in a basement, and taken to the ASPCA. Sofia listened without comment, gazing thoughtfully at Star; at the end of the story—the cat's rescue—she laid her face next to Star's. "See," Sofia informed her, "you're safe now."

Quiet, Stella watched her pet the cat, reflecting on the turning points, small and large, which marked the passage from child to adult. So much of who we are, she believed, was preordained; perhaps she herself had been born a stranger to her parents. Yet Maria's desertion had thrown Sofia's world out of balance, increasing the pressure on both father and daughter to deal with each other's hurt. It was striking how content the child seemed to spend time with a woman she barely knew.

"We can't have a kitty," Sofia said. "There's no one to take care of it."

Stella could not read the child's expression; beneath long lashes, incomparably lush in a seven-year-old, her eyes remained focused on Star. But her tone was not a bid for sympathy; it was a statement of fact, in which Sofia the child wished for a cat, and Sofia the woman, her father's partner, acknowledged their circumstances.

"Star's alone all day," Stella told her. "She doesn't seem to mind."

The child looked up at her. "But she has you," Sofia answered.

Michael, Stella realized, was standing in the entryway with a videotape. She did not know how long he had been watching them. "I thought I'd put on *Babe*," he informed Sofia. "Maybe Stella can show us where to play it."

THE TWO adults sat on Stella's couch, both sipping scotch on the rocks. Upstairs in Stella's bedroom, Sofia watched Babe the pig escape annihilation for, by Michael's calculation, at least the fifteenth time.

"She's into rescue fantasies," Michael said wryly.

But in which role? Stella wondered. To Michael, she replied, "She liked hearing about Star. But I think most children would."

Michael shook his head, demurring. "It's not just that. You're good with her."

No, Stella thought. *I'm just selfish, and needed company.* But she did not wish to explain. Instead she took another sip of scotch, feeling the glow settle into her.

"What were *you* like?" Michael asked.

Stella laughed. "When I was seven? A tomboy. Some people think I never got over it. I wasn't much like the girls in the neighborhood."

Michael smiled at this. "Did you want to be?" he asked.

"I never thought I could be," Stella answered simply. "But I was lucky. Growing up, no one seemed to dislike me for it."

She did not tell Michael what their neighbor Wanda Lutoslawski had called her, with a tone bordering on admiration—"the cat who walks alone." Nor could she describe the relief she had felt on discovering that—free of cliques or petty jealousies—others saw her as a natural leader, a girl who never looked back to see who followed. If the price had been loneliness, the appearance of needing nothing and no one, the compensation was to be respected as she respected herself. Only with Jack Novak had she looked at someone else to see who she should be; she had let no one since get close enough to harm her.

Michael watched her face. "You must still see people you grew up with."

"At church, mostly." Pausing, Stella passed over her years of absence from St. Stanislaus, stubbornly honoring her father's edict as if it were her own. "They tell me about children," she added with a smile, "and ask me about murder trials. Some of the women still call me Star."

Michael returned her smile. "From Stella, in Latin."

Stella nodded. "It started on the ninth-grade basketball team, after I told Margaret Stupak that I hated my name. It's funny the things people remember—outside Warszawa, no one calls me that."

"So you lent it to the cat."

Reaching out, Stella stroked Star on the forehead, the cat's favorite spot. "No," Stella answered. "She took it."

AFTER THAT, they were quiet for a time, sitting in the light and shadow of the living-room lamp. Michael did not feel required to make conversation for its own sake and, for Stella, this lent a sense of comfort. This was all that Sofia had needed from her, she supposed—the sense that being with the child was enough, and that Stella wanted nothing more.

"Maria," Stella said. "How much does Sofia talk about her?"

Michael examined his drink. "Not much. Memories mostly."

Stella pondered whether to pursue this. "Sofia knows," she said finally. "She knows Maria's not coming back."

"Why do you say that? Her insecurity?"

"That. And because I think she's looking out for you." Stella softened her tone. "It's as if she knows you're hurting, too."

Michael shifted on the couch, pensive; once more Stella was struck by the contrast between his maleness, the air of confident assertion which seemed part of him, and the uncertainty he felt as father to Sofia.

She leaned toward him, intent, though still speaking quietly. "Sofia makes me remember being her age, sensing things before I could put them into words. How unhappy both my parents were. That my father was angry because he was afraid.

"You understand Sofia, and yourself, in a way they never could. But she senses things, too. I don't think there's any hiding what Maria did to both of you. The trick is letting Sofia off the hook for it, the best way you can manage."

Eyes narrowing, Michael seemed to contemplate the couch. "Maybe that's a reason she likes being with you—you're fun, and you're pain-free." He looked up at her with sudden candor. "Maybe, when you're around, she doesn't worry about me, either."

"Which worries *me* a little."

"Why?"

Stella drew a breath. "Because I'm afraid somehow I'll end up disappointing her without meaning to. Which is exactly what she doesn't need."

Michael smiled at one side of his mouth. "That instead of having a Maria fantasy, she'll have a Stella fantasy."

To hear it put that baldly made Stella feel presumptuous. "We don't have to intend it," she answered, "for Sofia to want a surrogate. Those feelings have to go *somewhere*, Michael. That's why I wasn't sure about seeing you today."

In the shadows, Michael's brown eyes made his face, battered as it was, seem gentle. "Then maybe we should talk about that."

His tone was calm, matter-of-fact. But Stella felt an intuition, a flush crossing her skin.

"I didn't just ask you for Sofia," Michael told her. "I asked for me."

Stella looked at him, silent.

He tilted his head. "I hope that doesn't embarrass you."

She shook her head. "It's not embarrassment."

"But you have someone."

"No. There's no one." Surely, Stella thought unhappily, Michael would understand the rules of common sense, as impersonal as, to her, they were imperative. "We work together, Michael. How many office dating situations end up with two people who can't even look at each other?"

"Do you think *I'd* act like that?" Michael began, and then his tone softened. "I like being with you, and I'm attracted to you. It's the first time since Maria that I've felt that."

For a startling moment, Stella imagined how it might feel to make love with him. There was a catch in her throat: she had grown too able to delude herself, and so had been able to believe—wrongly, she now saw—that what she had felt for him was merely friendship.

"I like being with you, too," she finally answered. "And I like Sofia, very much. But if we tried to be more than friends, we'd only hurt each other. You're still in love with Maria—at least with who you thought she was. And I'm probably more self-centered than would be good for either of you."

Michael draped an arm across the back of the sofa. Quietly, he asked, "Do you really see yourself like that?"

No, Stella wanted to say. But she was not sure. "You chose Maria," she answered, "when you were twelve. Now you get to be with someone you've chosen in your thirties. But it's going to take some time to know who that person is."

Michael put his glass on the table, and then moved close to her, hand grazing her arm. She thought of New York, of the first time, the last time, he had touched her. "Can we try something?" he asked.

Stella did not answer. She could feel her own pulse.

Slowly, Michael raised his hand, gently bracing the nape of her neck. When her face was near his, eyes locking into his, she closed hers. She did not turn away.

His mouth was warm, generous, tasting faintly of scotch. She let herself be kissed and, for an instant, to kiss back. Then she lowered her head. But the warmth lingered inside her.

"All I'm asking for," Michael murmured, "is time."

She leaned back from him now, looking into his face. "I need time, too. To think. I wasn't prepared for this."

Gently, Michael touched her face. Stella mustered a droll look. "The pig movie should be winding down, Michael. I don't think Sofia needs a double feature."

Michael smiled. "I'll go check on her," he said.

When he came down the darkened stairway, a sleeping child was draped across his shoulder. "I guess she knows the ending," Michael said.

Smiling, Stella opened the door. "Thanks," Michael said, "for everything. From both of us."

"From me, too," Stella answered.

For a moment, she wanted them to stay, wished that she had told him about the shattered statue, her fears of being followed. Instead she watched them from the doorway, the shadow of a man and a child on the sidewalk below, until they reached his car.

Locking the door behind her, she found herself staring at the bare space where the Infant of Prague had been.

THAT NIGHT Stella could not sleep. Her mind swirled with thoughts of Michael and Sofia, and her senses, stirred by Michael, would not rest.

She was aware of every sound—the muffled noise of a passing car, the hiss of steam from her ancient heating system, Star awakening to lick herself, purring before she slept again. Then Stella heard someone parking below, the soft chug of a motor ceasing abruptly.

She listened for a slamming car door, footsteps on the sidewalk.

Nothing.

Without reaching for the lamp, she went to her closet, put on a robe, then walked to her window.

The sidewalk below was a shadowy pool, barely lit by a streetlight three houses down. But in the space left by Michael was a car she did not recognize—old, nondescript, perhaps a Japanese compact, dark in color. Not a neighbor's car.

Still, she watched it for minutes. Then she crossed the bedroom and switched on the hallway light.

The cat stirred, blinking. Stella paused before returning to the window. As she did, a motor coughed to life.

The space below was empty. There was a flash of red taillights, moving away. Just enough of a glimpse for her to see that the headlights were turned off.

Sitting on the edge of the bed, Stella reflected on the intruder two nights before.

How, she wondered, had the intruder gained entry without breaking in? The room around her suddenly felt cold.

SEVEN

AT DAWN the next morning, eyes grainy from fatigue, Stella went running.

The sun had appeared, bright and hard-edged, and her breaths were white puffs in a bitter wind which whistled from the lake in gusts. The road ran above the shoreline at the edge of a low cliff to Stella's left; waves smashed the rocks below, shooting a white spray into the air. Ahead, the towers of the city glistened in the distance, like a child's toy set. There was no one else in sight, no sounds but for the wind.

Still running, Stella glanced behind her.

Along the road, too far back for her to see its driver or a license plate, a brown, battered car was following, perhaps a Toyota, but so shabby in appearance that it looked like an abandoned junker the cops had towed away. Except that it was moving on its own, too slowly.

Stella turned away, facing the city, and counted thirty seconds as she ran. Then she looked back over her shoulder.

The car was still behind her. Moving at the same pace, maintaining the same distance.

She felt herself tense.

Quickly, she considered her choices. She could stop, see if the car stopped also. But she was alone—if this was not an oddity but a threat, she had little means of protection. Then she realized that the car could be on her within seconds.

Veering abruptly from the lake, she took a side street toward her home.

For two blocks, she did not look back. When she closed the door behind her, leaning against it, sweat ran down her wind-chilled face. The car was nowhere in sight.

ARMIN MARZ sat in the shadows.

Stella felt, as she always did, haunted for the first few seconds, as though in the presence of death. She could not account for the instinct to walk softly, speak gently—it would have made no difference had she shouted.

He had been like this for a long time now, sunk into the recesses of his mind, eyes unseeing, such movements as he made so painfully slow that, watching, Stella felt suspense as to whether he could complete them. Consuming a sandwich might take minutes, or hours; the remnants might remain in his hand, unnoticed, and then the hand would move again. The eyes stayed blank.

Gone were the spasmodic signs of struggle: the lists he made to remember something, the same word written over and over; the time spent staring at his photograph of Helen Marz, until his failure to recall had so upset him that Stella removed it; the querulous inquiries as to how Stella and he knew each other. "I'm your daughter," she had said, and the words had carried echoes of the years he had not acknowledged her.

Now she sat in front of him. A slight shifting in his posture conveyed a recognition of her presence, as though he had heard a distant, unthreatening sound. The once-fierce black eyes held no interest, or antagonism.

"Well," she told him, "here we are."

She wondered if her voice stirred memories imprinted too deeply in his senses to be lost, or whether it seemed to him as neutral as the drone coming from the hallway, someone else's television. The doctors could not tell her, and she supposed it did not matter—the visits were as much about her humanity as his. That was why it mattered to her that the nursing center was clean; his room bright; that the attendants, patient and well trained, still called him by his name. That was why she paid the bills.

"Hello, Dad," she said again.

He did not answer her. Stella smiled to herself: compared to the father she had known—the man who had come to reject and fear her—his silence felt benign. It had become her conceit, harmless and wistful, that the shell she sat with, stripped of anger, listened to her, and cared.

"Bad week," she told him. "I still can't figure out Jack's murder, or find the missing files. The only witness in Fielding's death had her throat cut. I've stopped trusting anyone, or telling them what I'm doing. I'm not even sure myself.

"Oh, and remember the Infant of Prague? Someone got into the house and broke it all to pieces. And now they're following me."

Armin Marz turned slightly, as if at the sound of her voice. That his eyes met hers was such a startling accident that—for an instant, brief as a shiver, he seemed like the man who had been her father.

She took his hand. Softly, she asked, "Can you hear me?"

He was very still. In her imagination, the revival of old longings, this was because he strained to listen. Stella looked away.

"There's a man," she said.

She knew he did not hear. With each stage of his descent, she had accepted something more: that he imagined she was a friend from Warszawa, someone he had known when he was six; then that the friend, too, was forgotten; then that the simplest choices upset him; and then, just before he lost the power of speech, that *nothing* upset him anymore. He had come at last to the acceptance Stella once had craved.

"His name is Michael," she murmured. "He has a daughter."

Still she kept his hand in hers. His other hand, she saw, began moving from his side, so slowly that it seemed to assume a life of its own, the sinuous gliding quality of a snake raising its head.

"I think I could care for him. I think I could care for them both. But I'm afraid to." Pausing, she still gazed at his lap, her hand holding his, then softly asked, "Is that how it felt to you?"

There was a long silence, Stella hearing the echo of her confession, the hopelessness of her question. And then, with the same painful slowness, her father's other hand began moving again, to cover hers.

Tears sprang to her eyes. When she looked into his face again, her father was asleep.

ENTERING HER house, Stella looked about her. Nothing seemed disturbed, and Star rubbed against her leg. The wall switch worked as it should.

When she went to fill the cat dish in the kitchen, she saw that there was a message on her answering machine. She was surprised how quickly the hope leaped to mind: Michael . . .

She pressed the button.

"Hi," Sofia said. "Dad and me had a nice time." There was mumbling in the background, Sofia asking if she'd said enough, and her father added, "*Really* nice . . ."

As the message ended, Stella smiled to herself. Then she went upstairs and switched on CNN.

EIGHT

STELLA HAD barely poured her first cup of coffee when the receptionist called to say that Dan Leary of the *Press* was waiting. "He knows the
way," Stella answered, and took the next half minute to prepare herself.

Her policy with the press was simple—never lie, and when you can't
tell them something, say so. Still, the Novak and Fielding cases were delicate, made more so by her own ambitions. Leary's beat was not homicide but city politics: a misstep could give Charles Sloan what he needed
to defeat her or, as bad, damage Arthur Bright. But Stella's expression
when Leary came through her door conveyed nothing except placidity
and the desire to be helpful.

"What's up?" she asked.

Leary took a seat. He was slender, sharp faced, graying and, unlike
some reporters, made little effort to ingratiate: his usual manner oscil-
lated between the watchful, the suspicious, and the peremptory. "Jack
Novak," he answered. "I've got some information, and it's only fair to
ask you about it first."

Stella heard a faint bell of warning. "All right."

He sat back, pad and pencil poised, looking at her. "You and Novak
were lovers," he said flatly.

Stella felt the nervelessness kick in; it was her reflex now, the result of
the inevitable rude surprises of the courtroom, to respond to danger by
thinking rather than feeling. "That sounds like a statement," she answered.
"But it *must* be a question. These days, Jack's keeping pretty quiet."

Leary's smile, such as it was, accented a bright-eyed inquisitiveness.
"Other people know about this, Stella."

"Oh? Who?"

"You know I can't say." His tone became more hectoring. "Look,
either it's true or it isn't."

"What's true? You toss out a gossipy little tidbit, which I'm supposed
to dignify by commenting." Stella kept her voice calm. "I don't play
hide-and-seek. Tell me what you think you have, and where it came

from, and I'll respond. For instance, *when* was this relationship supposed to have happened?"

Leary tilted sideways in his chair, as if dodging a punch. "You tell me. I'd like to see if my sources are consistent."

"Sources? I don't think you have 'sources,' Dan. I don't think you've got a thing." Stella let her tone harden. "You don't know me all that well. So let me help you out here. I don't lie, and I don't like cute. Somebody's using you."

Leary looked stung and then, like a smart reporter, seemed to back his own pride out of the equation. "I got an anonymous phone call," he said.

"Saying?"

"That you had an affair with Novak for a couple of years. That you were too involved with him to be objective about his murder."

Stella stared at him. "When did our 'affair' end? Just so I can jog my memory."

Leary's expression was calm and unabashed. "They didn't say."

"So what you want from me is an admission. No admission, no story."

Leary shrugged. "I came to you first, Stella. There are other ways."

"Oh, don't worry—I'll answer your question. But first I've got a few more of my own. Easy ones, like whether your caller was a man or a woman."

Pausing, Leary picked imaginary lint off his sport coat. "I don't know."

Stella prepared a scornful remark, and then a sudden image stopped her: Jack Novak hanging naked in a mirror as Kate Micelli said, "Whoever called disguised their voice enough that it could have been a man *or* a woman." Of Leary, Stella asked simply, "What did the voice sound like?"

"As though they were using a device to slow down the words, make them come out deep and slurred." Leary sounded curious now. "It was like listening to Boris Karloff."

Or Jack's murderer, Stella realized. "Do you have a private phone line?"

Leary looked intrigued, as though following her thoughts. "Yes."

"Did the call come in direct, or through the switchboard?"

"My line."

"Who has that number?"

"My wife. You—people I call for work."

"But John Q. Public has to get you through the switchboard." Stella thought for a minute. "You don't have 'nothing' after all. You've got a caller who wants to embarrass me, doesn't want his or her voice recognized, and is well enough informed to have your private phone number. What does all that suggest to you?"

"That the call was placed—or instigated—by someone who doesn't want you to get elected County Prosecutor . . ."

"*Or* just wants me off this case."

"Maybe." Leary's brief smile of acquiescence resembled a twitch. "Because it's true about you and Novak, and the caller *knows* it's true."

"And knows I won't deny it." Stella drew a breath. "Ready?"

Nodding, Leary struck the expected posture of a journalist, pencil poised over his pad.

"When I was in law school," Stella began, "I worked part-time in Jack's office as a paralegal. I left just before I graduated, in 1986.

"Up to then, for about a year and a half, we also had a dating relationship. I won't spell that out for you except to say that we weren't living together. After I came to work here thirteen years ago, we only saw each other by accident—I never worked in narcotics.

"Two years ago, I became head of homicide. Two *weeks* ago, somebody killed him, and so he landed on my desk. Period."

"Not 'period,' Stella. Novak's your ex-lover, your ex-boss, your current boss's friend, and he died the kinkiest death in recent memory. Doesn't that impair your objectivity?"

Stella thought of her painful memories of Jack; of Moro's visit; of the Haitian's murder; of the chain of aborted cases which had led her to the dead-records room. She *had* no objectivity—the case was part of her. Which was why, in the end, she might solve it, and why someone might want to stop her. Summoning a note of incredulity, she asked Leary, "Are you suggesting there's an ethical problem? Maybe you can explain what a relationship that's been over for thirteen years has to do with Novak's murder."

It was a probe. But either Leary's source had no idea, or Leary wasn't saying. "We're not talking ethics," he said bluntly. "Just common sense. In a case where the victim's so close to Bright *politically,* Arthur might want somebody running it who wasn't so close to Novak *personally.* For *both* your sakes."

Stella stifled her first, annoyed reaction: Dan Leary, the self-appointed tribune of good government. She and Bright had a problem, and she would have seen it coming were her own emotions not involved. She said, "If I'm getting in the way, this office will take care of it."

Leary raised his eyebrows. "Regardless, I'm printing this tomorrow. So you might tell Arthur to return my calls. In case he wants to share his thinking with the voters."

When Leary left, Stella stared at her desk.

Her day was in ruins; for now, it did not matter who had called Leary, or for what reason. She picked up the phone and told Brenda Waters to find Arthur for her, no matter where he was.

IT WAS noon before she caught up with him, in the mezzanine of the Steelton Palace Hotel, just before Arthur was to speak at a fund-raiser for the Family Violence Prevention Fund. The cause was important to both of them—Stella despised delaying him, and that her reason was so personal. Near the doorway of the ballroom, one of Arthur's staffers waited anxiously; Stella blessed Arthur for remaining calm.

"Thirteen years ago," Bright's voice was soft, sympathetic. "Who would even remember?"

"Not many people—my family, Jack's receptionist and secretary. You, because I told you. I guess whoever Jack might have told. But it was a lonely time for me; I never talked about Jack to anyone."

Bright's sidelong glance was at once delicate and penetrant. "At the crime scene," Stella told him, "it felt like Nat Dance knew. But I couldn't see how."

Through gold-rimmed glasses, Bright's look grew more reflective. "I guess there's no outrunning the past, Stella. You haven't outrun it yet. That's been Sloan's whole point about your digging into Jack's drug cases."

Stella folded her arms. "How far," she answered, "do you think he'd go to make that point?"

"Call Leary, you mean?" Bright straightened, and his face became stern. "Charles would never do that—first, because he's not the Machiavelli you've made him out to be; second, because screwing you is screwing me. Besides, I never told him you were involved with Jack. No need to—you didn't want to work in narcotics.

"No, girl"—this was said with a satiric black lilt—"time for us to clear our heads. We both got a Novak problem, and you never hid *yours* from me. So the buck stops here, like usual."

Stella did not comment: that there *were* things she was hiding made his absolution all the more uncomfortable. "Dump you now," Bright continued, "and it would have to be because of what you've done *since* Novak's murder. Otherwise, the *Press* is stampeding me over something

I knew all along. That would make me look bad, and you look bad. And we've both got places we want to be going.

"So here's what I tell Leary. You're the best of the best—which is why you're head of homicide. If you say you can do this case, then Leary has to show me why not. And dating Jack Novak before you took the bar exam doesn't get it."

Despite her gratitude, Stella thought of a frightened cat, a shattered figurine. "I think so, too," she said. "But someone's after me."

Bright glanced at his aide. Then he turned back to Stella, smiling slightly. "Do you really believe it's *you* they're after?"

Before she could answer, Bright turned and headed for the ballroom, a candidate with a speech to give.

"Hi," Michael said.

Stella looked up, and saw him standing in the doorway, regarding her with a tentative smile, an inquiring gaze. She felt at once pleased, disconcerted, and uncertain. "Not a great day," she told him. "Close the door, okay?"

He did, settling in a chair with a look of concern. "What's wrong?"

"To start, I have a little problem with the *Press.*" She folded her hands in front of her. "When I worked in his office, Jack Novak and I were lovers. An anonymous caller told Dan Leary."

Several emotions registered on his face—disbelief, curiosity, even jealousy. His eyes never moved from Stella's. "Then investigating his murder can't have been easy," he said.

"It hasn't been. His death dredges up a lot that I don't like to think about. Even then I knew—or suspected—too much about him." She paused, keeping her voice level. "Jack wasn't a good experience for me. It was a lousy time in my life—for a while I lost track of who I was."

He gave her a long sober look. "Because of Novak?"

"I had no one, Michael. Jack understood that, and understood my weaknesses. Though maybe I used him as much as he used me. He helped free me from my father, and get this job."

"And, in between, did a lot of damage."

Stella hesitated, unsure of what to say. She was not used to revealing herself, or to receiving compassion in return; her emotions seemed labile, a combination of fear and need which undercut her self-possession. "I think so," she said simply.

Michael leaned forward, as though he wished to touch her, but knew that he could not. "There's so much I'd like to know about you," he said. "I wish we could just bail, go somewhere and talk."

Stella shook her head. "That's one of the problems of working together. We've been sitting here with the door closed, talking about Jack Novak as if all I need is a hug." She tried to smile. "Maybe that's what I want, Michael. What I *need* is to figure out who killed him. And why. Not to mention why somebody's out to get me."

Eyes lowered, Michael seemed to reflect. "You told Bright, I guess."

"He knew about Jack, before I started working here. He's not taking me off the case."

Michael looked up, considering her.

"You think that's foolish?" she asked.

"As one friend to another? If something goes wrong—yes. Especially with your ambitions."

Though she knew this, to hear the truth from Michael was depressing. "I can't duck this case," she said.

"Someone clearly wants you to."

More than you know, Stella thought. "Then help me out, okay?"

"How?"

"I told you to put Jack's files on hold. Now I need you to dig back into them as we were planning, focus on the ones for the last few years. Look for funny outcomes, fixed cases, anywhere it seems like someone besides Jack was crooked. A cop, say, or a judge."

Michael touched the bridge of his nose, still appraising Stella. "You keep coming back to Moro, don't you."

"Until someone persuades me I shouldn't."

Michael was silent. "All right," he said at length. "I'll put this ahead of Steelton 2000."

Stella heard the undertone of frustration, his feeling of momentum interrupted. "Just for now," she answered. "Is there anything new about the ballpark?"

"Nothing much. I've checked into this guy Conrad Breem, the president of Lakefront Corporation. He's a tax attorney who dabbles in real estate, apartment buildings mostly. No obvious connections to Krajek—the reports on Krajek's donors don't turn up Breem or Lakefront." Michael paused, and his tone became pointed. "They *do* show contributions from the Alliance Company. As if *that's* a surprise."

"Rockwell's minority contractor? Not much of a surprise." This was the source of Michael's frustration, Stella realized. "I guess you're wanting to visit Hall Development, go over Fielding's records."

Michael nodded. "At least send them a subpoena. Especially for any bills for Alliance—we don't want them to go missing."

"Arthur has to clear a subpoena—it's too political. But I don't think anyone will be destroying invoices. Otherwise, there'd be no backup for MBE compliance."

Michael looked skeptical. Though he did not say so, in this instance he plainly questioned her judgment, and her priorities. It reminded Stella of the problems in letting their relationship go any further than it already had. Quietly, she said, "We'll get back to Steelton 2000."

With noticeable effort, Michael tried to appear untroubled, which made Stella feel more awkward. With an uncertain smile, she added, "See, you're not talking to me already."

To her relief, Michael laughed at this. Then his look grew more serious. "More than anything, Stella, I want to understand you. I never want to *mis*understand someone again."

Michael stood, reaching into his pocket and extracting a small rubber mouse. "This is for Star," he said. "From Sofia. She worries that she's home alone."

Stella was amused at the thought of her independent cat, so obviously ruffled by Sofia, becoming the object of the girl's compassion. But projection, she supposed, was second nature to a child. "Tell Sofia I'll call her tonight, to report on how Star likes it."

Michael smiled. "That would be nice. Unless Star's underwhelmed."

Stella returned his smile. "In certain matters, Star lets me speak for her."

Amiably, Michael left. Whatever tension had existed was, for the moment, eased.

Yet Stella felt uneasy. The Novak case was too entangled with her past—in which Michael, as a prospective lover, had an understandable interest. Jack aside, working together carried a heightened potential for tension, misunderstanding, and strain. Even that they had met with the door shut might not go unnoticed.

The telephone rang, interrupting her thoughts.

"This is Peter Hall," her caller said. "I have a favor to ask, and I hope that you'll say yes."

The sound of his voice, self-assured yet polite, was, to Stella's surprise, stimulating. But she did not have time to consider why. Dryly she said, "How large a favor?"

"Lunch. Say tomorrow?"

This, a further surprise, gave Stella pause. "I guess I'm puzzled," she said. "Is this about Tommy Fielding?"

"If you want it to be. But I hope we can talk about you." In the silence caused by Stella's bewilderment, Hall asked, "Can you indulge me until tomorrow?"

Stella stood, caught between caution and curiosity. In other circumstances, Peter Hall was someone she would not mind having lunch with, though she doubted he would bother asking. The problem now was one of appearances; however obliquely, Stella was investigating Hall Development. The opportunity was a chance to learn something—including what had caused Hall to approach her.

"All right," Stella said at last.

NINE

THE OFFICES of Hall Development were atop a forty-story glass-and-steel tower, and the view from Peter Hall's floor-to-ceiling windows framed the lakefront. From the corner, where they sat at a round glass table, Hall's vista included City Hall, the courthouse, the sullen gray surface of Lake Erie. Directly below, the drop so steep that it gave Stella a sense of vertigo, was the stadium.

Hall followed her gaze. "That's why we took these offices," he said. "For us, the ballpark's not an abstraction, or a series of blueprints. We've watched it rise from nothing."

This was said with a quiet passion, the way Stella imagined an artist or filmmaker might speak of his work. The impression was enhanced by Hall's blue jeans and denim shirt, the way his thick blond hair, carelessly falling over his forehead, suggested a man absorbed by the task before him. The apparent lack of self-consciousness made his good looks all the more striking.

"How does that feel?" Stella asked.

He faced her. "My great-grandfather built the mills. For the next three generations we lived off that; for the last two—my father's and mine—we turned our back as the city began dying. *This* feels like we're building something again."

His summary had an ironic resonance for Stella: Hall's father, comfortably rich, had left her father stranded. But Hall's vision of civic renewal and, perhaps, of self-renewal, conformed to her desires for the city.

"How about the waterfront?" she asked. "Do you have plans for that?"

As though gauging the purpose of her question, he paused, but only for a moment. "Tom Krajek does," Hall answered. "If the ballpark's a success, there'll be another project—restaurants, shops, perhaps a mall. The lakefront's a resource, he says."

So Michael could be right, Stella thought: the ballpark might be the first stage of a real estate play, enriching the landowners around it. She

picked at her salad, then looked around her. On his desk were photographs of a blond boy and girl in their early teens: briefly, she wondered about Hall's life outside of work, then returned to her own agenda.
"You must know all the developers in town," she said.

Hall gave her another quiet look, the cornflower blue of his eyes
showing beneath long lashes. What struck her most, Stella reflected, was
his naturalness. But perhaps the greatest artifice was to seem to have
none at all. "I know all the *commercial* developers," Hall answered. "At
least anyone substantial."

"Did you ever hear of Lakefront Corporation? Or a lawyer named
Conrad Breem?"

Hall tilted his head, smiling slightly. "No, and no. Why do those
sound like prosecutor's questions?"

"Because I am one. But they have nothing to do with you."

Hall sipped his mineral water. Though his manner was pleasant, he
made no effort to hide his curiosity. "Yesterday, you mentioned
Tommy."

Stella nodded. "It may be nothing, and there's no evidence to tell me
his death wasn't exactly as it appears. But did you know Fielding was
two months behind on his MBE reports?"

"Yes." For the first time, Hall sounded troubled. "I'm having to
catch up."

"Does that seem like him?"

Hall met her eyes. "No." He paused, then added bluntly. "You're
wondering about Alliance."

Hall was surprisingly direct. "Are you?" Stella asked.

Hall cradled his chin. Focused on the table, his eyes narrowed with
thought. "I'm just wondering how to put this," he said at last.

Stella waited; she had long since learned not to throw potential witnesses a life raft. As if recognizing this, Hall looked up and smiled.
"What I'm about to say won't shock you," he began. "I've got a ballpark
to build, and the mayor has an election to win, so Hall Development
needed to ensure thirty percent minority participation. So we turned to
Larry Rockwell.

"Is he the world's greatest minority contractor? I doubt it. Will dealing with Alliance cost us *and* the city money? I don't doubt *that* at all.

"Tommy didn't, either. His job was to make sure Alliance did its
share, and got its share. While minimizing the excess cost to us."

Hall's candor, Stella found, summoned forth her own. "*Has* Alliance
done its share? Or the MBEs it helped you find?"

Hall gave her a long, cool look. "Are you asking," he said at length, "whether Tommy Fielding defrauded Hall Development and the city compliance inspectors? Because he never would have."

Stella shook her head. "I'm asking if there's fraud. I don't have an opinion on how it might work, or whose it was."

Only her voice, soft with inquiry, kept this from being an insult. But Hall's self-containment did not waiver. "Your office has more resources than I do. If there's a question, you should get the answers." He paused, and for the first time his voice took on an edge. "As long as this is about civic virtue, and not mayoral politics."

Stella returned his unblinking stare. "This isn't coming from Arthur. It's coming from me."

He held her gaze, then slowly nodded. "Then what *I* can do is make our records available. I won't require a subpoena. All I'll need is a week or so."

He was admirably direct—no lawyers, no delay, no obfuscation. "Then I'll call you in a week," Stella responded.

"Good." Hall glanced at her plate. "You haven't eaten much. Can I get you anything else?"

"No. Thank you."

He had asked her here, he had said, to talk about *her*. But she had no intention of seeming eager to know more. She placed her napkin on the table, as though preparing to leave.

He sat back, appraising her with a quizzical smile. "I did have a reason for calling. But you've made it a bit more awkward."

Stella summoned a smile of her own. "If I have, I'm sorry."

Hall watched her, as if undecided, then plunged ahead. "I read Dan Leary's column. Someone's decided to make things hard for you."

This was a genuine surprise. The piece had not been as bad as Stella feared—the anonymous tip, her admission, Bright's support, a recitation of her record—and so far she had received only one further call, from a TV station. But Stella interpreted the tip as a warning shot, the article as an embarrassment. So, it seemed, did Hall.

"I'm glad," she told him, "that my life's so boring they had to reach back thirteen years. Never has the phrase 'skeleton in the closet' been more apt."

Hall steepled his fingers. "Do you still mean to run?"

Stella gazed at him with open curiosity. "Why are you asking?"

"Not to co-opt you, if that's what you're thinking. In fact, I'm much more reluctant to have this conversation than I was an hour ago. But let me say two things."

Stella hesitated, then felt the pull of temptation. "All right."

"First, Charles Sloan is a clever hack. He's everything that's wrong with politics in this city: self-serving, a favor swapper, and wholly lacking in vision." Pausing, Hall smiled. "Or would you care to argue the point?"

Pondering her answer, Stella thought of Hall's aversion to the prosecutor himself, and found the perfect response. "Let's just say," she said dryly, "that Sloan's no Arthur Bright."

Hall bit his lip, then began to laugh. The effect was completely charming, the look of a man diverted from his mission by a woman he found engaging. "Touché," he said. "Do you think I could try point two?"

"Go ahead."

"You're no Arthur Bright, either." Hall's expression became serious again. "I know you support the ballpark. That's why I trust you to be fair—which is all I ask, let me emphasize. And it's also emblematic of why I prefer you to Sloan.

"The politics in this town is moribund. Race against race, interest group against interest group, a gaggle of petty Neros fiddling while Rome burns. Even Tom Krajek—he's not a visionary, he's just someone who knows how to count to fifty-one percent, so he can pick an issue to run on. In that, I'll even give Bright some credit for principle. If enough other people do the same, he may become mayor." He leaned forward, adding more softly, "Which brings me back to you."

"How so?"

"If Bright becomes mayor, you've got a chance to take his place. Dan Leary aside, the *Press* might even back you. From what I've heard, your ideas are the right ones—protect consumers, prosecute domestic violence, go after deadbeat dads. Something besides playing cops-and-robbers.

"But Sloan's been gearing up for years. He's got contacts, exposure, and every black politician in the city. Except, maybe, the one that matters most." His voice lowered again. "Bright's keeping awfully quiet, Stella. Is there a chance he may support you?"

Stella debated whether to answer. But she was intrigued by Hall's candor, his knowledge of her proposals, his grasp of city politics. "Yes," she answered. "A chance."

"Bright's endorsement would help. But what you need to win, like it or not—and I don't, particularly—is money. Money for consultants, mailers, advertising, television, radio, organizing, office space. All the things a young, lesser-known candidate requires to compete with Sloan."

His analysis was as discouraging as it was accurate. Stella thought again of her diminished savings, her father's lingering senescence, her sister's bitterness. "There's no help for that," she said. "There's a five-hundred-dollar limit on campaign contributions in county elections, unless I lend the money to myself. If I run, I'll just have to slog it out as best I can."

Hall still watched her closely. "Who's giving you advice?"

"No one, yet."

"That's what I thought. Because there's a piece missing. If Bright's elected, how do they choose his interim replacement?"

"There's a special election. But first the Democratic Party chooses its nominee, by a vote of roughly two thousand precinct committeepeople." Reciting the difficulties made Stella feel testy. "I know all that—their vote will be tantamount to election, and most of them have known Sloan forever."

"True. So what are the campaign funding limits for a vote of precinct committeepeople?"

All at once, the realization hit Stella hard; she felt at once foolish, demeaned, and, despite her deepest instincts, hopeful. She looked directly into Hall's eyes. "What I think you're about to tell me," she said quietly, "is that there are none."

Briefly, Hall touched her hand, a calming gesture. "I know what you're thinking. So I want you to know how it looks to me.

"I've recommitted to this city. I don't want to see it run by the Charles Sloans. And I know that if an attractive candidate is all over television, and radio, and has a war chest ready to take into the general election, even the dimmest ward heeler might find her irresistible." His voice became emphatic. "It would change the race entirely.

"Turn over all the rocks at Steelton 2000 you care to. I wouldn't ever have mentioned this now, but I'm worried that something—this Novak item, money, or Bright endorsing Sloan—might drive you out of the race. I'm trying to keep you in."

Stella tried to sort out her emotions: her belief in law, her fear of seduction, her distrust of the privileged man in front of her, the sudden, blinding prospect that—for the first time in her life—her ambitions would not be circumscribed by money, or the lack of it. She wondered if

Peter Hall could imagine how that felt; when she looked into his face, all she saw was the desire, by his own lights, to be helpful. "I appreciate what you've said," she told him. "But I'm sorry that I heard it."

She waited for some sign of offense, of a powerful man rejected. Instead, Hall slowly nodded. "I know," he said. "Exploiting loopholes is not the ideal solution. But neither is electing Charles Sloan."

He stood, walking to the windows. In profile, slim and blond and tousle haired, he looked as if he were gazing out to sea.

"Do you know what money does?" he said at last. "It makes more money. I'd have been rich if I hadn't raised a finger. And once this stadium's built, I'll be richer yet.

"You're your own invention. I'm my great-grandfather's. No complaints, but what's left to me is to use the money in a way that matters. That's why I'm selling the house in Stonebrook, and moving back to Steelton. Except for my late wife, I'd have done it long before." He turned to her, speaking slowly and seriously. "This may sound unbelievably sentimental, even saccharine. But my ancestors got rich on the backs of yours, and put me where I am. It would please me to repay the debt, and do the city some good."

Stella felt both skeptical and moved. "I appreciate that. But we can't talk about this now. I can't let it affect what I do, either in my job or about running for County Prosecutor. Those things will have to sort themselves out."

Hall smiled a little. "If they do, Stella, could we at least have dinner?"

TEN

IT WAS close to ten at night before Stella returned home, and she had much to think about. But her first thought was that she no longer felt safe.

Star rubbed against her leg. All seemed in order. She went to the kitchen, fed the cat, poured herself a glass of wine, and sat in the living room.

Tonight's event, a speech to the Erie County Bar Association, had gone well. Hers was a careful balancing act: a review of the conviction rate for violent crimes which reflected well on Bright and Stella; an attempt to intimate that she could bring new perspectives to the office. But it was easier to impress a group of lawyers, her natural audience, than an auditorium full of precinct committeepeople who would have to be persuaded—against their natural loyalties—that Stella, not Sloan, was the best candidate to hold the office for the Democrats. Which brought her back to Peter Hall.

What she had told him was true enough: that she wished never to have heard his offer. But she had. And she would never think of Steelton 2000 without knowing that Peter Hall represented her clearest chance of succeeding Arthur Bright. Against her will, Hall's interests had become hers.

This was how it started, she supposed. The hesitance, the small compromises, the weighing of "the greater good." And wasn't *she* the greater good, her innermost self argued fiercely—she *was* the best, she *should* be County Prosecutor. But she had come this far by being who she was; if she became someone else, would she be any better, any different, than Sloan? She was not certain that, even now, she was the same woman who had entered Hall's office.

In certain ways, she had already lost her bearings. Because her suspicions were so formless, she had trusted no one—Bright, Sloan, Dance, Micelli, or Michael—with all that she feared. Her work had become a maze, and she was lost. Afraid of her job. Afraid of her house. Afraid of herself.

She went upstairs, undressed, and got into bed. For uncounted minutes, perhaps hours, she tossed restlessly in some twilight between sleep and waking. But when the phone rang, startling her, she realized that at last she had fallen asleep.

SHRILL, THE phone sounded in the pitch-black room. Stella sat on the edge of the bed, half-stunned. The red letters on her nightstand clock read 2:17.

How many times had it rung? She stood, afraid to answer, afraid not to. Before Jack Novak's murder, she would have answered without hesitance.

The caller ID, she saw, showed "private line."

Picking up the telephone, she was surprised by the calmness of her tone. "Stella Marz."

The voice was slurred, grotesque. "Hello, Stella Marz."

It was like a record played at the wrong speed. Then Stella thought of Dan Leary's description and corrected herself: it was the voice of a fun-house monster. Its aftershock was sudden nausea in the pit of her stomach.

"Let's talk about your boyfriend," the voice continued.

Stella felt herself swallow. She felt dirtied, invaded, exposed, fearful they were watching her now. "You wonder about his wife," the voice continued. "You wonder how she could have left her daughter."

Stella did not answer.

"But then," the distorted voice continued, "you don't take a child from a man who works for Vincent Moro."

Stella's eyes closed.

"Ask him to tell you who paid for his college and law school.

"Ask him why he works for Bright.

"Ask him why Maria left." The voice became a near whisper. "Maybe if you fuck him, he'll tell you."

Phone clamped to her face, Stella sat again. The whisper, for its quavering, was all the more chilling. The voice was distorted by a box, the reasoning part of her knew—an instrument of disguise. "Why are you telling me this?" she asked.

"Because we're worried for you. A woman like you, with no real friends, could die alone. It's time to cut back your caseload."

Stella drew a breath. "Which case?"

There was a deep, rumbling laugh. "That shows how little you know. You'll have to guess, and hope you're right."

Reflexively, Stella stood up. "Good night," the voice told her. "Don't forget to feed the cat."

The line clicked off.

She went to the bathroom and vomited.

STELLA STARED into the bathroom mirror. Her skin was sallow, clammy. Her forehead shone with sweat. Her stomach felt twisted, raw, emptied out. When she held her hand in front of her, it trembled.

Think, she ordered herself.

Head bent, she stared into the sink.

He had called to frighten her. But also, perhaps, to make her seek protection, to trust someone else she should not trust. Or to distrust someone she should trust.

If Michael belonged to Moro, why tell her? Unless it could never be proven, and the caller's purpose was to convince her that the betrayal all around her made her position hopeless. But then why was she a threat, and to whom?

"That shows how little you know." Including about Michael.

She could not go to Bright without more. She did not know where to start. She could not, anymore, act alone.

Shivering, she went to the bedroom window. The street was dimly lit; the dark beyond impenetrable.

"You'll have to guess, and hope you're right."

She reached for the telephone. On the rug beside her, Star, awakened, gnawed Sofia's mouse.

"Dance," the deep voice answered. Even at this hour, stirred from sleep, the Chief of Detectives was prepared for work—a murder; the death of a cop; an informant at risk.

"It's Stella," she said without apology. "I need to see you, now."

THROUGH THE window, Nathaniel Dance was a massive shadow on Stella's porch, rapping softly on the door. When she flicked on the light, his breaths were white puffs in the chill of night.

Silent, she let him in. He walked to the living room; perhaps because Stella focused on him so intently, she noticed for the first time that, well into middle age, he moved with a catlike grace and quiet. He sat on the couch, forearms resting on his knees, gazing up at her with a complete absence of expression.

"I've made coffee," Stella said.

He shook his head, dismissive, watching her.

"Someone got in here the other night," she told him, "without any sign of forced entry. I don't know who or how—they disturbed just enough to let me know they'd been inside.

"Tonight, someone called. I can't identify the voice; he—or she— used some sort of voice box. The message was simple: drop what I'm doing. They left me to figure out *what* I'm supposed to drop, or what'll happen if I don't."

Dance remained quiet. For an unsettling moment, Stella believed that he knew the rest—what her caller had said about Michael. At length, Dance said, "You've been fucking with me, Stella."

She sat across from him. "Fucking with you? Someone's been selling me out."

He folded his hands; to Stella, the gesture bespoke controlled anger. "And you think it's me."

Stella felt weary, still frightened; the lateness of the hour, the basilisk mask of Dance's expression, gave the moment a surreal quality. "Could be," she answered. "You've been 'fucking' with *me,* too. But I'm guessing it's because you don't trust me, either."

Dance's eyes narrowed. "You first."

Briefly, Stella hesitated. Then, in sequence, she told him about the missing drug files; her meeting with Natasha Tillman; her questions about Fielding's death; his tardy MBE reports. "I don't know what it means," she finished. "But the missing files and Tillman's murder are just too much coincidence."

Dance was silent, impassive. "Different cases," he finally answered. "There's no connection."

"They both involve *me,* Nat."

Dance remained quiet. His face and body were otherwise so still that his chest, moving with each breath, seemed like a bellows. "Who else knows all this?" he asked.

In the half hour between her call and Dance's arrival, Stella had realized the answer: only Michael Del Corso, the man to whom she had also loaned her keys. She shook her head, as if caught between dream and waking. "I'm not sure."

Dance scowled. "Someone knows. If we can't find out who, someone else is like to die. Maybe you."

Stella felt the protest trapped inside her: *It can't be Michael.* But her only basis for trusting him was to trust her instincts, and, at least in the case of Jack Novak, they had not been good. "Let's go at this another way, Nat. You haven't trusted me, either. Why?"

Dance considered the question, then gave her a look which seemed somewhat more equable. "Not because I thought you were dirty," he answered. "Because I thought you were right."

"About what?"

"Novak. For sure he fixed those cases—I've known *that* much for years. Just like I know he had to have help. But I don't know from who, and I didn't want you warning them off." He paused, finishing softly, "My guess is you already have, and that's what this call's about."

"Why so sure?"

"Because you've tried out pieces of your theory on Bright, Sloan, Curran, Del Corso, Saul Ravin, and me—"

"Bright and Sloan aren't talking it up," she cut in. "Believe me."

Dance gave her a perfunctory smile. "I know. But your suspicions are out there, so you can't assume whoever you're after hasn't heard about them. Or why the call?"

Stella pondered this. "*That* assumes Jack's helper—or helpers—is still around. And that it's the reason for what's been happening to me. But what if it's about Fielding somehow?"

Dance frowned. "Are you listed?" he asked.

"Of course not."

"Who has your number?"

"Friends. People in the office. You, of course. The other cops in homicide."

Dance leaned forward. Combined with the weight of his presence, his size seemed to dwarf the furnishings, make the room resemble a child's playhouse. "About fourteen years ago," he told her, "I got a call like the one you just got. Right after that Haitian dealer got whacked, when I was still working narcotics.

"I was after George Flood, too. Only *my* idea was to take the same cases you found, and try to flip Jack Novak. Any way I could."

Abruptly, Stella felt cold. "What I didn't know," Dance said softly, "is that Novak could give me Moro.

"I still didn't know *that* until two weeks ago. When you told us you'd seen Moro in Novak's office one night. You think Novak gave the Haitian up to Moro, don't you?"

"Do you?"

Dance did not answer. "*My* call was late at night," he told her. "Like yours. Voice was disguised, too. But he wasn't near as gentle." Dance's voice was flat, toneless. "He said my cover was blown, that the dealers knew who I was. Either I got out of narcotics, or he and his friends were gonna fuck my wife and daughters up the ass. Before they killed them.

"He told me where we lived, where Beatrice worked, where the girls went to school. He explained how patient they'd be, just waiting for their chance, and how safe I'd be until they caught up to my wife or kids. Because they wanted me alive to see who was raped and murdered first.

"*His* favorite was our youngest girl, he told me. Because she'd hurt the most, and scream the loudest." Dance paused, as though remembering, then finished, "Someone on *our* side tipped them off."

Stella's temples began to throb. "What did you do?"

"Buffalohead was one thing, Bea and the kids something else. When I tried to tell Bea, I couldn't." Dance slowly shook his head. "For twenty-four hours, I thought about it. Then I went to the captain and said I was burnt out on narcotics work.

"I was gone in a heartbeat. Until right now, no one knew why." Dance's voice was low and soft. "And you're not telling anyone, Stella. Not now. Not ever."

"And you still wonder who it was."

Dance stared at her. "Thanks to you, I've stopped wondering who gave the order. It was Moro. What I don't know yet is which of my 'friends' told him I was after Novak."

Graven on Dance's face was something Stella had never seen in him— an implacable hatred. She tried to imagine how it would feel to fear for one's own children. Instinctively, she thought of Sofia. Then her caller's words came back to her: "*You don't take a child from a man who works for Vincent Moro.*"

Shaken, she asked Dance, "Who do you *think* it was?"

"That part's simple. Anyone but Arthur."

Doubt flooded Stella's mind; Dance's history left no room for trust, or leaps of faith. Watching her, the detective seemed to read this. "I guess he never told you," Dance said at last. "Remember when you came to Arthur for a job?"

"Sure. Arthur didn't exactly make it easy."

"Before the interview, he called me. Said you came from Novak, that he wanted you checked out on the QT.

"So I poked around a little. Even followed you a couple of nights." His voice became ironic. "Can't say I found you real interesting. But I did figure out you'd been screwing Novak, and passed that on to Arthur.

"He didn't seem real happy to hear it." Pausing, Dance considered his nails, spreading his fingers, with surprising delicacy, in front of him like a fan. "Then Arthur called me back. Said you'd copped to being Novak's girlfriend, and didn't want a job in narcotics."

To Stella, several things became blindingly clear: why she had sensed at the scene of Jack's murder that Dance knew about their affair; why Bright had seemed so reserved at first meeting; why he had finally offered her a job. And perhaps the most important fact, which she spoke aloud to Dance. "Arthur didn't trust Jack, did he?"

"No way. He may have taken campaign money from the guy, but he didn't want Novak fucking around in his office, and he sure wasn't going to hire anyone who'd be leaking to him."

Stella had begun to imagine the three of them in compartments, concealing facts from one another, trusting no one completely. "Since Jack was murdered," she rejoined, "Arthur hasn't exactly been eager to explore all this."

Dance looked at her. "Why should he? He's running for mayor. Suppose the problem *was* in his office—now's a shitty time for him to be finding that out, isn't it?" He paused, adding quietly, "Of course, you never told him files were missing. Who did you think took them— Arthur? Or Sloan?"

Stella flushed, then thought of Michael again. "Someone in the office," she answered. "*Who,* I don't know."

"You know even less than that. There's no security in that room. Anyone in law enforcement could have gotten in there, at any time." His voice turned cold. "Me, for example."

Stella felt herself stiffen. "What *about* you?" she retorted. "You're Arthur's friend. You don't want problems for him, either." *And,* she did not add, *like me, you have ambitions of your own.*

Dance's eyes were hard, his tone quiet. "I want the guy on the telephone. And whoever sold me out. So I hope he wasn't Arthur's."

For a time thereafter, neither spoke. "Who killed Jack?" she asked.

"Don't know yet. But probably not Melissa Allen." Dance hesitated, then added bluntly, "More likely whoever broke in here, then called you up tonight."

Stella folded her arms. "Doesn't that point back to Moro?"

"Good chance." Rising, Dance walked to a window, looking out. "I'll tell the precinct captain you've been getting funny calls."

Stella watched him. "Let me try another question, Nat—Natasha Tillman. Why were you at the crime scene?"

Dance turned to her. "Same as you, more or less: two hookers in two weeks. That's a pretty high mortality rate for one block in the Scarberry." He paused, then added a second rebuke. "Especially since you tell me that Tillman saw Welch disappear."

There was something more, Stella sensed. But Dance seemed determined to keep her on the defensive. She felt quite sure that he was not prepared to tell her what else he might know, even as she could not, without more hard reflection, tell Dance about Michael. "So what do we do now?" she asked.

"We?" His smile, as always, was fleeting. "I'm Chief of Detectives, my kids are grown now. So *I* mean to square accounts. But you? Seems like you've got to decide how much farther to go. Just like I did fourteen years ago."

It was all too neat, Stella thought suddenly—first, the threatening call to her, then Dance's story of another call. Perhaps, instead of a pattern, Dance's account was a lie, an event that never happened, designed to scare her off. And then, a fresh suspicion seized her: suppose the caller had been Dance himself, and his story a test to determine how tied she was to Michael. Her only certainty was that she must go to Arthur Bright.

"I've got no kids," she said to Dance.

ELEVEN

WHEN STELLA finished her narrative, Bright was quiet. The office, too, was silent—even sepulchral, Stella thought mordantly. But then it was barely 7:00 a.m.

"You've changed my mind," Bright said at last. "You can't be running the Novak case."

The soft words shocked her. "Why not?"

Even to her, the response sounded foolish. Bright's expression was somber, concern warring with displeasure. "Several reasons. Maybe the case *is* too personal. But it's clear you've lost your judgment. You don't trust anyone." His tone grew quieter yet. "When you don't trust the man you work for, it's time to consider resigning."

Now Stella could barely look at him. He had stood by her in public, while she had wronged him in her thoughts. "I'm sorry," she said. "It's Charles I don't trust. Those files didn't walk out by themselves."

"No, indeed," he said firmly. "But Charles didn't take them."

His manner brooked no argument. "Except about the files," Stella temporized, "I never held out on you. You always knew that I suspected Jack was fixing cases." She paused, then finished. "*You* must have suspected him for years, Arthur. Or you wouldn't have had Nat Dance check me out."

Bright was quiet again, then gave a curt nod of acknowledgment. "You can fire me," Stella said with tentative humor. "But I won't resign. It was too hard getting this job."

Bright's smile was almost imperceptible, and his soberness of manner did not change. "There are other reasons," he said. "Beginning with your personal security."

Stella felt her anger of the night before returning. "Is that what we've come to, Arthur? 'Make a phone call, bump a prosecutor'?"

"Not when the prosecutor's doing her job." Bright's voice betrayed an anger of its own. "You haven't been straight with me. So worrying about your safety becomes far less of a luxury."

He was within his rights, Stella knew, though the remark was sting-
ing. She made herself stay silent.

Left without resistance, Bright seemed, almost literally, to deflate: the
next sound he made was a long expelling of breath. "All right," he said.
"Jack's murder shook me up, too—and I didn't see him hanging there with
his balls cut off. But this case is a danger to you, Stella. In several ways."

Oblique though it was, the allusion to Stella's own plans were clear.
She found it best to say nothing.

"Once you stop leveling with me," Bright continued, "you don't just
put your job at risk, or even your job *performance*. You put *me* at risk, as
County Prosecutor, *and* as a candidate for mayor. And that impacts your
future."

Stella considered how to answer and decided to speak what, before
deciding to come to him, she had concluded was the truth. "What future,
Arthur? Once I told you about the files, I knew I'd lose any chance for
your support."

The fractional smile returned. "I already gave you points for that.
Because I *knew* it's what you thought."

Once more, Stella found herself distrusting her own perceptions,
trapped in the hall of mirrors Saul Ravin had described to her. But she
believed, perhaps only from desperation, that Bright had just implied
that his help might yet be forthcoming. Once more, the moment coun-
seled silence.

"Your initial suicide attempt has failed, Stella. You're merely on the
critical list. I've decided to try and save you from yourself."

The tacit message was clear: Stella must put Bright's interests first.
And yet, even though she knew this, she was concealing what her caller
had said about Michael. "I should have told you about the file," she
acknowledged. "But taking me off the Novak case isn't saving me. It's
confirming that Dan Leary had a point, and giving whoever called him—
and me—what they want."

Bright nodded. "That's why I'm doing it quietly—no fuss, no muss.
A simple administrative transfer."

Which someone else, Stella was certain, would leak to the Steelton
Press. Perhaps her caller, perhaps Charles Sloan. A deeper fear overcame
her—that no one would solve Jack's murder. "Who would you give the
case to?"

"Sloan."

His voice and manner were implacable. Softly, Stella asked, "Give me
two more weeks, Arthur. Please."

Bright studied her with a curious mix of coolness and compassion. "One week," he finally answered. "And then Charles gets the file."

MICHAEL WAS in his office. At his back, a chill rain spattered the windows. Seeing her, he smiled.

"How's the mouse?" he asked. "Any pieces left?"

Despite her resolve, his banter threw her off. Feeling a fresh wave of tension and distrust, she could not bring herself to smile. "Still intact," she answered.

Michael cocked his head. "Is something wrong?"

Beneath the surface of his inquiry, one colleague inquiring of another, Stella imagined a muted tenderness, and felt that much more off-balance. "Yeah," she answered. "Jack Novak's still dead, and I'm still wondering why."

Her tone was so curt, Stella realized, that she could not tell whether his stare was that of a veiled enemy, or an offended friend. "I'm not done yet," he said, "if that's what you're asking. Combing through four years of your friend's drug cases takes more than a day. But if you're asking whether I've found any strange outcomes yet, the answer is no. Not for the half a year I've gotten through."

To Stella, the answer was defensive, though the reference to her "friend" had a distinct edge. But it was also a response she might expect from someone who was tied to Vincent Moro. Sitting, she said more evenly, "When will you be done?"

"Not right away. Even if I drop everything else, give me a week or two."

Anything he told her now was subject to multiple interpretations, and presented her conflicting choices. Did she push him to finish, believing him a liar, or signal her distrust by reclaiming the files herself—and, in the process, perhaps telegraph her resolve to Moro. "Let me ask you something, Michael. Suppose that Jack was fixing cases when I worked for him, just as I believe. Suppose further that you find nothing from the last four years that suggests he was *still* fixing cases. If you were me, how would you make sense of that? That Jack had repented his sins?"

"No," Michael retorted. "That Jack Novak had always needed help. And that Moro has no one left to help Jack anymore."

The ready explanation, delivered with a trace of anger, left Stella even more uneasy. She gazed at the floor, feigning thought. "I spoke to Peter Hall," she told him. "He'll give us access to Fielding's records. Why don't you prepare for that, dig back into Steelton 2000—Lakefront, Alliance, those MBE reports. I'll do the rest of Novak's files myself."

Silent, Michael appraised her. To Stella, each moment with him felt like a Rorschach test which reflected her deepening paranoia. His reaction might be puzzlement with a woman he cared for, frustration with her changing directives, or something far worse. "All right," he said at length.

Stella stood to leave. He looked up at her, his manner dutiful, businesslike, wholly lacking in warmth. "About Steelton 2000," he said, "Krajek's having a press conference this afternoon. Something about the next stage of development. I thought you might want to go."

Was this, Stella wondered, his professional curiosity, or a small diversion? The smile she summoned was an act of will. "Why don't we go together, Michael. I'd like your reaction."

KRAJEK'S PRESS conference was jammed and Stella and Michael, arriving late, stood at the rear.

They were greeted by a double image: Krajak himself, a small figure on a stage, standing in front of his own likeness amplified by an enormous television screen. The mayor was surrounded by eye-catching props: a relief map of the waterfront, with shades of blue depicting the various depths of the lake itself; an aerial photograph of the barren landscape surrounding the stadium in progress; and, most arresting, a scale model of that same landscape, with the ballpark at its core, as Krajek envisioned it in 2003. The mayor stood over it, microphone in one hand, the other pointing out each feature of his futuristic Steelton.

Lovingly, his fingers caressed a sprawling complex of glass and white marble. "*This,*" he said, "will be the Steelton Convention Center, a design as modern as our stadium. And, like the stadium, it will bring millions in new tax revenues to Steelton, and to our businesses, and to our people, millions more."

Krajek was in his element, Stella thought. The front of the platform on which he stood was jammed with cameras; boom mikes protruded from the crowd like spikes; technology magnified his face and voice. His proposal was a surprise: Krajek's slight frame seemed to swell, like a stage actor's, with the drama of the moment; his tone, which tended to be shrill, on this day projected gravitas. The pleasure he took in besting Bright—surely the main object of this display—struck Stella, even from a distance, as close to sensual. She entertained a thought which her contempt for her nakedly striving peer had not heretofore permitted: that she could be watching a future governor. Then a second realization struck her—that Peter Hall had told her the truth about Krajek's plans. The fact that she felt grateful to him, she supposed, was further proof of how little she trusted anyone.

Next to her, Michael stared straight ahead. Whatever he knew, he had divined her mood; he stood apart, as if she no longer existed.

"Surrounding the stadium," Krajek went on, "will be a four-sided mall, with its anchor to be the largest department store in our state's history."

Listening, Stella felt herself divide: the prosecutor was filled with questions, centered on the Lakefront Corporation; the woman who had watched her city's decline with such regret wished that she had no questions. "The lake itself," Krajek went on, "has been an untapped resource, its water despoiled, its potential unrealized." Turning, he walked to the relief map of the lake. "The bond issue I propose will make the lakefront live again.

"We will dredge the harbor, create more room for pleasure boats and cruise ships. And why will they come? Because the waterfront will be lined with restaurants and nightclubs and shops . . ."

"What is this?" Stella murmured. "What would bring anyone to Steelton in January? Ice fishing?"

Intently watching the screen, Michael said nothing.

LEAVING CITY Hall, Stella and Michael stopped on the marble steps, a bitter wind from the lake numbing their faces. Michael remained silent.

"What *is* this?" Stella asked again.

Michael turned to her, eyebrows raised, awaiting more. "I was with him," Stella said, "until he started dredging the lake. No way 'the harbor'—if you can imagine that—will ever be a tourist attraction."

Michael folded his arms, huddling against the cold. "Not based on what Krajek told us, anyway. Restaurants and T-shirt shops won't do it without something more."

"So what isn't he telling us? There'll be more skeptics than Arthur about floating another five hundred million dollars in municipal bonds. Even with federal grants and all the tax incentives Krajek's saying he'll offer to new businesses."

Michael nodded, and his manner eased a bit. "I know one thing Krajek didn't tell us: the stadium's the first stage in a real estate play, just like

I thought. If this second stage goes through, whoever owns the surrounding land gets richer. Whether or not the project is an ultimate bust."

It felt much better, Stella thought, to talk like this, to assume that Michael could be trusted. She assured herself that, because it did not involve Novak, it was safe for her to continue. "Before this press conference," she told him, "I thought Hall was using Krajek. Now I wonder if Krajek isn't using Hall, with the ballpark as the Trojan horse which got this whole thing rolling."

"How so?"

"Hall told me that the name Lakefront Corporation means nothing to him. I wonder what Krajek would say."

Michael frowned. "I wonder what *Arthur* will say—or Sloan. We started with an inquiry regarding Fielding's death, and branched out into questions about MBEs. If Hall and Fielding have nothing to do with the second stage of development, how much farther can we go?"

Stella hesitated. "Legally," she answered, "I'm not sure."

"I meant politically. But you're missing something. Has it occurred to you that maybe Peter Hall *is* Lakefront, or that Hall Development may wind up building most of the second stage? By the time this is over, Hall might make old Amasa look like an amateur. All from having friends in high places."

Stella had a brief shamed thought, mercifully hidden from Michael: that she, quite possibly, was a fool, co-opted by Hall in more subtle ways than money. And that, were Michael right, Hall would be well served to have his wholly owned subsidiary, Stella Marz, as County Prosecutor.

"No," she conceded. "It hadn't occurred to me."

Michael squinted, as though protecting his eyes from the wind. "Which brings us back to Arthur. What Krajek floated just now isn't really a concrete proposal yet—it's a dream, a ploy in mayoral politics. But it's an attractive dream, in Technicolor, with nice little scale models. Arthur may think twice before he stomps all over them. Especially with Krajek and Hall and Larry Rockwell winning the PR war on the ballpark."

It was a practical observation. But, to Stella, Michael sounded too much like Sloan. The thought quickened her doubts again—distrust had become an involuntary reflex. Which reminded her, unhappily, that she had one week left on the Novak case.

"For now," she said, "you focus on Fielding's records, and get me the rest of Jack's files. I'll talk to Arthur."

BUT BRIGHT, of course, was out campaigning. Which left Stella to wonder what he might have said, and how he was reacting to the fact that Krajek's new project would be the lead story on the evening news, the headline in tomorrow's *Press.*

She returned to her office. There was a stack of messages and unread papers: the press conference had cost her two precious hours and the price, as always, would be another late evening. Tomorrow morning, she promised herself, she would start in on Jack's files. Even if she had to go back to his office to retrieve them.

Staring at the pink telephone slips, she realized that fifteen minutes had passed in a near trance, her subconscious, as it often did, having claimed her. She picked up the phone to call Micelli.

"I've got a question about Novak," Stella told her. "Remember saying he wasn't unconscious when they hung him?"

"What I remember saying," Micelli amended, "is that for Novak to remain unconscious while somebody hoisted him up on a stool and hung him would, in my judgment, take more alcohol than he'd had."

"You're confident of that?"

"Stella, someone *that* unconscious is damned near dead. Which we know he wasn't, because the cause of death was asphyxiation by the belt we found him hanging from. Okay?"

Even if her words had not, the coroner's quickness of speech signaled her impatience. "Busy?" Stella asked.

"Yeah. Let's talk about this later—*if* there's anything more to talk about." Without waiting for an answer, the coroner hung up.

TWELVE

IT WAS past eight o'clock when Stella arrived home, and light glowed from the alcove.

Instinctively, Stella froze. An instant later, the fear, a tingling on her skin, became a thought—the light should not be on.

Standing on the porch, she searched her memory. Her routine on leaving the house each morning had the mindlessness of habit. Fill Star's cat dish. Run the dishwasher. Turn off the lights. She would only remember doing something different, and this morning she had not.

Turn off the lights.

Someone had been inside, and wanted her to know this. Perhaps was inside still.

"A woman like you, with no real friends, could die alone."

Irresolute, Stella remained still. Save for the alcove, the house was dark. The only sound was the far-off yipping of a dog.

Her hands were shaking. She had to leave, to run. Turning, she searched the street for strange cars, saw none. A new fear shot through her like a current.

Stella swallowed. Trembling still, she slipped her key into the lock. The sound of the dead bolt turning made her flinch.

Stella stepped into the alcove.

Her foot hit something soft, yet heavy. Her eyes shut, a reflex, and then she looked down.

Star lay at her feet. She was dressed in the robe of the Infant of Prague.

Stella shuddered. Even as she knelt, curled fingers touching Star's forehead, her eyes filled with tears.

"Don't forget to feed the cat . . ."

The cat's fur was cool. Her stare of fright was one Stella had never seen in life. A sob died in Stella's throat.

Gently, she took the cat and cradled it in her arms.

"I've got no kids . . ."

Tears ran down her face now. She forced herself to be still.

Star's killer could be anywhere. Gone, or in the living room. Or in the bedroom, waiting.

She should go to her car, call the police. But she did not move. Her thoughts, like her breaths, quickened.

If the intruder meant to kill her, would he have left Star as a warning?

Quietly, she rose, hugging her cat as if she were asleep and they were going up to bed. With soft footfalls, she walked to the kitchen, tormented by grief and anger and fear for her own life.

The room was silent.

Stella looked about her in the dark, letting her eyes adjust, listening for someone else. She could hear nothing.

Carefully, she laid Star on the kitchen table.

Only after a time could she bring herself to slip off the linen robes. Her eyes filled with tears again; her heart with love, and hatred. She had not backed away, and now they had done this.

Whoever they were.

She switched on the light. Preparing herself, she stood over her murdered cat, stroking her fur. Then she went to the telephone and called Micelli at home.

"Hello?" the coroner answered.

"It's Stella." Her voice was calm, but thin. "I want you to autopsy my cat."

MICELLI WAS waiting at the front door of the coroner's office. She looked haggard after a long day, and her dyed black hair made her pale skin more sallow. Glancing at the garbage bag in Stella's hand, she flicked on a light switch and led her to the basement.

At the end of a long corridor were two swinging metal doors. The corridor was dismal, with green tile floors and locked rooms: as a rookie in homicide, Stella recalled stifling her horror by asking Micelli if the rooms were for spare body parts. Now she said nothing. Their footsteps on the tile echoed through the empty hallway.

Silent, they passed through the metal doors, and Micelli turned on the light. The autopsy room glistened with steel—steel tables, steel sinks, Micelli's scale and instruments. The last time Stella had been here, she had covered Novak's face with a sheet and then watched the coroner eviscerate Tommy Fielding. Now she removed Star from the garbage bag and laid her where Fielding had been.

Micelli put on gloves and her white coat and stood over the cat. "I've never filled out an overtime report," she said, "on a dead pet."

Stella watched Micelli place her instruments on the table. Star stared up at her, as if in horror at this betrayal.

"I'm sorry," Stella murmured.

Micelli put a hand on her shoulder. "Sit over there," she instructed.

"Over there," Stella saw, was a metal stool beside the sink. She sat, arms propped on the sink, staring at the blank gray wall.

Sounds came to her: Micelli's scalpel. The swish of her coat against the table. When the sawing started, Stella closed her eyes.

When she had rescued Star from the animal shelter, the cat had been scrawny, frightened, unhealthy. Stella had taken her for her shots, found her food she liked, learned to love her well before she grew healthy and sleek, the companion of her nights, a warm ball lying next to her, the friend to whom she made ironic comments about another day in trial. These moments were as vivid as yesterday. What seemed hallucinatory was the steel room, the fluorescent lights, the scraping of Micelli's saw.

"Jesus fucking Christ . . ."

The words were Micelli's, uttered with something akin to awe.

Stella turned. Micelli stared down at the table. Beneath her gaze was blood, Star's fur spread open in flaps, her splayed legs. Seeing Stella, the coroner held up a hand, signaling her to stay where she was, to wait.

As the coroner returned to her work, Stella turned away, hands shaking. She hunched, tucking them beneath her arms, until the tremors stopped. Then she realized that Micelli was beside her.

Dully, Stella asked, "What is it?"

The coroner was composed again, her voice flat. "I'll run some tests," she said. "But your cat died of a massive respiratory collapse. Unless I miss my guess, someone shot her full of heroin."

"ASK HIM why Maria left."

Stella drove in a torrent of urgency and rage. Her thoughts were like fragments of a dream: a hanging corpse; a shattered doll; a dead cat's staring eyes; a prostitute sprawled in a Dumpster with her throat cut; a nightmare of missing files in a darkened room, then a hand on Stella's shoulder. The warmth of Michael's mouth; the stirring of her desire.

"Maybe if you fuck him, he'll tell you."

Self-contempt rose like bile to her throat. It was not Sofia who had the rescue fantasy but Stella herself, her need so obvious that Michael had barely needed to dangle the vision of love that Stella had never known, a man and child to go with her cat. He had betrayed her; she had betrayed herself in a way far more degrading than with Jack, corroding her hard-won self-respect, confiding in a man who must find her weaknesses—so easily touched beneath the professional veneer—amusing. Stella Marz, the head of homicide, County Prosecutor–in–waiting. Her rage was so consuming that she understood at last how her father must have felt when he had struck her across the face, seeking release from his own torment. Her car squealed to a stop in front of Michael's house.

"I had no one, Michael. Jack understood that . . ."

Slamming the car door behind her, she ran toward the house, not bothering to catch her breath as she reached the porch and jabbed at the button, causing a sharp buzz to break the still of night.

Silence. She stabbed the button again.

A light came on.

The inner door opened. Michael appeared behind the screen door, a semishadow in blue jeans and a T-shirt, with the dull puffy look of someone startled from sleep. Stella stared at him through the screen.

"Stella? What in God's name?"

Taut, she said nothing.

At last he opened the screen door. Stella pushed through the opening and swung her open palm with all the strength she had.

Her hand cracked across his face. The sound reverberated; Michael staggered, startled, eyes widening with astonishment and anger. He grabbed one hand as she twisted away, then the other, pinning her to the wall like a living crucifix. Blood trickled from his lip; she felt his breath, warm and sour, on her face. Her frenzy was such that his grip did not hurt.

She held herself straight, wrists straining against his grasp. "Moro," she spat out. "You work for him. You gave him my keys."

He stared at her, as though amazed, and then his gaze flickered toward the inside of the house. His grip tightened. Under his breath, he said, "You're out of your fucking mind."

"You told him what I knew about Jack." Her words were staccato. "You told them when I was working late, when to get into my house, how to scare me. You told them about Star . . ."

"Star?"

"You told him the phone call didn't work. So Moro had them kill my cat—"

"*Stella.*" His eyes widened, as though at the presence of insanity, but he spoke in a controlled whisper. "Think about Sofia."

"*You don't take a child from a man who works for Vincent Moro . . .*"

Instinctively, Stella glanced into the hallway, looking for the child. "Someone *killed* Star?" Michael asked belatedly.

Furious, Stella resumed struggling. "Moro owns you," she said in a strangled voice.

"Bullshit."

"He paid for your college, paid for law school, put you in Bright's office—"

He clamped his hand to her mouth, body pushing against hers. Stella writhed in helpless fury, unable to break free. "Listen," he whispered into her ear. "*Listen* to me. We can talk, I can explain. But not like this—"

"Why?" Her mouth covered by his hand, Stella was panting now, her words muffled. "Are you going to call the police?" This threat was a reflex; at once Stella remembered that she could not trust *them* either. Turning her face, she managed to say, "Why don't you call Arthur."

His body pressed into hers, shortening her breaths. Even as she struggled, Stella realized with bitter clarity that, a few short nights ago, she had *wanted* to feel him this way. Gripped by rage, she bit his shoulder through the cloth of his T-shirt. He gave a yelp of pain, then jammed his hand to her throat, cracking her head against the wall. "I don't want to do this," he whispered. "But I don't want Sofia to hear you raving."

Stella swallowed, throat constricted, head ringing. "*Listen* to me," he urged, "and I'll let you go. All I want is a minute. After that, do anything you want, as long as you leave here."

White spots flashed through Stella's vision. She refused to answer him.

After a moment, Michael's hand eased. His body still pinned hers, and their faces were inches apart.

"I worked for Moro two summers," he said. "Not him—for Dioguardia Security. But everyone knew he used Dioguardia to pay some of his leg breakers, maybe buy a little goodwill by giving a few kids from the neighborhood money they needed for college.

"I guarded a warehouse nights for Moro's food distributorship. I knew whose money it was. But I took it because I needed it."

She stared at him, breathing hard, windpipe raw.

"You worked for Novak," he said. "I worked for Moro. After a couple of years it was over for me, like it was over for you . . ."

The parallel enraged her. "It was *never* over for you," she shot back. "*You* stole the files. *You* got my key. *You* spied on me—"

"Spied on you? *I* didn't ask to be part of your obsession with Novak. You got me from Sloan, remember?"

"Because *he's* Moro's, too."

Michael shook his head, as if to clear it. "I don't know *who's* Moro's. But I'm not."

"That's why you didn't tell me about your 'summer job.'" Stella's voice pulsed with anger. "You were full of tidbits about Frankie Scavullo, but you left *that* one out . . ."

"I'm Italian, all right? How much trouble do I want?" His voice filled with resentment. "Look what you've accused me of. Everything from cat murder to being Moro's plant."

Stella pushed against his chest, giving herself space. "Not just Star," she said. "Natasha Tillman."

"Wait. Who's Natasha Tillman?"

"That's right, I didn't give you a name. I just told you about Tina Welch's friend."

"Tina Welch is *another case,* Stella. You're so screwed up you don't know up from down."

"I told you about Tillman," she persisted, "and then someone cut her throat."

Wearily, Michael shook his head once more. "I won't even ask. I don't really think I give a shit."

Stella felt the first interruption in her rage, the disconnection in her chain of accusations represented by Natasha Tillman's murder. "Maria knew who you worked for," she rejoined. "When she couldn't stand it anymore, she ran away. The price was Sofia."

Michael stepped back, freeing her. Stella stared at him in surprise.

In a tight voice, he said, "I've never hit a woman. But I don't trust myself not to hit *you.*" His chest was heaving. "What do you know about Maria and me? Where have you heard all this?"

"Someone called me."

"*Who,* dammit?" Michael folded his arms. "Someone's playing with your head. I wish I could feel sorry for you. But you make your own misery."

In the painful silence, Stella heard footsteps.

Sofia stood in the hallway, frightened, eyes moving from Michael to Stella. Even through her anguish, Stella felt, in piercing memory, the child's terror of a parent's anger.

"Jesus," Michael murmured. It was a muted accusation, directed at Stella, filled with his own anger and despair.

Sofia stared at them. "Go back to bed," Michael told her softly. "In a minute, I'll come get in with you."

Imploringly, Sofia looked at Stella. Stella felt helpless, sick, unable to speak or move.

"Go to bed," her father ordered.

Slowly, the child turned. The two adults watched until she disappeared.

Facing Stella, Michael said, "Take this to Bright, if you have to. Maybe you can cost me my job."

Stella felt a fresh wave of anger, intensified by shame; even now Michael knew how to reach her. "Sofia can always sell pencils," she answered.

Michael stiffened. "I don't want anything to do with you—inside the office or out. Whatever you decide."

Stella gazed at him in confusion, outrage, hurt. Abruptly, she turned and left. She could hear the door locking behind her.

The night was cold. Her cat was dead, and she had never felt so alone. She had nowhere to sleep.

THIRTEEN

STELLA AND Arthur Bright watched the crime-lab team, under
Dance's direction, dust her house for prints.

It was past seven o'clock in the morning. Stella had gone to the office
from Michael's house, afraid to go home. At dawn, despairing of her
alternatives, she had called Nat Dance and then Bright. Dance's response
was to search her house much as he had Novak's: as Dance pointed out,
the intruder could have murdered Stella instead of her cat.

Now, sitting beside Bright on the living-room couch, Stella drank
coffee and struggled to retrieve the strands of reason. "We need to talk
about Lakefront," she told Bright. "Whatever else is happening . . ."

Her voice fell off. Absently, Bright polished his glasses with his hand-
kerchief, speaking in a low voice so that others could not hear. "Let's talk
about you running for County Prosecutor."

Stella turned to him, startled, ignoring the noise and movement
around them.

He continued working on his glasses. "You support me for mayor,"
he began, "but you're not identified as an opponent of the ballpark.
Maybe that's good politics. Now Peter Hall wants to be your friend.
Why go looking for more trouble?" Pausing, he seemed to consider his
words. "I don't want to end up visiting you at the morgue. I don't want
you dead politically, either. That's no good for you *or* me."

Stella had no response. Her mind felt leaden: the last ten hours had
destroyed her equilibrium, and the mention of practical politics made the
serial invasions of her own house seem all the more unreal. Putting on his
glasses, Bright finished with the same directness. "What I'm saying is, let
Sloan worry about Novak, and let Del Corso and the white-collar crime
unit worry about Lakefront, the MBEs, and Steelton 2000."

"What about Fielding? Or Welch—or Tillman?"

Bright eyed the crime-lab technicians, then turned to her. "As far as
we know, Fielding and Welch were an accident, and Tillman was a
hooker who got killed like hookers do—an occupational hazard. *If,* and

it's a huge *if,* the white-collar team takes us through Lakefront or Alliance back to some problem with Fielding, it still doesn't make him a murder victim. And *murder,* not corruption, is the business of your unit. Show me evidence of a homicide and then we can revisit it. Right now, you and Dance have nothing.

"Someone doesn't like whatever you're doing, and it clearly has to do with Jack." Pausing, Bright briefly covered her hand with his. "On top of that, why risk pissing off Peter Hall and everyone who believes in Steelton 2000 and Tom Krajek's vision of the Steelton renaissance— borderline corrupt as it may be? Why not stay out of it, leave the dirty work to Del Corso and me? Why not let us cover for you?"

Stella felt lost. A speech this long, and this personal, was not typical of Bright. Tired though she was, she saw what Bright was offering: a road out of harm's way, avoiding political damage in a manner which, because it honored the jurisdictional lines between the homicide and white-collar crime units, was eminently defensible. This would lead to a further mercy Bright did not know about: a way of severing her work relationship with Michael Del Corso which required no action by either Michael or Stella. But that, in turn, would allow Stella to conceal her knowledge of Michael's past—or present—connections to Vincent Moro.

Silent, she stared at the carpet. How many times already had she relived her visit to Michael's home: her rage, her accusations, his admissions, his denials. The emotions—helplessness, bewilderment, fear— flickering across Sofia's face.

"*You make your own misery,*" Michael had said.

A bleak truth came to her: how tenuous the underpinnings of her contentment had always been. She thought of Star again.

"*Someone shot your cat full of heroin . . .*"

"Take a couple of days off," Bright was saying. "Dance will have your place guarded. Then I'll want your help with something different."

Stella turned to him. "What's that?"

"Can we step outside for a minute?"

On the way out the front door, Stella took a ski jacket from the closet. They stood on her modest front lawn, its grass stunted by winter, dusted with frost.

"I'm lagging on the West Side," Bright said. "Polling poorly among Poles, to be alliterative. I need you out in Warszawa. Elsewhere, too." He looked at her intently. "For you, it's valuable exposure. For me, it could make a real difference. You're white, and you're a woman. You can do for me what Charles can't."

Stella prided herself on quickness of thought. But her mind was over-taxed, her emotions unreliable: what struck her was Bright's reference to Sloan, as bald as it was gratuitous. "What are you saying, Arthur? That you'll support me if you win?"

Had she not been so weary, Stella knew at once, she would not have been so blunt. It was not the frankness of ambition; she was too heartsick for that. But not too heartsick to be curious.

Bright looked less surprised at her question than she was. But he seemed to measure his words. "If you help me win, and look like a strong candidate in your own right, that's two good reasons. But I'll need more campaigning from you than I thought."

The subtlety of Bright's offer became apparent. Not only was he pro-tecting her from the consequences of the Novak case, he was protecting himself: as her successor, Sloan most likely would put Bright's political interests ahead of the truth. But Bright's real achievement, Stella realized, was placing Sloan in this position instead of her—by also insulating her from Steelton 2000, Bright, to her amazement, was advancing both their interests at a potential cost to Sloan. Not for the first time, Stella won-dered if she had—or wished to have—the combination of suppleness, self-interest, and comprehension of others' motives to succeed in Steel-ton politics.

At length, Stella said, "I'm a little slow this morning."

While smiling, Bright looked at her keenly, as though divining her thoughts. "Practice, Stella. I came up a black man with aspirations in a white man's town. It sharpens the mind."

How long, Stella wondered, had Arthur wanted to be mayor? Had he dreamed of it thirty years ago, as valedictorian of his high school, when Stella was in second grade and no black politician in Steelton had ever won a citywide office? How many calculations had he made, each day, for all the years since then: hiding his ambitions; feigning an interest in one goal when he held another; pretending to like men he despised, of whom Jack Novak might have been one; waiting for another's weak-nesses or misjudgments to open up a path? As he might be now, with her. And yet she believed in Arthur, and what he had achieved.

"Have you ever dreamed you're falling from a building?" she asked. "Then, just before you're about to die, you wake up?"

Bright nodded. "My worst nightmare is where they find out I failed the bar, and can't be County Prosecutor anymore. They've discovered the fraud, you see—exposure scares me worse than death. But, yeah, I've had *your* dream, too."

She folded her arms, cold despite her jacket. "That's how I feel now. I just woke up, and I'm not sure where I am. The only way I know I'm still alive is that I'm scared to death."

Bright pondered this. "Sometimes I think about George Walker, running for mayor the last time. I honestly thought he'd make it. Instead, they nail him for possession of cocaine, and I become the great black hope." He held up his thumb and forefinger, nearly touching. "I'm like George Walker, Stella. I'm that close. Maybe you are, too."

As with Hall, Stella felt momentarily mesmerized, a child watching a magic trick. Then she thought of a dead ex-lover, a dead cat. "I work for you," she responded. "Just like in the Novak case, you can decide what I do with Steelton 2000. And if you want more help campaigning, I've got enough vacation hours saved up to take the time. But I still want to work Jack's murder for the next six days."

Bright's gaze was cool; he was opening Stella's future for her, his expression said, and she persisted in bargaining. But she had something *he* wanted, too. "All right," he said at last. "Just don't take any chances. By tomorrow, we'll get you a schedule of appearances."

He clasped her shoulder, looking into her face. Then, their mutual interests established, he walked briskly to his car to commence another day of campaigning.

When Stella returned to the house, Dance was at the back door to the kitchen. Near where he stood, illuminated by a crack of pale sunlight, was a cat dish, a few remnants of the last food Star had eaten. The thought that she need not fill it made her look away. Dance did not notice; he was bent over the lock.

"Still no sign of a break-in?" Stella asked.

Without turning, Dance emitted a negative grunt. His mood seemed as foul as Stella's was dark.

"How do you do that, Nat? Get in that clean without a key."

"You don't. Unless you're a genius at burglary. Do you have a maid, someone who comes here when you're gone?"

"Not for months." Not, in fact, since the cost of her father's care had required still more economies.

He turned to her, his dark eyes wholly without warmth. "Anyone else have a key?"

Stella felt herself tense—not only at Dance's manner, but at the decision she must make. Once more she thought of Sofia.

"You worked for Novak. I worked for Moro. After a couple of years it was over for me, like it was over for you . . ."

"I'll have to think," Stella answered.

"You will at that." Dance towered over her, his rough-hewn face as expressionless as an African mask. "It's like I said the night before last—you've got a decision to make. Someone keeps sending you a message, and they don't think you get it."

Filled with grief and distrust, Stella turned and left.

SHE WENT to Novak's office.

It was where both logic and emotion drove her. Logic, because Jack's files were the only evidence she had; emotion, because she would not have to see Michael. She sat in Jack's chair, fighting off the eeriness of memory. Then she called her secretary to leave a phone number and began reviewing files.

She started with the half year of files Michael had already gone over. It was seven hours later, four in the afternoon, before she finished.

Among these files she had found nothing suspicious. This either supported what Michael had told her—that Moro had no longer had anyone to help Novak fix cases—or perhaps showed that Michael had destroyed any files which suggested otherwise. And Stella could not know which.

Tiredly, she looked at the remaining storage boxes, jammed with paper and manila folders. Three and a half more years. At least it might keep her mind off Star, give her more reason not to go home.

The buzz of Jack's telephone, as soft as he had always kept it, nonetheless startled her.

It was Micelli. Without preface, the coroner said, "I got to thinking last night, after the cat. About Novak."

Stella sat straighter. "Okay."

"You were asking how someone could hang him up there. Ever hear of a drug called flunitrazepan?"

Stella searched her memory. "The date-rape drug," she answered. "Some guy slips it to a girl at a party. It makes her dopey and amnesiac—she doesn't resist, and doesn't remember whatever he and/or his friends did to her. Handy."

"It's also unlikely to show up in her blood. But it will in her urine. That is, if you test for it." Micelli cleared her throat. "I kept a sample of Novak's urine, of course. I had the crime lab check it. There were distinct traces of flunitrazepan."

To Stella, Jack's windowless office felt darker, cooler. "Then someone drugged him," she said. "Missy Allen, or the person she claims Jack was waiting for."

"Looks like. For sure it wasn't part of some autoerotic ritual: Novak wouldn't be taking flunitrazepan to heighten his sensations. But that raises another question—once he's like a hundred-eighty-five-pound sack of potatoes, how does a woman like Allen lift him up there?"

Stella considered this. "She doesn't. Unless Missy slips the drug in Jack's scotch and lets someone else in his apartment. Either way, whoever planned this was cool and very sophisticated. Probably a professional."

Even as she said this, Stella had several reactions, all instinctive: excitement at perceiving something important; fresh horror, before she mastered it, at what people can do to each other, at what someone had done to Jack; a more lasting horror that the same person might have entered her own home; the certainty that the crime lab would find no evidence of value. "So they could have drugged him," Stella said slowly, "then dressed him in the garter belt and heels."

"Could have. *Why* they'd go to all that trouble is your department."

"To make it look different than it was?" Stella posited. But this did not satisfy: why would a professional bother with such excess?

Micelli remained silent. "Thanks, Kate," Stella told her. "I appreciate this."

Putting down the telephone, Stella imagined Moro in the shadows. Her mind felt cold.

It's you, she thought, *you psychotic sonofabitch. The fixed cases, the Haitian, Jack, the missing files, Star. Even though I may never prove it, it's you.*

You, and someone else.

That was the real problem: someone else.

If she persisted, Moro might have her killed, and she would not even know why. Flunitrazepan. It was all too easy—after Jack—to imagine the death they might design.

She would have to tell Arthur about Micelli's call and, having told him, tell Dance, who might belong to Moro. Who might, in her worst fears, have been the last visitor to Jack's apartment.

The telephone rang again.

"Stella?"

Recognizing Dance's voice at once, she felt the now-familiar paranoia, and wondered if Jack's telephone was tapped. "Yes?"

"You decided yet?"

This was delivered with his usual flatness. Stella considered her answer. "I'm here, if that's what you mean."

"Suit yourself." The words carried no discernible emotion. "Then I've got something you might be interested in. A witness who says she saw Welch and Fielding together on the night they died."

FOURTEEN

LIKE CITY Hall, the town house across from Fielding's was from the beaux arts period, and its occupant—a thirtyish investment banker who affected horn-rimmed glasses and slicked-back hair—had accented its high windows and intricate moldings with a French provincial decor. He had been in Toronto when Fielding died, Roger Blechman explained to Dance and Stella, and had never known anything about him. But Roger's girlfriend, Susanna Patch, had stayed over to watch his house and walk his Doberman.

The night before last, over dinner, Susanna had mentioned something curious to Roger. A check of his appointment book confirmed the date of Susanna's memory: though she did not, Roger recalled the day's significance. Together, they had decided to call Dance.

Roger delivered this account with a somewhat officious air, suggesting that, even in matters for which he was not responsible, Roger Blechman was precise. Susanna, a graduate student in art history who used little makeup and wore her naturally blond hair skimmed back from her face, deferred to his air of certitude. As though he had heard enough from Roger, and was confident the man knew nothing important, Dance had switched on his tape recorder and addressed his questions to Susanna.

Serious and reserved, Susanna answered Dance with a faint New England accent. For a time Stella merely listened, trying to conceal her distrust of Nathaniel Dance, the theory which had begun to merge with a picture of the night Welch and Fielding had died.

IT WAS late; Susanna knew this because she was watching the weather on the eleven o'clock news. Belatedly, she remembered that it was the night to put out the garbage—given the spotty quality of trash collection in Steelton, Roger had admonished, it was not a date to miss.

Putting on her robe, Susanna went out the rear door and wrestled the plastic trash can to the sidewalk in front.

The night was cold to the bone, more harsh for its still, moonlit clarity, and garbage cans from the other houses already lined the street. Susanna made certain that the lid was secure—there were stray cats in the neighborhood, Roger had warned her—and began to scurry back inside.

There was a noise down the brick street, the quiet, almost imperceptible purr of a motor coming closer. Turning, Susanna saw two headlights easing through the light and shadow cast by the wrought-iron arc lights which Roger and his neighbors had raised money to erect. As it passed through a pool of light, slowing, Susanna noted that the car was white: though she had little interest in automotive design, she recognized it as a luxury car.

For no reason beyond the street's accustomed quiet, Susanna paused.

The car had stopped across the street and, perhaps, three houses down. Though there were streetlights, the driver had parked where the glow of one light dissipated and another began, and the car was the faintest of outlines in the reflection of a half-moon.

Susanna heard a hollow sound, the echo of a car door softly closing. From the shadow of Roger's porch, she watched and listened.

There were footsteps, even fainter, the form of someone moving in front of the car, then a second metallic whisper—the passenger door opening, Susanna guessed. Only after an interval, surprisingly long, did the hollow thud of a car door closing confirm this.

The footsteps, resuming, were slower, heavier. Curiously, though two car doors had opened, the steps sounded like those of a single person. Susanna felt sure of that: she did not drink, except for the occasional glass of Bordeaux with Roger, and from the Christmas of her third year, when she had heard the putative Santa Claus placing presents beneath the tree and come downstairs to apprehend him, her father had often remarked with a smile on how unusually keen were his daughter's senses.

Now her eyes were more accustomed to the night. Though colder still, she waited.

At the edge of a streetlight, Susanna saw two shadowy figures. They were illuminated, dimly, for only a few seconds. But the image surprised her: a man half dragging, half carrying a woman who must be drunk. They were headed for a town house with no porch light on, and no light inside.

Abruptly, they vanished. The last sound Susanna heard was a front door opening, then closing; the last she saw was a light coming on, a yellow glow through the front window of the house.

Shivering, Susanna went inside.

"THE WOMAN," Stella asked, "how tall was she?"

At this, Stella felt Dance's sideways glance. Susanna Patch considered her answer gravely. "Tall. Even though she was leaning against him, he was standing straight, and her head still reached his shoulder."

"Did you recognize either one of them?"

Patch shook her head. "I'd never seen him before." She glanced at her boyfriend, then Dance. "I know from the news that he was white and she was black. I couldn't have told you that, either—it was too dark. But it must have been him, because he let himself inside."

Stella paused at this. "Do you remember how he was built?"

Patch gazed up at the ceiling. "Big, I think. Thick across the shoulders. But maybe that's more about how thin she seemed to me, and how incapacitated she was. It was the woman who made an impression."

When Stella fell silent again, Dance resumed his questions.

AFTERWARD, THEY stood on the sidewalk. Though it was earlier, a little past eight, the night was clear and cold, the street as quiet as Patch had described. "I want to see Fielding's house," Stella said.

Dance nodded; before they had come, Stella had asked him to retrieve a copy of Fielding's house key. They crossed the brick street in silence.

Fielding's town house was dark. Entering, Stella flicked on the lights. The first few seconds unsettled her: two bodies had been found here, and the house, though illuminated, bore the unmistakable evidence of a place where no one lived now—the smell of stale air, the chill of a thermostat kept too low. It reminded her of the morgue.

She did not like being alone with Dance.

Ignoring him, she walked from room to room. The living room was sterile, with the functional decor of a busy man who had gotten divorced and left his furniture behind. The kitchen, too, was sparely equipped, just enough dishes for a father and daughter. Or, Stella supposed, Fielding and a guest.

Quiet, she stared into the stainless steel sink. The police had found a ham sandwich here, a glass of beer, left, incongruously, next to the heroin paraphernalia. It made less sense than ever. Or perhaps, and for the first time, more.

She went to the bedroom, gazing down at the queen-sized bed.

She remembered the crime-scene photos well: Fielding and Welch, naked, looking alienated from each other even in death. What the photos had not recorded was the picture of the child on Fielding's nightstand, as lovely, in her way, as was Sofia.

Stella felt Dance waiting behind her. Quietly, he said, "You're thinking she was already dead."

Tense, Stella did not turn. For the last two hours, she had wondered if Dance had asked her to help interview Patch so that he could ferret out Stella's theories and, if so, for what purposes. Now she must decide what to say, what to withhold.

"No," she answered. "I'm thinking *he* was already dead."

Circling Stella, Dance sat heavily on the bed, staring up at her. "That," he observed, "would explain some things. Like the sandwich."

"How do you explain Curran?"

"Curran?" Dance still watched her closely. "That's a hard one. But let's assume Fielding was murdered, and whoever did it had some way of borrowing his car.

"We know that two nights before he died, Fielding went home sick. Maybe the killer knew that, too. So he gets in Fielding's white Lexus and cruises the Scarberry for a prostitute.

"That's what Curran could have seen. And that's what your girlfriend Natasha Tillman saw two nights later—the killer picking up Tina Welch."

Stella folded her arms. Though she had seen many kinds of depravity, the cold-bloodedness that would plan a second murder as window dressing for the first, choosing the victim at random, was of a different order. "What Micelli would ask," she told Dance, "is how someone could shoot up Fielding without a struggle, let alone be certain that the overdose was sufficient to kill them both. That argues this was an accident."

Dance frowned. "What about Susanna Patch? We all know eyewitnesses are unreliable, especially the ones who pride themselves on remembering every detail. But if you believe her, Tina Welch arrived here at least unconscious. So does she wake up, inject Fielding, and *then* herself?"

Stella shrugged. On the surface, their exchange was professional, colleagues trading hypotheses. But it felt to Stella like a game played on two different levels: the theories themselves, and what each of them might choose not to reveal.

"The problem with a homicide is Welch," she finally said. "Not Fielding."

"How's that?"

"According to Patch, Welch arrived here unconscious. According to Tillman, Welch got in Fielding's Lexus roughly half an hour before, completely alert.

"She *knew* the man who picked her up—well enough to get in the car, and well enough to shoot up on the way. As I suggest, Fielding *could* have been dead already. But the idea that someone else drove his car through the Scarberry twice in one week is a stretch." Pausing, Stella was careful to look directly at Dance, hoping she sounded plausible. "If Curran saw the Lexus two nights earlier, it makes sense that Fielding was driving. *And* that Tina got in with him on the night they died because she'd been with him before. However strange that seems."

WHEN STELLA arrived home, there was a squad car in front, a uniformed policeman on her porch. Thanking him, she opened the door, then stopped abruptly in the alcove, staring down at the place where she had found Star's body.

She took a deep breath and went upstairs. Lying down on the bed, she spread a cold washcloth across her eyes, trying to ease the headache which shot through her temples from the base of her skull.

Her thoughts were confused. Star. Novak. Michael and Sofia, Fielding and Tina Welch. Natasha Tillman. Hall's offer, then Bright's. The Viking hardihood of her own ambition. The disquiet which made her mislead Dance.

"*Right now,*" Arthur had said, "*you and Dance have nothing.*"

But this might not be true, and—except for the murderer—only Stella knew why. Or how bewildering the truth might be.

She picked up her bedside phone, listening carefully for a click, for the unsteadiness of dial tone which suggests a wiretap. Though she heard nothing, she waited for a time before calling Micelli at home.

"I'm sorry," she told the coroner. "I don't like to make a habit of this. But I need to ask you some things."

"As long as you're out of cats," Micelli said evenly. "What is it?"

"Do you remember about how tall Tommy Fielding was? And Welch."

"Not exactly. But he was maybe six feet one, or six two. She wasn't short, either. Perhaps five eight."

This was Stella's memory. "By any chance, did you check their urine for traces of flunitrazepan?"

"I didn't see any need." The coroner's response, though prompt, reflected surprise. "Is there?"

"Yes," Stella answered. "As quickly as you can."

FIFTEEN

THE NEXT morning Stella went to Michael's office.

He glanced up from the papers spread in front of him. His first expression was surprise, then wariness and resentment; however angry he might be, his look conveyed, Stella was a threat to him. What this said about his guilt or innocence she could not guess. He did not speak to her, and seemed to have no wish to do so.

Nor was it easy for Stella to find words. She took a chair in front of his desk, neither speaking nor looking away.

"There's something I need to say to you," she told him.

"Unless you're going to Bright, there's nothing. Sloan tells me I'm not working for you anymore."

The bluntness of his challenge stopped her, but only briefly. "If you're looking for an apology, forget it—except about Sofia. Everything I said the other night is true." She kept her voice low, controlled. "When I applied for a job here, I told Arthur about my relationship with Jack. You concealed that Vincent Moro helped you pay for college. God knows what else you're hiding.

"No one broke into my house, Michael. Obviously they had a key. Tell me who you gave it to."

Michael stared at her. "No one," he answered, half rising from his desk. "Let's call Bright—right now. I'm not putting up with any more hysteria."

Every part of Stella felt taut now. "Tell your friends I intend to figure out who killed Jack Novak, who ordered it, and why. Then it's your turn." She paused, struggling to control her voice. "Before I came here, I wrote a letter and put it in a safe deposit box. It spells out everything I believe you did. So before they do anything to me, tell them *that,* too. So they can decide how important you are."

His look of anger changed to incredulity. In an undertone, stunned and low, he said, "You're serious, aren't you."

She stood, facing him. "Who's Lakefront, Michael?"

To a less cynical eye than hers, Stella realized, he would have looked genuinely bewildered. "Do you think I *know*? I was the one who asked *you* the question. If it weren't for me, you couldn't ask me now."

Stella gave him a hard smile, maintaining her resolve as if her life depended on it. Which, she feared, it might. "Then get me an answer," she said, and walked out.

THE NEXT few hours, futile ones, were spent at Jack Novak's office. Despite the urgency of her task, Stella found her mind drifting, first to Michael, and then to Jack, to their last humiliating stay at his weekend retreat, to her final memory of him, body slack, eyes bulging.

Whoever killed him had searched his apartment.

It was nothing she could prove. It was the knowledge of how Jack did things, culled from all the mornings she had awakened there and watched him close each drawer before leaving. Habits of neatness, however incongruous, which no slackness in his personal life seemed to erase. Even his last year of files was neat, orderly, sequential.

And told her nothing.

There were no sweetheart deals, no light sentences. No disappearing evidence. Unless Michael had known where to look, what files to destroy, Jack had lost his touch.

Unless, she amended, Moro had formed other goals, found better means of protection. Perhaps his friends in law enforcement had been promoted.

She picked up the phone and called Micelli. "How are those tests coming?" Stella asked.

"Give me two more hours." Instead of harassed, Micelli sounded uneasy. "Then I want you to come see me."

Stella did not ask why. Hanging up, she riffled through more files, killing time by finding what she now expected to find—no anomalies of justice, no favors for George Flood. Or Vincent Moro.

At a little past four o'clock she drove to the coroner's office.

RISING FROM her desk, Micelli looked grave, and the downcast fluorescent light made the lines and angles of her face more harsh. She told her secretary on the intercom that she would take no calls. Then she walked to the door and closed it behind them.

"This isn't one for the telephone," she said.

Stella felt queasy. "What is it?"

"Where to begin." Micelli's manner was sober, a scientist's, as though distancing herself from what she had learned. "You know our procedures, Stella. There are tests for all kinds of things, but we can't run every one of them.

"Take Novak. We tested his blood for drugs and alcohol, because that made sense. But those tests don't necessarily reveal the presence of other substances . . ."

"Like flunitrazepan."

"Exactly. There's a separate test for that. Until you gave me a reason, it didn't occur to me to run it. The same with Welch and Fielding." Micelli's voice became oddly gentle. "Welch was a negative, Stella. Fielding was positive."

Stella felt fear as a coolness on her skin. "Novak," she said slowly. "And Fielding . . ."

Micelli nodded. For once, her manner said, she was a step ahead of Stella. "Welch was a user—no one needed to make her shoot up. Not so Fielding. But that leaves the question of a lethal overdose. Someone sophisticated enough to put flunitrazepan in Fielding's beer would make sure the overdose would kill them both.

"I considered the possibilities. Then I remembered a rash of deaths in Baltimore, from street sales of heroin cut with a drug called fentanyl. Not a good idea: fentanyl's an anesthetic, but it's about one hundred percent more potent than morphine. An overdose of heroin and fentanyl will do the job for sure." Micelli folded her hands in front of her. "*That's* what killed Welch and Fielding."

Silent, Stella felt a design, intricate and terrible, move from suspicion to fact. The same man who had murdered Jack Novak had murdered Welch and Fielding, and only Susanna Patch had seen him. The same man, Stella was certain, who had cut Natasha Tillman's throat. Who had designed a series of threats, each more unnerving than the last, to assure Stella that she, too, was unsafe. But any motive she could posit for killing Novak—that somehow the corruption of his practice had led to murder—was irrelevant to the murder of the others.

"Let's talk about our killer," Micelli said.

"All right."

"College boys know about date rape. But fentanyl? I'd say he's in the drug trade, or someone with medical or other specialized knowledge."

The coroner paused. "The same man killed your cat, Stella. I'd keep that in mind."

Stella could think of nothing to say.

LEAVING THE coroner's office, Stella looked up and down the street.

A biting wind whined through concrete canyons—the rooflines of struggling shops, old office buildings, a diner which had already closed. Four blocks away was the Scarberry, and beyond that a steel pier beside the Onondaga River where the Haitian, Jean-Claude Desnoyers, had been found murdered. Stella shivered. Though close to the cluster of new office towers which, with the stadium, constituted the city's reason for hope, these downtown streets were dangerously quiet, the residue of white fear and white flight, families huddled in their neighborhoods or in the suburbs, with children who would never know these streets at all. Stella, like other women, was fearful of their emptiness.

She saw no one. Crossing the street to her car, she thought of Welch and Tillman vanishing, and then, abruptly, of Desnoyers's account of getting in his car, believing himself safe, only to feel Johnny Curran's gun to his head.

Stopping beside her car, she peered through the window, looking for the shadow of someone waiting inside. Only when she detected nothing could she acknowledge the pulse beating in her throat.

She needed a refuge, a place to reflect without fear, and now there was but one.

Stella got in the car and drove toward Warszawa, glancing in the mirror to see if she was followed.

AS ALWAYS, the massive doors of St. Stanislaus were open.

Stella's hand rested on the hand-carved wood. Like a century of priests before him, Father Kolak kept the church open at all hours, a sanctuary for those in search of peace; her great-grandfather, Carol Marzewski, had helped make it so, and now, although he could not have imagined Stella or the life she led, she had returned.

Quickly, Stella stepped inside.

Carol had spoken little English, she knew, and the Masses he had heard, as was Stella's first Mass, were in Latin, intoned through time. Now there was only silence, a woman from the neighborhood hunched before the candlelit altar, crossing herself. Stella's footsteps sounded on the stone.

In nomine Patris, et Filii, et Spiritui Sancti.

Stella at four. Huddled beside her parents at her grandfather's funeral Mass, her first clear memory. From child to prosecutor, the thread running through her life had been a thousand visits to this place, broken only by her father's banishment, the painful years when she had come here but once—after the last weekend with Jack Novak, looking from side to side, as she had tonight, to ensure that no one saw her. Then, as well, she had remembered the Mass for her grandfather Emil Marz.

Hail Mary, full of grace . . . pray for us sinners now and at the hour of our death.

That weekend, too, had felt like a small death.

"It's all right, Stella." As Jack had said this, she could sense the other man listening outside. *"Do this for me. For us . . ."*

Stella knelt, feeling the shadowy vastness envelop her. To have come so far and yet be here again, still haunted by Jack Novak, still groping for survival.

After prayer, she hoped, would follow reason, God's gift to her.

F O R S O M E time, she knew not how long, she let her prayers, this place, do their work. At last she searched for a prosecutor's logic.

The murderer had set out to kill Fielding, then Novak. To obscure his motives, he had designed deaths meant to demean the victims. Fielding would die using drugs with a black prostitute; Novak at the climax of a sadomasochistic ritual. Death as deception.

The women's deaths meant nothing in themselves. He had murdered Welch to serve as scenery. Tillman was an accident: the murderer had followed Stella to the Scarberry, seen Tillman enter Stella's car, and feared—wrongly, as it happened—for his own security. Because he had feared Tillman's knowledge.

That, Stella realized, must be what Fielding and Novak had in common—not drugs, or Jack's decade-old corruption. Knowledge, whatever it might be, and therefore the power to harm.

But what could Jack and Fielding have known in common?

Surely it could not involve sex, Stella reflected, not if one believed Amanda Fielding. She let her mind drift again.

When they had searched Fielding's town house, they had found pornography. The murderer had planted it, Stella was now certain, to corroborate a sexual interest which did not exist. But he did not need to do that with Jack Novak.

Novak was into scenes, Curran had said. Missy Allen had confirmed this—Jack's emptiness, his ceaseless craving for excitement, had taken over his life. And yet there must be a reason for the manner of his death.

Still Stella knelt, seeking.

The murderer had searched Jack's apartment, she believed.

What could he have been looking for? How could it relate to Tommy Fielding? Why, if he had found it, was Stella still worth threatening, her inquiries so dangerous that each threat came closer to her?

Perhaps he had not found what he needed.

In her bewilderment, Stella reviewed what she knew. The police had combed his office, opened the safe deposit box where he kept his will. Gone to his weekend place . . .

Remembering, she closed her eyes.

STILL HALF-NAKED, Stella began to cry.

Through the bedroom door, she could hear voices, Jack and the man he had wanted her to have sex with, the man's contemptuous laugh. At last the front door opened, then closed.

Silence.

In her relief, her misery, Stella quivered. The bedroom door opened.

Jack looked at her. "Diego's gone," he said.

Tears ran down Stella's face. In a muffled voice, she told him, "So am I."

He sat beside her on the bed, stroking her hair, her bare skin.

"*No.*" She stood abruptly, snatching at the top of her bikini. But she was so agitated that it slipped from her fingers. She bent, instinctively covering her naked breasts.

"You're way too scared," he said. "Nothing will happen unless you want it."

Turning from him, she managed to dress. His voice, coming from behind her, remained soft. "It's nothing, Stella—an experiment. We should have talked first."

She wheeled on him. "Talk? You wanted me drunk and helpless. The fun for you would have been watching me realize what I'd done."

He shook his head. "You're as suspicious as a peasant. As your father." At once, seeing her face, he said, "I'm sorry. That was unfair. But you're being unfair to me."

She stood there, transfixed by his quicksilver changes, her sudden startling desire to defend her father against this man. When he led her to the living room, a horrified fascination kept her from resisting.

They stood in the middle of the room. Gently, Jack kissed her forehead. "Next week is the opening of the symphony, Stella. I've never taken you before. You'll look beautiful."

What was so humiliating was his belief, even now, that she would be flattered. And, flattered, would come.

Releasing her, he walked to the bookshelf, reaching for a leather volume.

She watched this as a child watches something she does not comprehend. Her mind was still dull with alcohol: the moment seemed no more real, or unreal, than what had gone before. He returned to her, volume cradled in both hands.

"Here," he said.

Was he offering her a book to read? Then he opened it, and she saw that it was hollow.

Inside were three thick stacks of hundred-dollar bills bound with rubber bands—drug money, Stella knew at once.

"My Swiss bank account," Jack told her, "for emergencies."

Stella stared at the money, and then at Jack.

He smiled now. "It's for the symphony, Stella. For your new dress. And whatever you think goes with it."

Jack had just told her what she was to him. But there was something worse—her knowledge of whose money this was. Her memories of a frightened dealer who had confided in her. Then of Vincent Moro, a few days before the Haitian died, emerging from the shadows of Jack's office.

With a visceral rage, she struck the book from Novak's hand.

The piles of money scattered at his feet; the book fell face down, its spine turned so that Stella could read the title, Jack's heartless joke. *Crime and Punishment.*

She looked up into his flushed face, startled eyes.

"Take me home," she said.

AT THIS, Stella's eyes opened.

Turning, she studied a stained-glass window, recounting in colored fragments the martyrdom of St. Stanislaus. Now, as then, it helped her to remember who she was.

Outside the office, that weekend was the last time she had been with

Jack, or to that house. Even the thought of returning had haunted her, as if, by entering there, she would become the woman Jack wanted, the woman Stella feared. But, like a talisman, she had kept the house key Jack had given her when, in a last bid for her friendship, he had suggested that she use his place to study for the bar exam. It remained in a drawer, next to the shattered pieces of the Infant of Prague.

Still kneeling, Stella said a final prayer, and rose.

Outside, she scanned the street again. Then she drove home, retrieved the key, and started for Jack's house on the lake.

PART FOUR

NATHANIEL DANCE

ONE

ONE HOUR and forty minutes later, Stella turned off the main road, taking the long dirt and gravel drive to Jack's house.

She slowed, headlights illuminating the grassy field around her, glancing back to ensure that no other car had turned. She saw nothing. But this did not put her mind at ease—in this place she would be alone, at risk. For the last minutes she had done little but question herself; all that had brought her here was intuition, and the nearer she came the more intensely she questioned it. Yet she had not turned back.

At the end of the drive was a bare willow tree and, beside it, Jack's retreat, set against the dark waters of Lake Erie. Stella parked and got out. The susurrus of the lake had a deep resonance, evoking its enormity, its depth; above this, Stella heard the slap of waves spilling onto the narrow beach. The only other sounds were the stirring of branches in the wind, the crunch of her footsteps on ice and gravel.

The house loomed against a starless sky. It had been built by a Steelton plutocrat at the turn of the century; though one story, it was large, a rough-hewn wooden structure with a stone fireplace, lofty ceilings, exposed beams. Stella was not surprised by how distinctly she pictured the interior; whether she would see it again rested on whether a thirteen-year-old key still worked.

At least it fit.

Stella leaned forward, forehead against the grainy wood of the door. The key would not turn. Wrist straining, she jiggled it. There was an abrupt snap. The click of a latch made Stella flinch.

Slowly, she opened the door.

The interior was pitch-black. She found the switch by touch.

A wall sconce behind her cast a pale illumination toward the center of the great room, leaving its corners in shadows. Stella did not move.

All was as she remembered it: the fireplace, the stack of logs, even the teak model of a schooner Stella had given Jack for his thirty-eighth birthday. As old, Stella reflected, as she was now. The thought was at once eerie and sad, evoking the passage of time and the knowledge that now Jack would grow no older. The room felt like a museum.

Here were the remnants of all that Jack aspired to, the things which he had once imagined would complete him—the rich Persian rugs, the elaborate stereo system, the hundreds of recorded operas and symphonies, the shelf of expensive wines, the photographs of his trim white sailboat. Yet none of it had satisfied. For Jack had never mastered the simplest and most precious act—to occupy a space, a moment, and feel at rest.

Slowly, Stella crossed the room.

The shelves surrounding Jack's massive television were crammed with books—art collections, leather-bound classics, treatises on sailing or astronomy, food for Jack's omnivorous mind. Everything but history, Stella thought; even in his reading, Jack had been a creature of the here and now. Things he felt he could not use held no interest for him. Things, Stella amended, or people.

In her memory, Jack reached for a leather volume.

She found the book quite easily. Once more, Stella felt Jack Novak's presence; Jack had been orderly to the last, and its place had not changed. Stella read the gilt-edged letters: *Crime and Punishment.*

Inside was a videotape.

It was not commercial. Nor, uncharacteristically, had Jack labeled it. From the brand, identifying it as VHS, Stella surmised that it was relatively old—from the eighties, not the nineties. That, and the fact that Jack had concealed it, made the silence of the cabin more unsettling.

Tape in hand, Stella went to the front window. She could see little but, from what she could see, she was alone. Edgy, she drew down the blinds.

The VCR was beneath the television. Nervousness made Stella awkward; it took her a moment to realize that, without the power on, the machine would not accept a tape. Task completed at last, she paused, inhaling, then hit the on switch.

The television crackled. A white flash shot across the screen, and then the gray-and-white grain of blank tape followed. Cross-legged, Stella sat on the rug, waiting.

Abruptly, a picture appeared.

It was soundless, surreal—an empty room, a bed, a closet. The image was grainy, and the vantage point did not change, as if the camera was immobile; though Stella could not see all of the room, she guessed that it had no windows or, perhaps, that the film was taken at night.

For minutes nothing changed, like the picture on a security monitor.

But the unblinking focus on a lifeless scene unnerved her. She glanced over her shoulder at the room behind her.

When she turned again, a woman had entered the picture.

The woman was young, perhaps in her early twenties. On the dim-lit video, her naked body was silver.

Her back to the camera, she walked toward the closet, opening the door. Inside the closet was a footstool.

The woman removed it. As she did, Stella noticed the closet door, and squinted in concentration. Her breath caught in her throat.

Near the top of the closet was a metal prong—like a coatrack, but much larger. Looped around it was a leather thong.

With an air of expectancy, the woman gazed toward the room at something, or someone, beyond the range of what Stella now believed must be a hidden camera. Stella waited with mounting apprehension. As though to mirror her unease, the woman seemed to tense.

A man appeared, walking toward her.

He, too, was naked. Stella could not see his face. But what she could see made her start: the man wore a garter belt, silk stockings. His high heels made each step awkward, pitiful, like a prisoner walking toward his execution.

Instinctively, Stella stood.

She was watching a reenactment of Jack Novak's death, she suddenly believed, as his murderer had designed it. Except that this was a prediction, and the film had belonged to Jack himself.

Turning, the man removed his heels and stepped onto the stool.

In the dimness, Stella could not clearly see his face. As he placed the thong around his neck, his movements had the dazed quality of someone stunned by drugs or liquor. And yet Stella also sensed in them the familiarity of ritual, the inevitability of compulsion. He had been to this room before, she thought, to this psychic space long before that.

Kneeling, the woman took him in her mouth.

Stella folded her arms. She forced herself to keep watching: on the screen, the man stood on tiptoes, neck straining against the noose, as the woman did her work.

Twisting, the man kicked the stool from beneath him.

As though hugging herself, Stella's folded arms clamped tight. The man's slender body shuddered with his climax.

Suddenly the picture zoomed. In close-up, the man's face was a terrible rictus of ecstasy and debasement.

"No," Stella said softly. "No."

On the screen, Arthur Bright slowly closed his eyes.

He was younger, Stella recognized, than the man she first had met. A man whom she was never meant to know. Or had ever wished to.

The focus changed again, becoming wider.

The woman replaced the stool beneath Bright's feet, helping him remove the thong.

Stepping down, he reeled sideways, numbed by oxygen deprivation and whatever he had taken. Then he slumped against the wall.

When the woman turned again, facing the room, Arthur had passed out.

The second man could not have been more different.

Startled, Stella watched him fill the screen.

He was thick bodied, a bull: his nakedness was vital, vulgar. His movement toward the woman was not pitiful but ominous.

Stella edged closer. Though she could not see the man's face, there was something familiar in his lazy grace, bringing goose bumps to her skin. The woman, too, seemed apprehensive. As the man approached, she took a tentative step back, then another, until she had nowhere left to go.

The man stopped, saying something. The woman shook her head. Now her every gesture was fearful.

Cat-quick, the man stepped forward and slapped her across the face.

The woman's head snapped back. The man closed his fists. His next blow, short and brutal, was to the jaw.

The woman's neck snapped. Her head smashed against the wall. Even before she pitched face forward, Stella knew that something had gone badly wrong; her collapse seemed absolute, irrevocable, the result of a brain shutting down.

From his reaction, the man knew it, too. Just as Stella, appalled, realized who he was before he faced the camera.

Bending over the woman, Johnny Curran flopped her roughly onto her back.

Her eyes were open. Their fixity did not suggest unconsciousness but death. Curran's face showed only annoyance.

Watching, Stella felt sick.

She had just seen a woman murdered. But now she saw Curran react—not as she did, with revulsion, but with coolness. Each quick movement bespoke a clarity of thought, an absence of feeling: taking the woman's pulse, listening to her heart, placing two fingers to her lips.

Certain she was dead, he stood and lifted Bright to his feet. As Curran dragged him away from the body, Bright's head lolled to one side.

The picture ended abruptly.

Seized by shock and confusion, Stella sat again.

It took minutes, perhaps longer, for her to process what she had seen. Far longer than that to consider its implications. Only then did she weigh the danger to herself, the choices she must make—however uncertain their outcome or obscure their consequences.

Standing, she cracked open the door, as quietly as she could.

The night was still, windless. The sound of the lake, its deep implacable stirrings, had become menacing.

Locking the door again, Stella placed two phone calls. The second was to Arthur Bright.

He had just returned from a long night making the rounds of white neighborhoods, and sounded weary and dispirited. Even now, Stella did not know what she felt more strongly—anger, fear, or pity.

"I've got to see you," she said bluntly. "Now."

It was strange; now that she knew the truth, if only the smallest piece of it, a certain calm had entered her. She could hear it in her voice.

"Now?" Bright's tone was querulous. "It's midnight."

"I don't give a damn, Arthur. This is about Jack's murder, and it won't keep. You don't want it to."

In the silence, she envisioned him questioning, wondering. Finally, he said, "Let's meet at the office."

"Make it two-thirty. I've got things to do." She hung up without waiting for an answer or telling him where she was.

Retrieving the tape, Stella left the house. She walked softly, in the hope—so foolish as to be superstitious—that whoever waited for her would not notice.

But there was no one. Reaching the car, she locked herself inside. Then, hastily, she started the motor. She left without looking back.

On the drive to Steelton, she reviewed what she must do. Go home. Copy the tape. Put it in a self-addressed envelope, then drop it in a mailbox. Place another phone call from a secure line.

She did all that. Then, a little before two-thirty, she entered Bright's office. That he was waiting did not surprise her.

TWO

DEPRIVED OF sleep, of the adrenaline surge which propelled him through event after event, of the tailored suits which lent him dash, Bright looked slighter, as vulnerable as he must feel in his private moments. Only Stella's bitterness kept pity at bay.

"I've got something to show you," she told him. "In my office."

Her tone brooked no questions. Standing, Bright followed her.

She had wheeled the VCR from the main conference room. Once Bright saw it, he stopped, leaning against the wall as though he preferred to stand.

Stella closed the door behind them. As she turned on the VCR, Bright remained still.

On the screen, an empty room appeared.

Bright's mouth opened, but made no sound. He stared at the screen as if into an abyss.

Softly, Stella said, "I didn't much like the ending."

Abruptly, Bright rushed forward and switched off the screen. There was a sheen in his eyes, a mix of shame, anger, and humiliation so naked that Stella felt she was looking into his soul.

"In case you're wondering," she told him, "I've made an extra copy."

Bright folded his arms. He seemed to call on some inner reserve—the ability, almost frightening to Stella, to live his life in compartments. But his voice stuck between whisper and rasp.

"What do you want?" he asked.

The question was open-ended, a probe—perhaps this could still be managed, it suggested. Despite her anger, her sense of betrayal, for a brief, involuntary moment Stella imagined the potential benefits implied. Then she gave him the only answer she could give. "I want the truth. From beginning to end."

"'The truth'?" Bright echoed. "You've lived here all your life, worked for Novak and then in this office. And you still pretend there's only right or wrong, and that all you need to tell them apart is 'the truth.'"

"Fuck you, Arthur. At the least you're an accessory to murder. So you can shitcan the moral relativism."

Bright winced. In their years of working together, Stella realized, there had been a vein of mutual confidence which made stress more bearable, eased the friction of shared ambition. Now he seemed anguished that her belief in him was gone.

Stella felt it as well. Thirteen years ago, she had come to him as a supplicant. He had given her a job, honored her integrity. Now, suddenly, *she* defined his future, and hers. A feeling of disequilibrium overcame her: though, shockingly, his fate was in her hands, both were at risk.

All that she could do was force herself not to look away.

Finally, Bright did.

Turning, he sat in her chair, staring out at the city at night, its scattered lights, the black hole which concealed the stadium. "The truth," he repeated. "Do you mean the truth I discovered when I was home alone, wishing my mother was there, and started trying on her clothes? Do you want to hear about how ashamed I was, how afraid I'd get caught? Or about how aroused I got when I looked at myself in the mirror?

"Or maybe you want to hear about how much I needed to get straight A's, to succeed, to be someone who mattered in this godforsaken city. Just like *you* wanted." His voice held bitterness, anger warring with the need to reach her. "We *all* have secrets, Stella—things no one can know. You didn't hold Novak's interest all those years ago without doing things you don't want *anyone* to know."

"I got away, Arthur," Stella snapped. "Jack got you on tape. Only one of us sold his soul."

They stared at each other, and then Arthur seemed to deflate. "What I told myself," he said at last, "is that I'd only rented it. That somehow I could outrun this like I outran the ghetto, still be the person I hoped to be."

Stella was looking at a man on the brink of ruin: some part of her wanted to pause, to consider the question, at once irrelevant and intensely human, of why he had come to this. At length, she asked, "How did it happen?"

He rubbed his temples, as though dazed. "No one could know," he said at last, "especially Lizanne. I was a rising young prosecutor in the war against drugs. That was who I *wanted* to be. This other person just needed a night out every couple of weeks." Pausing, Bright swallowed. "The only way to do that was to get numb on drugs and alcohol. *Then*, I could let a prostitute give me what I wanted. Or what I hated myself enough to need."

"Bondage."

Bright's face twisted. "The rest of the time, I thought, I could lead a straight life. You just saw where it took me."

"To Johnny Curran. Among other places."

Bright sat straighter, steadying himself. "Curran made himself my friend—bought me drinks, helped me deal with the other cops. I got to trust him, God help me.

"One morning he came to my office. He closed the door, said he'd heard some things. Then, like we were talking baseball, he described what I'd been doing.

"I couldn't even look at him. All I could imagine was being exposed—the end of my career, Lizanne and our kids finding out. All I wanted was to die.

"Curran put a hand on my shoulder, like an uncle.

"There were other ways to get what I wanted, he said, from people too scared to fuck with us. Just like there were ways to ensure what I'd done would never get out."

Stella thought of Curran, laughing softly at Fielding's death. "I imagine he could have arranged that."

"That was why I went with him." Bright turned to her, as if trying to face his shame. "That, and because he could give me what I needed."

IT WAS the second time.

That was how Arthur knew what would happen. Curran taking him at night to a nondescript apartment. The woman smoking dope and drinking bourbon with him, until he was ready to dress.

That was how she knew his desires.

As if in a trance, he walked toward her.

He was drunk, drugged. His field of vision had narrowed; his fear of exposure had dulled. All he could see was the woman in front of him.

She would give him what he craved. He would do what she asked.

The rest was instinct. The last minute of clarity was the pressure on his throat; the lights exploding before his eyes; the shudder of shame and passion; the imagining of his death as a release. Spent, that was his deepest desire—to lapse into darkness.

He awoke, groggy, in a strange apartment.

He was lying on a couch. Johnny Curran sat in a chair across from him, his blue eyes slits. The look of cynical amusement was gone.

Bright felt disoriented. Feebly, he asked, "What happened?"

Curran watched him closely. "Your hooker's dead. She'll never talk to anyone."

Though the words were uninflected, Bright heard them as a threat. He could not bring himself to ask how the woman had died; whether Curran had silenced her; what had happened to the body. All that mattered was that Bright's secret had killed her.

He bent forward, swallowing, trying not to vomit. Curran's voice was etched with contempt. "It's taken care of. All you have to do is go to work tomorrow."

Bright felt his eyes shut.

The rest was a dream. The harsh bite of black coffee. Curran driving him home. Falling into bed with his sleeping wife, endlessly patient with his devotion to work. The image of a naked white woman flashing across his retina like spots from a flashbulb. The oblivion of sleep.

The next day was clear and bright. All that remained were nightmare flashbacks against the darkness of his blackout—hours lost to memory, a desperate need to believe that he had never left his bed.

He drove to the office like an automaton.

His secretary smiled at him. His new case file was on the desk where he had left it the night before, half-read.

Two days passed, nights without sleep. The third morning he went to the coffee station.

The County Prosecutor, a genial Irishman named Francis X. Connolly, was talking to the gruff veteran who was Connolly's chief of homicide. "Enough to gag a maggot," Connolly was saying.

"What's this?" Bright asked.

Connolly turned to him. "More water pollution. This morning they found a barrel full of body parts floating in the Onondaga. Properly reassembled, they add up to a naked woman. Had to ask some whore to identify her head."

Bright's stomach knotted. "Her head?" he repeated stupidly.

Connolly gave a short laugh. "Yeah. Fortunately, she was a redhead. Not too many of *those* in the Scarberry."

Bright went to the men's room and threw up.

LISTENING, STELLA swallowed.

"*What's the word,*" Natasha Tillman had asked her, "*arr-o-gance?*"

"*Yes.*"

"*Arrogance is picking up a whore, cutting her into pieces, stuffing her into an oil drum, and dumping it in the river. That was another friend of mine. Never found the one that killed her, did you."*

"No. We didn't."

"That's 'cause it was a cop."

"*You* know *that?"*

"The girl just disappeared. Someone that crazy, we can tell. No whore's gonna drive off with him. Unless the man's a cop."

Bright seemed to notice her expression. Softly, he asked, "Remember the case?"

"Yes."

He looked away. "By the time I was splashing water on my face, I made a vow—no more drugs or alcohol. That I'd kill myself before I let that side of me escape." His voice was soft. "Just put a gun to my head . . ."

"Maybe you should have."

Bright closed his eyes. "It never happened again, Stella. I started prosecuting drug cases like my life depended on it. A year later, Connolly made me head of narcotics."

Stella's anger, hard and cold, lent her a clarity of thought. "So you could work with Johnny Curran."

After a time, Bright met her gaze. "As far as Curran was concerned, it never happened at all. He never asked me for anything."

"And you never *said* anything to anyone. Because you'd 'outrun' a murder."

Bright stared past her. "Until Novak called," he finally said. "Just like you, he had something to show me."

THEY MET in Jack's office, at night. No one else was there. Though they were both in their mid-thirties, Novak had begun to age; there were pouches beneath his eyes, and it was rumored that Jack's practice was struggling. But then Bright had never liked him, even when they were classmates.

Novak seemed to know this. It made his smile broader, a parody of friendship. He waved Bright to a chair with the grandness of a pasha; Bright almost expected him to say "May you live a thousand years." He was stiff with apprehension.

Novak gestured toward his wet bar. "Drink, Arthur?"

Queasy, Bright sensed that Novak was aware that he no longer drank, and knew or guessed the reason. Attempting calm, he answered, "Just water, thanks."

Novak gave him a grimace of disappointment, as though, for an old classmate, he was showing a poor spirit. Then Bright noticed the VCR in the corner of the office.

"Ice?" Novak asked pleasantly.

When Bright shook his head, Novak passed him a crystal tumbler. "Château Onondaga," he said. "Amazing there aren't lumps in it."

Bright stared at him. A picture flashed through his head—a barrel, floating in a river. Novak raised his glass. "To clean water, Arthur. And clean living."

Arthur sipped, still watching Novak. He forced himself to wait.

Without a foil, Novak's grandiosity diminished. For the first time, Bright perceived the tension this had concealed. He felt pinpricks on the back of his neck.

With deliberate flatness, as though too bored to pretend genuine interest, Bright asked, "How's business, Jack?"

"Not what it could be." Novak's tone was mild. "But you can help. That's why I asked you here."

Abruptly, he stood and went to the VCR. "I'll turn off the light," Novak said. "I've already seen this, several times. But I somehow doubt you have."

Novak pushed the button, then a wall switch, plunging his office into darkness.

The blank screen became an empty room, Bright's nightmare.

With horror and fascination, Bright witnessed his other side.

Novak was silent. Together, they watched the stations of Bright's ecstasy and humiliation—the stool, the leather thong, the kneeling woman. When Bright's face appeared in close-up, he recoiled.

Novak pushed the stop button.

Helpless, Bright studied his own contorted face, frozen in time. At last Novak turned on the lights.

Crossing the room, he sat at his desk again. The only difference between this moment and the moments before was Bright's face on the screen.

His tone was leaden. "Where did you get this?"

"From a client." Novak's tone was quiet, as if he, too, were unsettled. "She was the one behind the camera. When things went bad, she took it for protection and ran. I accepted it in lieu of payment."

Bright could not help the tremor in his voice. "That isn't *me.*"

"It was." Novak's manner was patient; in another context, Bright might have called it kind. "Put your mind at ease, my friend. Any favor I ask will be judicious and occasional. You'll continue to prosecute drug cases with your accustomed zeal. All but a very few."

"And if I say no?"

Novak's face went cold. "First we should have a trial period, Arthur. There'll always be time for Lizanne to see this tape."

STELLA STILL looked at Bright. But what she saw was Novak, watching her in the mirror. The man she had defied her father for. The man who had betrayed Desnoyers to Vincent Moro.

"*What I never figured out,*" Saul Ravin had told her, "*was why Moro canned his old* paisan *drug lawyer, Jerry Florio, and started passing the word to big guys like Flood that Jack was the one to call.*"

Now Stella knew.

"Jack told Moro he owned you," she said. "All he needed was a 'trial period' to show what he could do."

Bright steepled his fingers. "I didn't know," he finally answered. "Until Jack called me about George Flood."

"And you came through. You made Jack Novak the biggest drug lawyer in Steelton." Stella stood, unable to contain herself. "*You* stole those files, damn you. To cover up how you fixed Jack's cases."

"Not all of them. I didn't destroy the evidence, or have Desnoyers killed—"

"Only because Jack didn't need you." She fought for self-control. "*You* sent me to Curran—for an education, you told me. Your real purpose was to have me educate Curran. He's no ordinary killer, is he. He's dirty."

Bright grasped her wrist. "I had to stop you—"

"You *played* me, Arthur. You're the one who told the *Press* I was Jack's lover. That way you could 'save' my political future by taking me off the case." Her voice held corrosive anger. "Did you make those phone calls, too? Or did you leave that part to someone with more guts?"

Bright's grip tightened. "*Listen* to me. I don't know who called Dan Leary. I don't know who called *you*. I don't know who broke into your place or murdered your fucking cat. All I knew was that I was as scared for you as you were."

"Not as scared as you were for *you*. Did *you* kill Jack? Or ask someone to do it for you?"

Bright still gripped her arm, as if afraid to lose her. "You don't understand," he said with quiet urgency.

"I understand. You're corrupt, and you'll do anything to save your own ass—"

"Then why do you think I had Nat Dance check you out before I hired you? I didn't want Novak to own my goddamned unit."

"Just to own you."

Stepping back, Bright released her arm, then inhaled deeply. "When I was elected County Prosecutor, Stella, I thought it was done.

"Winning was my ticket out. I told Novak we were done, that now I couldn't tamper with the drug unit without giving us all away. That I wouldn't try." Now he spoke in a rush. "All Jack had was drug cases; there was nothing else I could do for him. He was livid—he thought helping me get elected helped him. He never guessed I'd use it to break free. But I did."

"Not in the end," Stella retorted. "That was why Jack died the way he did."

Bright stared at her, and then he turned away.

"Yes," he answered.

THREE

"HELLO, ARTHUR," Jack Novak had said.

It had been night, past seven o'clock, when Novak slipped into Bright's office. Bright had been savoring a rare evening without an event, the prospect of a quiet dinner with Lizanne. They had survived so much, more than he hoped she would ever know; but for what she did know—that she loved him and believed in him, as a husband and a father and a leader of this city—he had grown more grateful every year. Though his undivided attention for a night was too small a way of saying thanks for her steadfastness, she would value it, an unexpected gift. And then Jack Novak had called.

This could not wait, Novak told him—it involved Bright's future, and his. Bright knew he had no real choice: although for the last four years he had avoided fixing cases, he could not very well refuse Jack Novak a meeting. He still possessed the film, their secret.

"Sit down, Jack."

Bright's manner was civil. He had learned to stop cringing: the line he had drawn had become part of Novak's knowledge of him. The balance of life was strange, Bright thought; those same years had not aged him, but Jack Novak looked like hell.

As he sat, Novak's body seemed to sag, as though overtaken by gravity and hard living. The pouches beneath his eyes resembled bruises; soon, Bright supposed, Novak would go in for plastic surgery. But nothing Novak could do would cure his hollowness. He had lived a life devoted to his own pleasures: now there was something pathetic about him even in moments of bravado, the look of a man haunted by the passage of time, who knew he had too little to show for it.

All this passed through Bright's mind in seconds. What remained was deep wariness and antipathy: Jack Novak was too dangerous, too amoral, for Bright to risk compassion. Watching Bright, a furtiveness, that unsettling glint, had appeared in Novak's eyes.

"You're running great, Arthur. You're about to be the first black mayor of Steelton."

The cynicism of this sentiment offended Bright. But what unnerved him was the proprietary undertone of a man about to collect an overdue bill. Evenly, Bright answered, "A great moment in black history, for sure. I mean for it to turn out okay for white folks, too. At least most of you."

The oblique rebuff made Novak pause. "Oh, I think it will," he finally answered. "But let me give you some advice. I've been very restrained about that—just sat on the sidelines and cheered. It's time for a modest suggestion."

Instinctively, Bright glanced at his door. Then he regarded Novak in the pale light. "Modest? What does it involve?"

Novak's smile resembled a twitch. His eyes remained watchful, apprehensive.

"Steelton 2000," he said.

Bright laughed aloud, a burst of nervousness and derision. "Tom Krajek's stadium? Are you about to tell me that I love it?"

Novak's smile vanished. "That's right, Arthur. You love it."

It was not a joke, or a request. Novak's tone left no doubt of his meaning.

Bright felt dread overtake him.

He was in the way of something, he suddenly understood, and Jack Novak had promised to change that. Bright wondered who else had seen the film: against his will, he imagined copies arriving at the *Steelton Press*. He had not outrun Novak after all; his enemy had simply waited until the stakes were higher, the opportunity riper. Bright's hands felt damp, his skin clammy.

"How *much*," he asked, "do I love it?"

"Very much. Beginning now you'll stop opposing it. Next week you'll decide it's good for the city, especially African-Americans. So good that, no matter what happens, you and your office will never, ever make any trouble."

Though his tone was calm, Novak's manner was at odds with it—tense, so watchful that it increased Bright's tension as well. "What kind of 'trouble'? What do you *expect* to 'happen'?"

Novak leaned forward. "This is serious, Arthur. You have no idea how serious this is. To both of us."

All at once Bright was truly afraid. The irony had vanished from Novak's voice and manner; for a strange moment, his persona was that of a friend, warning of a problem which could overwhelm them. Novak's eyes were bloodshot.

Quietly, Bright asked, "Who sent you?"

For a long time Novak simply studied him. Only after a time did Bright understand that Novak's silence was his answer.

Abruptly, Novak stood. He walked to the door without saying anything further. Bright stayed where he was.

Novak paused, hand resting on the doorknob. Then he turned to Bright again. "Refusal's not an option for you. Please believe that. Because failure's not an option for me."

Bright did not answer. For a moment, Novak studied him intently, and then left.

WHEN BRIGHT arrived home, Lizanne had lit the candles in their dining room.

On another night, he would have smiled at this. As it was he studied her across the table: the delicate features, the full mouth, the look of shy reserve, of quiet loyalty. Suddenly she looked so lovely that it stirred his deepest emotions.

"What is it?" Lizanne asked.

His eyes misted. "One of those moments, I guess. I was thinking about you."

About loving you. About two good kids, our son and daughter. About all that you deserve—and don't deserve. But Lizanne could not know this. She inclined her head, smiling at him, pleased. Then she took his hand.

They went upstairs. He made love to her with a sense of desperation. Afterward he held her until she fell asleep.

THE NEXT morning, the candles, unattended, had burned out.

Heart burdened, Bright went to a prayer breakfast, then to the opening of a senior center. He was driving to a strategy meeting when his cell phone rang.

"Something's come up," Dance told him. "I thought you should know."

Despite his preoccupation, at once Bright became alert—Dance always gave him warning when the police encountered anything of note. His motive was unspoken: for reasons of solidarity and ambition, Dance wanted Bright to become mayor. Watching the stoplight turn red, Bright pressed the cell phone to his ear.

"What is it?" he asked.

"A white guy named Tommy Fielding, lives in Steelton Heights. Maid found him dead this morning, along with a black prostitute. Maybe they ODed, but he's not your usual smackhead."

"Why not?"

"The man worked for Peter Hall. Project manager on your favorite ballpark."

Bright touched his eyes. Behind him, someone honked, announcing that the stoplight had turned green.

"Keep me posted," he told Dance.

THE MEETING centered on his debate with Krajek.

The debate was in Warszawa, only two days away. Distracted, Bright listened to his chief campaign consultant, a sharp-tongued black woman named Etta Rogers, analyze the opportunities and pitfalls for the others at the table: Bright, a speechwriter, a pollster, his campaign manager, and an aide—all men, two white, three black. That, by gender, Rogers was a minority of one seemed to make her all the more pointed.

"Krajek will push his stadium," she told them. "You know the pitch—he creates jobs and progress, you pander to pimps and welfare queens and dream of a world on food stamps. Never mind that this abortion is a playpen for the rich." Pausing, she turned to Bright. "Agreeing to Warszawa, Arthur, was practically retarded. Krajek knows these are *his* people—everyone watching on television will see *him* getting the applause, *you* sinking like a stone. Either you waffle on Steelton 2000, hoping at least they don't start booing, or you just decide to go for it."

Bright realized that he had been watching this discussion as if it did not involve him. "What's your best advice?" he asked.

Rogers flashed a sardonic smile. "You wanted this debate. I'm sure you had a reason."

Bright summoned his resources; the decision, so vivid once, seemed to have occurred in another life. "Warszawa's a risk," he answered. "But if I'm just another black politician, I can't win. Or if I manage to win, govern."

Rogers's look retained a certain bitter amusement. "So you've got this audience of rapt, open-minded Poles who love pierogies, bowling, and the Steelton Blues. What do you tell them?"

Bright looked around the table. He thought of Lizanne, the redhaired woman, the new and troubling death Dance had reported. In his mind, Novak said, "*Refusal's not an option for you.*"

But *he* was not Jack Novak, Bright felt himself cry out.

"That they're being taken," he told Rogers. "That Steelton 2000 is a fraud."

FILLED WITH hope and desperation, Bright went to the office. He forced himself to call Novak before the adrenaline wore off.

Novak came on the line. "Arthur?"

"You can take that videotape and stick it up your ass." Bright felt a strange exhilaration. "Tell your friends I said so. That way they'll know why you're walking so funny."

He slammed down the telephone.

Finally, perhaps too late, he had chosen his course. He hoped that he could bear whatever came.

THE NIGHT before the debate, the sharp ringing of a telephone jarred him from a fretful sleep.

Bright turned on the night-light, saw that it was two o'clock. Beside him, Lizanne had barely stirred; she was a politician's wife, her serene face said, and calls to him at any hour were part of their lives.

Bright snatched at the telephone.

"*Arthur.*" It was Novak. Even his first word, Bright's name, conveyed a picture of drug-addled, sweaty fear. "They're *coming* for me, you fucking queen—"

"Shut up." Walking quickly to the head of the stairs, Bright added in a hoarse whisper, "You *hear* me, Jack? You can play that tape on television before you call me at home like this."

"*You don't understand.* I have to give him something, or it may be over for *both* of us. I mean *over.*"

Bright sat at the foot of the darkened stairs. His voice was low, tight. "I don't know what's happening here. But I can't have any part of it—"

"*Fuck you.*" Novak's voice pulsed with hysteria. "For four fucking years you've hung me out to dry. Tell me you'll come through, starting with that debate tomorrow. Or I'll give *them* the tape—"

With sudden intuition, Bright understood it all. "I don't believe you, Jack. After that, what will you have to offer them?"

"*Arthur.*" There was a long pause, Novak fighting for self-control. "You *need* me between them and you. If—"

He stopped abruptly. Over the telephone Bright heard the faint rasp of a door buzzer. Hastily, Novak said, "I'll call you back . . ."

He never did.

As STELLA listened, she remembered another moment—three weeks ago, in Warszawa, moments after Bright's brilliant, scathing denunciation of Steelton 2000. A lifetime.

"How did it happen?" Bright asked.

"Badly." Stella's voice came out flat. *"He was hanged from the closet door, with his own belt, wearing stockings and high heels."*

Bright stared at Stella. His lips parted, but no sound came out. Then he turned from her, gazing emptily at the darkened windshield. He seemed hardly to breathe.

It was difficult for Stella to imagine how Bright had felt. Stella felt it, too: she could picture Jack Novak in his final moments, overtaken by the engines of his greed.

"They killed him as a metaphor," she said at length. "To tell you that whoever hanged him had the tape. After that, everything you did was to divert me. To save yourself from whatever they might do."

"To save us all," Bright said simply.

THE LAST call was on the night he learned of Novak's murder.

Bright was in the kitchen: for an hour, as Lizanne slept, he had drifted like a ghost from room to room. In his disorientation he thought it was Jack Novak, hoping for a different answer.

"Arthur?" The voice was distorted, eerie. "I'm sure you got our message."

Fearful, Bright paused. "Yes."

"Then you know what to do. Or else Lizanne and the kids will find out how nice you look in a garter belt.

"There's one copy for the family, and another for Dan Leary. Maybe we'll let you live to see their faces."

The phone went dead.

. . .

BRIGHT AND Stella stared at each other.

"It's gone too far," she told him. "You can't stop this now."

He seemed unable to argue or agree: the consequences were unfathomable, beyond his power to control.

Softly, Stella's door opened. Bright turned, startled.

Dance regarded him. It was some moments before he murmured, "Jesus, Arthur."

For once his impassive face held sympathy, his laconic tone a kind of awe. They seemed to tell Bright more about his downfall than Stella ever could.

When Bright looked away, Dance turned to her.

"Curran," she said.

FOUR

AT ROUGHLY 4:45 in the morning, Stella pressed the door buzzer of Johnny Curran's apartment.

She heard no movement inside. She pressed the button again, careful to stay in front of the peephole so Curran could see her. At the corner of her vision, Dance stood with his back against the wall.

The door cracked open. Through the crevice she saw Curran's face, his cold blue eyes above the door chain, a gun in his hand.

"What do you want?" he demanded.

Stella's heart pounded. "We can't talk in the hallway."

Curran appraised her, then peered into the hallway. She watched the calculations cross his face. "I keep office hours," he said.

Stella hesitated. "It's about Jack Novak."

Curran was still. Stella tried not to think past the next few seconds.

Slowly, Curran reached for the latch.

It rattled, fell loose. The door opened slightly. Curran stepped back a foot or two, his gun aimed at her stomach.

He nodded toward the door.

Dance moved from the wall. His hand replaced Stella's on the knob.

As she stepped sideways, Dance flung the door open.

Startled, Curran flinched. Dance hurtled toward him like a tackler, his head and shoulder crashing into Curran's chest.

Curran fell backward, gun flying from his hand. Then Dance was on top of him, one knee on Curran's heaving chest, the other on his throat. Dance pressed the barrel of his gun to Curran's forehead. Their faces were a foot apart. The Chief of Detectives was breathing hard; Curran's chill blue eyes stared back at him.

Slowly, Dance put the gun between Curran's eyes and cocked it. The barest pressure would send a bullet through Curran's brain. "Fuck you," Curran whispered.

Stella closed the door and latched it.

Crossing the room, she stood over the two men. "Self-defense," Dance said to Curran. "She's my witness."

Stella's face felt clammy, her brain fevered. Curran's eyes flickered toward her.

Softly, she said, "You murdered my cat."

With his free hand, Dance turned the cop's face to his.

"You killed Desnoyers," he said. "You took out Harlell Prince on Moro's orders. You sabotaged our cases. You threatened me and mine. You sold us out for twenty years."

Curran's gaze was blank, indifferent.

In one savage motion, Dance smashed the butt of his gun into Curran's mouth.

There was the snap of teeth breaking. Stella winced. Curran had made no sound at all.

A bubble of red saliva formed on his lips. "You won't shoot me," he croaked, "'cause you don't have shit. You *want* something."

Turning, Stella walked through the dimly lit room to where she had dropped her purse. She knelt and withdrew a videotape, then stood over him again. He stared up at the tape in her hand.

"We've seen your idea of foreplay," she told him. "I'm surprised you waited to cut her head off until *after* she was dead."

An angry tinge appeared beneath Curran's mottled skin. "*Look at me*," Dance demanded.

Curran did.

"Novak made a spare, Johnny. You're going down.

"They're waiting at the state pen—all the animals you put there. You know what happens to cops in prison. The booty lovers will keep gang-raping you. The sadists will cut off some fingers at the second joint. Some dealer will put out an eye. They'll use all the ways to make you half a man. Maybe if you're lucky for a while, three-quarters. And it won't ever end. You'll wish Stella had asked for the death penalty."

Curran's face hardened. "But I won't," Stella told him. "I believe in the sanctity of human life. Especially yours."

With slow deliberation, Curran mouthed a single word, "*Cunt.*"

Dance placed the gun, still cocked, to Curran's mouth. "Don't shoot him," Stella said. "Please."

Curran stared at her implacably. "Which one of you is wired?"

"No wires," she answered. "No record. You're ours."

Curran turned his head to Dance. "Not good enough."

Dance hesitated. Then he raised himself, still aiming the gun at Curran.

Curran regarded him with a half smile. He rose stiffly; as he did, Stella heard a knee pop. But he retained an air of latent power, grace mingling with brutality.

Facing Dance, he said, "You first."

Dance placed one hand on Curran's shoulder, the gun to Curran's ear. Softly, Dance admonished, "Take it slow, Johnny. Don't make me twitch."

Watching Dance's eyes, Curran patted Dance's chest, his back. Then he knelt, feeling the detective's legs. Dance's gun rested against the back of Curran's neck.

Curran rose. "Your turn," he told Stella.

He moved forward, his face close to hers. Dance stepped behind him. Curran's eyes were as cold as Dance's, which were trained—as was Dance's gun—on Curran's head.

Hands on Stella's waist, Curran considered her. A faint whiskey smell came from his bloody mouth. His hands began tracing her spine.

"Get it over with," Dance told him.

Curran bent slightly. Through her jeans, his fingers felt her thighs and the backs of her legs. Then he stood again, looking into her face, and slowly cupped her breasts.

Dance jammed his gun into Curran's neck. Curran smiled at her. There was only one man living whom Stella hated more.

"Nothing," Curran told her softly. "Nothing at all."

Stella stepped back. Her jaw was tight, her fists clenched.

Seeing this, Curran smiled again. "It's all right then." There was faint laughter in his voice, a trace of Ireland. "I can tell you every little thing I did, and you can't prove any of it."

The stakes were too high, Stella reminded herself, to let Curran cloud her judgment. She forced herself to survey the room.

It was small, bleak, relentlessly banal—green walls, nondescript furniture, a department-store portrait of a mountain stream, a beat-up television and, to her surprise, a tortured Jesus on a silver crucifix. Dawn had not yet come; the dim glow of a single light was reflected against the black of Curran's windows.

Stella drew the blinds.

When she turned again, the tension had become more subtle, a test of nerve. Dance sat in an armchair with his gun, Curran across from him on the couch, his posture one of ostentatious ease. "It's true what you said," he observed to Dance. "I made the rules, and the rest of you never even knew what they were. Drove *you* clear out of narcotics, didn't I?"

His voice held quiet arrogance. Stella had her first glimpse of Curran as he saw himself: slipping through the darkened city without any rules but his own, knowing—as did only one other man, his peer—where all the dots connected and where the power was, a power that he shared. Dance betrayed no anger, and yet Stella could feel it as deeply as she felt her own. "On someone's orders," Dance replied. "Who was it, Johnny?"

"Oh, we'll save that for a while. See how we get along." Curran looked from Stella to Dance. "So who would you like to hear about first—Fielding, Novak, or the two whores?"

Dance's manner was one of deadly calm; beneath this, Stella sensed his mind at work. "Why don't we take them in order."

Curran watched him closely. "That would be Fielding," he said.

CURRAN HAD one week to learn his habits; to choose a time and place; to design a death both "accidental" and demeaning. When the idea came to him, after Fielding's third trip to the gym in as many days, Curran laughed to himself.

Method aside, eliminating Fielding was no great challenge: whereas Desnoyers had known that he might die for snitching, Fielding was unsuspecting, an easy target. He worked long hours, had no social life to speak of, lived alone. His only visitor in the five days Curran watched him was his daughter.

Curran was not told why Fielding had to die. But he was certain that—as with Desnoyers and Harlell Prince—it was for business reasons. It was a measure of how life in Steelton was changing.

Once he was ready, Curran followed Fielding in an unmarked car.

It was night. Curran parked on the next block, put on a wool cap and gloves, took his gym bag from the trunk. Ambling down the sidewalk toward Fielding's house, Curran felt a faint contempt. Steelton Heights was not like Little Italy. These people existed in boxes, never knowing or caring who lived across the street: Curran's biggest fear was encountering a yuppie with a dog.

He knocked on the door.

Fielding opened it. He wore slacks and a short-sleeved shirt with a Ralph Lauren logo—all that working out, Curran thought, and Fielding still looked like some pussy in a men's fashion magazine. He regarded Curran with the furrowed brow of someone expecting a pitch for a dubious charity.

Curran smiled. "Officer Curran," he said. "Narcotics. Can I talk to you for a moment?"

Fielding gave him a wary, puzzled look. His eyes moved to the gym bag in Curran's left hand. "Can I see some identification?"

You're not such a fool after all, Curran thought. *I bet they taught you in grammar school never to trust a stranger.* He took out his ID and waited on the doorstep while Fielding studied it.

The man's face eased, and his expression became one that Curran always found amusing: an anxious eagerness to seem law-abiding. "Come on in," Fielding said.

Curran stepped inside, looking about the room as Fielding closed the door. "Is there some problem?" Fielding asked.

Curran nodded. "Someone in the neighborhood's using heroin."

"Who?"

Curran drew his gun and pointed it at Fielding's head. "You."

Fielding's shock was palpable: flinching, he stumbled backward, blood draining from his face.

"Where's your bedroom?" Curran asked pleasantly.

Fielding was shaking now, his Adam's apple working. "Don't wet yourself," Curran said. "Just show me."

Hands in the air, Fielding staggered down the hallway like a holdup victim in a silent movie. But what was funnier was to imagine the chaos in his brain. The man would die before he made any sense of it.

"Strip," Curran commanded.

There was sweat on Fielding's forehead, a red tinge on his face. He barely moved.

No percentage in scaring him, Curran thought. Resistance would spoil the plan. "Do it," he advised. "It's just a robbery, after all."

Fielding gaped at him. Like he was a Martian, Curran thought, but far more credible.

Undressing, Fielding turned his back, reminding Curran of a twelve-year-old in his first communal shower. His body was pale, smooth, muscled, without an inch of fat. Idly, Curran wondered if he was a faggot. The perfect ones usually were.

Fielding turned to Curran again, eyes averted. Curran nodded toward a framed photograph on the nightstand. "Cute kid."

Fielding's lips trembled. "Thank you."

From deep within, Curran began to laugh. The spasms made his gun hand shake.

Fielding looked sick.

After Curran regained his self-control, he said, "Now the kitchen."

Naked, Fielding shuffled to the kitchen with Curran at his back. On the sink were the remnants of a sandwich and a glass of beer.

Perfect, Curran thought.

Still watching Fielding, he reached into his gym bag for the fluni-trazepan. Then he emptied the drug into Fielding's beer glass.

"Drink it," he instructed.

Reaching for the glass, Fielding's hand trembled. "Are you going to rape me?"

Curran shrugged. "I wasn't. Want me to?"

For an instant Fielding's eyes shut. Then he stared into the glass.

"Don't worry," Curran said. "It won't kill you."

Fielding's expression became at once pitiful and hopeful—*Maybe it's just a sedative,* Curran imagined him thinking. Fielding hesitated, then took a hasty gulp of beer.

Curran nodded toward the kitchen table. "Have a seat," he said, "while I do a little cooking."

Fielding sat, as heavy as a bagful of dead cats. He could not look at Curran.

Curran laid his gun on the sink. Taking out his chemistry set, he began to prepare the heroin.

By the time he finished, Fielding was groggy. It was all Curran could do to walk him to the bedroom. As Curran laid him on the bed Fielding's eyes fluttered, like those of a child struggling to stay up past bedtime.

Curran jabbed the needle into his arm.

The fentanyl shot through him. Moments later Fielding's body twitched, as though he were running from an enemy in a nightmare. He died in his sleep.

Curran gazed down at him. *Not a mark on him,* he thought. *Sort of like that statue by Michelangelo.*

STEELTON WAS a funny place.

A half hour's drive from yuppie Valhalla, you wind up in hell. The Scarberry.

Curran had always savored it—the furtiveness, the stench of urine, the throb of human desperation, of violence just beneath the surface. Curran was too often bored: like his secret life did still, the Scarberry had helped give him his edge.

As he cruised the street in Fielding's car, a man and a woman slipped into an alley.

Once that could have been him. He could make them do what he wanted, maybe rough them up a little, all as easy as a free cup of coffee. But the redhead had made him careful. Killing her was an accident, and what immediately followed had nearly unnerved him—finding the woman who ran the video camera gone from the next apartment, along with the tape meant to entrap Arthur Bright. He had dismembered the redhead as subterfuge, and as a warning to the woman who had fled. For years afterward, Curran had feared that the tape would surface.

Now he was back, looking for a woman again.

On the next block a hooker shivered in the cold.

Slowing, Curran watched her. She had the jittery movements of an addict, and she hugged herself as though hanging on tight. He thought of Fielding's pale body: that the whore was black appealed to his sense of humor.

Farther down the block was a second whore.

Curran felt the tug of caution. A witness who could identify Fielding's car would be helpful. But the second woman increased the odds he might be recognized: though few hookers lasted long, there might still be one who recalled the redhead, perhaps had seen the man who had picked her up. This new woman would be mere artistry: the bona fides of Fielding's accident; a stage prop in Curran's theater of the absurd.

She stepped forward, tentative, as though mesmerized by his headlights.

Curran felt a connection form between them. With a sense of the inevitable, he slowed the car, then stopped.

She leaned forward, trying to see him through the windshield. Down the block the second whore still watched them.

Stay there, Curran thought. *Memorize the license plate.*

He touched a button.

The passenger window lowered, a whisper. The whore took two more steps forward, her boots scuffing against the dirty cement. Her eyes had a smackhead's desperate avidity. Her face was that of walking death.

"Want some fun?" she asked.

Fun, Curran thought. *Like fucking corpses.* He smiled at her. "Want some smack?"

The whore's lips quivered. At the periphery of Curran's vision, her colleague served as sentinel.

Silent, Curran took two hundred-dollar bills from his wallet and placed them on the passenger seat.

She looked from the money to Curran, torn by the inner war between addiction and fear. Then she slipped into the car.

The door closed with a soft, expensive thud.

The woman looked haggard, anemic. With or without him, Curran thought, she would not live out the year.

As the car drove away, the two whores gazed at each other through the darkened glass.

He kept her from shooting up until they got to Steelton Heights. After that there was no choice: dead, she was merely awkward; alive, even *she* could recognize a corpse. For the coroner's benefit she should die without a struggle.

Reaching inside his gym bag, Curran passed her the needle.

Eyes closed, she stuck it in her arm and then leaned back against the headrest. She was still shuddering when he parked in front of Fielding's.

Curran put the needle in his pocket. By the time he pulled her from the car she had stopped breathing. Her skin was still warm.

He looked up and down the street. Saw nothing.

Awkwardly, he leaned the whore against him, like a date who had passed out.

It was a struggle getting her inside. Dead women, he noticed, don't walk well.

He laid her on the bed next to Fielding. With the blood retreating from the surface of his skin, his first victim looked like marble.

"Don't mind *her*," Curran told him. "She's just dead."

Death made undressing her awkward, as well. But not as distasteful to Curran as the end result, her nakedness. He felt a little sorry for Tommy Fielding.

STARING AT Curran across the room, Stella wished him dead.

Despite his bloodied lips and broken teeth, his eyes glinted; each admission made him more valuable. Stella felt acutely aware of everything: the dim light, the dismal apartment, Dance with his gun trained on the man across from her.

"So far," she told him, "you've murdered five people."

Curran examined his nails. That he held power over them was so obvious, his manner suggested, it required little comment. "That's five life sentences," he answered. "I hope you'll make them concurrent."

There was buried laughter in his voice. Watching him, Stella could see Natasha Tillman, an angry presence in Stella's car.

"*Vice,*" Stella had told Tillman, "*is where they send cops too crazy for narcotics. But the ones who hate women volunteer.*"

"*The special one that takes you for a ride, beats and rapes you at night in Steelton Park, and dumps you by the side of the road. Because he can.*"

"*Give me names.*"

Even through the half-light obscuring the woman's features, Stella felt her black eyes smolder. "*No way, Ms. Prosecutor. That trip to Steelton Park was my lucky day. The man told me what would happen if I wasn't grateful for his attentions. So I am.*"

"You also murdered Natasha Tillman." Stella kept her tone impassive. "You followed me to the Scarberry. When Tillman got into my car, you recognized her. So you cut her throat and tossed her in a Dumpster. Not just because of Welch but because Tillman knew what you are—a pervert who can't get it up without inflicting pain."

Curran's look of amusement vanished. His ice-blue eyes betrayed his hatred of Stella, and of women. "Perversion," he said softly, "is a relative thing. I never fucked Jack Novak."

"What stopped you?" Stella asked. "That he was dead?"

It took Curran a moment to smile again. "Would you like to hear about that?" he asked. "Or is it time for you to leave the room?"

WITHOUT WAITING for an invitation, Curran pushed Novak aside and closed the apartment door behind them. Softly, he said, "These days, Jack, you're worthless."

Novak's eyes changed. "Bright will come around. I still know how to reach him."

Curran shook his head. "Time's up."

Novak noticed the gym bag in his hand. Instinctively, he backed away. "Let's talk about this."

Curran appraised him. "Pour us some Irish whiskey," he answered. "By the time I've finished mine, you'll have told me what I need."

There was a sheen on Novak's forehead, and his movements betrayed the cocaine jitters. "I can give you scotch. A single malt."

"You do that, Jack."

Novak went to the kitchen.

Curran sat in a wing chair. There was a residue of coke on the coffee table; Curran had seen Novak's blond armpiece scurrying from the building, looking disarrayed. Torn from the diversions which numbed his fear, Novak would open like an overripe peach.

The lawyer returned with two glasses, ice tinkling against crystal. Curran studied him. His mustache was dyed, his paunch showed beneath his cashmere turtleneck, and his eyes were those of a coward, clever and wary. But then women would fuck anything for money.

Novak handed him a glass. Only then did he notice that Curran wore a surgeon's transparent gloves.

As Novak stared, wordless, Curran sipped his scotch. "Very smooth, Jack. I'll finish this in no time at all."

Novak seemed mesmerized by his hands. "Please," he managed to say. "Arthur still listens to me."

Curran's voice was silken now. "Influence is all a matter of relationships. Is that it?"

Nervously, Novak sipped his scotch, licking his lips. He gave a quick nod of his head, like a hiccup.

"Bullshit," Curran said softly. "You've got Bright on videotape. You never told our friend that, did you?"

The question made Novak shift. "No," he said at last.

"Not that he didn't guess—taping Bright *was* his idea. He just never knew what else was on it." Finishing his scotch, Curran put down the empty glass. "Only you know why I'm really here. You and me."

He took out his gun.

The blood drained from Novak's face. "Remember Desnoyers?" Curran asked. "Having him killed was easy, wasn't it, Jack."

The look in Novak's eyes was one Curran had seldom seen: the slow, horrific appreciation of what his life had come to, of the danger of invoking powers which knew no limits. "You're the sorcerer's apprentice," Curran told him. "That's all you ever were. But you forgot."

Novak's face seemed to sag. He was a slow learner, Curran thought. Jack had just realized that, whatever his intentions, he himself was far more than a blackmailer. Novak was also a witness to murder.

Slowly, Novak went to his bookshelf. He took down a leather-bound King James Bible and placed it on the coffee table.

When Curran opened it, he saw the tape.

"Okay," Novak implored him, "I've given you what you want . . ."

"Not quite." Curran reached into his gym bag for the garter belt and stockings. "Put these on, Jack. They should be about your size."

Novak looked utterly disoriented. "What are you doing, Johnny?"

Curran heard this for what it was: a plea, the hope, however vain, that all Curran wanted was to humiliate him or, perhaps, to blackmail him. "It's an experiment," Curran answered. "To see if you still want to live."

Novak still did. Curran watched him undress.

Naked, Novak quivered. It took him a while to put on the stockings.

With a jerk of his head, Curran motioned him to stand.

Novak did that, too. Curran appraised his soft torso, the incongruous black nylons. "I hear you make your women wear a garter belt," Curran remarked. "Now I can see why."

Novak seemed ill. "This tape," Curran added brusquely. "You make copies?"

Novak closed his eyes. Then, slowly, he shook his head.

Curran watched him narrowly. "Don't lie to me, Jack. Ever."

Novak swallowed. "I'm not," he said in a hollow voice. "Believe me."

After a moment, Curran handed him the tape. "Then you should play this one last time. After all, I've never seen it."

Curran watched the terrible question forming in Novak's eyes. "*Play it,*" he commanded.

Abject, Novak went to the television. The stockings seemed to make his tread dainty, a parody of a woman. It put Curran in mind of a beauty contest staged by Monty Python; it was too bad the high heels would have to come later.

The tape began playing.

"Stay there," Curran instructed. "I'll tell you when to stop it."

Novak knelt, his finger on the stop button, watching Arthur Bright walk toward the woman. As Bright climaxed, Curran snapped, "Now."

Bright's contorted face froze on the screen.

"Erase the rest," Curran ordered.

Novak could not seem to move. Curran watched him try to remember how to erase a tape and, at the same time, wonder what would follow. As he did, Curran placed the drug in Novak's scotch.

Finally, Novak pushed two buttons.

"There," Curran said. "Now you can finish your drink."

Each directive seemed to strip Novak of his will. From his demeanor, he had nothing left.

"Coke wearing off?" Curran inquired pleasantly.

Novak sat in near collapse. He did not touch his scotch. The look on his face was comic—wide-eyed, openmouthed, like a fish jerked onto the dock.

"Drink," Curran said.

Novak stared at the amber liquid as though it were hemlock. Raising his head, he looked around his apartment, as though taking in every detail. Then he gulped the scotch in one jerky swallow.

Curran cradled the gun in his lap. "By the way," he said conversationally, "you're a dead man."

Novak seemed to know this. He lay back on the couch, head lolling.

Efficiently, Curran searched the apartment for a second copy of the tape. By the time he returned to the living room, Novak's eyes were shut, and his breathing was shallow.

Just another naked man in stockings, Curran thought.

He put the tape in his gym bag, then went to work.

STELLA FORCED herself to breathe slowly, evenly. Curran watched her face.

"I'll skip the rest," he told her. "Seeing how you respect the sanctity of human life. But cutting off Novak's balls was a nice touch. A valentine to Arthur Bright."

"The nice touch," Stella answered, "was Jack lying to you. So here we are."

Curran sat back, his eyes slits. Stella's voice was staccato. "Desnoyers. Prince. Fielding. Novak. Who gave the orders?"

Curran looked from Stella to Dance. The bargaining, this signaled, was about to begin.

"Vincent Moro," he said calmly. "In person."

FIVE

DANCE LAUGHED out loud. "Of course he did. So you could deal him later."

Curran gave him a cool, appraising look. His posture suggested he had time to spare—that Dance and Stella could play these games all day. The first light of dawn, Stella saw, illuminated the blinds.

Dance turned to Stella. "Johnny wants to *testify*. But he's waiting for you to beg him."

"Why should I?" she asked Curran. "Did Moro invite corroborating witnesses?"

Curran's eyes were cold. "No one knew," he said. "Not you, not Vincent's wiseguys. Just him and me."

Once more Stella was struck by his narcissism: Curran believed himself surrounded by people who lacked his nerve and resources, and there was only one person whose respect he cared about. The one he proposed to betray.

"So," Stella said, "I put you on the stand. Then you tell the jury, 'I'm a serial killer who chops whores into little pieces. But Vincent Moro made me do it.'" Contempt crept into her voice. "What's your price for getting me laughed out of court? Those concurrent sentences you mentioned? You're not even worth *that*."

Curran merely shrugged.

"How did you meet with him?" Stella demanded.

The inquiry produced, in Curran, a fleeting smile. "Safe houses. Secure phones. I'd call him, or he'd call me—no intermediaries, just long enough for him to give me a code. The code was for one of four or five apartment buildings with an underground garage. I'd go to an apartment and wait. Vincent always came last, and left first."

Dance leaned forward, voice flat. "The missing cocaine, the blown raids, the murders—the same way every time. You and Moro meet in private to plan it all out."

Curran's eyes glinted again. "Scaring you out of narcotics, too. Vincent and I planned that." He turned to Stella. "Just like we figured out how to fuck with your head. And it all worked." His tone became softer, mocking. "But I guess I can't prove how stupid you are. No jury would believe me."

Stella kept calm. "You want *us* to believe you? Set up another meeting."

Curran twisted the ring on his finger. "What will that prove?" he asked softly. "That I can do it?"

"No. You'd be wearing a wire."

Slowly, Curran looked from Stella to Dance. "Fuck you both. Vincent's too smart."

"And you're not smart enough." Dance's tone was ruminative, almost nostalgic. "Remember the prisoner rebellion a few years ago—what happened to the crooked ex-narc? The inmates cut his dick off and stuffed it down his throat. But it was the spike through his head that killed him.

"Security's tighter now. You'll probably die more slowly, of AIDS. That'll suit us fine."

Curran seemed barely to move. Softly, he asked Stella, "What's your offer?"

"Fifteen to life. The redhead only. Give us Moro and I'll sell it to the judge."

Curran's eyebrows rose in incredulity, and then his stare became hard. "That's bullshit. Once I'm in, the parole board never kicks me loose. Vincent has me killed in prison—"

"Time's running," Dance cut in. "Tell us what you want."

Curran gazed at the floor, considering his chances. "Out of the country," he said at last. "I set up Vincent and come out alive, you give me a week's head start—no one comes after me, no bulletins to Interpol or Immigration. After that, I'm on my own."

It was an offer of startling amorality: a week for Curran to take whatever money he had hidden and find a place which would not extradite him. "No way," Stella answered. "Not even in Steelton."

"They do it all the time, lady. Remember Sammy 'the Bull' Gravano?"

So here it was, Stella thought. Gravano was the classic case—a Mafia killer who had executed twenty or so people, and then traded in his boss for refuge in the federal witness protection program. "Gravano did time," she rejoined.

Curran shrugged. "By my count, I'm about fifteen bodies behind Gravano. Even if one of the corpses was your boyfriend."

Stella saw Dance's finger caress the trigger of his gun. "You're a crooked cop, Johnny. You kept Moro running the East Side for twenty years—"

"And that's not all," Curran interrupted softly. "There's more."

Was there something else? Stella wondered. She forced herself not to ask.

"Ten years," she said. "Federal prison. *If* you give me Moro."

Curran smiled at this. "Federal time? What did I do? Violate that redhead's 'civil rights'?"

Stella forced herself to think only of prosecuting Vincent Moro. "You'll set Moro up, and you'll tape him. Then you'll testify to that *and* to everything you've done for him. If Moro gets the death penalty—or life—you get your deal."

Her flat statement of the stakes—for Vincent Moro and for him— erased Curran's smile. Stella watched him weigh the risks. "No prison time," he said at last. "The feds commit to witness protection—as soon as I'm through with Vincent, they take me into protective custody.

"After that I testify, and then the feds take me to a plastic surgeon and help me disappear. Any money I have, I keep."

"Ten years," Stella reiterated.

Curran shook his head. "You want Vincent Moro. You need me to deliver him. But that's not worth ten years of my life."

Stella braced herself. "That's right. It isn't."

Curran sat back. At length, he said, "Then let's find out what is."

There *was* something more, Stella knew. Dance became as attentive as she.

"Four years ago," Curran told them, "I planted coke in George Walker's apartment. *I* made Tom Krajek mayor. On Vincent's orders.

"Vincent Moro runs this town." Finishing, Curran's tone was matter-of-fact. "He owns Krajek like he would have owned Bright. He kept that jive-ass Walker from being Steelton's first black mayor."

Dance leaned toward him, eyes hard, a portrait of suppressed violence. "Fuck you, Johnny." Dance's expletive was soft, involuntary, angry. Stella simply stared.

"No jail time," Curran repeated calmly. "Or no Moro."

GAZING OUT at the lake, Stella and Dance were silent.

They had left Curran at his apartment, guarded by two cops Dance trusted—it was unsafe to put him in jail. Nor could they talk in front of him. So they had driven Dance's unmarked car to Steelton Park.

It was shrouded in trees; only at its edge, a narrow beach, did the foliage end. Dance and Stella stood on the sand, hands jammed in their pockets, their breath puffs of mist in the air. Somewhere in this park, Stella reflected, Curran had raped Natasha Tillman.

"You always suspected him," she finally said. "Didn't you?"

Watching the wind-tossed lake, Dance nodded. "It was either a conspiracy, or Curran. He was the smartest, the only one with enough slack to do it on his own." He expelled a deep breath. "I wanted him bad."

She turned to him. "Why didn't you trust me?"

"I thought there was a problem in your office. And Bright sent you to Curran." He paused, then murmured, "Fucking Arthur . . ."

The muted sorrow in his voice betrayed blasted hopes—first Walker, now Bright. Steelton never changed.

Stella hunched against the cold. "What you thought about Curran," she admitted, "I suspected about you. That you were in a position to fix those cases, and smart enough to do it. That maybe you'd whacked Buffalohead for Moro."

Turning, Dance gave her an unamused smile. "Yeah," he said. "In the world of Vincent Moro, that would make sense."

Drizzle had started, blowing hard in Stella's face. "This is huge, Nat. If Moro owns Krajek . . ."

"You're thinking we have to make this deal. Just let him go."

Though it was true, the words stuck in her throat. "The prick counted on this," she said. "That's why he dealt with Moro directly. So he could trade him if he had to."

Dance laughed softly. "You don't think *Moro* doesn't know that? Remember what he's survived all these years, and everything he's done."

That was the answer, Stella knew. If the world was imperfect, Steelton was more so. As matters stood, it belonged to Moro, and only Curran could change that.

She turned her face from the rain. "So how does Curran trap him for us?"

Dance shrugged. "I don't know yet. But if he tries and fails, he dies. That's our consolation prize."

Stella was certain Curran knew *that,* too.

SHE FOUND Bright in his office, alone.

He had canceled his appearances. He stood by the window, gazing down at the steel frame of the stadium: since Fielding's murder, Stella realized, it had taken form, with the relentlessness of the day-to-day. Soon it would be done: in time, if the second stage of Krajek's plan was realized, it would be the center of a five-million-dollar development which would change the face of Steelton.

When Stella closed the door, Bright still watched. "What does it all mean?" he asked. "I keep wondering."

He could have been thinking of Steelton 2000. But Stella imagined that what he saw was his life: years of striving, and of hiding, come to the brink of ruin. She could not imagine he had yet accepted this. Nor had Stella quite accepted that Bright had become her pawn in a plan to destroy Vincent Moro which, if it succeeded, would destroy Arthur as well. But she had no time to feel anything. All that she could do was tell him what had happened.

When she got to Krajek and George Walker, Bright looked away.

Stella could follow his thoughts: that despite their political maneuvers, their calculations of power, the cut and thrust of personality and ambition, Moro had reduced all three of them to playthings. The Bright who had existed short hours ago might have savored the thought of Krajek's ruin, his own ascension. Now he looked as hollow as he must feel.

"What do you want me to do?" he asked.

"To contact the feds. We need an up-front commitment they'll process Curran into witness protection, make sure he doesn't get whacked. This deal with Curran will take some work, and no one but us can know. For now, you don't tell the feds about *you,* and *we* don't tell anyone.

"Nat and I will handle Curran. You'll act like nothing's happened. And keep Sloan out of our way."

Bright went to his desk. He laid both palms on its surface, as though testing its reality. His voice was toneless. "What about Lizanne?"

"You can't talk to her yet. In everyone's eyes but ours you're still a candidate for mayor." She forced herself to speak without sentiment. "Don't fuck this up, Arthur, intentionally or unintentionally. Moro doesn't own you—I do. Cooperate and I'll make this as easy as I can. But don't ever let yourself imagine you'll be better off if Moro murders Curran and I've got no case against him. I'll crucify you."

Bright's eyes signaled anger, then a bitter resignation. "Jack was right, Stella. You were perfect for the job."

"And you hired me to do it. Look how far we've come."

Bright seemed to gather himself. His decision to live with dignity and purpose, at least for the next few hours, was palpable to Stella. "I'll do whatever I need to," he said. "Just don't *you* fuck up. You'll never have a second chance at Moro."

There was nothing more to say. She left, taking the elevator down and crossing the wind-blasted street to Dance's car.

WHEN THEY reached Curran's apartment, Dance sent his two guards to the bedroom. He sat with his gun turned on Curran.

Stella remained standing. "We're working on your deal."

The merest smile touched Curran's eyes, vanishing as quickly as it came. "Good. Come back and tell me when it's done."

"First things first," Stella rejoined. "Tell us your plan."

Curran began twisting his ring. "Oh," he murmured, his Irish lilt satiric now, "I thought I'd ask him to confess. A small favor to a boyhood friend."

"No plan?" Stella asked. "Then no deal."

He looked up at her with chill humor. "*You* want me to tape Moro implicating himself in murder. *I* don't want to die. So meeting Vincent in the usual way doesn't strike me as very safe.

"I have to tell him something that makes him deviate from the pattern, and yet persuades him that we have to meet." His eyes widened in mock inspiration. "It comes to me now. You have a *witness*. Someone who believes she saw a man leaving Novak's who sounds suspiciously like me. And now you're testing poor Jack and Tommy for traces of flunitrazepan. I might get Vincent to believe that, even if it makes you way cleverer than you are."

"I'm grateful," Stella said. "I assume you're leaving the country."

"It seems my time is up. I need a half million in cash and a hiding place in Italy. If I don't get it . . ." Curran's humor vanished. "I'm just as likely to get it in the head—Vincent isn't trusting, and he'll know passing money implicates him. So perhaps he'll understand when I feel safer meeting him in the open.

"The virtue of meeting outdoors, from his point of view, is that it makes electronic surveillance harder. Unless I'm wearing a wire." Pausing, Curran seemed to envision their contact, step by step. "He'll think of all that, of course. That's why he won't say *where* we're meeting till the last."

Stella reviewed her doubts. "Why wouldn't he just send someone?" she asked.

"Then he'd be exposing another witness to me, and me to him. Someone else for me to turn. Doubling the chances of betrayal." Curran's voice became softer. "We've been doing this for decades, the two of us. It won't change now."

Stella glanced at Dance. It had to be, his expression said.

"All right," Stella told Curran. "We'll let you know when to call him. And how."

Silent, Curran shrugged.

"There's one more thing," Stella said. "Michael Del Corso."

At once, Curran smiled again, and his eyes seemed to dance. "I was wondering when you'd get to that. You want to know if he's dirty."

"Yes."

"Do you want him to be?"

Stella crossed her arms. "I want the truth."

"I thought you *knew*. Vincent runs him. His wife left because she had to, abandoning that poor little girl. He gave me a copy of that key you lent him, because my skills at breaking and entering are so inferior. He kept me informed because I'm just not up to following the subtle workings of your mind. Or your car, running from Micelli to Novak's office to the Scarberry." Curran's voice was tinged with laughter. "You gave the boy his walking papers, I hope."

Stella did not trust herself to respond. With casual cruelty, Curran finished, "Del Corso's an innocent, like you. Making him look dirty was all Vincent's little game. He remembered you from Novak. So he knows what a poor judge of men you are."

SIX

FOR STELLA, the next few hours were difficult—a terse conversation with Bright confirming that the feds had made the deal; conferring with Dance to ensure that Curran and his guardians remained invisible; pretending to Sloan that all was normal; struggling with her pain over Michael; reasoning through the implications of Fielding's death and Krajek's supposed corruption. She had started with a single murder, drugs, and case fixing, and found something very different. *What*, precisely, she was not yet sure. But the thing she sensed was ugly and enormous.

Twice she went by Michael's office.

She did not know why—there was nothing she could say to him. And Michael was not there.

She found herself thinking of Sofia. Then of Fielding's daughter, and of the man who had killed the girl's father. Whom Stella might set free.

Vincent Moro belonged in jail, she had told Jack Novak. She had been too young to imagine the price.

A LITTLE before four o'clock, Michael appeared in her office.

He tossed some papers on her desk. "You might want to read these," he said.

Stella was not prepared for this. Quietly, she said, "Close the door. Please."

He did that, slowly enough that every movement conveyed how little he wished to be there.

"You wanted to know who Lakefront is," he said. "This is the paper trail—six private companies, each owned by the other, with no legal obligation to list their stockholders, ending with a corporation in the Netherlands Antilles. But I knew someone there from another case."

Mechanically, Stella riffled through the photocopied pages. The last document was on fax paper: a registration form for the Malta Company, N.A., of the Netherlands Antilles. Its president was Richard Flack.

"Who's Richard Flack?" she asked.

"The law partner of my old friend and classmate, Nicholas Moro."

Stella stared at him. "*Vincent's* son?"

"That's right." Michael's voice was cold. "I thought you'd want to know. That way you can mention my relationship to Nick Moro when you take all this to Arthur."

Stella picked up a pen. She turned it in her fingertips, watching it, her thoughts in turmoil. But there were two that she fixed on. In all likelihood Vincent Moro, or his son, controlled Steelton 2000 and Krajek's plan for developing the waterfront. By accident or design, Peter Hall was fronting for them.

She would not have known this without Michael.

At last she looked up at him. That he seemed less angry than indifferent pained her even more.

No apology, she thought, could be abject enough. Nor could she make one without explaining Curran.

"You can take it to Arthur yourself," she said.

WHEN MICHAEL left, Stella turned on her computer.

For a moment, she found it hard to concentrate. Then she began typing a document she wanted no one else to see: an application for a court order permitting the police to wiretap Peter Hall. When she was done, she called Dance at Johnny Curran's.

"Steelton 2000 is Vincent Moro," she told him, and then explained why.

When she was finished, Dance was quiet. Finally, he asked, "What do you want from Hall?"

"To break him, if I can. It's another way of getting at Moro."

"What if Hall tries to phone him? Or Krajek?"

"That's what the wiretap is for. And if we're questioning Hall it makes Curran more credible."

There was silence on the other end. "I don't think I should leave here," Dance said.

"You don't need to. I'll go to Hall's myself." She paused. "I want Del Corso with me. He understands the financial stuff, how Moro works. I won't tell him about Curran."

Stella felt him pondering the risks and, perhaps, her motives. "We need Curran to make that call," he said. "Soon. I don't want Moro figuring out we've got him."

"I'll be there in an hour," Stella promised, and hung up.

Briefly, she tried to imagine the problems of the next few hours: the uncertainty surrounding Curran's call to Moro; the complex operation required if Moro agreed to a meeting; her chances of unnerving someone as poised as Peter Hall. Then she went to Michael's office.

He was throwing papers in a briefcase, preparing to leave.

"I need your help," she said.

He glanced up at her, then continued filling his briefcase.

"I'm going out to Peter Hall's. I don't want to question him without you."

He snapped his briefcase shut, not looking at her. "What does Bright want?"

Stella hesitated. "He wants us both to do it."

Michael propped the briefcase on his desk, regarding her with undisguised resentment. "Then I guess it's compulsory."

Stella wished she could apologize for asking on such short notice, and for making him leave Sofia at his parents'. But to do this felt too personal now. "I'll pick you up at home," she said.

He put on his coat and walked past her without answering, or even looking at her.

Stella went to the courthouse and found the duty judge. Though his eyebrows raised at the mention of Peter Hall, she told him as little as she dared. She left with a wiretap authorization.

She called Dance to arrange the tap. Then she drove to Curran's.

WHEN SHE arrived, Curran's living room contained two extra telephone extensions, headsets, and a tape recorder, installed by the police. This made her edgy: each step, however necessary, meant that someone else would know that they had Curran.

Curran himself lacked his usual composure. He looked dyspeptic, like a man whose dinner had not agreed with him: fidgeting with his ring, he kneaded his swollen fingers, then picked imagined lint off his Irish fisherman's sweater.

"It's time," Dance said to Stella.

Curran did not look up at them. He was suddenly still, as though retreating deep within himself.

"Think about prison," Dance told him. "It'll help."

A series of emotions flashed through Curran's eyes: anger; a last weighing of his chances of survival; a cold estimate of what prison life would hold for him. He stared at the phone beside him.

Finally, he reached for it.

Stella and Dance sat across from him. Though there were headsets for each of them, they did not pick them up.

From memory, Curran stabbed out a number. He waited for a ring, then hung up, and redialed.

Listening closely, his eyes narrowed. Someone had answered.

"It's me," Curran said, and hung up the phone again.

The apartment was silent. Stella imagined Moro taking out a cell phone reserved for this, with a number no one knew. But it was difficult for her to conceive of the vigilance, the constant fear, which Moro's life imposed on him. Even in the simplest acts, like the placing of a phone call.

Curran's hand rested on the telephone.

Stella stared at her watch. The second hand measured the quiet. A minute passed, then two.

Ring, she silently implored. She heard Dance expel a breath of suppressed tension. Without raising his head, Curran moved his eyes to Dance, his pupils like ice.

The telephone rang.

At once, Dance jabbed at the start button on the tape recorder.

Trying to keep her hand steady, Stella reached for her headset. At the edge of her vision she saw Dance do the same. Both of them looked at Curran.

The telephone rang for a second time.

Slowly, Curran nodded.

He snatched the telephone, creating a click which covered Dance and Stella gently lifting theirs.

"Yes?" Curran said.

There was a long silence, and then there was a voice that Stella would have known anywhere, though she had not heard it in fourteen years.

"What is it?" Vincent Moro asked.

His tone was soft, polite. Yet it contained a subtle admixture of imperiousness and suspicion. It was the voice of a survivor, the lord of his own dark world.

Curran's face was tight with concentration. "There's a problem. I've had a warning from our African-American friend."

Curran paused, waiting. "A warning?" the soft voice asked.

"Someone thinks they saw me at the apartment of a well-known lawyer. Now our lady lawyer's running drug tests."

"And so?"

"It's finally over for me here. I need half a million in cash and a place in the old country. Yours, not mine."

"I see." The voice remained calm; only the silence which followed conveyed surprise. At last Moro said, "That will take some arranging."

There was sweat on Curran's forehead. With quiet urgency, he answered, "We're out of time."

His use of the plural, Stella knew, was a reminder. That they knew each other well. That they were bound by forty years of betrayal, and of what passed for friendship in a world which permitted none. That one could destroy the other.

"Then we should meet." As before, Moro's tone was matter-of-fact. "As we always have."

Curran licked his lips. "I don't think that's good now. I want somewhere new, in the open, where I'd know if I was followed. I don't want anyone around."

The silence was longer now. Stella felt herself swallow. She was reluctant even to breathe, fearful that Moro would hear her.

When Moro spoke at last, his voice was softer yet. "Is this a matter of trust?"

Curran became still. To Stella, it was as though he had heard the muffled footsteps of an intruder. "Of prudence," he answered.

"I see. Then I shall be prudent, too. Wait by the telephone."

The line went dead.

SEVEN

ON THE way to Michael's, Stella felt herself shutting down.

She had barely slept since finding Star's body. In the past forty-eight hours she had barely eaten; in the last twenty-four the only care she had taken of herself was to shower and change clothes. The tension of Curran's call to Moro had burned the last of her adrenaline. Her lids were heavy; the city streets at night—the lights, the traffic—seemed distant and abstract, as though she were drunk. The crosscurrents of sleeplessness and betrayal, all that she had seen and learned but wished were not true, eroded her grasp of reality.

She clung to the hard facts of the last half hour. That Dance and Curran were waiting. That Dance had arranged police backup if Moro set a meeting. That Peter Hall was home. That she had forty minutes to prepare for him, the time it took to drive from Michael's duplex to Hall's estate. That she was half-crazy with fatigue.

Perhaps this was a mercy, she thought. It kept her from dwelling on Michael.

When he opened the door, Michael gave her a long look of appraisal, as though stepping back from his own antipathy. Finally, he said, "You look like hell."

She shoved her hands in the pockets of her overcoat, huddling against the cold. "Can you drive?" she asked. "I'm tired."

Michael held out his hand. She fished out her keys and gave them over.

They got in her car. She leaned her face against the passenger window; though it chilled her face, she did not care.

Michael drove coolly, without haste. "What's going on?" he demanded.

She tried to consider how much to tell him. "Fielding was murdered," she said at last. "Someone drugged him, then shot him up with bad heroin. Welch was cover."

Michael glanced across at her. She could sense him gauging what this meant. "Does Hall know that?"

"He knows *something*."

Michael fell quiet. She felt him wondering, as she did, about the depth of Hall's involvement. Then another thought came to her: to pursue Vincent Moro, she was taking down Arthur Bright, and now, if she had the resources, Peter Hall. But the only certain consequence was not to Moro: Stella was destroying all hope of becoming County Prosecutor.

She turned back to Michael. In profile he seemed preoccupied, his head—the curly hair, broken nose, heavy lids—dim in the half-light of passing cars.

"I need to sleep," she said.

He looked over at her, then nodded.

She slumped back in the seat, closing her eyes. The car moved on.

Sleep began to overtake her, with its drowsy, deceptive sense of well-being. From her subconscious came a long-ago memory. It was Christmas, and their parents had driven Stella and Katie downtown to see the department store lights. They had bought hot chocolate from a street vendor; on the way home, huddled with Katie in the backseat, she could feel the warmth in her limbs, taste the sweetness on her tongue, see her parents' heads, listen to the murmur of their voices. Katie's mittened hand held hers . . .

Stella fell asleep.

A HAND nudged her shoulder.

Stella started, and then opened her eyes.

At night, ground lights lined the stone drive of Hall's estate like a landing strip. The snow at its edge was silver-gray.

As they parked, Stella gathered herself.

Michael, too, regarded the house. Neither of them, she supposed, could ever approach such a place without remembering where they came from, feeling that seed of self-doubt which, in Stella's case, was amplified a thousand times by all that was at risk. But the few minutes' sleep had helped her.

"Thank you," she said.

"For what?"

"For driving."

They got out. Except for the searing wind off the lake in Steelton, it seemed even colder here: the elevation was higher, and there was nothing—buildings, or sidewalks, or people—to blunt the edge of winter. The path to Hall's door was pebbled with salt.

Peter Hall opened the door himself.

He wore a tuxedo. This was the opening night of the symphony, he had reminded Stella when she called, and there were guests in the box owned by Hall Development. He had heard Stravinsky's *Firebird* many times before—surely better played, he added dryly—and would happily sacrifice this pleasure at Stella's request. But he was hosting a table at the gala afterward, which was where inattention to his guests, and thus his time for her, must end.

He had related all this with a polite incuriosity as to her mission, as though her desire to see him was sufficient. But it also served to remind her that whereas she occupied one plane in Steelton, Hall occupied many. A request which might seem imperative to her was, to him, an imposition and a courtesy.

His manner upon seeing Michael reflected all this and something more: irritation, conveyed by raised eyebrows when he turned to Stella. He had time for her, the look said, but meetings with her fellow prosecutors were reserved for business hours. She remembered again what she had felt in his presence—the drift toward compromise, the sense of being favored and favoring in return. But she was far too tense to feel it now.

Hall led them to his office.

Once there, he waved them to a couch and sat across from them in a wing chair. He did not—as she believed he would have had they been alone—offer a drink.

"So," he said to her.

Stella paused. The rest of her life—all that she had worked for, her idea of who she was—might flow from this. Part of her wished she had no choice; instead she was about to make one.

"Tommy Fielding was murdered. On Vincent Moro's orders. I want you to tell me why."

Hall was utterly still. Only his eyes, as blue as Curran's, showed surprise. "I don't know anything about murder," he said. "I don't know Vincent Moro."

Michael leaned forward, his presence in the room heavy and masculine, as out of place as a club fighter's at a charity ball. Softly, he said, "He's your partner."

Hall turned to him in anger and, it appeared to Stella, with genuine distaste. "Explain that to me, Mr. Del Corso."

"Why tell you," Michael rejoined, "what you knew from the beginning?

"You knew Larry Rockwell was Moro's pawn, and that Alliance was Moro's front.

"You knew Moro was skimming the MBE money, and you helped him cover it up.

"You sold the concession rights for parking, food, and novelties to 'local' vendors no one had ever heard of. So Moro could use them to launder more cash from gambling, drugs, and prostitution by reporting it as legitimate income." Michael's voice was low and biting. "When it comes down to it, Mr. Hall, I've seen you all my life. You're like Frankie Scavullo—a stooge in a tuxedo. Only richer."

Hall stood. "No one talks to me like that," he said. "Not in this house, or anywhere. I don't know anything about Vincent Moro. Say any of this in public, even once, and I'll make your life as miserable as you're threatening to make mine." Pausing, he turned to Stella. "I don't know why you're doing this. But I've had enough. It's time for you to leave, and for me to call my lawyer."

"You do that," Stella said calmly. "I'll have you arrested as an accessory to murder. After that I'll make sure you're released on your own recognizance, and leak it to the press that you're cooperating with us. I'm sure Vincent Moro reads the papers." Standing, she picked up a cell phone from the table beside her. "You can use this phone. If you're still alive for the preliminary hearing, maybe we can talk again.

"Your only other choice—besides prison—is ending up like Fielding.

"You know all about *that* part. So let me define accessory for you. That's someone who knows why Fielding was killed, then lies to me about it." Fighting her own nerves, she looked up into his face. "There's an accessory before the fact, or after. Ask your lawyer which one you are. I think you're both."

His anger vanished. His gaze became irresolute and, she thought, imploring. He had never looked more attractive.

She took his wrist, and placed the cell phone in the palm of his hand. "A hundred years ago," she finished, "your bastard of a great-grandfather owned this city. Now you're selling it to Vincent Moro. No one can say you lack a sense of continuity.

"Call your lawyer, Peter. We're leaving you to Moro."

Hall's fingers closed over hers. "I don't know Vincent Moro, Stella. I don't know anything about that."

His touch was cool. Slowly, she removed her hand. "Then tell me what you *do* know," she said. "All of it."

· · ·

SHORTLY AFTER his election, Tom Krajek had asked to see Peter Hall, alone.

Peter was not surprised. Though he was vague as to specifics, Krajek had pledged his best efforts to keep the Blues from leaving town: Hall had quietly supported him over George Walker, who had spoken in scathing terms of "welfare payments to millionaires." That was the crux of the problem—Peter wanted the new stadium to be built with public money. Chary of controversy, Krajek was unwilling to commit himself before the election. But he had passed private hints to Peter of a willingness to deal. Now he was free to talk: his insistence that no one else attend was, to Peter, nothing more than caution, the belief that a meeting so preliminary should not leak to the media.

Why not meet at his home, Peter had suggested. But the sight of Krajek in this place reminded him of what his late wife, Alix, for whom he still grieved, had said: "Tom Krajek has the eyes of a bird. You look into them and there's no one looking back."

It was true. Krajek's pale eyes were small and cold—Peter saw nothing to suggest a soul. His face, too, was birdlike: beaky, callow, given to darting glances. But it would not do to underrate him. He had great energy, a gift for rhetoric, and, Peter suspected, a thirst for power that would repel a normal man. For Tom Krajek, a moment not focused on self-interest was wasted: perched on a chair in Peter's office, Krajek spent little time on small talk.

"I want to keep the Blues here," he said abruptly. "You're demanding a new stadium, built with public money. There has to be a way to meet your needs without killing my career."

Though Krajek was not given to irony, he concluded this remark with a glance at their surroundings—the Miró print, the sylvan landscape framed in Peter's window—which suggested that the world had favored Peter Hall too much already. Equably, Peter said, "I'm open to ideas."

Krajek took a pen from his pocket, touching it to his lips. "I've only been mayor two months," he began. "And I'm already hearing footsteps.

"Last November, George Walker could have beaten me—except for his drug problem, he probably would have. Arthur Bright's next in line.

"He's already sitting on a bloc from the East Side: forty percent of registered voters, all black, thinking it's time one of their own was mayor. Another ten percent and . . ." Krajek snapped his fingers. "I need to keep whites from crossing over. I need more blacks to realize I'm their friend. And I need to do all that without pissing either of them off."

If Krajek believed that confiding this rudimentary formula would impress him, Peter reflected, he was truly self-absorbed. Then he grasped what Krajek was telling him: that the price of his ballpark was to serve Tom Krajek's interests. Wryly, Peter remarked, "I'm not exactly the East Side's poster child."

Krajek nodded curtly. "That makes you a burden, Peter. Your job is to lighten the load."

"How do I do that?"

Krajek smiled—although, to Hall, it resembled a nervous tic. "You want two hundred twenty-five million dollars of public money. You'll have to settle for fifty million more than that."

Peter stifled his astonishment: suddenly only Krajek knew where this conversation was going, and this made Peter wary. Mildly, he said, "I appreciate your compassion."

"You're joking. But I'm not. Hall Development will manage the project itself. For two hundred seventy-five million, you'll build the premier ballpark in America. You'll also be liable for overruns, and split half of any savings with the city."

Peter made a swift calculation. He could bring the project in for between two hundred and two hundred twenty-five million: that Krajek was offering an enormous tip, with only a cosmetic benefit to the city, made him more cautious yet. "What else?" he asked.

His phlegmatic response seemed to please Krajek—perhaps because the mayor sensed, as he did, that Peter was being drawn into Krajek's plan. "The city owns the ballpark," Krajek said. "You sign a twenty-year lease at a million a year. In return, you keep all revenues from the naming rights, luxury boxes, and ticket sales, and get a fair share of parking and concessions."

For months Peter had studied the complex economics surrounding a new ballpark: now he could run the math in his head. What unsettled him was that Krajek had clearly mastered them, too—the mayor knew, as did Peter, that in principle no one who owned a baseball team could turn him down. "And your political problems?" Peter asked.

Krajek smiled again. "*Our* political problems," he amended.

Peter found himself wishing that he had resisted the tug of curiosity. "Such as?"

"Bright will say I'm giving away a fortune in public money to an extortionist—a rich one. *That's* the perception we need to change." Krajek's voice took on the public cadence of a debate. "It's not *your* stadium—it's *my* start on saving Steelton. It's the first stage of a master plan to bring new jobs to the inner city and new life to its waterfront. And it benefits every member of our community.

"*That's* where you give me what *I* need.

"You'll build the ballpark near the lake. Every company on this project will be from Steelton, and thirty percent of the companies and the workers will be drawn from minorities. Every dollar spent goes to our people, and every dollar of tax revenue stays." Krajek pointed his pen at Peter, like someone throwing a dart. "*That's* how we sell this deal and trump Arthur Bright."

"What about competitive bidding?" Hall asked. "The best construction company for sports complexes is in New York—Megaplex."

Krajek no longer smiled, or pretended to persuade. "There won't be any competitive bidding," he said. "*I* choose the general contractor. *I* choose the minority contractor. *I* choose who gets the concessions, and the parking. *I* negotiate their fee structure." Pausing, he gave Peter the hard, shrewd look of a politician dispensing favors. "This is a turnkey deal, Peter. Take it or leave it."

Peter stared at him. The deal was too good not to come at a price, and Peter was not yet sure what the price was.

For a time, Krajek waited him out. Then he reached into his briefcase, withdrew a three-page memo, and placed it in Peter's hands.

It was undated and unsigned. But all the terms were there: Peter's profits; Krajek's prerogatives; the precise location of the stadium itself. Who owns the land? Peter wondered, and then a measure of comprehension came to him.

Softly, he said, "You called this the first stage. What's the second?"

"Complete waterfront development," Krajek answered crisply. "Dredging the harbor—"

"Dredging the *harbor*. What on earth for? The Love Boat?"

Krajek gave a brief laugh. "If we're lucky."

There was something wrong here, Peter knew, and now he felt determined to learn what it was. "I'm all for revitalizing Steelton," he said. "But the waterfront in winter is as barren as the tundra. And the notion of dredging the harbor borders on hallucinatory."

Krajek sat back, his gaze level and, to Peter, hostile. "Do you want this deal?" he asked.

"Before I answer, I want to know what it is. And where it's going."

Krajek tented his fingers, as though pondering his answer. At last he said, "Waterfront gambling."

Of course.

Suddenly Peter felt quite dull-witted. But it was easy to calculate the windfall to whoever owned the land, or to whomever Krajek quietly advised to buy it. Just as it was all too easy for Peter the developer to imagine the waterfront transformed by the lure of excitement, the power of greed.

Krajek leaned forward. "This is a depressed area, Peter. The only cure for it is gambling. You've been to Atlantic City. Before gambling it reeked of decay."

Now it reeks of criminality, Hall thought. But Krajek was right: only gambling would fulfill his vision.

"You'll need legislation," Peter said at last.

"It'll be easier with your support. It's in your interest, too." Krajek smiled briefly. "Especially as a developer."

So that was the ultimate carrot, Peter thought. He chose to let Krajek interpret his silence however he wished.

Placing the memo in his lap, he began to review its terms.

He stopped on the second page.

"What's this about minority ownership?" he asked.

"Before we go to the voters, you bring in Larry Rockwell as five percent owner of the Blues, at a price set by an impartial appraiser. We can't put you in blackface, Peter. Rockwell's the next best thing."

Krajek's cynicism was a weapon, Peter saw: his private coarseness was a form of control, meant to remind Peter that he had entered Krajek's domain. "Truly," Peter said sardonically, "this is the land of opportunity. I assume you've picked out my contractor and subcontractor, too. As well as the vendor."

Krajek's eyes narrowed. "I haven't worked that out yet."

"You're going to have to—at least the majority general contractor—to make this deal with anyone. A ballpark isn't Chipper and Muffy's starter house."

Slowly, Krajek nodded. "That's fair. Anything else?"

Peter hesitated. He felt Krajek measuring him, imagining his estimate of gain or loss. Krajek's weakness, he suspected, was an inability to imagine motives different from his own. But Peter had them: his dream of a stadium, of a city which bore his imprint. Of giving back some of what his family had taken, restoring life to a place which had begun dying with Amasa's mills. It was what losing Alix had done to him—made him reflect, hard, on what his life would mean without her, and would mean to their children when, as adults, they judged him. That this deal was one no businessman could refuse only made his hopes become more vivid, seem that much closer to reality.

But there was Krajek to consider. So Peter paused, imagining the version of himself that Krajek saw.

"This second stage," he finally said. "Would I be the developer?"

Krajek's smile was quiet, satisfied; in the end, Peter had conformed to expectations. "For the right price. That seems to be no trouble here."

"Then I want that to be part of our deal—a two-month right of negotiation with the city before any other developer gets to bid."

Krajek's gaze was unreadable. "You want this ballpark," Peter said. "You want gambling. You want to develop the waterfront. You want us to be as inseparable as Siamese twins." He passed the memo to Krajek. "Draft something, Tom. I trust you. Because you need me."

PAUSING, HALL turned to the darkened window. Stella watched him, a slim, elegant man in a tuxedo, and thought of Dance, waiting in Curran's miserable apartment, gun trained on Fielding's murderer. She kept hoping for Hall's phone to ring, for Dance to tell her that events were set in motion. And yet she felt the past unfolding, the hidden corruption of her city, the inexorable chain of events which tied Hall to Johnny Curran.

"Tell me about Fielding," she said.

EIGHT

SOME MEN were perfect for their job.

That was what Peter Hall had always known about Tommy Fielding. Tommy was smart, hardworking, and borderline obsessive. There was a curious purity about him: the day-to-day performance of his task, the mastery of detail, sometimes seemed more important than the end result. To Tommy, Peter thought wryly, project management was more than just a handsome living—it was an aesthetic.

But that was fine. Peter himself could serve as both pragmatist and visionary, and let Tommy nag the details—the change orders, the over-charges, the subcontractor who was running late, the endless shepherding of forms through stultified bureaucracies. Peter suspected that Tommy's dedication was also flight: that there was something beyond work, perhaps within himself, which Tommy dearly wished to escape. If so, the pragmatist in Peter—the user and the motivator—dearly hoped that Tommy Fielding would never find a cure.

Until Steelton 2000, and a bleak November day.

Peter remembered it well—better than he had realized until the morning that Tommy was found dead. After that, their meeting recurred in his mind, over and over, as haunting in its own way as the memory of his late wife's fatal accident. Of which, unlike this death, Peter was wholly innocent.

Tommy had come to his office. With his perfectly pressed slacks, tasseled loafers, crewneck sweater, and slick jet black hair, he had looked to Peter like a Fitzgerald character on the way to a regatta. Except for his seriousness, almost painful to witness.

"Peter," he said, "I can't keep signing these reports."

Peter knew the reason. It was only to probe the depths of Tommy's resolve that he asked, "Why?"

"Because we'd be guilty of a fraud."

Tommy's voice had always been light, a college boy's. Now it held the collegian's utter lack of irony.

"In politics," Peter said dryly, "fraud is a relative concept. Of necessity."

Tommy faced the window, staring down at the scarred earth, the steel outline of the stadium. "You sit up here," he told Peter, "and you see a dream. I've begun to see a project more corrupt than we've ever imagined."

This bluntness both nettled Peter and worried him. "What I see," he answered, "is a project as good for the city as it is for us. We don't get to dictate the terms, or the people we have to deal with. To coin a phrase, you're in danger of letting the perfect be the enemy of the good. As if we even have a choice."

Tommy put his hands on his hips. "We're submitting lies, Peter."

Tommy's sheer simplicity brought Peter to his feet. "There's nothing for it, Tommy. Do you want Arthur Bright to become mayor? Then there really *will* be trouble."

"I know. And my name is all over those reports."

"Which you signed in good faith."

"Not anymore." Tommy's voice rose, and his dark eyes fixed Peter with new resolve. "Let me recite the facts, and see if you're still so goddamned blasé.

"Our minority contractor, Alliance, is a shell—a trailer with an accountant and someone to answer the phone. Larry Rockwell knows as much about construction as I do about hitting a curve ball. The only thing they're good for is cashing our checks—"

"I don't mean to be cynical," Peter interjected, "but that may have been the whole idea. If so, it wasn't ours."

"Then whose is it? Alliance bills for work they don't do. Then the general contractor covers for them by *doing* the work, and submitting padded bills and phony change orders. So we pay twice. The city's getting screwed, and we lose money off the savings clause. Who's making out here?"

Peter walked from behind his desk and stood beside Tommy. Deliberately, he focused on the stadium below them; it was one of those moments, rare for Peter, when he had no wish to look Tommy in the face.

Softly, he said, "That's not ours to know. The city compliance inspectors say that Alliance is doing its job, and that the project's swarming with minorities. That's what I see from here. That's what the paper *you* see tells you. That's what gets this stadium done." He turned to Tommy. "Do I like it? No. Be grateful you didn't have to decide between feeling like you do and staring at an abandoned patch of earth in a dying city. All *you* have to do is sign some papers."

Tommy placed a hand on Peter's shoulder. His eyes were wounded. "How can you do this?" he asked.

Peter tried to smile. "You've been ten years in real estate development, dealing with politicians and every interest group on earth, and still you ask me that? Name one project where we never had to give someone with their hand out something they didn't earn. That's the nature of free enterprise."

Tommy did not smile. Softly, he asked, "Who's the 'someone,' Peter? Just Larry Rockwell? Do you even know?"

Peter could not answer.

Tommy's grip tightened on his shoulder. "This isn't just a little graft, looking the other way while some bogus outfit steals another ten grand or so. It's millions upon millions.

"Someone's getting the money. Someone's screwing legitimate MBEs out of work. Someone's stealing from the city. Someone's bribing the inspectors—"

"How do you know *that*?" Peter interrupted.

"What I see, they can see. Does Larry Rockwell have *that* much juice? Is he *that* important in attracting black support? Is Bright *that* much of a threat?"

They were all good questions. Listening, Peter knew how deeply Tommy had considered this. He had seen the big picture at last.

Reluctantly, Peter ventured, "If your share of the savings clause concerns you—"

"You think this is about bonus money?" Tommy dropped his hand, stepping back to stare at Peter. "What 'concerns' me is jail. I don't want my seven-year-old visiting the pen on Father's Day. But I'll tell you what 'concerns' me even more."

"What's that?"

"You. You're a good man who's somehow being corrupted. If it's happening to you, it can happen to me." His voice grew quiet again. "I'm not signing those reports. I'm not authorizing Alliance's bills. I'm not paying twice for the same work. I'm not covering up for people I don't know.

"I'll give you two months to decide, Peter. Tell whoever it is that I've dug my heels in, that I'll go to Bright if I have to, that you can't go along anymore. Get yourself out of this . . ."

"I can't, Tommy. We've got a project to finish."

"Fine. They wanted minorities? Let Rockwell hire some real ones. Because when somebody starts turning over the rocks on this deal, God knows what they'll find."

LISTENING, STELLA felt anger, and a useless pity. The pity was for Fielding: he had transcended Hall's place for him, and the price had been his death. The anger was at Hall, and at herself for being drawn to him.

"Who did you tell about Tommy?" she asked.

Hall's eyelids lowered. Perhaps it was theatrics, as cool as Hall was, but Stella had the impression, not of an accessory to murder but of someone steeped in regret, reliving how all his false choices, wrong turns, led to the murder of someone for whom he felt affection and respect. But with a man this polished it was hard to know: from Hall, even candor seemed double-edged. And she had Michael's presence to remind her how skewed her judgments could be.

"No one," Hall answered. "I stalled him. A month passed without a signed report, then two. It was like a war of nerves. No one said anything. We just both got in that much deeper."

Silent, Stella turned to Michael. "That's all?" Michael demanded. "You just woke up one day and found out Tommy was a smackhead. Just another of life's surprises in an imperfect world."

Hall did not look up. Once more, she felt him weighing his course. The practical course of calling his lawyer. Or the course Tommy Fielding had pleaded for.

When he raised his eyes, it was to look at Stella. "Krajek called *me*," he said. "Five days before Tommy died."

"WE NEED those reports," Krajek said. "Alliance tells me they're not getting paid."

Despite his own worries about this, the mayor's peremptory tone nettled Peter. "They're not getting paid," he answered, "because they're not doing work. Something about that bothers Tommy Fielding, and he's naive enough to expect it to bother me."

"In Steelton," Krajek retorted, "certain things need to happen if you're going to get what you want. Do *you* believe we're doing good?"

"Yes. And Tommy believes he's doing good."

"He's not. Not if we want this stadium."

Peter stood, walking to the window. Though winter, it was a rare bright day: across the river, he could see the smokestacks of his great-grandfather's dying mills. But hundreds of feet below him, the pristine angles of a ballpark were appearing out of nowhere. Its steel framework glistened in the light.

"Tommy won't bend," Peter said at last. "If he has to, he says he'll go to Bright."

There was silence. Coldly Krajek answered, "That can't happen. Ever."

At once, Peter felt cowardly. It was he who had put Tommy in this position; he who had not wished to know what Tommy had discovered. However distasteful, his responsibility now was to salvage the ballpark and keep Tommy Fielding clean, at whatever risk to himself. "I'll take over Tommy's job," he told Krajek. "I'll approve the invoices, and sign the reports. That'll get his name off the paper trail."

Krajek sounded dubious. "Is it enough to keep him away from Bright?"

"Yes," Peter said firmly. "*I'll* make sure of it."

"You'll have to." The mayor's voice rose in anxiety, in warning. "There's too much at stake here, Peter. Not just the ballpark but the entire second stage. Including your place in it."

Peter cursed himself for giving this man reason to see him as he so clearly did. "I can deal with Tommy," he said. "Now you back off."

Peter hung up.

That would be the end of it, he thought.

THE AFTERNOON before Tommy died, Peter told him.

Tommy's eyes filled with doubt and disappointment. Peter felt a fissure open between them which might never mend.

"Why are you doing this?" Tommy asked.

"So you won't have to."

Frowning, Tommy appeared more troubled yet. "And you do?"

"To build this ballpark, yes. So I have a favor to ask you."

"What?"

"Stay away from Arthur Bright. If you don't, you won't just ruin our project. You'll ruin *me* with it."

Tommy gazed at him, and then slowly shook his head. It was not refusal, Peter knew, but sorrow and disillusion. Whatever damage this did to him, he would not betray Peter.

"Go home," Peter said softly. "Get some sleep. There'll be other projects."

Tommy went home. It was the last time Peter saw him.

The call had come from Amanda, Tommy's ex-wife. Putting down the phone, Peter thought of Alix.

She had hit a patch of ice and skidded into a telephone pole, dying on impact. Her one fault in life had been driving too fast; in all other things she had been flawless, a dazzling wife, a caring mother. So that Peter knew, even before the police told him, that both of their children were safe. Alix was only careless when alone.

Frightened, Peter sat at his desk and prayed that Tommy's death was as senseless as Alix's. An accident.

"HE DIED for nothing," Stella said. "Just so Moro could be sure."

Hall appeared devastated. Stella supposed it was hard to face that his ambition, not heroin, had killed Tommy Fielding.

"If I'd known about Moro . . ." Hall began.

"Yes?"

"I thought it was politics as usual, Krajek taking care of his future, his constituent groups, his supporters. I figured some would get paid for nothing, others might buy and sell the land on inside information, still others might kick cash back to Krajek. That this was the kind of graft associated with public works. Not the stuff of murder." Pausing, Hall spoke quietly, "Now I know. If I'm going to help you, I'll need secrecy and protection."

Edgy, Stella thought of Curran, still her only link to Moro, and wondered why the telephone had not rung. "How can I believe you?" she asked.

"About Moro? Maybe you can't. But one reason I didn't call my lawyer is that I'm telling you the truth. That's exactly how it happened."

"Yeah." Michael's voice was skeptical. "Without witnesses."

Hall turned to him. The dislike between them was instinctive, Stella thought—a male antagonism which went deeper than their roles. Then, as if dismissing Michael, Hall turned his back and walked to the bright Miró on his wall.

Carefully, he lifted the print from its hook.

Behind it was a wall safe. Hall placed the print on his desk and then, head cocked, opened up the safe.

Stella could not see what was inside. Hall withdrew a document and flipped the first two pages. Turning to Stella, he said, "Here it is."

She took it from him. Scrawled at the bottom of the third page were some phrases about the waterfront, a two-month negotiation. It was meaningless, Stella knew—unenforceable. But now she understood that this had never been Hall's purpose.

"Krajek's handwriting," she said.

The trace of a smile formed in Hall's eyes. "Krajek's handwriting," he answered. "In case I ever needed it."

THEY WERE driving past Hall's guardhouse before Michael spoke again.

"It's incredible," he said.

"Moro?"

"Yes. He's taking his family 'legitimate.' He sees crime lords like John Gotti going to prison and senses his time is up. Drugs have become too nasty and too dangerous. And he knows that the next generation, guys like Nick Moro with law degrees, don't have the stomach to do what he's done.

"None of this will be easy to nail down. But I'm right about the concessions, I'm sure. That's how he's laundering more money for the second stage. And that's just for the interim. I think his real plan is to clean up on the land and the phony MBEs, invest in waterfront development, and wind up holding the casino licenses. It takes nerve, and it's brilliant. Worth killing for, in fact." Michael's voice became soft, scornful. "Moro may have murdered Tommy Fielding. But his grandchildren will be as respectable as Peter Hall. And as slick."

"You don't believe him?"

"No. But I can't prove it. In the end, he'll skate—these guys always do."

Stella stared out the windshield. Their headlights cut the darkness of a lonely road at night. "I'm going to need him," she said. "For Krajek."

"Don't think he doesn't know that. He didn't need a lawyer. He'd already set up Krajek, as insurance. The only reason he talked was to save himself, and because you made him believe you'd put his life at risk if he didn't. But you wouldn't have, would you?"

"No."

He glanced across at her. "What is it with you and Hall?"

Stella smiled briefly. "I'm his candidate for County Prosecutor. Or used to be."

"And Krajek was his candidate for mayor."

It was not a gibe, Stella realized, but an admonition. What they had learned was awe-inspiring, and frightening, dwarfing the anger between them. The damage Vincent Moro had done to others involved far more than murder.

"Moro's insulated himself," she said. "That's why I believe Hall's basic story. Hall sees only Krajek and only Krajek sees Moro, just like a drug network. And Krajek's like a dealer—he'll never admit his orders came from Moro. He's too scared, and there's too much to lose."

She did not tell him the rest—that her only hope of getting Moro, and Moro's only risk, was Johnny Curran. But she could not return to Curran's apartment: the call from Curran had put Moro on notice, and his people could be watching.

Her car phone rang.

She snatched at it. "Go to your office," Dance said brusquely. "Use the underground garage, and make sure no one sees you. I'll phone you there."

Stella tensed. "What's happening?"

She felt Dance hesitate. "Your friend called back," he said.

NINE

ENTERING HER office, Stella was startled to discover Arthur Bright.

He was sitting in her chair. "Nat called me," he said. "At home."

Stella found his presence as pitiful as it was disturbing. Though it was past eleven o'clock and the office was dark, Bright wore a suit, as if clinging to an identity which was slipping away. He looked wasted—the inexorable progress toward exposure, the strain of not telling Lizanne, must be toxic.

"What did he say?" she asked.

"That Moro told Curran to go to his office, then wait for a call."

"That's all?"

"Nat thinks they want to see if we're tailing Curran. Maybe that Moro's people will try to stop him, or kill him."

Stella sat on the edge of her desk. "Where *is* Nat?"

"Lying on the backseat of the car, with his gun aimed at Curran's head. Assuming they get out of Curran's garage alive."

Stella considered this. She sensed that Curran had been right: to send anyone else to meet with him, or to execute him, would increase Moro's exposure. "Moro wants no witnesses," she said. "He needs to see if Curran's alone."

Bright nodded. "Nat's got backup ready, two teams from Special Operations. One precinct on the East Side, one on the West. Nothing downtown—Nat's afraid Moro's watching headquarters. But he doesn't know what to tell them to do, or where to go."

"Has he called the Chief of Police?"

Bright looked away; perhaps, Stella thought, the question reminded him of how quickly his own secrets would be known. "No," he answered.

Stella said nothing. The situation involved the risk of lives, reputations, careers, requiring a series of decisions which had no certain end. Operations of this importance should be cleared with the chief, Krajek's man. But to do so here might be fatal. This made Dance's position more delicate yet: unless Curran succeeded and Moro went down, there would be much for Dance and Stella to answer for.

Turning, Stella surveyed the city.

Next to her building, the beaux arts structure which housed the courts and the police was nearly dark, peopled only by a skeleton crew of cops and janitorial workers. By directing Curran there, Moro had also sent a warning: should this be a trap, any extraordinary police activity would give Curran away.

Minutes passed.

Stella began pacing. Except for his fingers tapping softly on her desk, Bright was still. Something about their trapped intensity reminded Stella of prisoners in an exercise yard.

"I'm sorry," she said at last.

Bright appraised her, then slowly shook his head. Stella did not know whether to interpret this as anguish or as dismissal. Finally Bright asked, "Tell me this, Stella. Do you think I've done more good than harm?"

Watching him, Stella pondered her answer.

By most measures, Arthur had been a fine prosecutor. He was a symbol to the black community and yet, within the confines of Steelton politics, had avoided the uglier aspects of race. He had hired and promoted on merit; Stella would not be here without him. Yet, against his will, he had helped Vincent Moro maintain his deathlock on Bright's own community. And by advancing his ambitions in spite of this, he had offered Steelton another mayor who, though not corrupt, was corruptible.

At length, Stella said, "I wish I knew."

As soon as she spoke, she felt renewed sorrow, both his and hers. Arthur looked away again, as if shunned: in his despair he had been searching for something elegiac, absolution from the agent of his destruction.

Was that too much to ask from her? she wondered.

The telephone rang.

Bright started, then reached for it, a reflex. Stella took it from his hand.

"Get over here," Dance told her. "Curran's office. Use the tunnel." He hung up before she could ask questions.

Stella glanced down at Bright. "I'm going over to Curran's," she told him, then paused. "Don't panic, Arthur. Rat us out now, and your only hope is they kill both Dance and me."

Bright shook his head. "I'll just be here," he answered.

His tone was dispirited, as if the assertiveness had vanished, that he now recalled he no longer mattered. But Stella felt there was something more: he could not face Johnny Curran or what they had done years ago, more vivid on Novak's tape than it had ever been in memory.

Stella left, the videotape still in her purse.

THE TUNNEL between Stella's building and police headquarters dated back to the era of civil defense, when some underimaginative city planners had decreed that, in case of nuclear attack, the County Prosecutor should maintain contact with the police. But its major practical benefit was to protect both parties from the natural disaster of Steelton winters. Or, tonight, to let Stella's movements pass unnoticed.

The concrete passage was narrow, bleak, ill lit. Stella was alone. She moved as quickly as she could; when she finally reached the stairwell, emerging into the shadowed marble lobby, it came as a relief. She took the elevator to Curran's office.

Dance and Curran were alone. Though Dance glanced up at her, Curran took no notice. His expression was so intent that it seemed that his head was in a vise. Dance had his gun in his lap.

"Still waiting," Dance told her. "Phone's tapped."

Because Curran had given his permission, Stella knew, no court order was required. What puzzled her was why Moro, so carefully cryptic on the telephone, would risk calling here.

Still Curran did not look up.

His eyes had the opacity of thought. Stella could imagine the tension of descending to his underground garage, then driving downtown, then entering the garage below them where he and Dance could not be seen. Even worse than it was for Stella, waiting in a darkened corner of the police station with Tommy Fielding's murderer.

At last Curran looked at Dance. "Whose chances do you like, Nat? Vincent's, or mine?"

Dance shrugged. "It's hard to pick a favorite."

Arms folded, Stella leaned against the wall.

Krajek was hers. She would put Hall in front of the grand jury, then squeeze Larry Rockwell, the city inspectors, and the white general contractor. Even if she could not send Tom Krajek to prison—and Stella believed she would—she could ruin him. And, with him, ruin the second stage of Vincent Moro's plan.

But not Moro himself. He would have to take a hand in his own destruction.

She tried to think as Moro would.

He had not yet attempted to murder Curran. Perhaps this was twisted loyalty; more likely he had calculated that, without careful planning, Curran would be too hard to kill. Or, worse for Stella, Moro had judged it more risky to meet with Curran than to let her arrest him: without corroboration, Moro must know, a witness like Curran was damaged goods.

Against all this she weighed the power of his dream.

Dreams. Bright's. Stella's. Dance's. Hall's. Krajek's. For a place so blighted, Steelton was rife with dreams or their mutations. But, if Michael was right, none were as powerful, as audacious, as Vincent Moro's. The transformation of a family. The takeover of a city.

In Moro's mind, if he remained ignorant of Hall's involvement, Curran was the major obstacle to this design. Curran alone knew that Fielding had died on Moro's orders. That knowledge, shared with Stella, could unravel Moro's plans.

For the first time, Curran turned, acknowledging her presence.

"Vincent's not biting," he told her. "He's smelled you out."

The words bore a faint rebuke and—as desperate as Curran's future might be—a perverse satisfaction. Moro, as always, had been too smart for them.

Coolly, she answered, "Pray you're wrong."

Curran did not reply. But the hatred in his eyes showed that she had left no doubt: unless she needed him, she would make the rest of his life, however long it was, a nightmare. Nor did Stella doubt this.

Curran resumed staring at the floor.

The room was getting to her. The cinder-block walls, the metal desk, the dirty tile. Curran himself.

What was Michael doing? she wondered.

She tried to dismiss the thought—her friendship with Michael was beyond repair. Except at work, she doubted that she would ever see him. She would see Sofia only by chance, if at all.

A muffled buzz surprised her.

Still intent, Curran opened a metal drawer. The phone inside rang again.

A new cellular, Stella realized. An unknown number. Meant for Curran to use once, with Moro, before he threw it out. In this case, Moro's signal that he remained one step ahead.

Curran put the cell phone to his ear. Listening, he was still. He said nothing.

A few seconds later he placed down the phone. In the merciless fluorescent light, his face was pallid.

"We're meeting," Curran told Dance. "Or so Vincent tells me."

"Where?"

"The new stadium."

Stella was startled. But the dullness of Curran's tone betrayed his fear. Though spacious, the stadium was surrounded by a fence and patrolled by a security company which, she was now certain, Moro controlled. The police could not enter without Moro knowing. Nor could they plant eavesdropping equipment or infrared cameras. The only surveillance device would be Curran himself, and there would be no other witnesses.

"When?" Dance finally asked. "And how?"

"Now." The lines at the corners of Curran's eyes deepened. "There's a gate at the southwest corner. It'll be open. I'm supposed to pass through and walk to the middle of the field." His soft voice took on a note of irony. "Jimmy Hoffa's buried in an end zone at the Meadowlands, they say. But then football's a rougher game."

Dance regarded him steadily. "We'll have backup."

Curran's answer was swollen with contempt. "Sure, Nat. But far enough away that his security can't see you. You wouldn't want to spoil the joke."

Dance reached into his pocket, then held out his palm. It contained a miniature microphone, a device from a TV sound set. "Pin this to your T-shirt. As soon as anyone starts talking, we'll hear you."

"With the right equipment, so can Vincent. I'd be safer just taping him."

Dance was silent. Harshly, Curran said, "You're signing my death warrant."

Dance's face was hard, his voice flat. "If you try to tape him, we can't hear you. We already can't see you. There's no way we could respond. If he pats you down, he finds the tape. After you're dead, he takes it."

"That's not what I'm after, Johnny. I can kill you without his help."

Even with all she had seen, Stella felt a chill on her skin: as likely as not, they were sending Curran out to die. Calmly, Dance finished, "You can make a run for Canada. I give you about ten minutes. If you're lucky, my people will shoot you down."

Facing Stella, Curran's eyes bore into hers. "Put this bug on," Dance repeated. "If we stop hearing you breathe, we forget about Moro and come after you."

Curran kept watching her. Stomach tight, Stella nodded.

Time seemed to stop.

Turning, Curran stared at the gun in Dance's other hand. After a moment, he took the clip.

Pulling up his sweater, he pinned it to the T-shirt stretching across his belly. Stella saw an inch of bare skin, a roll of fat, and thought of the younger man on the videotape, naked and bestial.

"Where will *you* be?" Curran asked Dance.

"In a sound truck."

Once more, Curran's gaze turned inward. Stella sensed him gauging his alternatives, calculating the odds. Perhaps wondering if Vincent Moro, his friend from youth, would spare his life.

Dance angled his head toward the door. "He's waiting, Johnny. If you believe him."

Curran pursed his lips. Quite slowly, he looked from Dance to Stella.

"Take your time," Dance said.

Curran turned from them. He vanished in the darkened hallway.

Stella stared after him. "I'm going with you," she told Dance.

TEN

WAITING INSIDE the command post, Dance and Stella listened to Curran breathe.

The post was disguised as an ambulance. But its rear windows were opaque from the outside, concealing surveillance equipment, police technicians, telephones with scramblers. On Dance's instructions, the truck glided from the garage beneath Stella's building.

"Stay back," he said into the telephone. "I'll tell you when to seal it off."

The truck came to a stop. Over the monitor, Curran began to whistle "Danny Boy," so softly they could barely hear.

"Where *are* we?" Stella asked.

"Beside your building—six blocks from the stadium."

Curran stopped whistling.

Stella envisioned him, alone in the dark and bitter cold, walking in the barren no-man's-land between the courthouse and the stadium. At night, the area had no light; Curran would be as hard to see as would whoever might attack him before he reached the gate. Taut, Dance and Stella listened for the sound of gunshots.

They heard nothing but Curran's footsteps, his steady breathing.

He might run for it. She imagined him looking at the steel skeleton ahead, looming in a starless sky. In his place, she was not sure what she would do.

Beside her, Dance gripped the telephone.

In the dim light of the truck, a sound technician, listening intently, turned up the volume.

Footsteps, then a whisper of wind from the lake.

Curran's gun was empty.

How must that feel? Stella thought. She imagined him wondering whether Moro was near. Perhaps weighing the consequences of betrayal.

Curran might be dead in seconds. Or he might live for years, absolved by Stella of at least six murders, enjoying the proceeds of the Swiss bank accounts he surely had, his blood money from Vincent Moro. Laughing at them all.

Perhaps it was this, as much as fear, which drew him toward the stadium. The allure of winning one last time, and for good.

There was a metallic creak, like the swinging of an iron gate.

Dance's eyes narrowed. From the monitor came the first spoken words.

"I'm inside." Curran's voice, a murmur.

Stella turned to Dance.

He shook his head.

Curran was passing beneath the steel girders, Stella supposed. Where anyone could ambush him.

Abruptly, there were no footsteps.

Now he was on dirt, Stella guessed, moving toward the middle of the field. Or perhaps had stopped to look about him. All she heard were his breaths, slow and steady.

Dance put the telephone to his mouth. "Get ready," he ordered. Scrambled, his words would become incomprehensible except to the police who listened.

Head bent toward the monitor, Stella could hardly breathe.

A grunt, but softer. The sound of Curran's tension expelled.

"Hello, Johnny."

Stella closed her eyes.

In the same quiet voice, Vincent Moro asked, "How long have we known each other?"

"Forty-nine years." Curran's voice was lower, a baritone to Moro's tenor. "Since second grade, at Our Lady."

"Yes. And in all that time I never saw you afraid."

The very softness of Moro's tone made it, to Stella, insinuating. Still Dance gave no orders.

Curran, too, said nothing. His breathing was harsher, more audible.

"Why now," Moro asked, "when you've lived like this for twenty years?"

More silence.

"It's your friend," Curran said at last. "The Dark Lady. She's figured out Novak and Fielding."

The Dark Lady, Stella thought.

Turning, she whispered to Dance, "Bring them up . . ."

"Not only her," Moro was saying. "Tell me what else worries you so much."

For a time the only sound was Curran's breathing. "That it worries *you,*" he answered. "Enough for you to be here."

In the truck, Stella stared at Dance. "Give the order, Nat."

Briefly, Dance shook his head.

You want *him to die,* Stella thought.

On the monitors, Moro's voice remained soft. "You're important to me, Johnny. That's why I brought the package. Look inside."

There was silence. Stella heard a click, the sound of a latch.

"What are you doing, Vincent?" Curran's voice had changed now. Thick and low, fear breaking through.

Quietly, Moro said, "Hugging you, like a brother. Saying good-bye."

An image came to Stella, vivid and frightening—Curran, bent over an open briefcase, Moro's gun to his head, Moro's hand sifting his clothes.

"Don't," Curran whispered. "I'm wired."

There was silence. "I hope you're more loyal, Johnny." Moro's tone was lethal now. "If you are, I'm safe. If you're wired, I've got nothing to lose."

Curran's breathing was rapid, hard. He made no answer.

Moro's voice was quieter yet. "You didn't think of that?" he asked.

Watching Stella, Dance placed the phone to his mouth.

There was a soft cry, as if at a blow. Dance's face strained with the effort of listening.

"Damn you," Stella said. "Send them in."

A gunshot echoed in the truck.

"*Now,*" Dance snapped.

The truck started, squealing forward, pitching Stella against the wall. Its siren shrieked, converging in the night with others, more distant. As Stella gripped a metal hand railing, the truck careered, gaining speed.

"What are we doing?" she demanded.

Dance, too, gripped the railing. "We're going in."

The ambulance leaped a curb.

Through the back window, Stella saw the gates of the stadium, the base of steel pillars. The truck lurched to a stop.

Jerking open the rear door, Dance jumped out. Stella scrambled after him. Her feet hit frozen earth.

What she saw then stopped her.

The field glowed with the headlights of police cars. By the gate a uniformed cop aimed a semiautomatic rifle at a security guard. The beams surrounding the field were like yellow eyes; the steel pylons glowed with light and then, as they rose, became shadows. Voices called out all around them.

Ahead of her, Dance, too, had stopped.

He stood over a body. Motionless, it curled sideways, like a giant fetus.

Approaching, Stella recognized the Irish fisherman's sweater.

Curran lay on his side. His right eye stared back at her, but his left was missing. In its place was a trickle of blood.

Beside him, lying open, was an empty briefcase.

Dance regarded the body without expression. Only the duration of his stare betrayed emotion. He did not move.

"It's better this way," Dance said at last. "Now you've got him for Curran's murder."

Silent, Stella looked up.

At the center of the field police with weapons surrounded a dark silhouette. The lone man was slight, still.

Stella walked toward him.

When she was a few feet away, he turned to her, and his face came into the light. As it once had in Jack Novak's office.

Moro straightened. He was older, his skin seamed, and his hair had turned iron gray. But even now he maintained a chilling dignity. He looked into Stella's eyes.

"Such a pretty lady," he said softly. "Still."

Fourteen years, she thought. So much corruption, so much death. But she had no need to say this.

The next time she saw him would be in court.

Turning her back, Stella walked away.

ELEVEN

LEANING AGAINST the base of a steel pylon, Stella fought to absorb all that had happened. Her limbs were heavy, the crazy energy of the last hour gone. The noise and motion around her seemed to come from a great distance.

Curran was dead. With Dance's help, and Michael's, she had linked Jack Novak's murder to those of Fielding and Tina Welch. Krajek's ruin would follow and, with it, the end of his plans for the waterfront.

Now Vincent Moro was in custody.

She had wanted this desperately. But it was the force of Moro's own desperation, his dream of power transformed, which at last had warped his instincts. That, and his fear of Curran, the one man who had known him too well.

There was still much to do. Moro would build a defense; his trial would not be simple. But she believed she would win. And, as with Curran, she had already achieved a measure of justice.

It took a moment to register that Dance was beside her.

"We need to talk," he told her.

Stella shoved her hands deeper into the pockets of her coat. "About what?"

He moved closer. "Arthur."

She turned to him, her mind sluggish. Dance's voice was quiet, calm. "Curran's dead. You've got Moro for his murder. You've got Hall to use on Krajek. Arthur and his videotape add nothing."

Dully, Stella said to herself, *You're always a step behind*. But there was one thing she understood: Dance's ultimate reason for wanting Curran dead had been to protect Arthur Bright.

"Moro," Dance finished, "is the only one left who knows. And he's not telling anyone."

Stella stared at him. "*We* know."

Dance's tone was patient. "You wanted Arthur to be mayor. There were good reasons. I say they still apply." His voice lowered to ensure that only she could hear. "With Arthur's support, you could be County Prosecutor instead of Sloan. But you can't make it yet on your own. If you take him down, you're blocked."

It was true.

Stella felt this realization wash over her. Softly, she answered, "And if Arthur's mayor, you're Chief of Police."

Dance appraised her. "Is any of that so bad? Are things still so black-and-white to you that it only matters *how* something happens? By now, you should know better."

Stella weighed his questions, his plain reference to using Curran to get Moro. She became aware of the structure around them, the mass of cement and steel. "Perhaps I'm *learning* better," she answered. "But *Arthur* tried believing that he'd fixed cases for the greater good. I wonder what he'd tell me now."

Pausing, Dance looked into her face. "Why don't you ask him, Stella."

She stood straighter. "Did you and Arthur work this out?"

"No." Dance smiled faintly. "Unless Moro killed Curran, it was academic."

Stella was silent. Nathaniel Dance was more subtle than she, his motives more various. But none of them, she was sure, involved her own advancement. "Do you want a black mayor *that* much?" she asked. "Or do you want Arthur?"

For a moment, Dance did not answer. "Both," he said at last. "It's time. So now it's your time, too."

Stella shook her head, as if to clear it. "You don't even know if Arthur still wants to be mayor. He damned sure doesn't want *me*."

"He *needs* you. So you can forget Charles Sloan." Turning, Dance gazed through the steel framework at the darkened building where Bright waited for them. "We have to tell Arthur what's happened before Krajek or the press finds out. See what you think then."

As STELLA waited, Dance gave orders for booking Vincent Moro. Then, in the biting cold, they silently walked toward the building.

It was past two-thirty. The city was hushed, the lobby ethereal—dim lights, a single guard. As they took the elevator, Stella tried to imagine what Bright would say to her, or she to him.

The floor was dark. Only the glow of light from Stella's office, its door ajar, guided them. Its hinges creaked.

Stella stopped, shuddering in horror and disbelief.

The outline of a man hung from her door. His feet did not touch the ground.

"*No-o-o.*"

It was Dance. He rushed forward, Stella behind him. The door swung toward them, carried by Bright's weight.

His eyes, as Novak's had been, were bloodshot. His face was a mask of agony.

Moaning softly, Dance hugged Bright's body to his, lifting him from the noose which had been his belt. Awkwardly, Stella slid the belt from beneath his neck. His skin was still warm.

Dance laid him on the floor, and pressed his mouth to Arthur's. Nauseated, Stella hurried to her telephone and called 911.

When she turned again, she saw Bright's belt, still twisted around the metal coatrack affixed to the inside of her door. Then Dance raised his head. Tears were running down his face.

Stella slumped in her chair.

Bright had died as Jack Novak had. Except that he had hanged himself in Stella's office, for her to see. Though it was not cold, her teeth chattered. The anguish in Dance's eyes made her look away.

"Now we know his answer," she murmured.

Far below, the thin wail of an ambulance issued from the street. In a thick voice, Dance asked, "Where's the videotape?"

"In my purse."

Dance went to the hallway.

Her purse lay by Bright's body. Quickly, Dance extracted the tape.

"I made a copy," she told him.

TWELVE

FIVE DAYS later, Stella went to Bright's funeral.

She found it hard. When she asked Michael Del Corso to sit with her, he agreed.

They said little, and Stella did not explain herself. She was not certain if she ever could. To do so would involve revealing Bright's secrets, and her own: that she would always feel responsible for his death.

But life went on. The day was sunny, and First Baptist Church—built, as was St. Stanislaus, from the savings of struggling newcomers—was filled with light through its stained-glass windows. Seated in the third row, Stella studied Lizanne Bright, and pondered her obligations.

Sitting between her son and daughter, Lizanne held their hands. She did not weep. But she looked haggard, a different person. Without an explanation for her husband's suicide, Stella knew, she would wonder what signs she had missed, wherein she had failed. And never know.

Would she be better off knowing? Stella wondered. And what of Arthur's children? Stella had it in her power to soothe them, or scarify them, and she did not know which would happen.

Standing in front of Arthur's coffin, Acting County Prosecutor Charles Sloan spoke softly.

"Arthur Bright," he said, "brought to public life the stainless ideals of his private life . . ."

For once, Stella envied Sloan, if only for his ignorance.

But life went on. Sloan's statement was more than a eulogy—it was his claim to be Bright's heir. Even now, politics swirled all around them: across the aisle from Stella, sitting with two aides, was Mayor Thomas Krajek.

But not mayor for long, and Krajek knew it. His stricken look was for himself: Stella and Michael had sent Larry Rockwell a grand jury subpoena; Peter Hall, on the advice of his lawyer, was not returning Krajek's calls. The first leaks to Dan Leary, Stella's doing, had produced headlines predicting Krajek's indictment, and panicky compliance inspectors were looking to cut deals. Hall had already made *his*—the only call he had placed was to his lawyer, and Stella had agreed to bring no charges. Hall's task, like Stella's, was to contemplate in private his role in someone's death.

Next to her, Michael listened to Sloan.

His expression was sober. But his thoughts, she sensed, were elsewhere. Stella wished that she knew what they were.

Was it meant that she should feel so alone?

Heart leaden, she tried to attend to Sloan. But, once more, what she knew and saw was more telling than Sloan's words.

Sitting behind him was George Walker. The next mayor, Stella was certain, of Steelton.

The indictment of Vincent Moro for Curran's murder had been followed by a press conference. The speakers were Stella and Sloan, taking credit where he could. But it was Stella who had broken the case, and Stella who revealed that Walker had been framed by Moro and Curran. It was the first, telling blow to Krajek, but George Walker was a man redeemed.

Now Walker's interests, like Sloan's, were potentially affected by Stella's secret. For Bright to be tarnished by drug use, deviant sex, and complicity in the murder of a prostitute would surely damage Sloan, his closest aide; to a lesser extent, and even less fairly, this would also stain Walker among white voters enmeshed in racial stereotypes. But Stella guessed that, unlike Sloan, Walker was preparing for this.

The thought made her seek out Nathaniel Dance.

Dance was not hard to find: he and his wife were seated with Arthur's family. His grief was genuine, as was his concern for Lizanne Bright. But he had other concerns. Which was one reason that Stella believed Walker knew what she knew.

The other reason was that Walker had called her.

He wanted to meet with her, he said, to thank her for what she had done. He did not say more than that, or suggest that he was aware of anything. But he had passed the word through Stella's consultant: what he wanted to ask, what Stella should be prepared to answer, was whether she would support him in exchange for his support in the precinct election.

So Stella, too, might be served by her own silence.

She did not yet know her answer. But she could appreciate Walker's logic. In the mistrust which would flow from what had happened—

Walker's framing, Krajek's ruin, the corruption of Steelton 2000—he needed to reach across the Onondaga. He had already taken the first step: if Walker became mayor, he had let it be known, he would see the ballpark through to completion.

None of this had surprised her. What surprised and troubled her was the revival of her own ambition.

Five days of mourning, she said to herself, *and you're back to coveting the office of a man whose death you caused.*

A shard of dark humor came to her. She could always talk to her father.

Stella closed her eyes.

She would go to see him. The last time had been two weeks ago.

When she looked up again, George Walker was at the podium.

He was wholly unlike Arthur in appearance—fleshy and confident, with white hair and a look of good humor—and his voice, with its preacher's cadences, belonged to an earlier generation. He could not have risen to City Council President, Stella believed, without doing things which would not bear scrutiny. But he also could not have come this far without being able, and shrewd, and gifted at compromise. And he was as unsentimental as events required: moments before, he had exchanged handshakes and whispered words of condolence with Charles Sloan, whose political throat—unbeknownst to Sloan—Walker proposed to cut.

Now, though he spoke to Lizanne Bright, his voice filled the room.

"Arthur," he said, "gave and gave, and so did you. You gave him a place to rest, so that he could give to us again. And if, in the end, we wore him out, we have you to thank it was not sooner . . ."

Perhaps, Stella thought, that was as good as anything. But it was hard to know. And neither George Walker nor anyone else could discharge the obligation she felt to Lizanne Bright.

The choir was singing "Amazing Grace," rich voices carrying each note to the rafters. Then, at last, it was done.

Six pallbearers, Sloan and Walker among them, bore Arthur's coffin from the church. Passing, Walker caught her eye, and briefly nodded.

Instinctively, she touched Michael's sleeve. "Can we go somewhere?" she asked. "Please."

Michael hesitated, and then, from compassion or the sadness of the moment, nodded.

There was one more thing to do.

"Wait for me," she said.

She found Dance outside the church. At the bottom step, she waited until he noticed her, then separated from the others.

They had not spoken of Bright since his death. Nor did Dance speak now.

"I have something for you," she said.

Reaching into her purse, she removed a padded envelope, mailed to herself. "What is it?" he asked.

"The last copy of Novak's tape."

Dance considered her—perhaps moved, perhaps only curious. But he did not ask why. Nor did Stella understand all of her reasons. But one was clear: in whatever Walker did, whatever she decided, this tape, and her knowledge of it, must have no place.

"It's done with," she said.

THIRTEEN

STELLA AND Michael sat on a bench in the courtyard of St. Stanislaus.

In winter the garden was bare of flowers, its grass stunted. But the sun lent warmth and Warszawa was quiet, a refuge from the reporters who had pursued them outside the First Baptist Church, asking, as they had for days, questions about the death of Arthur Bright. As she had for days, Stella professed a mystified sorrow: though Dan Leary and the others were suspicious—the timing of Bright's suicide in itself aroused their instincts—Stella believed that they would never learn the truth. She no longer had reason to help them.

Michael, alone, was different. "I don't even know," she told him, "how to begin."

He turned to her. "I understand some of what you've been through, Stella. But you accused me of working for a murderer. I can tell you that 'I'm sorry' isn't enough."

What *was* enough? she wondered. Probably nothing. But what she could offer, if she chose to, she had been too fearful to offer anyone—the truth, not simply about her job but about herself as far as she knew it. The choice, and its consequences, kept the words inside her: her deepest instinct was to go on as she had, and yet now she feared this as well.

She bent forward, arms resting on her knees, staring at the ground in front of her. Then she began where she knew she must. Something of her father, then of Jack Novak. And then all that had happened since Novak's murder.

Michael fell quiet. She did not know what to expect from him: distaste; indifference; or, perhaps, the rote assurance she had done as well as she could. Instead, he asked, "Do you really think *you* killed Arthur?"

The bald question made her guilt more painful. "In a way. I should have told him I'd try to protect him, just let him serve out his term. He'd tried to overcome so much—he deserved at least that much hope. I didn't give him any."

"But *would* you have protected him," Michael asked, "after Dance offered you a deal?"

"I don't know." Stella paused; it was what she had asked herself, again and again. "If Arthur had dropped out, I wouldn't have exposed him. That much, I'm sure of. But help to make him mayor? Moro would still have something on him, and me. I'd already seen what that did to Arthur. So I can only hope I'd have walked away."

Michael's expression was hard to read: what Stella saw was less kindness than objectivity. "Do you care what *I* think?" he asked.

"Very much." Her voice was low, uncertain. "I'd started caring for you, not just Sofia. It scared me. Believing you'd betrayed me was about more than Curran's mind games. It was what I *knew* would happen." Slowly, she turned to him. "I didn't know how to trust you—not with a case, but with me. Now, at least, I'm trying."

Michael appraised her. "Okay," he said at last. "One thing at a time."

"First, Arthur killed Arthur. He'd never come to terms with who he was, or what he'd done—he just sat on it. You *had* to show him that tape. It wasn't your fault Arthur couldn't face that. You didn't put him where he was.

"You wouldn't have gone along with Dance, either." Michael's tone was quiet, level. "You have the virtues of your faults, Stella. You judge people too harshly—yourself included. But you can see a moral choice for what it is."

Stella felt the pain inside her ease. His questions were not meant to avoid the personal; they had gone to the heart of what she must live with. What he had said was better than false comfort—it was fair. She could only pray it also held the seeds of acceptance.

"What do I do now?" she asked.

He could have interpreted this in several ways; even Stella was uncertain how she meant it. All that Michael said was, "I can only tell you why I think this happened. The rest is up to you."

In a sense, this was true. She was free, as always, to choose for herself. That was the path she had taken. But it saddened her, now, that her choices mattered to no one else. "Not all of it," she said. "I've tried to explain what I did to you, the things that make me who I am. What else *can* I do?"

Looking down, Michael seemed to measure his words. Softly, he said, "I felt absolutely blindsided. It's not just about Maria. I don't want Sofia to ever hurt like that again. You understand that, don't you?"

This, too, was wounding: it was easier for Stella to understand a frightened child than a man she cared for. "Yes," she said simply. "I do. But I feel even worse about you. And I don't know how to make you believe that."

Michael tilted his head. "Have you ever talked like this before?" he asked.

"No. Since Jack, I've never wanted to."

"Then it must mean *something*, Stella."

This much, he seemed to grasp. Perhaps, in time, she could trust enough to help him understand the rest.

But that was in the future. The only thing she knew was that Michael had given her a measure of peace. And, with it, an answer to one question.

If George Walker still wanted her to run for County Prosecutor, she would. If not, there would be other years. No one had promised that what she wanted, whatever it was, would come without effort.

Quiet, she thought of her father, of Jack Novak, and then of the man beside her now. "It means everything," she answered.

ACKNOWLEDGMENTS

Dark Lady was a complex undertaking. Among other things, it required me to write about a woman's life, urban politics, racial conflict, political corruption, organized crime, the construction of a baseball stadium, and a city which does not exist. Little wonder I needed help.

Fortunately, I got it. In Cleveland, the following friends contributed their advice: County Prosecutor, now Congresswoman, Stephanie Tubbs Jones; Assistant County Prosecutor Carmen Marino, Chief of the Criminal Division; Dr. Elizabeth Balraj, the County Coroner; Dr. Mandy Jenkins and Dr. Sharon Rosenberg of the Coroner's Office; and Assistant U.S. Attorneys Roger Bamberger and James Wooley. Writer Gloria Brown shared her knowledge of the neighborhoods I used as starting points in imagining Steelton, and Father William Gulaf of St. Stanislaus generously explained the history of his church and its parish. I also owe a grace note to Cleveland itself: while I liberally borrowed on its history, geography, and neighborhoods, its revival as a city is as impressive as Steelton's decline is depressing. Steelton is *not* Cleveland—it's what Cleveland might have become had its people not decided otherwise.

Friends in San Francisco also bailed me out. Sergeants Richard Correia and Ron Kerns kindly agreed to speculate on the world of Nathaniel Dance and Johnny Curran, and Assistant District Attorney George Butterworth discussed his knowledge of schemes to misappropriate public monies. My usual "board of directors" helped me through the labyrinth I'd designed: Homicide Inspector Napoleon Hendrix; Medical Examiner Boyd Stephens; Defense Attorney Hugh Anthony Levine; and, especially, Assistant District Attorney Al Giannini. And, in New York, former Assistant U.S. Attorney Dick Martin, lead prosecutor in the "Pizza Connection" cases, gave me his unique insights.

Byzantine, as well, are the politics and economics surrounding the construction of a baseball stadium. Special thanks to Tom Chema, the driving force behind the Cleveland Indians' stunning ballpark, Jacobs Field; Michael Kerr, whose firm has designed the best parks in America, brilliantly combining old and new; Steve Agostini, who has been part of this process in several cities; and Clint Reilly, Jim Ross, and Doug Comstock, who shared their perspectives on stadium politics.

Of course there is the human side to all this. I'm grateful to community activist Margo St. James, and psychiatrists Dr. Ken Gottlieb and Dr. Rodney Shapiro, who helped me perceive the inner landscape of such diverse characters as Stella Marz, Arthur Bright, Johnny Curran, Jack Novak, Tommy Fielding, Tina Welch, and Natasha Tillman. And Michelle Wagner of the Goldman Center—which treats Alzheimer's patients with such wisdom and good humor—was invaluable.

I also want to thank the others who helped but wish to remain anonymous. You know who you are.

I'm particularly grateful to those whose comments made this novel much better: my wife, Laurie, and my dear friends Philip Rotner, Anna Chavez, and Fred Hill. My valued assistant, Alison Thomas, raised the level of my game, and hers, with her daily editorial suggestions on every aspect of the novel. And, as always, my splendid publishers at Knopf and Ballantine were wonderfully encouraging: special thanks to Sonny Mehta and Linda Grey.

Finally, a word for George Bush and Ron Kaufman. My debt to you is incalculable, both for your friendship and for your help with *No Safe Place*. I don't claim to have discharged it by dedicating a book, let alone *this* book, a darker piece of work than either of you may care for. I look forward to other opportunities in the years ahead.

Richard North Patterson's ten novels include the international best-sellers *Degree of Guilt, Eyes of a Child, The Final Judgment, Silent Witness,* and *No Safe Place.* His novels have won the Edgar Allan Poe Award and the Grand Prix de Littérature Policière. A graduate of Ohio Wesleyan University and the Case Western Reserve School of Law, he studied creative writing with Jesse Hill Ford at the University of Alabama at Birmingham. He and his wife, Laurie, live with their family in San Francisco and on Martha's Vineyard.

A NOTE ON THE TYPE

This book was set in Garamond, a typeface originally designed by the famous Parisian type cutter Claude Garamond (1480–1561). This version of Garamond was modeled on a 1592 specimen sheet from the Egenolff-Berner foundry, which was produced from types thought to have been brought to Frankfurt by Jacques Sabon (d. 1580).

Claude Garamond is one of the most famous type designers in printing history. His distinguished romans and italics first appeared in *Opera Ciceronis* in 1543–1544. While delightfully unconventional in design, the Garamond types are clear and open, yet maintain an elegance and precision of line that mark them as French.

Composed by NK Graphics,
Keene, New Hampshire
Printed and bound by Quebecor Printing,
Fairfield, Pennsylvania